Snowy

A sequel to The Cheerleader

What happens when ex-cheerleaders grow up?

For Snowy, the cute, blond, ponytailed cheerleader at Gunthwaite High School in the 1950s, did anything ever match the glory of those days?

This is the story that the multitudes of fans of the best-selling THE CHEERLEADER have clamored for, a story that new readers will respond to with equal eagerness.

While chronicling Snowy's next thirty years, it explores the nature of friendship as it follows the lives of her best friends, beautiful Bev and outspoken Puddles, and her first love, Tom.

What happens when the Silent Generation grows up?

SNOWY describes how she and her friends, who came of age in the security of the 1950s when roles were defined and accepted, develop in the next decades, coping with college, marriage, and careers, their experiences unique and universal.

The Cheerleader

This is what it was like to grow up in the 1950s in the years of ponytails, pajama parties, proms, and "parking," when to be popular was important and when, if you were a girl, being important meant being a cheerleader.

"One of the truest portraits of an American girl ever written...Everything works in MacDougall's book. She captures the times, the attitudes, the emotions with the authority of one who was once there and knows the route back by heart."
—*DETROIT FREE PRESS*

"A classic."
—*PUBLISHERS WEEKLY*

"If future historians and sociologists are ever impelled to find out what it was like to be a high school student in America at mid 20th century, they will need go no farther than *THE CHEERLEADER* for documentation and enlightenment... Utterly honest, accurate, and sympathetic."
—*KANSAS CITY STAR*

"A devastatingly accurate portrait of the '50s."
—*LIBRARY JOURNAL*

"It isn't often that you get to the last page of a book and are aware that you have just finished a real reading experience. But that's how you'll feel when you finish *THE CHEERLEADER*. A terrific book. Really terrific."
—*UNITED PRESS INTERNATIONAL*

Snowy

Ruth Doan MacDougall

Gift to the
Shrewsbury Library
from the
Angelica P. Allan Fund
for Young Adults

FRIGATE BOOKS

Visit the author's website at:
http://www.ruthdoanmacdougall.com

Reprinted by Frigate Books 2002

SNOWY. Copyright © 1993 by Ruth Doan MacDougall
Foreword Copyright © 2002 by Ann V. Norton

PRINTING HISTORY:
St. Martin's Press edition published 1993

Cover photograph: Kirk Dougal, "Snowy's House"
Cover design: hannusdesign.com

Library of Congress Cataloging-in-Publication Data
MacDougall, Ruth Doan
        Snowy / Ruth Doan MacDougall
            p. cm
        ISBN 0-9663352-3-6
            1. Women—New Hampshire—Fiction
    I. Title
    PS3563.A292S66 2002
    813'.54—dc20   2002090036
                                                          CIP

12345 06 05 04 03 02

Foreword

FEW BOOKS have been born by popular demand, but *Snowy,* the 1993 sequel to Ruth Doan MacDougall's classic 1973 coming-of-age novel *The Cheerleader,* is one of the few. So many fans were eager to hear what happened to "the Gang" who grew up in 1950s New Hampshire that they begged MacDougall to continue their story. And *Snowy* not only lives up to its predecessor; it enriches and complicates our understanding of this engrossing group and their world. Lovers of *The Cheerleader* will find the same minute accuracy, wild humor, and lyrical, sympathetic perceptions. Both novels satisfy as only the best realistic fiction can, by fascinating us with characters who come alive in their unique complexity and context, but also as people whose experiences mirror our own. *The Cheerleader* tells the story of adolescent ambition and longing. *Snowy,* with the same blunt but poignant veracity, exemplifies that old adage: be careful what you wish for, because you just might get it.

MacDougall deals brilliantly with the challenges of a sequel, skillfully weaving the past into the present with a judicious use of expository memory and dialogue. As in *The Cheerleader,* the unobtrusive narrative lens focuses on Snowy, but expands effectively at key moments to other characters' trenchant reactions; and while its protagonist is Snowy, the novel also chronicles the evolution of her friendships with Bev and Puddles. *The Cheerleader* covers only two years of their lives, as befits the intense, formative experiences of a coming-of-age novel. *Snowy* covers thirty years, and the Gang's encounters with marriage, parenthood, and death, its narrative skipping ten and fifteen years at a time as the characters mature and settle into the lives they have chosen. Realistically, they hear from each other only at intervals, through phone calls that prove MacDougall's uncanny ear for dialogue. As always she gets the details of each decade exactly right, as the dark comedy of the 1987 "Fabulous Fifties" party shows: its hostess, determined to serve hamburgers and French fries, nevertheless cannot omit the shrimp or the Brie.

The Cheerleader ends, like *A Portrait of the Artist as a Young Man,* with Snowy's ecstatic expectations of new freedoms and unfettered artistic expression. At Bennington College, where *Snowy* begins only months later, she is determined never to go "backward," as she had told Tom, her true love, on their haunting last night together. Yet just as *Ulysses'* first chapter reveals a Stephen Dedalus still struggling with religious and familial nets, *Snowy*'s first hilarious scene shows her literally and metaphorically begrimed by the same traps she had hoped to elude by leaving Gunthwaite, her hometown. The smug belief still lingers that all girls, even those attending Bohemian Bennington, go to college to catch a husband. Despite her desire to be an "enigmatic eccentric," Snowy finds that her status as ex-cheerleader impresses "even the most blasé." Moreover, Snowy is still Snowy, working frantically at her studies and "being a good sport, wagging her tail at praise." Here Snowy begins to learn the lesson that she cannot escape herself, despite changes of home or occupation; each character learns this hard truth.

Critics have praised MacDougall's quiet but devastating portraits of young women's lives—seen also in her novels *Wife and Mother* and *One Minus One*—that make her one of America's most telling contemporary feminist novelists. Her vivid portrayal of the "triumvirate" bears this out. In Boston, where as students the three glory together in big-city life, Bev and Puddles serve again as foils for Snowy, pursuing the stereotypically female jobs of secretary and nurse. Yet poetic Snowy, an intern at a publishing company, mostly types, and the male bosses expect her and the other "girls" to get them coffee and doughnuts. Bev's mother, Julia, always Snowy's mentor and model, sees very clearly these cultural forces when she fumes that "it's a damn shame that girls who ought to be doctors must settle for nursing" and laments Bev's desire to marry a millionaire rather than pursue acting in New York.

Relentlessly, but without fanfare, the novel explodes 1950s

viii

myths about marriage, work, and motherhood. Snowy views impending maternity with fear as well as joy, never losing sight of the constraints motherhood will have on her writing. Bev discovers that the ever-larger house, more children, do not satisfy her need for expression, for selfhood. Puddles, still restless after becoming a nurse and a mother, pursues professional advancement and erotic adventure. Significantly, *Snowy*, like *The Cheerleader*, portrays sexuality realistically and joyfully, as a part of life vitally important to women as well as men. Yet the openness with which this is admitted—and, enormously, the birth control options that enable Snowy to live her poet's life in control of her fertility—are new.

Still, MacDougall's genius for feminist fiction lies partly in her sympathetic portrayals of men who are equally hindered by social and cultural nets. Tom—whose enduring appeal inheres in his essential decency—begins teaching idealistically, but ends defeated by student apathy and stingy taxpayers. Dudley Washburn, class president and Snowy's only academic equal, lives her nightmare and goes backward. Nonetheless, Dudley's consistent devotion to Snowy is a moving portrait of friendship between men and women. In fact, the early mistake that begins his surprising reversal is rooted in his love and respect for women, and in a tragedy that could have been avoided fifteen years later. Indeed, the limitations of a particular time pervade *Snowy* as they do *The Cheerleader.* These men and women came of age in the 1950s, and by the 1960s and early 1970s were married, working parents. *Snowy* barely touches on this most famous decade, the 1960s. Its rebellions were not theirs, though they were fostered by the deadening conventions that MacDougall subtly exposes in both novels.

Just as "the Gang" depicts individuals within this generation, small-town New Hampshire typifies the cultural and geographical changes in the rural United States from the 1950s to the present (a subject MacDougall explores at length in *The Cost of Living* and *A Lovely Time Was Had by All*). Snowy's recurring image of the Stage Manager from *Our Town* (Bev's starring vehicle in *The Cheerleader*) ironically symbolizes these rapid changes and the threat to her small village's idyllic beauty as strip malls encroach. Snowy's awareness that this beauty masks lives of quiet desperation implies that the passing of the 1950s and all they stood for has not brought forth paradise. Yes, women have more opportunities; cheerleading lacks its old symbolic force for the triumvirate's daughters. But 1950s Gunthwaite was a more individual place, less crowded, with a more human pace. In this, as in so much else, MacDougall highlights an American paradox.

Snowy ends like a Shakespearean comedy, however, with all the major players on stage for the wedding of two members of the next generation. MacDougall's sure humor enlivens this scene even as it emphasizes the novel's realistic messages: that life does not follow a predictable narrative; that habit and routine are inevitable, sometimes life-enhancing, sometimes deadening; that in friends and family we find joy and solace, but not safety. It promises hope and continuity, despite the tragedies that precede it.

Those of us who consider Snowy, Bev, Puddles, and Tom our good friends—those fans who have been so haunted by their stories that they implored Ruth Doan MacDougall for more—will welcome this reprint of *Snowy* and cherish the continuation of this extraordinary ordinary saga.

ANN V. NORTON
Saint Anselm College

To Gloria Dibble Pond

Death:
Save it will wait
Until this life
That moves so fast
Gives time
For dreams to last
And least of all
Be something more
Than merely dreams
Dreamed before.

—Henrietta Snow, age 16
The Cheerleader

SO HERE SHE was, on Wednesday, October 9, 1957, about to strip off her Pig-Pen costume consisting of dried-muddy sweatshirt and Levi's, in a bathroom in a sleazy motel across the Vermont line in New York, with a little party going on outside the bathroom door whose lock didn't work, her roommate and her roommate's date and her own impromptu date lolling around watching loud TV and imbibing rum-and-Cokes out of paper cups. Henrietta Snow, known as Snowy, had definitely not expected to find herself in such a situation when she'd been accepted at Bennington College last spring. A scholarship student, too!

Someone tapped on the door. She froze, head inside the filthy blue Bennington sweatshirt. "Who is it?"

"Me," said her roommate, Harriet Blumburg. "Okay to come in?"

Dennis, Harriet's date, shouted, "Hey, Snowy, want us to help scrub your back?"

Harriet opened the door just wide enough to dart in and slammed it behind her. "Shit, the lock's broken?"

From the interior of the sweatshirt, a muffled wail: "You promised you'd keep them at bay!"

"I will, I will," Harriet said, "but I need some Dutch courage," and she grabbed Snowy's rum-and-Coke off the cracked toilet tank and took a deep swig.

"Huh?" As Snowy tugged her sweatshirt up over her dark blond hair pinned up frowzily to approximate Pig-Pen's and plastered with mud like a bird's nest, chunks of dirt pattered down on the scuffed linoleum. Her emerging face had been slathered with a facial of real mud, now also dried and crumbling. "You've already got a drink, has Dennis run out of refills?"

"There's a slight problem I haven't mentioned, I have trouble drinking or eating anything in front of a guy."

"Really?" Snowy said, amazed.

Harriet began laughing. "God, you're a mess—you, of all people."

3

Small and cute, with a heart-shaped face and turned-up nose, Snowy had been frantically trying to change her squeaky-clean look ever since she'd arrived at Bennington a month ago, but she'd realized she hadn't succeeded when, amid gales of mirth, the girls in her house had decided she would be perfect for the Pig-Pen part in the *Peanuts* skit. She said, "I tested the shower, it's hardly a trickle."

Exploring the dank sour room, Harriet picked up the wrapped midget bar of soap. "At least the management changes the towels and soap, be glad you don't have to use a sliver with someone's pubic hairs on it."

Snowy retched, a noise she'd learned from her high-school best friend, Bev Colby, and gingerly draped the sweatshirt across the washbasin. "This is crazy, I should be showering at the house."

"Any shampoo samples?"

"Are there usually?"

"Sometimes, but maybe these motels back East—" Harriet stared at Snowy, once again stunned by her lack of experience. "You've never been in a motel before?"

Harriet, a California sophisticate; Snowy, a New Hampshire hick. Hideously embarrassed, Snowy said, "Nope."

Harriet said quickly, "I've just been with my parents, no big deal, I haven't ever been to a motel with a guy."

"Plural! We've got two of them out there!"

"Try anything once, that's my motto."

Snowy's laugh was nervous, Harriet's bravado. But they were all supposedly only here so Snowy could wash off Pig-Pen and look reasonably presentable for what Dennis had termed a "pub crawl" of the beer joints over the line in New York, where you could drink at age eighteen. Yet Snowy doubted that that toy soap would make a dent in the dirt, and she'd need plenty of shampoo even under ordinary circumstances because since last spring she had been letting her hair grow, rivaling Rapunzel, and nowadays she usually wore it cascading straight to her hips in a Bohemian Bennington style, after having spent her high-

4

school years as a perky cheerleader in a long ponytail curled into an upside-down question mark. She unzipped her Levi's and asked, "If you can't eat when you're out on a date, what do you do at the Top Hat or the State Line?" Despite her size, Snowy possessed a lumberjack's capacity for food, and although she was shy, the presence of a boy had merely made her mind her manners with extra care. How Freudian, she thought vaguely, her major not psychology but literature, how Freudian that Harriet, who was thin and dark and angularly pretty, an art major, had become fascinated by fat women, painting nothing else. Harriet called it "my fat-lady period." The canvases hanging on the walls of their room would have daunted anybody's appetite but Snowy's.

Harriet guzzled rum-and-Coke. "Oh, I can fiddle with a piece of pizza all evening, I can nurse a beer for hours and hours."

Besides never having been in a motel before, Snowy hadn't ever gone to a beer joint. And this was her first date since coming to Bennington. Last spring, after breaking up with Tom Forbes, her high-school boyfriend, she had sworn off boys, so at Bennington she hadn't taken advantage of the tradition decreeing it socially acceptable to investigate and respond to stag boys who would enter a house and yell, "Anybody want a date?" Harriet had met guys from Williams and Union and Rensselaer this way and offered to fix Snowy up, Snowy always begging off, her excuses her reading assignments or a paper or a poem she was writing, and actually these excuses were the truth, in addition to that determination not to get involved with a boy again until college was over. She read and reread, wrote and rewrote, scared stiff she wasn't smart enough to attend a school which didn't have exams. Hard work and a photographic memory had been the reasons she'd graduated first in her class at Gunthwaite High School in Gunthwaite, New Hampshire, a mill town four hours away. Because of her terror of exams she had hated school; this and the pressure of having to be the fastest gun in the West, always having to get A's, had made her choose Bennington, where there were no grades at all. It was turning out to demand even harder work.

But tonight Harriet had provoked her into consenting to this date, and now beyond the bathroom door awaited Whit Bennett, a Williams boy. Whitney Bennett. Williams. He'd probably even gone to prep school. Well, Harriet had gone to a private school, albeit as a day student.

Dennis shouted, "Rub-a-dub-dub, two girls in a tub!"

Harriet reflected, "He *looked* like the sensitive type—compared with Ray and the others, anyway."

"Hah," Snowy said, laying her Levi's on the sweatshirt. "You're always complaining that Ray takes you to westerns and yells, 'Cut 'em off at the pass!' and throws popcorn all over the place, and at fraternity parties Jim specializes in pie beds and Stan adores his plastic hand that jumps out of toilets, and then there's the fraternity couch, but they never duped you into a motel."

"So Dennis *is* more imaginative." Harriet picked up Snowy's sweatshirt and Levi's. "I'll shake these outdoors."

"Thanks. Please, though, please don't let the guys pull any old-swimming-hole stunt with them."

"Good grief, you're such a worrier you should've played Charlie Brown." Harriet opened the door a slice and dodged out.

In motels, or at least in this motel, the bathmat was made of paper. Better than nothing, Snowy thought, to protect bare feet from this linoleum. She took off her right sneaker and hopped onto the bathmat, took off her left, peeled off her socks, plucked bobbypins out of her hairdo, turned on the reluctant shower, clumsily adjusted the nozzle, shucked her underwear, and, glancing over her shoulder at the door, leapt into the tin stall, where the ragged plastic curtain slid against her, slimy and suspect. Her parents would die if they knew what their darling daughter was doing. Well, it was a milestone. She and Bev had always kept mental lists of milestones, like their first bras (which neither of them had needed and still didn't) and their

6

first kisses, but she couldn't write Bev at Katharine Gibbs school for secretaries about this Williams-date milestone complete with motel because they were no longer best friends, to Snowy's shame. Nonetheless, as she held up to the dribble her mask of mud she began telling Bev about it in her head—and she began telling Tom.

She tried to lather her hair with the ridiculous soap. Dirt dripped down her body, a mud slide.

Breaking up with Tom hadn't cured her of talking to him in her head every day, telling him her news, even a Williams date, for Christ's sake! She still fought against the temptation to talk to him on stationery instead, and the telephone was another magnet she strained against, especially during Saturday nights alone. Give in, sang the sirens, give in, write him, a friendly note, not a billet-doux. If he doesn't write back, a twirl of the dial and the operator will connect you to his fraternity house at Rumford Teachers' College in New Hampshire, where he was now a sophomore. Why not phone? He certainly wouldn't be there, he'd be out on a date, so a call would only cost her money, not pride and independence. But what if he was there and they made up? The future would consist of writing him daily and waiting for his letters, waiting weekends as he drove the maybe two hours over to Bennington, then bliss: Depending upon his schedule of washing pots and pans in the college kitchen, she could be here in this motel Saturdays or Sundays with Tom, in that double bed out beyond the dubious barricade of the bathroom door. This prospect, however, was exactly why she'd broken up with him. He had understood their dilemma first. They had begun dating in March 1955, just before her sixteenth birthday. She had been yearning for him, Tom Forbes, handsome, funny, a Catch, and his finally noticing her seemed a present from the gods who bestowed on her the happiest birthday ever, followed by the happiest time of her life, making the Varsity cheerleading squad, cheering him at football games, going steady, discovery. What ended their romance was, of all things, Girls' State. At the start of the summer of 1956, she went

7

off to a week of Girls' State at the University of New Hampshire to learn about government, leaving him to grow scared about how much he missed her, this absence a preview of the college years ahead when he'd be trapped by love, fate sealed, opportunities closed. Upon her return he had broken up with her at the drive-in theater, saying they almost ought to make a date to begin again after they'd finished college. At home, she'd nearly drunk iodine. But on a cold April night a year later, having stolen him from Bev and lost her virginity, she had refused the fraternity pin he assumed she'd accept, because she realized her passion for him would ruin her future. She couldn't get pinned to him; she loved him so absorbingly she wouldn't have cared about anything at college except his visits and letters. She couldn't plan to take up where they left off after college, either; she had to be free of him totally. She needed a fresh start, unencumbered by Tom.

Her decision was like a murder, and she remained in shock. He had been her great love, but he'd also been her best friend. She had killed off her best friends, Tom deliberately, Bev a casualty of her Tom preoccupation. Yet on and on she talked to their ghosts.

Although handsome, this Whit Bennett didn't resemble Tom, thank God; Tom was five-nine, stocky, his eyes behind his horn-rimmed glasses a clear blue instead of her own denim blue, his lashes long and straight, while Whit was perhaps six feet, lean, dark-eyed, and whereas Tom had always chosen pretty girls (and got them—hadn't the "Superlatives" page of his high-school yearbook labeled him Most Flirtatious, plus Best Line, Best Dancer, Best Dressed, Friendliest, and Best All-Round?), Whit had chosen tonight an unknown, a Pig-Pen in a poke. If Bev were listening, still her best friend, Bev would exclaim, "Your inner beauty shone through!" and they would collapse into giggles. Was Whit on tenterhooks out in the bedroom over what the removal of mud might reveal? He was taking the risk, Snowy guessed, because he was intrigued by having a date with Pig-Pen to joke about with his fraternity brothers. The novelty had even made him sacrifice the upholstery on the passenger seat of his car to the dried mud on the seat of her Levi's. Those clothes! Tomorrow would have to be an unscheduled Blue Wash Day. The Bennington catalog read, "External disciplines are avoided, as interfering seriously with incentives and active learning," and one of the external factors you could rid yourself of at Bennington was clothing. That is, emphasis on clothing. This resulted in a campus of unhomogeneous outfits, Bermuda shorts, tights and leotards, slacks, an occasional skirt, usually dirndl over those tights, and the most casual, which Snowy and Harriet had adopted, Levi's and Bennington sweatshirts, the sweatshirts worn backward, nonchalant. The irony wasn't lost on Snowy that she, who hated going backward, who had broken up with Tom because it meant going forward, was walking around in a backward sweatshirt, except on the occasions they'd designated Blue Wash Days, traumatic occurrences when she and Harriet bundled up all their Levi's and sweatshirts and trudged over to the washing machine in Commons, wearing Bermudas and sweaters and feeling far too formal, feeling like the girls they called Circle Pin Types who looked as if they were at Smith.

And the announcement of a Skits Night, with girls from each house putting on some sort of show on the stage in Commons, had seemed the brainwork of Circle Pin Types. In McCullough, Snowy's house amongst the two matching double rows of white houses separated by the lengthy stretch of Commons lawn, the twenty-six girls agreed, "Too gung ho," deciding not to partici- pate, but then at the last minute they'd got silly and the house chairman had suggested *Peanuts* and thus it was that earlier this evening Snowy had stood in another shower, the bathtub- shower in the bathroom nearest the upstairs room she and Harriet shared. Fully clothed in sweatshirt and Levi's, she'd allowed herself to be smeared by Harriet and friends head to foot with mud made from the bucket of dirt Harriet had dug up with a kitchen spoon out behind the house. (Lucky Harriet and the other freshmen were cast only as extras, playing kids in the

9

background.) On a rack in front of the radiator hung some underwear belonging to girls who had rooms in this section of the hall, a rainbow of nylon underpants accented with white bras and white socks; the familiar domestic sight began to Snowy to emanate an aura of immaculate innocence she would never again achieve, while she became increasingly begrimed.

She had chattered, jittery, "The last time I was in a play, I was an oyster in our high-school production of *Alice in Wonderland,* it was a Christmas show for grammar-school kids and I danced the Lobster Quadrille, I had a big gray canvas shell on a wire frame and there was a veil that allowed me to see, theoretically." At one point, tears of laughter had also hindered her vision, but mercifully she was offstage then. Beautiful Bev, tall and green-eyed, with naturally curly auburn hair worn in a DA, ought to be going to drama school instead of Katharine Gibbs, and she had played the ugly Duchess to the hilt with such success that one impressionable child in the audience started crying, embarrassing its mother enough to hustle it out, not throwing Bev off her stride—this was nothing; her performance as the Witch in the previous year's *Hansel and Gretel* had sparked satisfying screams of terror throughout the auditorium—yet almost causing a mishap in the corridor where Snowy and a lobster beside her, the friend who completed their inseparable triumvirate, Jean Pond, known as Puddles, choked on giggles, Puddles moaning that she was going to pee in her costume, which she fortunately didn't. Snowy added, "From oyster to Pig-Pen, I guess you can't say I've been typecast."

"Stop talking," Harriet had said, "or you'll be eating a mud pie."

Back in their room at the top of the stairs to the right, a location handy for Harriet to inspect over the banister any guys in the hall below, Snowy had surveyed the mudlark in the mirror of her bureau. Their bureaus and twin beds and small one-drawer desks had come with the room, but the rest of the décor they'd purchased secondhand, having been approached their first day here by two enterprising sophomore roommates who

10

had decided that paisley and wicker were more suited to their new status and therefore wanted to sell some of their freshman stuff. So on Snowy's and Harriet's beds were dark green linen slipcovers and on the windows hung dark green drapes, the color reminding Snowy of Gunthwaite High's green-and-white school colors, and on the floor lay a green-and-brown braided rug, another reminder of her past because her parents had a multitude of braided rugs in their house, an old white Colonial with black shutters across the river from downtown Gunthwaite. Snowy wasn't homesick, except for her Shetland collie, but she still wished that when the sophomores were freshmen they had chosen different-colored slipcovers and drapes, a different rug. She highly approved of the orange canvas butterfly chair she and Harriet had also bought from them even though it had begun to rip. Her parents, accustomed to armchairs and rockers in that house which was their obsession, probably wouldn't recognize it as a chair at all, and they'd be befuddled too by the bookcase, a far cry from home where her parents' *Reader's Digest Condensed Books* were proudly arranged on the shelves of maple end tables, and her own library, in which Emily Dickinson and Edna St. Vincent Millay had replaced *The Bobbsey Twins* and *A Date with Marcy,* was kept in the white-painted bookcase in her pink-and-white bedroom. There were gaps in that bookcase now, for she'd brought here the most precious books, poetry collections and Agatha Christies, the former to fuel her ambition, the latter providing the reward of cozy murders after her studying was done—not *done,* but, as Valéry said of a poem, abandoned in despair. At Bennington, cinderblock-and-board bookcases were de rigueur, and Harriet had secured theirs when she answered an "Anybody-want-a-date?" yell and selected, out of the group of Williams boys, hefty Ray, owner of a car, who drove her to a lumberyard and then lugged everything up to this room and set up the bookcase under her direction, his heroic effort aimed toward torrid gratitude back in his car. What Ray earned instead was the privilege of giving Harriet a tour of the area, including the Bennington

11

monument, an obelisk visible from the campus which inspired many comments about the perversity of a phallic symbol on the horizon of a women's college.

Whenever Harriet's glance fell upon the bookcase, she would brood, "I've *got* to convince my dad to let me have a car here, I'm going nuts without one, he can't really believe Vermont roads are more dangerous than freeways, cow paths full of herds I'll run into." For Snowy, the bookcase was another reminder, of Tom. Lazy, he had tried College Prep and business classes and settled on shop because woodworking came easy to him, and what a bookcase he would have built! Yet he had lived outside the high-school caste system, being pals with both football players and National Honor Society members, and despite Superlative labels he'd escaped categorization and he continued unique; astonishing her, at Rumford he had changed last year from shop major to English major and was doing okay, thanks to her influence, or so he'd told her that April night. How many shop majors made such a switch?

Looking at the mirrored Pig-Pen, Snowy said, "The only good thing is I don't have to speak any lines."

"You couldn't," Harriet said. "When that dries, you'd crack."

"I feel like I've been mummified."

Harriet reached for her sketchbook. "Posterity demands a record, I'll call this 'The Transformation of Pure-As-The-Driven-Snowy.' "

It had taken Snowy longer than she'd expected to get used to sharing a room, especially with a roommate who turned her half into a studio reeking of oil paints and turpentine. Although Snowy was an only child, she had figured that rooming with someone wouldn't be difficult because she and Bev had slept over at each other's houses very often, but constant sharing was initially a strain, altering her envy of the twins in her high-school class who were never alone. She kept imagining Bev in Boston gossiping with the roommate who'd replaced Snowy. Ann Wilmot. Snowy's source of news, Puddles, in Boston too, going to Massachusetts General Hospital School of Nursing, wrote that Ann came from Fitchburg, Mass., wanted to be a private secretary to a globetrotting boss, and—Snowy's eyes skidded over the words—Bev had told Puddles she seemed "a kindred spirit." Puddles also was happy with her own roommate, finally finding a friend who didn't puke at the thought of nursing.

And despite adjustments, Snowy and Harriet had hit it off from the start, Snowy overwhelmed by the marvel of Harriet's coming from California. The powers-that-be who paired freshman roommates must have decided that New Englanders would best help Californians adapt, and Snowy had briefly felt the way she had back in eighth grade when the homeroom teacher asked her to take care of a new girl from Portland, Maine: Puddles. Deceptively fragile, taller than Snowy, shorter than Bev, the one out of their triumvirate who grew up to be stacked, Puddles hadn't really needed care. Neither did Harriet.

California! Harriet had brought with her on the airplane all her painting equipment, not trusting what she'd find back East in the boondocks of Vermont, and she had also brought, hidden in her paintbox, a silver flask of tequila, and she promptly introduced Snowy to margaritas over which she and Snowy got acquainted, Snowy thinking Harriet might as well have opened one of her bottles of turpentine. California equaled Hollywood to Snowy, so she had hoped Harriet's family was in the movie business, but when she learned that Harriet's father and older brother were instead in real estate, disappointment vanished after she next learned, without Harriet's telling her directly, that Harriet's family had money. Harriet was Snowy's first experience of wealth. It hadn't yet occurred to Snowy to be jealous; she was dazzled, a child at a circus. Harriet left things lying around, and Snowy had glimpsed a check from her father for a hundred dollars, but near the end of September Harriet had to bum cigarette money from Snowy until her October allowance arrived, and thus Snowy learned too that she couldn't budget her monthly fortune. All this learning! Snowy's new knowledge

13

now included the information that Harriet and lots of other girls at Bennington were Jewish, which she hadn't realized. Last names meant nothing to her; she simply assumed they were foreign, more exotic than the French-Canadian names she'd grown up with. And Harriet, never dreaming of the depths of her small-town naïveté, had thought it went without saying— besides, since Snowy's last name was sometimes an Anglicized Jewish name, who knew what her genealogy might hold? Then in Commons one night at dinner, the only non-cafeteria-style meal, an odd appetizer appeared on the tables, big thin white crackers and bowls of brown mush. Snowy's delight in encountering new food from the Bennington kitchen had at the beginning been clouded by her mortification over having reached the age of eighteen before tasting Eggs Benedict and prime rib of beef with Yorkshire pudding and varieties of fish that weren't the single kind her mother deep-fat fried, calling it "filly of sole," but eventually she had decided to stress her ignorance instead of trying to hide it, and she would proclaim Swiss steak a milestone. (She used the same tactic to cope with her embarrassment at being relatively a local yokel, describing herself as almost a native though she'd never been to Vermont until her Bennington interview.) Peering at the crackers and mush, she said, "I didn't check the menu, I haven't ever seen these crackers, I've read about pâté, is that pâté?", and Harriet said, "Matzo and chopped liver, for Rosh Hashanah," and Snowy looked so totally blank that Harriet fell back into her chair laughing, saying, "Where *is* this Gunthwaite of yours, on another planet?" Snowy blushed crimson, pleading, "Explain." Later, she got wondering what her parents might think. Had she used Harriet's last name in any of her dutiful letters home? If so, her mother hadn't reacted in her weekly replies, concentrating as usual on news of their house, like the new wallpaper for the living room and their hopes for new braided rugs someday. When her mother's letters arrived, Snowy took out the five-dollars-a-week allowance and skimmed the letters and tore them up, ashamed of her mother's grammar. But then she would

14

unfold the five-dollar bill and feel guilty about depriving her parents of new braided rugs immediately, picturing her mother slaving away in the office of Cinderella Shoe Company and her father doing whatever the foreman of the lathe department did at Trask's, a big weathered brick factory that made the machinery that made something else; during her younger years Snowy couldn't be bothered to remember what, but now she knew they made gear cutters, whatever *that* was. Snowy, though, was also working, as scholarship students were expected to. Having waitressed summers at Gunthwaite's Sweetland, a restaurant on Main Street, she had prayed she wouldn't have to be one of the girls waiting on table in the Commons dining rooms, and to her relief another part of her past came to the rescue; she had been the editor of her high-school newspaper, so it was suggested she write a column of college news for the local newspaper, forging a town-and-gown link. The salary permitted such luxuries as cigarettes and an occasional Milky Way, yet the deadlines were a further worry above and beyond studying for Bennington's version of freshman English, Language and Literature (Lang-and-Lit), Economics, Music Theory, and Russian, which she'd chosen because she'd had enough of French in high school and it was more unconventional than Spanish or German, but as she struggled with Cyrillic she wondered if she had been rash not to take a language that at least had the same alphabet.

Harriet said, "Done!" and held out the sketchbook. Snowy groaned, and somebody in the corridor yelled, "Ready?"

"The coffee table." Harriet cleared off books, an ashtray, a Nebbish, a Chianti bottle encrusted with candle wax. Their coffee table, shaped like a boomerang, another secondhand purchase from the sophomores, had been pressed into service as Schroeder's piano.

"God," Snowy said, "how I wish this were over, I am *repulsive.*"

But when they arrived downstairs carrying the coffee table and Snowy's prop, a bowl of dirt, her appearance was greeted with acclamation from the girls gathering in the hall, approval

15

which she found so gratifying she finally admitted to herself that she was still concerned about popularity. In high school she had striven to conform, yet she'd always been different, and by choosing Bennington she had announced that difference, vowing to discard the old high-school social values along with marks and exams. She would become an enigmatic eccentric! Instead, she was being a good sport, wagging her tail at praise.

"All set?" the house chairman asked them. Playing Snoopy, she had a real tail in the form of a scarf (Liberty) safety-pinned to her pajamas. Two freshmen hoisted up the trunk that had been brought down from the attic to represent a doghouse, and a sophomore said, "I can't believe we're doing this," and the junior who was playing Lucy said, "Skits Night, sheer sublimation—five cents, please."

Laughing, out of their house they sallied. The full moon made the autumn foliage seem to glow at nighttime too, and the girl who was playing Linus swung her security blanket and began singing "Moonlight in Vermont" as they joined girls from other houses walking up the path toward the pillars of the brick-and-ivied Commons. The moon was so bright that at the far end of Commons lawn could be seen an abyss looking more eerie than ever in such primitive light, an optical illusion named "The Cliff," an eye-deceiving brink over which girls claimed they were going to fling themselves to their deaths when papers were due or boys didn't phone. The true result would have been much less spectacular, a headlong sprawl onto a field.

At Commons, McCullough met more girls from other houses wearing makeshift costumes, some self-consciously, some with Bev's verve, and they went inside past the Co-op store and the L-shaped bank of mailbox pigeonholes, up the stairs to the second floor where the dining rooms and kitchen were located, up to the third-floor theater, Snowy becoming increasingly edgy. Cheerleading was less intimidating than stage performances, because the fear got lost in the excitement of the game. Cheerleading tryouts, however, were something else again.

16

They parked their bigger props and sat down. The show began.

Everyone seemed to have gone from silliness to punchiness, and skits were howled at and resoundingly applauded. Snowy alone sat immobile. Harriet figured she was preserving her costume from crumbling, and she was, but she was also rigid with stage fright and with the memories of the agonies she had endured on the stage of Gunthwaite High School's auditorium, she and Puddles trying out first for the JV and later the Varsity squads. That they'd succeeded didn't sweeten those memories. She had yet to meet another ex-cheerleader at Bennington— would such a species be as rare here as Miss America aspirants?—and she'd planned to keep her cheerleading a dark secret, only she had inadvertently spilled the beans while explaining to girls that she'd gone to a public high school over in New Hampshire, rattling on and, using the emphasis tactic, making a joke about having been so revoltingly honest-American she'd actually been a cheerleader, a head cheerleader at that. When she had seen a certain flick in their eyes as they laughed with her at such nonsense, she realized cheerleading impressed even the most blasé, including Harriet.

"McCullough? Next?"

"Eek," Snowy said, a word she and Bev had copied from comic books.

"Let's go," Harriet said. "Break a leg."

As Snowy ran toward the stage amid the other McCullough girls and applause, momentarily it wasn't a stage but a football field, a basketball court, her bowl of dirt a megaphone, and all her old training carried her up onto it where she settled herself on the floor to play in an imaginary sandbox, praying she was inconspicuous. No such luck. The audience now had a clear view of her.

"Pig-Pen! Pig-Pen!" Laughter, clapping. "Pig-Pen!"

What would Bev do? Snowy emptied the bowl of dirt over her head.

17

Pandemonium, which Lucy's scolding slowly brought down to giggles.

The last-minute script had been mostly written by McCullough's philosophy major, a senior; though much of it mystified Snowy, she was sure it was very clever, and out in the audience the superior amusement of the enlightened gave the signal to laugh to the other girls who didn't know Kierkegaard from a hole in the ground. Relaxing slightly, Snowy began telling Tom about tonight. Then she looked up and met the gaze of a shadowy guy standing in the doorway. A gate-crasher? A second guy materialized beside him. She blinked, and they were gone.

She hadn't had a date for so long she was hallucinating.

"Good grief!" said Charlie Brown, and the skit ended.

As Snowy helped Harriet carry down the coffee table which miraculously hadn't broken from being sat upon by the girl playing the bust of Beethoven, Harriet said, "You're a star!"

Mud cracking, Snowy said, "I think I'm seeing stars, or did you notice a couple of guys over in that door?"

"I've been warning you, your celibacy will rot your brain."

Snowy always blushed guiltily during these warnings, though Harriet couldn't know what went on in Snowy's bed because Snowy only did that terrible thing when Harriet was safely out of the room, on a date. Snowy suspected Harriet herself was more celibate than her worldliness suggested, but they hadn't candidly discussed how far she went with Ray, Jim, Stan. When Harriet had hinted in an early conversation that she wasn't a virgin, Snowy had hinted also, for even though there'd been just the one time with Tom, one time was all you needed, the culmination of the steps which had led her to this: the necking sessions on the front seat of Tom's 1949 cream-colored Chevy convertible (Tom had been too cool to use a blatant back seat), the Getting Fresh, the jerking-offs, the blow jobs, the rapture!

Still keyed up, McCullough sat back down. Snowy glanced at the doorway. The first guy had appeared again, and he wasn't

18

watching the next skit, he was searching the audience for— He found her.

"Hey," Harriet whispered. "Is he supposed to be here? I've seen him at fraternity parties, he's one of the quiet ones. He's giving you the across-a-crowded-room treatment with a vengeance."

"Why? I'm Pig-Pen!"

"He must like the earthy type."

They laughed, and the second guy moved into the doorway.

Harriet said, "Wow, I've had my eye on him, Dennis somebody, he looks so sensitive," and she leaned across Snowy and whispered to the house chairman, "Gotta get Snowy into a shower before she suffocates, we're leaving," and then she tugged Snowy and her bowl along the row toward the doorway, which went empty.

Snowy whispered, "What are you up to?"

"Shh. Hoist the other end of Schroeder's piano and act frail." But the guys weren't in the hall. "Hot pursuit!"

As they seesawed down the stairs, Snowy said, "I'm not just going to take a shower, I'm going to take a bath too, a bubble bath and soak until I'm a prune."

"You can soak all you want later, but now you'll take a fast shower and we'll be off to the State Line if we can find them—"

"Harriet."

"You're here to get an education in more than poetry, aren't you? Beer joints are an essential part of your curriculum, and these guys are nice quiet types *and* handsome, what a combination."

"If they're such shrinking violets, how come they were at the skits?"

"We don't know if that's illegal. Snowy, compared with other guys at parties, they're perfect gentlemen. I bet Dennis is someone I could discuss art with at long last, I do not understand why I attract jocks."

Snowy refrained from commenting that Harriet chose jocks.

"This isn't a weekend, it's a Wednesday night, I've got studying for tomorrow."

"Remember my Coffee Cake Therapy?"

So far, pancakes had been served every Sunday at breakfast, but only twice had coffee cake been served, on weekdays, making it extra special, a great event; Snowy and Harriet watched each breakfast menu for news of it, and the night before the second Coffee Cake Morning the subject of their gabfest was exclusively the joy the morrow would bring. Usually in the dining rooms Snowy was apt to be the lone early breakfaster, but on Coffee Cake Mornings the place was packed with girls who'd dashed to Commons, their beds unmade, their hair unbrushed. And Harriet had evolved the idea of Coffee Cake Therapy: Any deviation from the norm of studying, classes, writing papers, painting, more studying, was extremely important to your mental health, since small pleasures helped keep things in perspective. As examples Harriet listed Snowy's Agatha Christies, a six-pack bought for them by a senior, memorizing the Tom Lehrer songs on Harriet's records, and interesting mail, but a date was, Harriet maintained, the ultimate Coffee Cake Therapy.

Snowy said, "Because of this foolish skit, I haven't even got time for an Agatha tonight."

"My hunch is you've already finished studying, you'll be restudying."

"I can't breeze through Malthus, I never heard of him before!"

"Shh." Harriet opened the front door and they carried the table along the path, and there ahead the quarry stood talking. "Hi," Harriet said. "Enjoy the show?"

The second guy said, "What show?", but the first one smiled at Snowy and asked, knowing she'd seen them there, "Did you have your choice of roles?"

Unless the moonlight was deceiving, he was indeed very good-looking. He wore a V-necked sweater and chinos. Flustered, Snowy replied, "No." Scintillating repartee!

20

Harriet said, "And she couldn't rehearse either, for obvious reasons which she's about to wash off before she smothers."

The second guy said to Harriet, "I'm Dennis Crowley, may we be your piano movers?"

"Ooh, thank you, it *is* getting heavy." Coffee *Table* Therapy. "I'm Harriet Blumburg and this is my roommate, Henrietta Snow, she's called Snowy."

Snowy winced. Harriet was the reason she was still saddled with her hometown nickname; Harriet's first name and Snowy's were so close that when the other girls had asked them about nicknames and Snowy had answered without thinking, "I used to be Snowy," everybody had seized upon it.

The guys took the table, the first guy's hand gently bumping Snowy's glove of mud. He said, "I'm Whitney Bennett. Whit."

She brushed dirt off her face. "Um, how do you do."

"Are you a freshman?"

"Yes."

Dennis said, "We were thinking about a pub crawl, like to join us?"

"Great," Harriet said. "Ten minutes for Snowy's shower, you can wait in the living room."

Dennis and Whit exchanged glances. Dennis said, "Why waste time? There's a place we could go to that comes with a shower and we could get a head start, I carry my portable bar everywhere. Which house are you?"

They went into McCullough, and in the hall Harriet said, "A place with a shower?"

"All the modern conveniences," Dennis said. "Let's see, too late for us to be allowed to take this to your room, isn't it."

How scrupulous, Snowy thought, after the Commons escapade. She said to Whit, "Thank you, but I've got studying to do."

Harriet said to the guys, "Give us a moment."

Whit and Dennis strolled into the living room, and Harriet and Snowy maneuvered the table up the stairs, Snowy shaking her head violently at Harriet who said, when they reached their

21

room, "Okay, you told me you got too involved with some guy so you wanted to be footloose and fancy-free, but that means playing the field, not taking the veil."

Snowy didn't explain that throughout her senior year she had played the field, while longing for Tom. At Rumford Teachers' College right now, no doubt Tom was tomcatting even if it was a school night. Although he'd become an English major, she couldn't picture him burning the midnight oil; the Superlatives page hadn't labeled him Most Likely to Succeed. She looked at herself in the mirror. Disgusting. She must be a college stunt to Whit, like swallowing goldfish. "Does 'pub crawl' mean American beer joints?"

Harriet said enviously, "Dennis probably spent a summer in Britain, plus maybe Europe," such a tour being another thing she had yet to talk her father into.

"What's this place with a shower?"

"I guess they know somebody who has an apartment somewhere. An adventure! Education! Therapy!"

Snowy said, "I've got studying . . ."

"Damnit, you're so *compulsive!*"

At that word, Snowy put her chin up, a gesture which indicated pride. "Okay."

"Hooray!"

She was popular with her roommate again. "I have to pack a change of clothes and—"

"Snowy, you can't walk out of here carrying a suitcase, the night watchman might find it a trifle suspicious, we'll shake yours clean enough, look at me, I'm in my oldest."

"At least underwear—"

"No time." Harriet scooped up Kents and a lighter. "We don't have to sign out if we're back by eleven, hurry."

Snowy raced around the room, snatching her own Kents off her desk, her matches, and—genius—her comb off her bureau. Downstairs in the living room, she explained to Whit, "I rearranged my agenda."

"I'm glad," he said.

She felt suddenly warm, as if she'd emerged from an igloo into a tropical paradise.

They all walked to the parking lot. The guys stopped at a beat-up Studebaker, and she was relieved that Whit opened the passenger door for her while Dennis and Harriet got in the back, because driving might preoccupy Whit enough so he wouldn't notice that Pig-Pen didn't know how to talk to a Williams boy. She said, "Thank you," brushing covertly at her bottom before climbing in. He slid behind the steering wheel. She sought poise by tapping forth a Kent. He whipped out a lighter. She'd been a sophomore when she started bumming an occasional Lucky Strike from Tom, and since then she'd had plenty of practice in lighting a cigarette off a proffered flame, but now her hand trembled, very un-Bette-Davis. "Thank you," she said again. Whit must be bowled over by her extensive vocabulary. He lit his own Pall Mall.

Down the long drive they went to the main road, Snowy excited and scared. This was the first time she'd been off campus at night and only the third time since her parents had driven her here on her first day, humiliating her with their presence. (She had never wanted people to know she had parents, ordinary parents who were bewildered by and proud of her successes and who made her feel like a paper doll.) The local taxi company ran rides to and from town in an old car that smelled of rotting leather and greasy cigarette smoke, and last month she and Harriet had taken it in together to buy scatter pillows to jazz up their beds, Harriet afterwards going often, on shopping sprees, but Snowy had just gone in one other time, to arrange with the newspaper about her column. She stayed on campus partly because she hadn't the money to do much more than window-shop, partly because the taxi schedule necessitated waiting around in the taxi office where the squawking switchboard distracted her from the studying she'd brought along, and mainly because the Outside World made her jumpy, wistful for freedom. You could manage fine remaining cloistered; the town merchants came to the college to sell their wares, displaying them in Commons, a custom which, Snowy had thought when she and Harriet bought themselves Bennington Potters ashtrays and coffee mugs there, lent a disconcerting gypsy atmosphere to the Vermont setting.

Whit asked, "Have you decided on your major?"

"Lit. Yours?"

"Biology. I'm interested in entomology."

"Ento-?"

"Bugs."

He laughed, so she laughed and asked, "What year are you?"

"A junior."

She knew they weren't exchanging information. They were doing a mating dance, anticipating intimacy. The warmth tingled inside her, itchy, like when your foot went to sleep and started to sizzle.

In the back seat there was the clink of a bottle opener against a bottle and then the whoosh of spray, and Harriet shrieked, "The ceiling!"

Dennis said, "That road over from Williamstown always shakes up my portable bar, if we're ever stranded and want a drink we can wring out this ceiling."

Whit asked Snowy, forestalling Dennis's being funny about wringing out the car's upholstery if either girl wanted to get pregnant, "Where are you from?"

Snowy said, "Oh, I'm practically a native, here all the way from New Hampshire."

Dennis said, "Señorita, señor," and handed over two paper cups.

"Thank you," Snowy said, passing one to Whit, their hands lingering, her trembling smoothed by his touch, dried mud drifting. She sipped. Rum-and-Coke. She'd only drunk beer and hard liquor in cars at the drive-in theater or parking, the cars stationary. Another milestone! Feeling that she really was a college kid now, wild and reckless and devil-may-care, she looked out the window at the headlights' glimpses of country-

24

side where everyday people like her parents lived, except her parents were residential.

Whit said, "At least you changed states. I'm from Massachusetts. Colburn."

"Where's that?"

"Down near the Connecticut line."

State lines. "Are we in New York?"

"Uh-huh."

Harriet was discoursing on Rubens, and Whit and Snowy listened in until Snowy, emboldened at last by booze, decided to risk trying to entertain this Williams boy who might finally make her forget Tom. But what to talk about? She returned to the subject they'd left, using the emphasis tactic again. "Harriet's from California and she can hardly understand me, I didn't know I had an accent. For instance, we were reminiscing about getting our drivers' licenses and the big moment when you asked to borrow your folks' car keys—" Snowy was the one who'd done the borrowing; Harriet, she'd gathered, had been presented with keys to her own car. "—and after I said 'car keys,' Harriet gave me this peculiar look, she thought I'd gone crazy and was saying 'khakis,' you know, pants, chinos." She blushed. Like the chinos he was wearing, with It lurking within.

He said, ignoring all r's, "I parked my car in Harvard Yard."

Dennis shouted, interrupting Harriet, "Harvard? Traitor!"

Whit and Snowy laughed, and more dirt flaked off her face, and Whit pulled into the empty parking lot of a hunched building whose once-gaudy sign read SLEEPYTIME MOTOR LODGE. FLUSH TOILETS. TV. VACANCY.

Snowy had ten million heart attacks.

"Hey," Harriet said.

Whit parked a distance away from the office. This place couldn't care less about who its customers were and what they did, but you might as well maintain a semblance of discretion. He switched off the headlights.

Harriet said, "It's a *motel*."

25

Dennis opened his door. "Whit, explain how honorable our intentions are."

As they watched Dennis walk toward the office, Whit said to Snowy, "We'll just have another drink while you get cleaned up, and we'll be on our way."

Snowy jumped out of the car, spilling dregs of rum-and-Coke. The moon was gone behind clouds now, and except for the curtained office window the only light came from that tawdry sign, showing nothing except this decrepit motel no foliage-tourist in his right mind would stop at—and none had.

Harriet got out, slamming the car door, and said, "Snowy. God, what are we going to do?"

"Back from Yonkers, we're the ones who had to walk. Do you know where we are?"

"I wasn't paying attention."

Snowy crumpled her cup. "Where we are is, the middle of nowhere. Let's get started walking, I guess we could hitchhike, that wouldn't be any worse than this. Or would it? What if we're picked up by an axe murderer? Have you ever hitchhiked before?"

"No."

"Me neither." Off Snowy's face dropped more caked mud, reminding her. "And the minute a driver saw me, he'd step on the gas. A Pig-Sty!"

Harriet said, "Maybe the guys' intentions really are honorable."

"Maybe I'm Mamie Eisenhower. Harriet, people who go to motels are supposed to be married, we could get arrested and expelled, and intentions wouldn't matter a damn."

Dennis was sauntering back from the office, twirling a key. All at once Snowy wondered how much of his portable bar he and Whit had consumed tonight.

Harriet said, "They've obviously done this before and they haven't got arrested or else they wouldn't be here again."

"Criminals return to the scene of the crime."

"They'd've been kicked out of school. Okay, we can't hitchhike with you like that, and if we walk we'll be late and have to tell why, *if* we manage to get there and don't end up in Albany instead. Better take our chances with these guys. You've got to admit, they show a kind of creativity."

"Nice quiet perfect gentlemen. Still waters run deep."

"Running water! You can shower, and I'll keep them at bay, I promise." Harriet pointed at the sign. "TV! I miss TV a lot."

So did Snowy. The living room in McCullough had sofas, armchairs, a piano, everything a regular living room should have except a television set.

"Wednesday," Harriet tempted her, *"The Millionaire, I've Got a Secret—"*

Whit climbed out of the car and walked over and looked down at Snowy. "You want to go back?"

Her policy: Don't go backward.

"We'll drive you back," he said, touching her small hand gripping the paper cup, "but this isn't what it seems, we just stop sometimes to have a drink and remind ourselves of the real world."

"The Outside World," she said, warm.

And thus she found herself across a state line in a motel shower. A while ago, Harriet had come into the bathroom and said, "I did a Blue Wash by shaking, how're you doing?" and she'd replied, "Mud wallow," and Harriet had said, "They're planning to watch the *Wednesday Night Fights* next, hurry up and help me talk them into *Armstrong Circle Theatre,*" and left.

The little cake of soap was now as thin as a Necco wafer about to dissolve. She would never get any cleaner. She turned off the taps and whisked open the shower curtain. "Eek!"

Dennis said, holding the flimsy bath towel wide, "The TV went blooey."

"Harriet!"

"So I thought I'd watch you instead."

Snowy pulled the shower curtain around her, slime and all. *"Harriet!"*

27

"There's snow on the TV," Dennis mused, "and Snowy in the shower—"

Whit bounded in and shoved Dennis into the bedroom, wresting the towel. "Jesus, I'm sorry, I was fixing the TV."

"Thank you."

He gave her the towel and hesitated.

She saw that Harriet had left her clothes on the toilet lid. Then she saw that Whit, gallant rescuer though he might be, had a colossal hard-on in his chinos. Khakis!

Harriet called, "Snowy?"

"It's okay." She pushed aside the shower curtain, began toweling herself, and said to Whit while he goggled, "Would you believe I'm so honest-American I was even a cheerleader, the captain of the Gunthwaite High School cheerleading squad, State Champions of 1957?"

"You were?" He closed the door.

Stepping onto the paper bath mat, she stood on tiptoe to kiss him, and as he gasped and squeezed her against him, swooping his hands from her shoulders to her bottom, she certainly felt It, which almost overwhelmed her determination, but she could feel her true goal also jabbing into her and she slid her hand down his right front pocket and yanked out his car keys. "A motel isn't an appropriate place to take an honest-American cheerleader. Call me if you want a proper date." She grabbed her sneakers and clothes and Kents and wrenched at the bathroom doorknob. In the bedroom, Harriet had stuck Dennis behind the television set to work on the horizontal hold, imprisoning him with instructions, "Down, farther, no, up—"

Snowy said, "Harriet, run!"

They ran. A place like the Sleepytime Motor Lodge, Snowy supposed, had probably seen stranger sights than two girls, one stark naked, sprinting out of a room. Gravel stabbed her feet. She tossed Harriet the car keys and said, "You drive, I'll dress," and they dived into Whit's car and screeched off.

Harriet said, "A clean getaway!"

"Not *that* clean," said Snowy, one leg in her Levi's.

28

Harriet dithered, "I'm sorry about Dennis—Whit and I were fixing the TV and he—I'm sorry about everything."

"Nope, you were right, an education." And a thaw.

"Which way home?"

Snowy opened the glove compartment. "Is there a dashboard light? Whew, he's got a road map, New England. Eek, what have we here?" She held up a pack of Trojans. Just like the emergency equipment in the glove compartment of the cream-colored convertible.

" 'Be prepared,' " Harriet began, and after they'd finished singing Tom Lehrer's "Boy Scouts' Marching Song," she added, "Don't tell me. I never thought to ask. You were a Girl Scout."

"Of course," Snowy said.

☙

"WE WON'T EVER find a parking space," Harriet said. "You jump out and I'll keep driving."

Snowy said, "Around and around Boston, maybe an hour?"

"I wanted to visit Boston, didn't I? It's heaven."

Snowy screamed, "There, that car's leaving!"

When Harriet did talk her father into something, she sure got results. The car with which she captured the empty parking space was a white Jaguar. Snowy imagined the dazed salesman boring his progeny to tears, endlessly repeating down through generations of children, grandchildren, great-grandchildren, his tale about the day these two Bennington girls came into the showroom and one of them just—

"If you hurry," Harriet said, "you won't be late."

"God, how I hate high heels." Wearing her new camel's hair coat, her own hair in a laborious French twist, Snowy hopped out and ran wobbling along Commonwealth Avenue, a street so wide it had a median strip. The last week in October, and the city trees were still filled with the colors which had fallen and withered up north. This was the second time in her life she'd

29

been to Boston, the first her first train trip, occurring when she, chairman of the Junior Prom Decoration Committee, and three other kids rode down here to have decorations designed at Dennison's for their prom's theme, *Ocean Fantasia*. A juvenile mission; now she was here to go to a job interview. Along past imposing buildings she ran until she saw on a brownstone a brass plaque modestly acknowledging: COMMONWEALTH PUBLISHING COMPANY.

Bennington had a Non-Resident Term each year from January through early March. NRT. There were jokes about how its real purpose wasn't to get the students out of the ivory tower into the workaday world but to give students and teachers alike a chance to flee the Vermont winters, and such jokes made Snowy, a survivor of New Hampshire winters, feel smug, though NRT scared her, another adjustment, another new life. During NRT she couldn't waitress, the only job she knew, because you should find a job connected to your interests. What could an aspiring poet do? Her counselor suggested that learning about the publishing world might be useful, an idea which appealed and had future possibilities, for she was going to have to get a job when she graduated since you certainly couldn't earn a living writing poetry, and a publishing career would be better than a waitressing career—she assumed. So she went to the NRT office and read the listings. Several typist jobs in New York publishing houses, one in Boston.

Boston? She had sat in the NRT office pondering. The conventional though braver choice would be New York, which she'd glimpsed at age sixteen when her Girl Scout troop, en route to Washington, had gone to Radio City Music Hall. But Bev and Puddles were in Boston. Would it be anticlimactic to attempt to revive the triumvirate? Would it be going backward? Would it, she asked Bev in her head, would it fail? New York, she asked Bev's mother, or Boston?

Snowy and Bev, also an only child, had been best friends, practically sisters, since second grade when Bev and her widowed mother, Julia, had moved from a chicken farm outside

30

town to a house in Snowy's neighborhood. Julia and Bev's father were both from Bedford, Massachusetts, Julia working as a secretary two years in Boston before becoming the wife of an inexperienced but Depression-determined poultry farmer. Bev's father had died at Iwo Jima. When Bev was in sixth grade, Julia remarried and moved again to the country, and Snowy planned to hate the new place because it took Bev away, but Julia kept her promise that the move wouldn't change things, and thus Bev didn't have to transfer to another grammar school or ride a school bus, her stepfather dropping her off at Snowy's house on his way to work and picking her up after work—Fred was the head teller at the Gunthwaite Savings Bank, not a farmer—and Snowy and Bev walked to and from school together, same as always. And, surprised, Snowy loved the farm. She already loved Julia, even though Julia and Bev were very different except for their height. Prematurely white-haired Julia was gawky, the opposite of fluid Bev, giving such a gaunt impression of being all elbows and collarbone and awkwardness that you expected her to get snarled up in her warps and woofs as she worked at her looms in the dining room of the old Cape where she made the place mats and handbags which the New Hampshire League of Arts and Crafts sold like hot cakes. Reclusive, in the mornings Julia wove; she spent afternoons gardening, walking in the woods, reading. Julia was the only woman Snowy knew, besides teachers, who had gone to college, Mount Holyoke. It was Julia who'd suggested Bennington when Snowy told her she dreaded having to prove herself again in college, striving once more to be a big-deal A-student.

Did Julia know what had happened last spring? Julia must wonder why she hadn't seen Snowy since then, why Fred drove Bev directly to school and drove her home from there if she didn't have a ride with some guy. Julia must wonder why this closest of friendships had shattered.

Because: Bev had briefly gone steady with Tom before he started dating Snowy, and she had fallen madly in love with him after he broke up with Snowy, dating him whenever he came home from Rumford. But that night last April, Tom brought Bev back from a date to a pajama party at Puddles's house and Snowy had unintentionally appeared on the doorstep while they were kissing; Snowy did not withdraw, and gradually Bev realized she herself was the third person in this tableau. Bev went into the house, and Tom and Snowy drove off. Afterward Snowy told Bev it was over, but Bev acted aloof, and when no phone call came from Tom asking Bev out again, Bev stopped speaking to Snowy altogether, dramatically avoiding her.

Agonized, Snowy sought Puddles's help. Any fights had always previously been between Bev and Puddles, Snowy the restorer of peace, like when Bev had stolen football-captain Jack O'Brien from Puddles, nearly destroying the triumvirate. Puddles tried, yet even she, crazy fearless Puddles, blunt Puddles, was foiled by Bev's total refusal to discuss the situation. "For Christ's sake," Puddles would scold Bev, "stop this stupidity, we're grown-up now!", suggesting, since Bev was almost as famous for her forgetfulness as for her swinging way of walking, "Can't you just forget it, forgive and forget?" Bev would reply, "*Why* did Miss Hubbard take until the end of French Two to admit, in front of the whole class, that my nasals are good? How belated! They've been superb all along, vocab and grammar are the minor difficulties." Sometimes Puddles attempted subtlety, saying things like, "What a drag, having to go to the Senior Banquet with a senior boy, but I guess I'll go with Norm instead of Ron, Gene won't get jealous over him, Snowy's going with Dudley, it'll be her first date since the pajama party, she's still claiming she's too busy, *I* call it penance, have you chosen between Frankie and Joe?" Bev replied, "Another movie in chemistry tomorrow—the discovery of Orlon, simply asking for trouble, the guys and their sweater wisecracks," and made a Marilyn Monroe moue, then crossed her eyes. Bev adored making faces. Exasperated, Puddles eventually gave up.

After graduation, for the first time Snowy and Bev didn't have summer jobs together at Sweetland.

Bev, through a friend of Julia's, got a job waitressing at a

32

hotel in Camden, Maine. Waitressing again, yes, but amid wealth in a gorgeous setting, with new boys, the ocean, sailboats, and, most thrilling, here the movie version of *Peyton Place,* whose true on-location site should have been New Hampshire, was being filmed. Bev had intended to become an extra and get discovered—*that* would show Tom and Snowy!—yet far from Gunthwaite her résumé of school plays seemed kid stuff and she felt too insignificant to compete. Anyway, everyone and his grandmother were signing up. If she didn't try, she wouldn't fail. This was the same reasoning that had made her not go out for cheerleading with Snowy and Puddles. Trying out for a Dramatics Club play was different, because if you didn't get a part (though she always had) it wasn't final, there would be another play.

Back in Gunthwaite, at Sweetland Snowy concocted frappes behind the soda fountain and lugged trays laden with hamburgers and toasted club sandwiches to clerks and businessmen in booths, imagining Bev's adventures which they could be sharing if they'd remained best friends. Many a night Snowy almost drove to the farm to see Julia, then didn't, ashamed of confessing betrayal, incapable of mentioning sex to any adult, Julia no exception, but hoping Julia might phone her; Julia stayed silent, apparently having decided against interfering. Snowy counted the days until she would leave Gunthwaite, this hell where she couldn't keep herself from being constantly on the watch for Tom, and how could you miss a red Texaco tank truck, Tom delivering gas, his summer job, or a classic cream-colored convertible with a continental tire on the back and a series of girls in her seat? The most excruciating moments of the summer occurred one time when she and a carload of other girls went to the drive-in theater. "Broading around," such outings were called, and during the second feature the girls got frisky and ran along the rakish back row banging on car hoods, and there was Tom's car. Nancy Gordon thumped the hood and up popped the head of Gail Perkins and then Tom, looking blind. He always hung his glasses over the sun visor at the onset of necking. Nearsightedness did not, however, prevent him from recognizing Snowy. While the girls yelled, "Tom! Gail! We thought this car was empty! Abandoned!", Tom and Snowy stared at each other. She could hear radio music. They used to turn the movie speaker off and the radio on and—kisses, popcorn spilled onto the floor, Tom spilled into his handkerchief. Gail said, "Oh. Snowy." Tom said nothing. The other girls ran farther along the row. Snowy followed.

That summer Puddles was, as usual, a cashier at the Gunthwaite A&P, working wicked hours and probably making more money than Bev and Snowy combined, minus Bev's fat tips from admiring men; Bev dated some of the younger unmarried guests, but they received, hopes dashed, no extra service.

With their savings Snowy and Puddles shopped for school clothes at Yvonne's Apparel and Dunlap's Department Store on Main Street, asking anxiously, "Is this *collegiate?*", Snowy teasing Puddles about the angel-of-mercy uniform she'd wear when she began the bedside-nursing part of her training six months hence. A cloak, perhaps? After Bev came home, Puddles went shopping with her, and because at Katharine Gibbs the students had to dress as if they were going to an office, Bev kept asking, "Is this *secretarial?*", but she just bought enough for the first week, until she could get a chance at the bounteous sophisticated selection offered in Boston stores. Puddles demanded details about her summer, and Bev, who loved telling stories, embellished every incident, knowing whatever she said would be repeated to Snowy and wanting to make Snowy suffer great torments of jealousy over Camden and glamorous men and yachts, although she became vague whenever Puddles prodded her about *Peyton Place*. Puddles reported to Snowy, "She says she didn't have time to try out, what with dates and parties and clambakes." Snowy saw through that, as Bev feared she might, and only excitement over leaving for Mass. General caused Puddles, who always said what everyone else was thinking, to accept this explanation and not remark, "Bullshit."

New clothes, new lives. Puddles had wept sentimental tears

at graduation but had long since recovered; Bev had missed her mother awfully this summer, despite their many phone talks, which didn't comfort because Bev was unable even over faceless long-distance to pour out the tale of Snowy's perfidy, but Bev had indeed made the break from home by living two months in Camden and she was raring to depart again to try the grander stage of Boston (Snowy might be going to an expensive four-year college, but Bennington was in Vermont where, it was a well-known fact, the cows outnumbered the people); Snowy had packed and repacked her white Skyway luggage with everything that wouldn't wrinkle. Yet Snowy's and Bev's eagerness to flee Gunthwaite differed from Puddles's, and to them these last urgent days seemed a kaleidoscope whirling too fast their eighteen years of growing up together here, with now separate futures lying ahead in foggy unreality. And they couldn't discuss this, the way they would have before. They couldn't, one last time, sit around Snowy's bedroom or Bev's, leafing through *Seventeen* magazines, talking, talking. They couldn't say au revoir and exclaim, "Another milestone!"

Bev and Puddles had assumed they'd be a mutual-support duo in Boston, so they were nonplussed to find that they gradually phoned and met less and less as they became acquainted with their roommates and made new friends. They did manage to meet Thursdays for a beer at a bar on Charles Street, Puddles using her old driver's license on which she had altered her date of birth to make her twenty-one, and Bev, who hadn't learned to drive, successfully trusting her appearance. Bev had always looked more mature than other girls, and now she had abandoned her DA—too high-school—for a secretarial gamine cut.

(Puddles had also been experimenting with her hair lately, placing a Dixie cup on her head and considering the effect in the mirror, trying to decide which style would look best beneath a nurse's cap, but she kept returning to her old tried-and-true hairdo, her brown hair almost touching her shoulders, its tips curled under. Snail-curls, Snowy long ago had named them, to herself.)

In addition to news about Bev's roommate, at Bennington Snowy received reports of Bev's love life via Puddles, whose own love life meant being pinned to Gene Chabot, a Gunthwaite boy now a sophomore at UNH. Gene and Jean; Puddles had always thought that their sharing the same first name was a sign that their romance was meant to be. So far this fall, Puddles had only been able to leave school one weekend, which she and Gene spent at home in Gunthwaite, mostly parking at the sandpit, Gene insulated inside the two Trojans she'd insisted upon at first when they started screwing a year ago and she now required again after months in which she'd allowed him to use only one. Puddles had heard abortion stories at nursing school. Laboring over her, Gene thought of a girl at UNH who didn't ask a guy to use any skins, who even permitted Sloppy Seconds. Seconds with Puddles meant two more goddamn Trojans; he ought to buy them by the case.

In high school Bev's biggest romance besides Tom had been with Roger Lambert, now a scholarship junior at Dartmouth. When Bev had started dating Roger, before Snowy began dating Tom, Snowy had been scared to death of him, a senior, the co-captain of the basketball team, the president of the National Honor Society, jaunty, smooth. Going out with Tom had ended her intimidation, and by the time she graduated she'd realized that she and Roger had more in common with each other, in a way, than with Tom and Bev. Hers was the female equivalent of his high-school success; she understood scorching ambition. Puddles wrote Snowy, "Bev has gone back to her plan of marrying a millionaire instead of Tom, but Roger is on the scene again. He wrote her a letter and last Saturday he drove down here in the Heap and they walked around Beacon Hill. Bev has decided she's going to live in Louisburg Square when she marries her millionaire. Swanky! Then they drove around trying to find a place to go parking, but they couldn't, which was FRUSTRATING, Bev says. I expect Roger drove back to Dartmouth with an extra stick shift, ha ha. She's dating other guys, natch. Same as at home, she draws guys like flies. And to think she's the one of us who's still a virgin, or so she claims—I know, you're keeping mum about you and Tom that time last spring, but I'm not STUPID. P.S. My brother Malcolm is playing JV football. Do I feel OLD."

I'm to blame, Snowy thought in the NRT office. She had ruined friendship.

"Boston," she said to the NRT advisor. "I want to apply for that job at Commonwealth Publishing."

Bennington's Long Weekend at the end of October was the time when most girls had their NRT job interviews. By mail, Snowy made an appointment to meet Mr. Palmquist, an assistant editor, on Monday, October 28, intending to take a bus from Gunthwaite to Concord, where she would get the train. Harriet didn't have to bother with an interview, for she'd be working at a New York gallery owned by a friend of the family, but she was going to New York anyway to see the city. Emily Post kept nudging Snowy, who finally asked if Harriet might prefer coming home with her instead and seeing some of New Hampshire. Harriet said, "Sure, New York can wait until Thanksgiving." "Wonderful," Snowy said weakly, consternated, "I'll call my folks and tell them they don't have to pick me up." Harriet said, "And I'd like to see Boston too, I'll drive you to your interview."

Long Weekend began at one P.M. Friday. They packed the Jaguar and headed northeast, Snowy growing more embarrassed about her parents and Gunthwaite the closer they got. Harriet had once mentioned a swimming pool; she probably lived in a mansion. During the drive, which seemed both twice as long and twice as short as before, Snowy spelled Harriet for an hour, and the first wisp of envy curled into her soul when male drivers honked and waved at *her,* thinking she owned the glorious car. She drove debonairly, under false pretenses.

Harriet drove barefoot. In October.

Their talk, mixed with radio music, always returned to boys, Harriet's dates—and Snowy's. On the two weekends since the Sleepytime Motor Lodge episode, Snowy had begun dating,

37

choosing guys who didn't look like Tom and whose majors bored her, guaranteeing she wouldn't fall in love (though hadn't she fallen for a shop major, head over heels?). Twice she had gone out with the best-looking, Whit Bennett. After he and Dennis had hitchhiked back from the motel and picked up his Studebaker she and Harriet had left at the end of the driveway, he had sent her a note of apology—and a dozen red roses! Their first date had been admirably respectable, movies and a good-night kiss, but last Saturday night, on their way back from a fraternity party, the Studebaker meandered off onto a dirt road and soon they were parking and her pent-up celibacy burst and she let him Get Fresh; although he didn't have Tom's ability to unhook a bra one-handed, he otherwise managed maneuvers with practiced ease.

"Have I told you," Snowy said to Harriet, "that he bites his nails?"

"Anything else?"

Snowy blushed. "Where I come from, where we're heading, Hicksville, you're not supposed to let a guy Get Fresh until you're going steady." She'd also broken that rule with Tom.

"Hickeyville!" Harriet laughed. "And you can't screw until you're pinned? This music is for the birds."

At least when Harriet dismissed Pat Boone and changed stations, she didn't stop at the Everly Brothers but went on to find Elvis Presley. Snowy agreed that Elvis's singing, not his looks, was sexy, and the Everly Brothers' efforts were callow; Whit *liked* the Everly Brothers, another point in his favor. Snowy said, "I am never getting pinned."

"That guy you were too serious about, you weren't pinned to him?"

"He asked."

"You broke his heart?"

"Only temporarily."

"I'm," sang Elvis, "all shook up!"

Books had warned Snowy that she would find her home-town smaller than she remembered, and the old mill town on

38

the river had indeed shrunk. In the middle of Main Street, Snowy said, "There's the restaurant where I worked." As Harriet slowed and they looked at the storefront, the sign saying SWEETLAND, they thought of how Harriet had been taking art lessons summers while Snowy slung hash.

Snowy said, "Sweetland was better than working at Hooper's, the dairy bar I told you about. Hooper's stays open late and interferes with dating. Sweetland is just open until six, nine on Fridays."

Harriet slipped her feet into her loafers, Snowy's parents imminent, and drove onward. "Did you have to wear a cute uniform?"

"Plain white nylon. This is State Avenue now, turn here, right, at Chestnut Street." The tall old houses seemed shorter. "That's Gowen Street, Puddles lives there, we'd meet at this corner when we walked to school and bid farewell when we walked home." She pointed at a yellow house. "Bev lived there, before she moved to the country. Before *that,* she lived on a chicken farm that's long gone." It had been impossible to delete Bev during gabfests with Harriet, but she couldn't bring herself to talk about the estrangement, so she'd explained the lack of letters by telling Harriet that Bev wasn't a letter writer, and Harriet had said, nodding, "Do I get complaints!" They came to Emery Street. Snowy quailed. "Turn here," she said.

Emery Street ran alongside the river, and the view of warehouses and the backs of Main Street stores had always made Snowy think of ports and faraway places. Her parents found the view slummy; this had almost caused them not to buy the big neglected Colonial on the low hill above the river when in 1946 they had saved up enough to put a down payment on a house and move out of the apartment a few streets over, yet they convinced themselves the Colonial could become a showplace, despite the view, and they had gone ahead and bought it and begun fixing it up, and they'd been refixing and refixing ever since.

Snowy said lightly, "That's the old homestead." It had shrunk too.

"Beautiful," Harriet said.

The Jaguar glided up the driveway into the small backyard of bushes. Snowy's parents didn't waste any time or money on this yard, because it was hidden from the street. Snowy heard the familiar explosion of high-pitched barks, and as she jumped out of the car to catch the Shetland collie hurtling at her off the back steps, she saw, distressed, that Annie Laurie, whom she'd owned since she was twelve, had not shrunk, had got fat, Snowy's departure depriving her of exercise. Kit, the black-and-white cat, descended the steps with dignity; he had always been heavy, neutered. Snowy hugged Laurie, patted Kit, tried not to cry, and braced herself.

The front door was only used to bring in mail. Her father opened the back door, and her parents emerged together. In the evenings while they read and watched television in the living room, they seemed to Snowy to be posing for a portrait of family life, and now Harriet could title them "Parents Welcoming Daughter and Roommate Home from College," but their expressions supplied an involuntary subtitle: "Parents Bowled Over by Jaguar."

"Henrietta!" her mother exclaimed, recovering, hugging her, Laurie and all.

Her father said, "Henrietta."

Snowy's nickname dismayed her parents.

They also had shrunk.

Snowy thought, I won't actually perish of embarrassment, and introduced Harriet to these people. Her mother, Charlotte, was a Gunthwaite native whose travels had never taken her farther than Manchester, New Hampshire, until Snowy's interviews at Mount Holyoke and Smith and Bennington. Plump, her brown hair nearly completely gray now, she appeared a serene woman, but inwardly she was constantly worrying, about whether or not the sofa needed a new slipcover and why Snowy hadn't gone to a coed college where she'd be a popular cheerleader dating popular athletes again and whether or not to buy that rooster wastebasket for her kitchen rooster collection (which Snowy loathed). Hank Snow, slight and gray-haired, had grown up very poor in Manchester, his widowed mother waitressing to support him and his sisters. He had been determined to create a perfect family of his own in a perfect house, envisioning himself the patriarch of a brood of rosy-cheeked children who would sit quietly at a long dining-room table, hanging onto his every word, profiting from his wisdom. But miscarriages had made Snowy the sole offspring. He did have a dining room, where he insisted every meal be served, even breakfast, and he did have a fine maple table at which Snowy sat quietly (her mind a million miles away), and he pretended his vision was achieved.

Harriet said, "What a lovely house."

Snowy's parents looked up at it, the way they did on summer evenings on the front lawn, standing there looking at the house, not the river. Snowy's father said, "We're going to buy a flagpole."

Oh God, Snowy thought.

Snowy's mother said, "Did I write you that? Come in and see the wallpaper."

Snowy expected Harriet to act like Margaret Mead amongst the Arapesh of New Guinea, but Harriet behaved as if she found it natural to have Snowy's mother lead her and Snowy straight through the shiny white kitchen and the gleaming maple dining room into the living room to see this wallpaper—Colonial eagles had replaced the green herringbone—and next, a bathroom-dash upstairs permitted, to sit down immediately to supper. Served on the good china from the maple hutch, blue Currier and Ives scenes, the meal was chicken and dumplings, a time-consuming dish Snowy's mother rarely made after she had returned to work when Snowy started high school. Snowy remembered that Harriet had once remarked that her father was the gourmet cook in their house, his specialty Chicken Kiev, which Snowy had never heard of. Since Snowy's parents weren't a boy, Harriet could eat, heartily, answering Snowy's father's

41

questions about her car (Snowy prayed he wouldn't ask how much it cost and he didn't, with obvious restraint), and then Harriet listened to him and Snowy's mother tell the tales of their latest purchases, endless tales that always maddened Snowy, but shopping was her parents' recreation, their drama, and on and on they went right through the apple pie topped with a slice of Velveeta.

No matter what Harriet's last name might be, they didn't have any curiosity about her except for her car; she was important only because she was Snowy's roommate.

A social squabble over doing the dishes ensued, Snowy's mother saying, "You had a long drive," Harriet saying, "So we need to stand up," and Snowy saying, "You worked all day, Mother, and made supper, I mean dinner." The girls prevailed. Afterwards they went upstairs to brush their teeth, and when Snowy came out of the bathroom she found Harriet examining the rows of pictures on the hallway wall, Snowy's school pictures from first-grade pigtails to her graduation yearbook photograph in which she'd worn her hair not in a ponytail but formally, loose curls, her scalp sore from a night of being stabbed by bobby-pin pincurls.

Harriet said, "A Girl Scout uniform. A Brownie Scout!"

"The doting parents' gallery. I've blinded myself to keep my sanity. Want some TV?"

"Do I ever."

Downstairs, Snowy's parents were posing in the living room, Snowy's mother reading the *Gunthwaite Herald* and Snowy's father reading the Manchester *Union-Leader*. The *Union*'s ultra-conservative reputation, Snowy told herself firmly, couldn't possibly have reached California. She touched middle C on the piano which was still tuned, still part of the living room furniture although she'd quit lessons in junior high because she hated recitals.

Her mother said, "You wrote you're taking piano lessons again, we're awfully glad. Play us something."

"I'm taking Music Theory." Bennington being Bennington,

however, the real thing was included besides theory, so she *was* taking piano lessons. She had wanted guitar lessons, to aid her Bohemian aspirations, but everyone else had the same idea and the openings were filled in a flash.

Her father lit a Camel. "I know you mentioned lessons."

"Yes, Daddy." Snowy sat down on the piano bench and played a scale. And although stubbornly she kept on just playing scales, her parents listened impressed. Then she crashed a chord. "May we watch TV? We're starved for television."

Her father said, "We aren't paying to have you waste your time on TV there."

Snowy couldn't look at Harriet.

"She's here now," her mother said. "Henrietta, I got you and Harriet some Coca-Cola, it's in the refrigerator."

"Thank you," Snowy said. She turned on the television set and fetched two Cokes, and she and Harriet settled down for an evening of westerns and dramas, Snowy mentally begging her parents to go to bed early. Harriet, in her mansion, probably had her own private television set. But Snowy's parents read their newspapers and watched along with Snowy and Harriet; it was the girls who began yawning and went upstairs first, to separate bedrooms instead of a shared, Snowy carrying Laurie.

Snowy's parents hadn't yet redecorated the spare room, a daisy-wallpapered room which was even more neat and on display than the other rooms—and bleak, until Bev had descended upon it to sleep over, festooning it with bras and crinoline petticoats, and sometimes Puddles slept over too, all three of them in the double bed at the outset but only two by morning because elbows and legs would eventually wake Snowy and she'd sneak out to sleep on the green-and-yellow braided rug with Laurie, wrapped in the puff. Now Harriet did the messing up of the room and fell asleep consulting afterimages of daisies about her latest jock: "He loves me, he loves me not . . ."

In her bedroom, Snowy gazed around at the rosebud wallpaper, the white bureau and bookcase, the mahogany veneer desk, the toy animals on the pink chenille bedspread, and realized that for once she wished her parents would redecorate a room, this room, this going backward. Maybe they would when they could afford it, maybe change it into a den or a sewing room since they had resented the time she spent here in her pink-and-white hiding place, studying and reading in the evenings while they kept asking why she couldn't do her homework downstairs with them. "Sanctuary," she reminded herself and Laurie.

Coming into the dining room the next morning, Harriet said, "Is Gunthwaite the duck capital of the world?"

Snowy was setting the table. Hooray, she'd hoped Harriet would awaken before her parents, so they could breakfast alone. "Oh, the ducks, did they wake you?" Down along the river, people with bags of bread were feeding ducks in the water, ducks on the riverbank and sidewalk. "I created a monster," she said. "I wasn't the only person to feed them, but I was part of it, I used to feed them every weekend morning. It's unnatural, they stay through the winter instead of flying south." She had renounced her weekend ritual one Sunday last summer, when the ducks had swarmed off the sidewalk onto the street and an oncoming car didn't brake, the driver laughing. Snowy had run screaming toward the house to tell her parents, to phone a veterinarian, the police, somebody, then glanced back and saw another car stop and the driver jump out and wring the necks of the crushed ducks.

Over instant coffee and English muffins, Harriet asked, "How about a tour of your old haunts before we drive around the lake?"

Dismayed, Snowy could hear Emily Post instructing her to obey her guest's request, so after they did the dishes and brushed their teeth, Harriet fetched her sketchbook, Snowy left a note for her parents, they went outdoors, and Snowy said, "The high school, good old GHS?"

"Then Hooper's," Harriet said. "Brr, this must be the coldest day yet."

"Winter's on the way," said Snowy, an authority.

44

They got into the Jaguar. Going backward, a drive backward. Haunts, yes, haunted by Tom.

"Which direction?" Harriet asked, lighting a Kent.

"Farther up State Avenue." When they came to the big brick factory, Snowy swallowed and said, "That's where my father works," hurrying on, "ahead, past the Congregational church, beware of whistles from the guys at that gas station."

Varney's was where Tom and other popular boys had worked after school and weekends, tinkering with their cars and whistling at girls. (Tom hadn't been a whistler, which made him seem very sophisticated.) The tradition continued, and this morning there were already boys' legs sticking out from underneath jalopies, boys leaning against the gas pumps; as she'd predicted, whistles saluted the Jaguar, driver, and passenger. Snowy always ignored whistlers, her chin up, but Harriet waved, receiving an encore.

"Guys," Harriet said. "The same coast to coast."

Once during a snowstorm, Snowy and Tom had gone parking behind Varney's. It was here, horrified, she'd let him Get Fresh for the first time, on only their second official date.

After Varney's and a supermarket, the high school stood beyond a long lawn. Two brick buildings, a world Snowy had conquered in order to earn a college scholarship.

"Handsome," Harriet said.

There was so much to say about the school that Snowy just said, "My classes were in the main building, except typing and junior-high home ec. The right-hand building is Practical Arts, the cafeteria in the basement." Practical Arts: shop, Tom. "Hooper's next?"

"Yes," Harriet said.

But instead of directing her straight back to Main Street, Snowy said, "Turn here," onto a circuitous route of side streets, one of which was Morning Street. Snowy did not point out the narrow white clapboard house with dark-green shutters, Tom's house, or the upstairs window of Tom's disconcertingly anonymous bedroom to which once, while baby-sitting his much

45

younger brother, they had retreated for a blow job, a change of setting from the front seat of his car but never repeated because Snowy was too scared of getting caught by his brother or parents, so during subsequent baby-sitting they'd just necked in the living room, watching television or listening to the radio in the record-player-radio-cabinet he had built.

Harriet said, "Which way?"

"Huh? Oh." The Jaguar was crouched at a cross-street. "Left."

And eventually they reached Main Street. Past the stores they came to Hooper's Dairy Bar, a small white clapboard mecca where everybody went after the movies, where Snowy had had her first cup of coffee on her first date with Tom, and Harriet wasn't content to observe it from the outside, she wanted more coffee, so Snowy had to go in with her and sit on a stool at the horseshoe-shaped counter and have a cup without Tom, feeling as if she were smothering in the Hooper smell of milk and grease. Harriet drank her coffee leisurely, the guys here strangers.

"The lake next?" Snowy asked. She could shut her eyes to the dance hall there, and the rest would be the planned touristy two-hour drive around Lake Winnipesaukee.

But Harriet said, "You've made Bev's house sound like heaven."

"It's not unique, only an old Cape."

"You mentioned it has a view of the lake. Is it on the way to the lake?"

"Well, yes, a detour." Snowy heard Emily Post.

They drove up North Main Street to the outskirts of town, past a group of tar-paper shacks called Frog Hollow. The name drifted into Snowy's mind, then froze her. Since childhood she had assumed that that "frog" meant creatures who hopped; she had never associated it, as she grew up, with the other meaning. French-Canadians. Thank *God* she hadn't said the name aloud to Harriet.

As they drove through woods, Snowy did not bring to Har-

46

riet's attention a little dirt road dubbed the Cat Path, where she and Tom and other kids went parking. More woods, this trip so familiar. Tom had driven her to Bev's so many times after dates, her face on fire with beard burn, her clothes askew. At another narrow dirt road Snowy said, "Turn here," and they drove along across a brook, up a hill to a mailbox that read MILLER, Bev's stepfather's last name. "Turn here," Snowy said again, shakily. What if Julia was outdoors raking leaves or doing autumn chores in her vegetable and flower gardens?

Harriet asked, driving up the driveway, "That the lake?"

"Yes, part of it." Far below the spiderweb of bare tree branches lay the deep October blueness against grizzled mountains. Tom's eyes were the lake's shade in summer, and swimming clumped his long eyelashes starry. Snowy looked away, to the old white shutterless Cape set on a wide field, the gray barn and stooped apple orchard behind it. Nobody in sight. She said, "Bev's folks must be off shopping," and maybe they were, but probably Fred was tinkering with his beloved Jeep in the closed barn and Julia was weaving in the warm shambles of the cluttered house.

Harriet said, "Sure like to draw this."

"It isn't a fat lady."

"I'm on vacation from them." Harriet suddenly sensed, however, Snowy's nervousness. Were she and Snowy trespassing under New Hampshire law, although Snowy knew the owners? "Like to draw the lake too, let's get going."

"Okay," Snowy said, trying to mask relief as they backed up and drove down the driveway. If Julia and Fred should happen to glance out a window they would think the expensive car contained confused tourists who'd missed both the correct turning and the foliage season.

On the main road, Snowy didn't indicate one of the routes to another landmark, the sandpit where she and Tom had sometimes gone parking instead of the Cat Path. At the sandpit last April, she had lost her virginity.

Oh, she could run around this town placing historic markers everywhere!

The arcades at the lake were boarded up for winter, and the dance hall on the end of the pier was closed. Impossible to shut her eyes. Some of the happiest moments of the happiest summer of her life, the summer between her sophomore and junior years, had been spent in that dance hall, dancing with Tom (Best Dancer) beneath gossamer bunting through which blinked pink and green and blue lights, singing Old Favorites along with the band: "Heart of my heart, I love that melody—"

They toured the lake, Harriet stopping now and then to draw. When they got home, they dutifully studied, but after the Saturday night supper of baked beans, brown bread, hot dogs, came the Coffee Cake Therapy of *Perry Mason; Perry Como; Have Gun, Will Travel; Gunsmoke.*

The next day, to prevent any more haunted sightseeing, Snowy suggested they be thorough tourists, and they drove farther north, detouring to Woodcombe, which Snowy had heard was the prettiest village in New Hampshire and where Harriet whipped out her sketchbook, on up through the White Mountains, where the sketchbook got a workout.

And today she and Harriet had driven down to Boston.

In the lobby of Commonwealth Publishing, oriental rugs led toward the receptionist's desk. Snowy set forth across them, trembling. Under her camel's hair coat she was wearing her most adult outfit, a blue Jonathan Logan plaid suit bought from a Lana Lobell catalog, its top not a jacket but a dressy over-blouse, yet she felt an infant. "I'm Henrietta Snow, I have an appointment with Mr. Palmquist."

"Fourth floor. Elevator to your left."

Snowy had hoped that Mr. Palmquist would look like an editor should, rumpled in a tweed sport jacket, smoking a pipe, his office topsy-turvy with books, his desk piled with manuscripts, but Mr. Palmquist was a tidy nonsmoking young man whose desk was as clear as a school desk during summer, and although there were a lot of books in his office, they were restrained inside glass-fronted bookcases.

He stood up. "Won't you sit down."

"Thank you." She sat; he sat. She remembered her college interviews, when she had sought the right balance between self-assurance and modesty. Now she was worrying about having to take a typing test. The only C that unmechanical Snowy had ever received had been at the beginning of Personal Typing her junior year, and despite achieving an A— the final quarter, she feared she was far from professional.

But Mr. Palmquist just inquired if she liked Bennington, and after she'd waxed eloquent he said Commonwealth hadn't been aware of the NRT program until a Bennington alumna, the wife of a new editor, had mentioned it, so Snowy would be their first. Then he said, "The salary is fifty dollars a week. Is the amount adequate?"

My God. She had never made so much money in her whole life. "Yes," she said.

He stood up again, and that was that.

She ran back to the car. "I got the job!"

Harriet had put aside her sketchbook and was studying the Boston map Snowy had asked Puddles to send. "Great! Now, the rooming house. I wish this map told which street is one way which way. I guess we can get to Beacon Street by—"

"We could walk."

Harriet looked as if she'd proposed crawling there on their stomachs under machine-gun fire. In California, Snowy had gathered, you didn't walk, except on beaches. Harriet started the car.

After they located the NRT-recommended rooming house in the long line of dark buildings on Beacon Street, they found a parking space, and Snowy climbed the stone steps and rang the bell. An elderly woman wearing a lavender cardigan over a dress opened the door and invited her into the hallway, where a curving staircase sloped out of sight. The rooming house must have been somebody's home once. When Snowy arranged to

49

rent whatever room would be available during NRT, the full realization struck her that she'd have to pay rent, ten dollars a week, and she'd have to buy groceries too, so the fifty-dollar salary didn't seem a fabulous sum anymore. But it was *money*, and money was, as she had learned while spending her Sweetland paychecks, wonderful, though working was hell. Waitressing was hell, at least.

Leaving, she stood for a moment on the sidewalk thinking of Bev and Puddles here in Boston, probably sitting in classrooms this very moment, in their separate new worlds. Her world, come winter, would be Commonwealth Publishing. They had their roommates; she'd be on her own. Loss, that's what was welling up in her, a sick sensation of loss. Mourning.

Damnit, she should have chosen New York, where she and Harriet could explore the city together.

"I WAS AWFUL," Snowy said when she and Harriet met at lunchtime at their mailboxes in Commons. "I stumbled through the poem as if I'd never seen it before, much less written it myself."

The Lang-and-Lit assignment for this December day had been to write a sonnet, which you would read aloud in class. Although she'd had fun doing the writing, Snowy had been dreading the reading, having discovered she hated hearing poems performed. One evening last month she'd gone to her first poetry reading in the living room of a house across campus, to cover the occasion for her column, and there teachers and upperclassmen had solemnly presented their own poems while she grew more and more embarrassed, appalled; not even the cookies afterward tempted her to stay longer than she had to. It was like masturbating in public! She'd fled back to her room and wailed at Harriet, "What happens when I have to read a poem of mine aloud, in class or at a reading? Tonight I found out I'm of the silent-reading school of thought!" Harriet had said,

"You'll have to do it somehow." Then had come the sonnet assignment. Snowy rehearsed the reading over and over with Harriet, who didn't have the same Lang-and-Lit class so wouldn't be there for moral support—and Harriet hadn't been any help with a last pep talk this morning because she was too excited about the season's first snowfall, running back and forth from the windows to the closet shrieking, "It's *snowing*, what do I *wear?*" In class, Snowy's reading of her sonnet had turned into a nightmare of nerves, her typewritten page soggy with sweat, her eyes struck blind.

Snowy said, "I think I'll change my major to ceramics."

Harriet checked her mailbox. "Nothing," she said, vastly disappointed. The morning mail was more likely than the afternoon delivery to contain such diverting missives as a letter from the boy Harriet had left behind in California, or for Snowy a letter from Puddles or from another of Snowy's ex-boyfriends, Dudley Washburn.

Snowy said, startled, "A letter from Bev's mother."

According to the menu, today's lunch would be Italian grinders, a lunch equivalent of coffee cake. She and Harriet were early, but as they climbed the stairs to the second-floor kitchen and dining rooms, they learned they weren't early enough to avoid an eager waiting line. They queued up at its tail, and while they waited for the kitchen to open Snowy pulled the letter out of the envelope and caught a newspaper clipping.

Julia wrote: "Dear Snowy, In case your folks didn't notice this, I'm sending it along. You must be encountering many firsts nowadays, and I'm terribly sorry about this first."

Snowy's eyes flew from the stationery to the clipping.

"Oh no," she said.

Harriet asked, "What's wrong?"

It was an obituary in the *Gunthwaite Herald* for Ed Cormier, the boy she'd gone steady with most of their freshman year to guarantee she would always have a date. He wasn't the ideal boyfriend she desired, and she had broken up with him when going steady began to mean Getting Fresh. Big Ed Cor-

51

mier, a fullback who had been paralyzed during a football game their junior year. Ever after, Snowy had visited him as he lay in a hospital bed in his small bedroom in his parents' duplex, listening to the radio and leafing through magazines and not doing any schoolwork, but she'd forgotten to visit him Long Weekend.

She said, "I should have been writing him. Too damn busy." Yet she had been finding time to write her parents, Puddles, and Dudley Washburn.

Harriet said, "What happened?"

"A boy in my class died."

"God. Car accident?"

"I think the expression is 'he turned his face to the wall.' "

"What?"

"He'd been paralyzed in a football pile-on." Tom, the center, had been in that pile, had heard the crack when Ed's backbone broke, had pulled the other guys off him.

Harriet asked, "Is he the first in your class to die?"

"Yes."

"I had two last year. Car crashes. Did you go out with him?"

Snowy nodded, reading Ed's name again.

"He wasn't the guy you got too serious about?"

"No. But."

Here came another kind of mourning. Through tears, Snowy looked back at the letter. Julia knew quite well that Snowy's parents wouldn't have noticed the obituary; Ed had meant nothing to them after she stopped dating him.

Julia, whose first husband had died for an island, had once told Snowy that Bev's ambition to marry a millionaire was make-believe. Julia had said, "She's never dared imagine a real marriage because she knows real men die," and now in the letter Julia spoke of Bev.

"One can eventually become used to an absence," Julia wrote, "just as one became used to a presence, though the pain remains. This happens not only with deaths, but I do hope you and Bev won't continue to absent yourselves from each other.

52

Bev hasn't mentioned what occurred between you last spring. I suspect Tom realized he was dating her simply because she was close to you and she discovered this.

"Unlike me, Bev enjoys Boston. During our phone talks, she certainly seems her old self—except she's doing much better at Katie Gibbs than she did in high school. She's getting A's instead of B's and C's! So, she says, is Puddles.

"Perhaps I've managed not to meddle too long. I wish you and Bev had got together at Thanksgiving. I'm planning to ask her at Christmas to let bygones be bygones. Will you also try? As Henry Adams writes, 'Friends are born, not made.'

"That reminds me of Henry Adams's shattered reaction to the cruel death of his sister, when the idea that a beneficient omnipotent God would cause such torture as lockjaw drove him to consider atheism a comfort. I've written to Ed's folks, and I hope for them their religion is a comfort.

"Love, Julia."

Ed was dead. An absence forever. Snowy couldn't believe it.

Harriet said, "Want to go back to the house? I'll go with you."

"You have lunch. I'm okay."

"Preferring to be alone. I'll smuggle you out a grinder in the Pimpernel, you'll want something later." In the vast pockets of Harriet's red car coat, known as the Scarlet Pimpernel, Harriet had so far smuggled out sweetness, napkin-wrapped pieces of cake and slices of pie and once an entire sugar bowl for Harriet's study-time coffee.

On their first date, Snowy had copied Tom and she still drank her coffee sugarless, black. And, as she ran sobbing back to McCullough, she berated herself, her despicable self who was thinking how Ed's death could provide an excuse to get in touch with Tom. Probably Tom's parents hadn't sent him the clipping. She could forward him hers. She wouldn't even have to add a note, he'd recognize her handwriting on the envelope, and maybe he would write back.

Instead, after she had cried herself empty in her room, she sat down at her desk to write a letter to Ed's parents.

❦

THE TRAIN BEGAN passing other trains, and the noise and soot increased. Eek, she was here already, she was arriving in North Station, and when the train slackened speed Snowy willed it to turn around and choo-choo her home. Her father could help her find a job at Trask's, a job she could justify to the NRT advisor by saying she wanted to be a poet of the people. A female Carl Sandburg!

The prospect of working in Boston at a publishing house had seemed extremely glamorous until the time drew near, and then the whole NRT concept seemed extremely terrifying again. She'd hoped to travel there on the bus and train protected by Puddles, but Puddles wanted to prolong her farewell with Gene, who would drive her down on Sunday, as Roger would drive Bev, and although she could have hitched a ride with Puddles and Gene she'd be a fifth wheel, and anyway, she had planned to arrive early to get her bearings. So she was making the trip alone, on the Saturday before the Monday she was to start work. Her parents had tried to prevail upon her to let them drive her down, yet she preferred being scared alone to having them fuss over her (and having people see them and know she had parents), but she'd almost wept when, in the smoking car, she had opened the lunch bag her mother had pressed on her and discovered that her mother had made her favorite winter sandwich, raspberry jam and marshmallow fluff, two of them, which she ate while studying the Boston map. Tuna fish was her favorite summer sandwich. Over the years, she and Bev must have whipped up together an acre of such sandwiches.

She should *never* have chosen Boston!

During Christmas vacation, if Julia had asked Bev to phone or visit Snowy, Bev hadn't listened. Of course there was always the possibility that Julia had indeed asked and Bev had simply forgotten; Snowy had long ago concluded that Bev's forgetfulness was a result of Bev's saving her memory to store her lines in, but did Katharine Gibbs put on plays? And could even Bev forget to attempt a reconciliation with a best friend? Snowy herself kept trying, yet every time she picked up the phone to call Bev and apologize and invite her to spend the night, her courage failed her. Bev would hang up on her, and the sound would reverberate in her ears until her dying day.

There had been no reunion with the rest of their Gang, either. Puddles tried to talk her into cheering at the annual New Year's Eve Alumni-Varsity basketball game, when traditionally the Alumni team was cheered for by the JV cheerleaders and last year's available Varsity cheerleaders anxious to relive glory. "No," Snowy told her, "it would be going backward." Puddles said, "So what? Snowy, you were the *captain* of the squad, it's your *duty!*" "Besides," Snowy said, "I've forgotten how to do a cartwheel."

Needless to say, Puddles cheered at the game, rooting for her Gene, co-captain of the '56 team, and afterward she'd reported to Snowy all the news: The twins, Charlene and Darlene Fecteau, were there, as quick and hectic as ever, their hair still in identical brunette DA's, but they were sidelined from cheerleading. In high school they had both gone steady fast; after graduation they'd both got married fast, Charl to Jack O'Brien, Darl to Bill LeHoullier, and now they were twin blimps, because they'd also both got pregnant fast. "Holy shit," Puddles said to Snowy, "do you suppose they arranged to do it the exact same night? Their clothes, too, they're still buying the same clothes, they were wearing matching maternity clothes!"

Snowy laughed, determined not to ask Puddles if Tom had been there.

Puddles said, "And Joanne came into the gym office when we were all bumping into each other changing into uniforms or Bermudas."

"Oh?" Snowy said, her tone remote. Joanne Carter. Lovely,

with movie-star cheekbones and long glossy dark brown hair, the '56 Junior Prom Queen and co-captain of the '56 Varsity squad, Joanne would be a sophomore this year at Rumford Teachers' College, an elementary major.

Puddles continued relentlessly, "I saw that the frat pin on her sweater wasn't the same pin she'd worn last year, not Chris's, and I asked her right out whose it was."

"You would."

"She said it was Tom's."

Snowy nearly fainted.

Tom and Joanne had been friends since grammar school, classmates in Gunthwaite and at Rumford. A year ago last fall, Snowy had learned via the grapevine that Tom had taken Joanne out, her supposedly platonic escort to the movies because Chris had left Rumford to hide from the draft in the Coast Guard. Now—now Joanne was wearing the fraternity pin refused by Snowy! And Tom wouldn't be acting platonic anymore, if he ever had. That time last April, Snowy had suddenly guessed that Tom's expertise with a Trojan had been learned with Joanne, for although Joanne was the type to hold out until the wedding night, Tom was irresistible, but Snowy had since suppressed the images of Tom and Joanne in the cream-colored convertible, not truly believing that Tom had slept with anyone except her.

Snowy put her chin up and said to Puddles, "I hope you congratulated her."

"She's cheering at Rumford this year, she's the only sophomore to make the squad. She said she had to learn a whole new style, more athletic. They build pyramids, do stunts."

The Gunthwaite cheerleading style was vigorous but feminine, Joanne's personal style elegantly graceful. Of course, Snowy thought, of course Joanne would want to cheer at Rumford Teachers' College even if it meant wearing a clown suit and being shot out of a cannon. Thank God she herself had decided to go to a women's college and had picked Bennington, where

56

the closest thing to an organized sport was modern dance. She imagined Tom watching Joanne's cartwheels.

Puddles said, "Tom isn't playing football at Rumford. They don't have a football team, only basketball, and Joanne says he says he's through with sports anyway."

Snowy murmured, " 'When I became a man, I put away childish things,' " pierced by the memory of how she'd raced onto the football field after that terrible pile-on, the doctor kneeling beside Ed, and how Tom had hugged her, tears coursing down his charcoaled face while he said over and over, "This fucking stupid game."

Puddles added, "But Tom came to the Alumni game."

Had Tom, Snowy wondered, been hoping to see her there amongst the cheerleaders? It's *finished,* she told herself. Yet would they always be together mentally, in the wings of their minds?

Puddles said, "He sat with Joanne, and I could see Bev sitting with our gang with her eye on them, not on Roger out on the floor doing his best like Gene."

Despite Roger's and Gene's efforts, the Alumni had lost.

"But," Puddles said, "after the game Bev came to Charl and Jack's party with Roger. Dudley was there stag, saying he'd been spurned by you."

Another possibility: Maybe Bev was just plain too busy to phone her. Puddles had told her that Bev had a booked-solid social calendar this vacation, chiding, "Why haven't you? You aren't being faithful to Whit or any of the others, are you?" Snowy hadn't been sure why she was behaving during Thanksgiving and Christmas vacations the way she had last summer, turning down dates. Maybe, she decided, the trouble was that the references had changed, and if in Gunthwaite she said, "The Barn," her date would think she was talking about a place to shovel manure, not the building in which most of Bennington's classes were held—though some classroom discussions seemed to amount to the same activity.

Dating Dudley would be different, however.

Classmates, he and Snowy had been friends since their sand-box days (Had she got as grubby as Pig-Pen with him?), and he had grown up still blond and pink-cheeked but very tall. After Tom broke up with her and she began playing the field, he had become her most serious boyfriend, if the word "serious" could be applied to Dudley; yes, it could, the time he'd told her he loved her and asked her in vain to go steady, and since last April a steadfast determination hid beneath his blithe pleas for a date. "Ah, Snowy," he'd say, "O Belle of Gunthwaite, 'There is no Frigate like'—a movie, won't you go to the movies with me and we'll frigate?" Her excuses this summer were an imaginary reading list. Then he had gone off to Yale, on a scholarship. In grammar school he'd set his goals, to be both a baseball star and President of the United States, preparing for the latter by getting elected president of their class every year, and now a poli-sci major, he intended to go to law school before continuing on his way to the White House. The Red Sox would just have to do without him. He too had decided to take Russian, but his reason was practical, for he figured an end to the Cold War would be more likely if the President of the United States could shoot the breeze with the Soviet leader in his native tongue directly. When he'd written Snowy a letter from Yale and she'd replied, they learned they were both taking Russian, and a correspondence developed in which they interspersed first Cyrillic characters and then words, making fun of their ineptness. Eventually they were exchanging phrases at the start of their letters before lapsing in relief into English, Dudley once observing that since the Russian language didn't have articles, even fluent Russian must sound like babytalk or Movietone News.

Because of their letters, Dudley understood her new references and she his, and they also had undergone the realization that, unlike Bev and Puddles, who were doing better in college than high school, they themselves weren't the smartest people in the world. So why refuse his invitations? During Thanksgiving vacation she told him she was working day and night on a paper, knowing he wouldn't dare say, "It isn't as if you're going to get a *mark*." Then last week he'd phoned just as she returned from taking Laurie for a walk, and when he began reciting in Russian what she realized must be a stab at translating Emily Dickinson's "Hope is the thing with feathers," she started laughing and he said, "Doesn't that finally earn your hopeful swain a date? The movies? The Christmas Dance? Charl and Jack's New Year's Eve Party?"

And suddenly Snowy had known why she hadn't wanted to go out with him Thanksgiving and Christmas vacations. She hadn't dated him after the Senior Banquet through the summer only because she'd sworn off men. But now their correspondence these past months had transformed him back into her friend from childhood, making him no longer a boyfriend, and he was simply her dearest Dudley again, not the person with whom she'd spent many a night steaming up his 1950 black Ford, prostituting what had been special with Tom. She and Dudley should have played doctor in that sandbox of their youth and got it over with; they shouldn't have superimposed sex on friendship.

She'd be dating him under false pretenses now, so again she had begged off, saying, "I'm no good at reunions," although she wished she could see Charl and Jack's apartment. She had always liked to look in the windows of houses she walked and drove past, and she particularly enjoyed the apartment windows of young married couples, which showed self-conscious cosiness, new domesticity. But she could imagine Charl and Jack's slipcovered three-piece living room set, the Formica dinette set. The rent for this newlywed nest would be paid by Jack's job at Gunthwaite Oil Company cleaning furnaces. She and Bev and Puddles had constantly over the years made fun of the twins, with Bev's imitations of how they gasped and clutched and Puddles's comments about the unfairness of the cheerleading competition because twins were too cute for the coaches to resist, so she'd kept secret from Bev and Puddles her longing to be a twin, the core of the Gang, popularity guaranteed, social success on a silver platter.

Puddles said, "Jack passed, natch." A party tradition was

Jack O'Brien's passing out. She added, "Well, okay, you're going forward. Have you got that map of Boston I sent you?" She traced on the map the way to get from North Station to Beacon Street and then said, "Hell, grab a cab instead, you'll have a ton of suitcases. Splurge."

Snowy forced herself to stand up and tug her two suitcases and her vanity case down off the rack, remembering the arrival in Boston of the Decoration Committee and how Dudley, who'd been here before, had remarked, "The only route I know to anywhere is through Scollay Square," and had led them onward.

As the train stopped, she staggered. People pushed past her, everyone suddenly in a hurry, and the conductor who helped her off the train was so brusque she feared he would shove her under it, an involuntary Anna Karenina; apparently courtesy went out the window in a city. She found herself caught up in the rush of people into the big building where, once inside, she couldn't recall which of the many exits Dudley had taken. She tightened her grip on her suitcases and headed for the nearest one. Outdoors, the street was shadowed, the overhang of the building cutting off the wan sun that felt colder than home despite the lack of snow down here. In her boots, dressy though they were, she must appear a complete hayseed. Through the smell of exhaust fumes came a smell of food, of greasy onions. Taxi drivers clamored. She tried to look worldly-wise, getting into the next taxi that pulled up, and when she gave the driver the address of the rooming house he didn't stare at her, he accepted her by ignoring her, and away she went on her first taxi ride.

The route he took was evidently Dudley's or else another seamy side of Boston. Then she saw trees and knew they'd reached the Common or the Public Garden. They drove down a street of dark buildings—okay, this was Beacon Street—and the driver braked in front of a door and said, "Here you are, miss."

"Thank you." She fumbled in her pocketbook for her wallet, wondering how much to tip him, thrust an extra dollar into

60

his hand, splurging indeed, and climbed out. Another milestone!

Grasping her suitcases, she checked the street number. The right address. Inside, the elderly woman, again wearing a lavender cardigan over a dress, ceremoniously presented her with a key to the front door and the key to her room, telling her it was on the fifth floor. No elevator. By the time she reached that floor, her knees were trembling almost as much as when she and Bev and Puddles had, instead of taking the elevator, hiked up the miles of stairs to the top of the Washington Monument, just so they could say they'd accomplished that feat, Puddles's bright idea. She let herself into the room.

Well, she thought, it's smaller than our room in McCullough, but I have it all to myself. Yet there weren't any fat women on the walls or any sophomores' secondhand rejects or a cinderblock-and-board bookcase, and she unpacked quickly, trying to disguise with her belongings this dreary cell of gray walls, scarred bed and bureau, table and chair. Unlike Harriet, who'd brought to Bennington canned Mexican food which she cooked on the hot plate in McCullough's little kitchen for midnight snacks that were a fiery milestone, Snowy hadn't brought canned-goods supplies to Bennington, fearing what people would think and assuming that at the price she was paying, her scholarship notwithstanding, she would be given sufficient food and wouldn't be expected to eat it off the floor with her fingers. To a Boston rooming house, however, she had brought in her suitcases amongst her clothes some staples, a jar of instant coffee, a can of tomato soup, a box of pilot crackers, a jar of crunchy peanut butter, a can of baked beans (appropriate for Boston), and also some camping equipment, her Girl Scout mess kit and her Girl Scout nest of knife, fork, and spoon.

Exploring, she discovered the bathroom two doors down, beside a kitchen that reminded her of McCullough's except that McCullough's usually had a burned-on saucepan soaking in the sink, and then she put her coat back on, armed herself with the map, and explored farther, repeating silently, "I am in Boston. I am walking on Beacon Street."

61

The next street parallel to Beacon was Marlborough Street, where she stared at the two beautiful old buildings occupied by Katharine Gibbs. Bev and her roommate would doll up in their room here and go to classes dressed to the teeth. Uncomfortable! Garter belts! Snowy still adored clothes, as Bev did, but Bennington had spoiled her and she was dreading having to get gussied up every morning for Commonwealth Publishing; probably, though, Bev and Ann Wilmot had fun, playing with different effects, and maybe they wore the same size and could borrow. Walking on, Snowy missed Harriet. What would Bev make of Harriet? Bev wanted to marry a millionaire. For all Snowy knew, Harriet *was* a millionaire, in trust or something.

Always doing her homework thoroughly, Snowy double-checked the location of Commonwealth Publishing on the avenue parallel to Marlborough Street, and, that mission accomplished, consulting her map in peeps, embarrassed at being a country mouse, she ventured out of these dignified streets to Boylston Street, and now the city smelled oniony again and there were stores and restaurants and Saturday shoppers. Charles Street divided the Public Garden and the Common, and after it crossed Beacon Street it was lined with little shops. She got very brave and went into an artsy place and bought a Monet print, having fallen in love with Monet in the National Gallery of Art in Washington, so much so that when her Girl Scout troop had swarmed into its gift shop she had even invested part of her hoarded spending money in a postcard of a Monet springtime painting. Continuing along Charles Street, she came upon what must be the bar where Bev and Puddles met Thursdays. It looked excitingly depraved. She turned there and started back and went into a hardware store and bought a roll of masking tape, and then she went into a delicatessen and bought a pastrami sandwich which she hoped she'd manage to save until suppertime. Reaching the limit of her courage for the day, in a tiny grocery store she bought breakfast, bread and margarine and marmalade and milk. When she didn't get lost finding her way back to the rooming house, she felt she really was in Boston. A career girl, on her own.

Later, after hanging the Monet with masking-tape loops and rewarding herself for her daring expedition with an Agatha Christie she'd brought, she fetched her sandwich from the kitchen refrigerator and met two full-time career girls, who were about her age and who both worked in insurance offices. They'd been out shopping, and their conversation concerned purchases, boys, and hopes of marriage. She returned to her room telling herself, "I'm neither fish nor flesh, nor good red herring"—though the pastrami, when tasted, was good.

Sunday, wishing for Laurie to exercise, she walked to Mass. General and contemplated Puddles's new terrain, *huge* compared with the Gunthwaite hospital, and then she sought out small quiet Louisburg Square, a fenced-in park surrounded by haughty old houses, their wrought-iron balconies looking so delicate that Bev couldn't play Juliet if she did marry a millionaire and live in one. But here Bev would dine on meals she hadn't made (and not pastrami sandwiches, either), wearing silken dresses and diamond earrings that glittered like the crystal chandelier above the gleaming table, and after dinner she and her millionaire would stroll in the park, which seemed too exclusive to allow Snowy a closer investigation of its two statues. Snowy realized she needed a guidebook as well as a map, because this would be how she spent her spare time in Boston, walking and walking, looking, looking.

When she walked on, she heard herself mentally describing everything to Tom.

Since the rooming-house telephone was on the ground floor, there was lots of yelling and running up and down stairs. That evening a relay of shouts summoned her to the phone, and Puddles said, "Welcome to Beantown."

"You didn't warn me I didn't have to wear boots, hooray." In Snowy's opinion, boots were inconvenient and unromantic. "I've been exploring, I located Mass. General, it's gigantic!"

"Did you locate Katie Gibbs?"

63

"Well, yes, it's nearby, I couldn't help walking past."

"Damnit, if you two wouldn't bottle things up—" Puddles had a brainstorm. "Bottles, I always feel so awful after saying goodbye to Gene I want to go drown my sorrows, but I've got to hit the books—what are your hours at Commonwealth?"

"Eight-thirty to four-thirty, lunch hour from noon to one."

"My schedule—let's meet Wednesday for a beer, if you found Mass. General you found Charles Street. Did you spot the bar?"

"Uh-huh. Wednesday?"

"That's one good thing about you and Bev not speaking, I'll get to go beer-drinking twice a week. Wednesday, quarter of five, and remember to bring your fake driver's license." Puddles hung up and phoned Bev, inventing an exam, moving their Thursday meeting to Wednesday. Next she must figure out a way to keep Snowy from balking when she saw Bev, or Bev from making a dramatic exit; she must corral them there in the bar and force them to consume more than one beer so they'd get drunk and let their hair down and cry and kiss and make up.

Snowy carefully set the alarm on her travel clock, Bev and Puddles's birthday present last March.

MONDAY: A DAY fraught with peril. Wearing under her camel's hair coat her second-most-grown-up outfit, a brown knit suit, Snowy teetered to Commonwealth Publishing on brown suede heels, a first-day-of-work concession, planning flats in the future if other typists wore them.

Ah, the luxury of the elevator to Mr. Palmquist's floor!

"Henrietta," he said, stuffing a dust rag in a bottom drawer. (She later learned he dusted his desk every hour on the hour.) "Well. You're here."

"Er—yes, I am."

"Have you got settled in at your rooming house? Is everything satisfactory?"

"Yes."

"Will your probation officer be visiting soon?"

A hesitant joke. She laughed, noting his wedding ring, a detail she'd missed during her interview because of nervousness.

Mr. Palmquist said, "I suppose Frances and the others have arrived," and without further ado he escorted her along the corridor into a big corner room with tall windows where three women were taking off their coats, chatting. A stranger in their midst, Snowy wanted to die, but as he made introductions she managed to memorize who was who. Frances, middle-aged; Barbara, maybe late twenties; Lynn, maybe right out of college. Barbara and Lynn wore flats. There were four wooden desks and metal typing tables, one desk and table separated from the rest in a glassed-in cubicle, two under windows. In the middle of the room was the fourth desk, its typing table at right angles to it. On the desk were piled boxes like those that reams of paper came in. Mr. Palmquist tapped the desk and said, "This is yours. Frances will show you the ropes."

He hurried down the corridor back to his office.

Frances said, "He's bashful." She was buxom and rouged, and, to Snowy's everlasting gratitude, she wasn't big-city tough, she was motherly. She took Snowy's coat and hung it on the coat rack, admiring aloud the coat and Snowy's suit, asking if she owned snuggies, which were necessary both to keep warm in during the walk to work (she herself, she said, had to walk from North Station, commuting from a suburb whose name Snowy didn't catch) and because the office was chilly, a corner room having the advantage of more windows and light but the disadvantage of being at the mercy of the gales. Then, seeing Snowy's bewilderment, she pulled up her dress to display what snuggies were, long flannel underpants. Lynn, removing a typewriter cover, laughed affectionately, as did cubicled Barbara. And then while Snowy stood looking in consternation at the desk's mysterious little machine with a little record player apparently waiting to be played, Frances gave the desk an inspection and declared, "I guess everything's here. Usually only temps have this desk, regular temps, I mean—that's temporary help when we get too busy. Have you ever used an Audograph?"

"No."

"Nothing to it. Stationery, carbon paper. Let's see, you're doing rejections today. Put on the earphones, press the button, listen to Mr. Palmquist say, 'A letter to So-and-so,' and he'll give you the name and address, some people don't, they just say, 'Dear So-and-so.' Bang on the button and stop the record and type what he said. Mr. Palmquist spells out the hard names, but if you're not sure—" Frances opened the top box and held up a letter. "Mr. P. always has the boxes in the right order. Check it with this. Start the record again and listen to what he says next, bang on the button, type what he said, start the record again, type some more, and that's all there is to it. Pretty soon you'll be going like a bat out of hell. And Mr. Palmquist, he talks so you can understand what he's saying, some people mumble, and he gives you all the punctuation, you don't have to guess. Make one carbon unless he tells you otherwise. Type an address label, here they are, and put it with your finished letter inside the box. When you're doing letters with envelopes, he likes them in a pile face up, every letter slid under the flap of its envelope—" She demonstrated; Snowy's mind was a merry-go-round. "And if you have to paper clip anything for him, he likes the short end of the paper clip on the right."

"Anal retentive," said Lynn, lighting a cigarette.

"Huh?" Frances said, and Snowy laughed, momentarily back at Bennington.

Frances patted her shoulder. "Holler if you need me." She went to her desk.

"Thank you." Snowy sat down. Alone in the middle of the room, she felt cast away on a desert island. The desk was aimed toward the corridor, so she could see who was coming, but in turn as they approached they could see her, just her, stranded.

The Audograph. God, a mechanical device! The typewriter

was a Remington, and she was used to her Royal portable; in her typing class, she'd had a Smith-Corona. Inserting paper, she tried to remember what the typing teacher had taught the class about setting up a business letter, knowledge she hadn't foreseen she'd need, taking typing only to be able to type schoolwork and poems. Then she timidly put on the earphones and did what Frances had instructed, and eventually Mr. Palmquist's voice had directed her through the first letter, including commas, periods, and paragraphs. Yet she'd made so many mistakes on the unfamiliar typewriter that she had to retype it, but luckily it was a short letter. She had to retype the next letter too, though it was almost the same as the first. When, however, Frances announced a coffee break, she had mastered both the damn typewriter and the damn Audograph.

Frances came over to her desk. "Going okay?"

Snowy handed her the latest letter, realizing that because of her intense concentration she had scarcely smelled the percolator of coffee bubbling on a hot plate on a filing cabinet. She hadn't even noticed the box of doughnuts there.

"Hey, what a good job," Frances said, "you're a quick learner," and Snowy blushed, reminded of how the headwaitress at Sweetland had praised the neat way she arranged her trays.

"Thank you," Snowy said.

Frances said, "Help yourself to coffee and doughnuts," and she and Lynn left to deliver cardboard cups of coffee and napkin-wrapped doughnuts to, presumably, Mr. Palmquist and another editor. Barbara started sipping her coffee in her cubicle, reading something. Snowy stood up, stretched, and went to the filing cabinet for sustenance and sat back down at her desk with her coffee and doughnut and wondered what to do, regretting her choice of a honey-dip. She couldn't keep working if her fingers got sticky, and a bathroom would be useful for another reason too. Would she have to ask, cringing, where it was? As a distraction, she began reading that latest letter, with a certain amount of pride until—She stopped, shocked. The Audograph and Remington had so preoccupied her she hadn't comprehended the gist of the words she was typing. Frances had said "rejections." These were rejection letters, the kind of letters she knew about only too well, having accumulated a collection herself from sending out poems last summer. She reached into the nearest box and hoisted up a manuscript. A rejected manuscript, all four hundred and twelve pages of it.

And she had typed the polite concise letter that would make the author want to throw himself off a cliff, not Bennington's Cliff, but a real live precipice.

She was consorting with the enemy!

Frances and Lynn came back, fetched their own coffee and doughnuts, sat down at their desks, and office gossip commenced, Barbara joining in. Listening, Snowy figured out the hierarchy. Barbara was the assistant to a full-fledged editor, and Lynn was her secretary. Frances was Mr. Palmquist's typist and did typing for other editors in a pinch. Ambition budded within Snowy while she sipped and chewed: After graduation she would have a job like Barbara's, complete with cubicle.

Barbara and Lynn, Snowy next gathered, were single, because Frances started teasing them about dates, and then when Frances lit a cigarette and began talking about the imminent arrival of her first grandchild, Barbara and Lynn turned their attention to Snowy, who'd been hoping to remain invisible. The questions Barbara and Lynn asked revealed their alma maters, Wellesley and B.U., and their third degree also showed their belief in Bennington's wild Bohemian reputation.

"No," Snowy said, "no, we can't have boys in our rooms overnight, only until six or, if the house votes to, until nine—yes, the houses are our dorms, it sort of looks like a village, some classes are held in the living rooms of the houses but most classes are held in the Barn, yes, a converted barn—no, we don't all major in dance. Yes, I'm a literature major."

Finally Barbara glanced at her watch, a signal for Lynn to wipe her hands on her napkin and hit the typewriter keys again. But Lynn had had a plain doughnut.

God bless Frances, who said to Snowy, "If you care to freshen up, the bathroom is just one flight down, no need to take the elevator, it's the door on the left."

Snowy fluttered her honey-dip fingers. "I guess I'd better. Thank you."

When she was out of sight of open office doors, she dashed down the staircase as fast as high heels allowed.

Then, freshened up, she returned to the business of breaking authors' hearts.

She hadn't brought a money-saving sandwich to work for lunch, in case this wasn't done, deciding she would try to find the Waldorf Cafeteria where the Decoration Committee had dined. Come noon, she learned that lunch at your desk was permitted, because although Lynn left immediately amid dating jokes from Frances, in her cubicle Barbara could be seen eating a sandwich while she read, and Frances took a paper bag out of a bottom drawer of her desk and asked Snowy, "Did you bring your lunch, dear?"

"Not today. I thought I'd go for a walk and get a bite on the way."

"It's much cheaper."

"I will tomorrow."

"If you're doing any shopping, you can buy snuggies at Jordan Marsh, Filene's. Do you know where those stores are?"

After the Decoration Committee had eaten lunch, Snowy and Carol Tucker had been led by Dudley to Jordan Marsh and left there while he and the other guy on the Committee went exploring, and she and Carol had proceeded to get lost *inside* the place, so wouldn't she now get lost just plain trying to find it—and the Waldorf Cafeteria? Putting on her coat, she said, "Yes, I've been to Jordan Marsh."

She did locate the Waldorf Cafeteria, but she hesitated at the door, daunted; she should have brought a book for a companion or bodyguard. Anyway, the place smelled like vegetable soup, which smelled like sweat. She walked on, then stopped dead in her tracks and gawked. A theater! Not a movie theater, a real theater. She read the posters with awe. This was what Bev ought to be striving toward instead of a make-believe millionaire, Bev ought to be in New York taking acting classes, waitressing between casting calls, struggling and starving (well, Julia wouldn't allow the latter) to attain stardom. Julia, however, had once pointed out that Bev wouldn't consider such an ordeal because Bev simply wanted to have fun. Snowy had always thought this was caused by the death of her red-headed father, making Bev aware that life was short, while the certainty of death had made Snowy want to be famous so she'd live forever, although she hadn't decided what to be famous at until she read Emily Dickinson. Reminded of books, jolted into the realization that she was gaping, a bumpkin, she continued on, hurrying like the other people, keeping the Common in view and, when she couldn't see treetops anymore, memorizing street signs. In a bookstore, she bought a guidebook, all she purchased during her maiden-voyage lunch hour; lo and behold she came upon Jordan Marsh but she only toured it, resting on escalators, studying each floor, mapping the plenty through her dazzlement and not buying any old-lady snuggies, though they sure would've been more practical for cheering at football games than Lollipop underpants, the drawback being they would show, pantalettes below the jumpers.

She didn't get lost in Jordan Marsh, and despite moments of panic she didn't get lost returning to Commonwealth Publishing. Her feet were killing her, yet she had broadened her horizons farther, as she would every day. By four-thirty, her typewriter barely drowned out her growling stomach.

An umbrella, she thought the next morning, running to work through the rain, I'll have to buy an umbrella during my lunch hour, I saw some at Jordan's, fashionable ones. But when Frances announced the coffee break and she looked up from typing Mr. Palmquist's memos, she realized she should buy a snow shovel. Out the tall windows, the gray rain had changed to dense whiteness. So it snowed in Boston, after all. At noon she ate her peanut-butter sandwich at her desk and did her

70

exploring in the office copy of the *Literary Market Place,* listening to Frances and Lynn and Barbara. The snow came down purposefully.

By four-thirty the storm was still going strong. She fought her way through it back to her rooming house where she put her soaked flats near the radiator and stood at the window, which was etched with fern-frost. A Boston blizzard. Did she take more than a normal interest in snow because of her name? She sat down and wrote her first Boston poem:

> On frozen windows
> I have spelled my name,
> Breathed myself away
> And cooled my tongue.

Then she went to the kitchen to heat up a can of Chef Boyardee ravioli, and later, choosing her skirt and sweater for tomorrow, she set out her boots, sadly deciding they'd be necessary although the sidewalks of course would be plowed by then.

Ha! It was still snowing the next morning, but she was astounded to find the sidewalks unplowed, the streets a mess. In Gunthwaite, even such a big snowstorm would have been kept up with overnight, the drivers of snowplows stopping in at Jimmy's Diner for coffee to stay awake. Floundering over snowdrifts, her second-best flats squashed into her pocketbook, she reminded herself that Boston was rather larger than Gunthwaite.

"Schools canceled everywhere," Frances said, arriving late from her suburb, carrying a brocade bag in addition to her pocketbook and lunch bag, "some places have already got as much as twenty inches." She pulled a pair of heels out of the brocade bag, removed her boots, eased her stockinged feet into them. "You must feel right at home in such weather, dear."

Snowy laughed.

The storm began letting up and gradually stopped, but again everyone stayed in the office for lunch. Snowy considered the

71

phone on her desk, wondering about calling Puddles to ask if they should postpone the bar; she imagined, though, Puddles's response: "The weather, shmeather, we've gone *parking* in worse than this!" So she started looking through the office copy of *Books in Print* and nearly dropped her deviled-ham sandwich when she saw a great long list of Agatha Christies, in paperback, many whose titles were new to her. A bonanza! She could afford to buy them, she was a career girl.

Shyly, she took *Books in Print* to Barbara's cubicle and said, "How do I order something from this?"

Barbara said, "Write the publisher, tell them what you want and ask what the shipping charge is. Incidentally, tomorrow is payday, we get paid on Thursdays, and Lynn and I always celebrate by going out to lunch at an Italian restaurant near here. Would you like to join us?"

Overcome, Snowy said, "Thank you." She bet she'd learn there was more to Italian cuisine than pizza and grinders and Chef Boyardee ravioli.

"A shoe bag," Frances told her at four-thirty. "You need to buy a shoe bag."

Snowy was cramming her flats into her pocketbook. "A shoe bag?"

Frances held up the brocade bag. "Specially made for carrying shoes to the office. Jordan's, Filene's."

"Oh. Thank you." Discoveries abounding.

Outdoors, the early dusk was colder, and people were shoveling fat pillows of snow off stairs and either trampling down paths on the sidewalk or walking in the street on snow crumbled by tires into pie-crust dough. When Snowy reached the corner of Marlborough and Arlington Streets, she registered she was telling Tom about the Boston blizzard. Raging at herself, she looked up and saw Bev coming out of the Katharine Gibbs building, wearing a new tailored gray wool coat.

Bev hadn't yet recognized her. Snowy could hide in her turned-up collar and keep trudging through the snow.

Snowy stopped and waited. One day this winter she had

noticed on the Bennington campus a bush of red berries completely iced and preserved. Now determination iced her like those red berries. She put her chin up and said, "Hi."

Ever since they were children, Bev had seen Snowy make the chin gesture.

Snowy said lightly, "I'm meeting Puddles for a beer, but cocoa would be more appropriate."

Caught by surprise, Bev spoke. "So am I."

They stood looking at each other.

Snowy said, "Today's Wednesday, not Thursday. Did you forget?"

Bev said slowly, "Puddles switched days because of an exam."

Snowy said, "Puddles," and they said in unison, "Puddles."

Snowy took a step, waited, took another. Bev began walking beside her.

"This storm," Snowy said. "Do you suppose Bostonians know that the snowplow has been invented?"

"Snowplows? Oh horrors, too modern."

They walked on toward Charles Street, Snowy observing that Bev had tamed her famous hula walk. Did Bev fear that in Boston it would incite an attack? Gunthwaite boys had just ogled.

And as they walked, Snowy and Bev both were thinking of all the walking together they had done, to and from school, to and from Main Street. Now they were walking together in Boston, Gunthwaite the past, their shared past.

They clambered over a snowbank, and Bev said, "How cosmopolitan!" and crossed her eyes, which Snowy had seen her do since they were in second grade. They started giggling. Yet Boston *was* a city, albeit snowbound, and they had grown up to live here, in the same neighborhood once more but in Back Bay. Boston! The splendor of it!

Snowy said, "We're really here."

These words, instead of increasing the contrast, seemed to erase the gap between their former Gunthwaite best-friend selves and their present estranged selves walking down a city street.

Bev thought, I've been wanting to tell her my New Year's Eve milestone; you couldn't tell Puddles such intimate news because God only knew when she might blab it out, and Ann was still, comparatively, a stranger. Had Snowy passed the Big Milestone with Tom that night last April? Why did I just let him Get Fresh? Don't think about Tom, think about Roger. After Charl and Jack's New Year's Eve party, she'd gone parking with Roger on the Cat Path in his 1941 Ford known as the Heap. With boys, Bev always indulged her moods, and she had been melancholy at the party, but now when the necking began she tried to shake this blue mood caused by Joanne Carter's fraternity pin. She reminded herself how remarkable Roger was, pulling himself up by his own bootstraps out of a French-Canadian family who thought he should be working at Trask's instead of going to college. And Roger was planning to be a lawyer, while Tom was at a hick college and would end up a poverty-stricken teacher—if he managed to graduate. So that night Roger's lawyerly powers of persuasion prevailed, and at long last Bev had relinquished her virginity.

Snowy said, "Remember how we used to play Sergeant Preston of the Yukon on the snowbanks?"

Bev bellowed, "Sergeant Preston and his Wonder Dog, Yukon King! On, King! On, great husky!"

People stared at them, and by the time they came to the bar they were weak from the giggles that jiggled just above relieved tears.

The bar was satisfyingly seedy, with an oiled floor and an empty barren atmosphere. Puddles sat in a booth cracking her knuckles, her particular accomplishment; Bev's was the ability to bend her thumbs over backward, while Snowy's was to raise one eyebrow.

I'll be damned, Puddles thought, they met on the way. She hadn't taken that possibility into account. But neither had retreated, they were laughing, and as they toppled into the booth

74

she saw she could scrap her fiendish plot, an invented engagement to Gene which they'd have to keep toasting until she'd drunk them under the table. Obviously, they had somehow made up; they'd only needed distance from Gunthwaite.

Bev said to Puddles, "Very crafty, aren't you."

Puddles whispered to Snowy, "Did you remember your driver's license? The waiter's coming."

"Eek," Snowy said. During Christmas vacation, in preparation for Boston, she'd followed Puddles's example and altered on her old license her date of birth from 1939 to 1936. More criminal acts! But she should have entered the bar with mature dignity. Her hands began to sweat.

The waiter asked, "What'll it be, ladies, the usual?"

"Yes," Puddles said casually. "Thanks."

"Sure thing." He left.

Puddles said, "Jesus, Bev and I are such regulars he didn't bother checking you."

"Barflies!" Snowy said.

"Habitués!" Bev said.

Puddles said, "Or else the bartender doesn't want us kicked out because he's getting his thrills feasting his eyes on Bev. Well, Snowy, how's it going at work?"

Snowy hesitated. This might prove a delicate subject, since Snowy was actually doing what Bev was studying to do, although Bev must be studying more things than simply typing, such as shorthand, probably, and accounting, and maybe even good grooming. "Oh, no big deal. I type letters and stuff, I'm just a typist, not a secretary."

Bev asked, "Do you hitch your skirt up? I'm majoring in skirt-hitching. Remember how Mrs. Moulton in Latin and English used to perch on her desk with her foot on the wastebasket and the boys drooled? I'll make her look as sexy as Little Lulu."

So that was okay, too.

The waiter brought their beers.

Puddles said, "To Boston!"

Afterward, walking back, Snowy and Bev saw a man lurching and weaving along Charles Street, his head bleeding from a fall or a fight. People gave him a wide berth.

Bev said, "We're really here. Ughy-pew, let's cross the street."

BEV AND PUDDLES's friendship would have faded if Snowy hadn't appeared on the scene. NRT saved the triumvirate.

Snowy occasionally visited them in their rooms, meeting their roommates and reluctantly admitting to herself that Ann Wilmot was nice, a pretty girl who was indeed Bev's clothes-swapping size. Thelma, Puddles's roommate, was so stalwart you knew you'd lose any battle over, say, having your temperature taken rudely—as you would with Puddles, despite her fragility.

However, Bev and Puddles found it simpler to come visit her, and more fun, the rooming-house room a haven from school, grown-up, independent. They and Snowy would loll around having what Puddles called bull sessions but Bev corrected, "Heifer sessions!", talking some about school, Bev and Puddles proud of their marks, but then always moving on to other topics which would provide better common ground because their school experiences now differed greatly, and Snowy was mightily relieved when the subject did change, ashamed of feeling superior, a liberal-arts student at a college that rose above exams and marks, though she wasn't a grasshopper and they ants, for wasn't she too learning a trade, at Commonwealth Publishing? They discussed sex. Swearing Snowy to secrecy, Bev had told her, "New Year's Eve, the Big Milestone with Roger," and Snowy had blushed guiltily and said, "That night I behaved badly and T-Tom and I went off, it was my Big Milestone," and Bev said, "Fallen women!" and they escaped into embarrassed laughter. They continued to bow to skeptical Puddles, pretending to be virgins, saying she was their authority on sex, which

76

she was. They discussed life and clothes and food. Snowy bought a chafing dish, to eliminate waiting in line for the kitchen's hot plate, and they experimented, fussy-eater Puddles usually declining the results but hopeful about fudge; unfortunately, they learned, you couldn't make fudge in a chafing dish, it didn't get hot enough. Puddles fearlessly went into liquor stores with her fake license, stashing her purchases in Snowy's room where in her closet Snowy amassed ingredients for other experiments, whiskey sours, daiquiris, Brandy Alexanders, Bloody Marys, stingers. Puddles said, "Just like hammering tent stakes," banging towel-wrapped ice cubes with her shoe. "Just like Sweetland," said Bev, pouring from an improvised cocktail shaker that consisted of a vase, bought by Snowy to hold the street-vendor flowers she couldn't resist, and the mess kit lid.

On weekends they went window-shopping, and Snowy produced her guidebook and coerced Bev and Puddles into skipping the subway and taking long walks, the North End, Chinatown, seeking out historic sites, and going to museums. "For culture!" Snowy said, without explaining that this was a variation of a joke of hers and Harriet's: The first time asparagus was served at Bennington, Harriet remarked, "Asparagus is heaven, but I hate peeing afterward," and Snowy said, "What?" and Harriet said, "You're kidding, you never noticed the smell?" and Snowy said, 'Well, actually, my mother doesn't serve asparagus, Bev's mother grows it, I've had it there, but I never—" Harriet said, "After dinner, go to the bathroom and inhale a good whiff. Confirm my conclusion." Snowy said, "I don't *want* to." Harriet said, "You must! For science!" So Snowy had stuck her head in a toilet, for science.

Whit Bennett was introduced to Bev and Puddles when he drove all the way across Massachusetts to take Snowy to dinner and a play, a round-trip journey he repeated until the Studebaker broke down. Her other dates were double dates Bev arranged with guys from B.U., Harvard, M.I.T.; at parties, at the movies, in bars, Snowy once again coped with being dimmed by Bev's presence, as she had on double dates in high school, but now she also had to cope with—sometimes strenuously—the guys' assumption that a Bennington girl was an easy lay. (The Williams boys she dated knew better or soon found out, Whit still being the only one she permitted to Get Fresh.) Eventually her indignation became disgust and she told Bev, "Thanks, I guess not, I guess I won't go out anymore, I'm feeling unfaithful, these dates have shown me I'm maybe in love with Whit." A bald-faced lie which Bev didn't detect, saying reflectively, "I'm in love with Roger, but he's so far away and that's no fun." Then they began discussing what Bev should wear to the Dartmouth Winter Carnival.

Often it seemed to Snowy as if she led a double life, as a member of the triumvirate in one existence, a student like Bev and Puddles though a student whose homework just consisted of an NRT reading list, and as an office worker in the other, enduring the daily grind for the sake of the paycheck. And on paydays she was part of a new triumvirate, going out to lunch each Thursday with Barbara and Lynn at the Italian restaurant and discovering lasagna, manicotti, spumoni, zabaglione.

One afternoon near the end of NRT, when she took a stack of typed letters into Mr. Palmquist's office he said more than "Thank you." He asked, "What do you think of Commonwealth?"

"I've learned a lot."

"Have you learned if you want to go into publishing?"

"My ambition is a cubicle."

He grinned. "Then you'll be coming back next winter?"

"Could I?"

"I don't see why not. What are your summer plans?"

Snowy hated confessing her restaurant background, but her plans did involve a more exotic spot than Gunthwaite. "My best friend and I are going to waitress at a hotel in Camden."

"Is it definite?"

"No," she said, puzzled. "We've only been talking about it. Summer seems ages away."

"If you'd like to, you could work for Commonwealth this

78

summer, doing what you're doing now and filling in when people go on vacation. You're very quick—and neat."

Mr. Palmquist's highest accolade.

Stunned, Snowy said, "Thank you, but—"

"No need to decide right now. Just let me know before you return to Vermont."

Back at her desk and later in her room, Snowy balanced Boston against Camden. She'd kidded Bev about being mad at the Camden area because Bev reported that it didn't have a statue of Edna St. Vincent Millay, who was born in nearby Rockland, but her education lacked ocean experience, for she'd gone to the coast just once, when she was a child, her grandfather taking her and her grandmother on an autumn day. The wind, and the fierce waves thundering! (Her mother's parents, these were the grandparents she'd grown up with, until Grandpa died and Grandma moved to Florida. She could hardly recall her father's mother, whose early death was caused by the struggle to bring up a family alone after her husband died of—Snowy had overheard this when her mother and Grandma were talking about her father's family—drink.) Camden, ocean. Boston happened to be a port, she reminded herself, and the triumvirate ought to visit the docks during their weekend tours, Puddles scaring off sailors.

But the next Saturday, as planned, she and Bev and Puddles walked to the Fens, en route to the Isabella Stewart Gardner Museum, which Snowy wanted to visit again. Puddles began talking about her nursing outfit, a black-and-white-checked uniform, white apron, black stockings and shoes. "I've heard," she said, "they're horrible in the summer; your shoes and stockings stink when you sweat and black dye runs down your legs."

"Ughy-pew!" Bev said.

Nursing school went three years straight through the three summers. Puddles complained, "I'm going to be sweltering and stinking in Boston while you two are splashing in the ocean—"

It would be less awkward, Snowy thought, to tell Bev with

Puddles present. "As a matter of fact," she said, "I've been offered a summer job at Commonwealth."

Although Puddles wanted to do a cartwheel at the prospect of a fellow sufferer sharing her misery, she said, "Are you nuts? Everyone says summer in the city is *hell*."

"An inferno," said Bev, surprised by a swirl of gladness. Snowy had never been any competition when it came to boys, except for Tom, but her waitressing efficiency emphasized Bev's forgetfulness.

Snowy said, trying not to sound sententious, "I know. The problem is, a summer job here would probably further my career."

They walked along, musing.

Bev said, "Snowy, waitressing in a Camden hotel is still waitressing."

Going backward.

Bev said, "And there's the split shifts, every day. I love having the afternoons free for suntanning, but you hated the split shifts on Fridays at Sweetland."

"Yes." Snowy preferred to work straight through and get the damn thing over with.

"Then there's lobster," Bev said. "Did I tell you about the first tray of lobster dinners I had to carry in, tray carried *high above shoulder* as instructed, claws dangling over the platters, drawn butter sloshing, and when one of the claws seemed to grab out at me, I said, 'Eek!' rather loudly but luckily in front of a table where a gorgeous man was sitting"—Bev always thought of strategy, no matter what the situation—"and he came to the rescue, and it was worth being reprimanded later by the headwaitress, since he invited me to a party on a boat—"

This story of Bev's got them to the Gardner Museum, the summer decision acknowledged.

ON THE LAST Wednesday of NRT in the first full week of March, at the bar Bev and Puddles paid for Snowy's farewell beers, and the next day at the Italian restaurant Barbara and Lynn treated. Friday evening, Bev canceled a date to join Puddles in Snowy's room where they made Crème de Menthe frappes while Snowy packed, and on Saturday Bev and Puddles rode in a taxi with her to North Station and saw her off.

Walking back, Bev said, "After Boston, peace and quiet in Vermont will be like the grave."

Puddles said, "The boondocks aren't the grave, Beverly Colby, if you'll recall. God, how I miss the Cat Path."

Bev missed Snowy. Already.

So did Puddles, who said, "Well, at least we won't be getting dragged to museums anymore. For culture!"

In Gunthwaite, Snowy's parents met the bus and collected her and her luggage, curious about a big carton that accompanied the Skyway. Snowy had brought them Jordan Marsh presents, her mother a new wall can opener adorned with a rooster, her father a table cigarette lighter, but the carton held her Coffee Cake Therapy, the plentitude of paperback Agatha Christies she'd ordered.

Home. A rest stop between Boston and Bennington. Classes began Wednesday; her father would take Tuesday off from Trask's to drive her there. In between were these days of limbo that she planned to devote mainly to exercising Laurie.

Sunday afternoon they were walking along State Avenue when up ahead the doors of the Congregational church opened and out came a wedding party, the bridesmaids' pink dresses bursting into the bright winter sun like a magician's trick flowers. Then Snowy saw that the groom was Tom. Dark blue suit. White boutonnière. Stopping abruptly, she yanked Laurie's leash so tight Laurie yelped, and Tom glanced up from the bride.

As Snowy spun around, Tom thought, Why the hell is she home, she can't have flunked out, is she okay?

Snowy conquered the urge to run away headlong down the

81

street. She walked normally, saying to Laurie, "The radiant bride was a vision of loveliness in white satin with a sweetheart neckline, and she was also knocked up." Why else would Joanne and Tom be getting married on a Sunday in March?

She heard the sound of cold cars starting, the wedding party probably proceeding onward to the Gunthwaite Inn for the gala reception. She could ignore them. She put her chin up, and when the first car passed her, the back seat a billow of white satin, she smiled and waved.

Joanne waved, a queen. Sitting beside her, Tom looked at Snowy.

She got home without making a fool of herself by crying in public, but she didn't cry in her bedroom either. She went into the bathroom and picked up the container of razor blades and slid one out. There was a little arrow on the blade, showing which way to push it to remove it, and she idly observed that the arrow on the next blade pointed the other way. They were packaged at the Gillette factory with only one way you could slide each out. She remembered how, in this bathroom, she'd almost drunk iodine. Studying her wrists, she remembered that when Bev was dating Tom, he'd written Bev from Rumford about a girl who'd cut her wrists with a razor blade because she had flunked some test.

Snowy dropped the blade in the wastebasket and went downstairs and asked her father if she could borrow the car.

It was a 1955 black Ford her parents had bought in 1956; concentrating on the house, they didn't spend money on new cars which, Snowy's father always said, depreciated whereas a house appreciated, words that had considerably confused young Snowy, for she knew that her parents appreciated the house (did they ever!), yet how could the house appreciate back? You're babbling, she told her brain, driving out of town past Frog Hollow, on through woods and woods, and even the sight of the Cat Path didn't slap tears into her eyes. When Tom had brought her to Bev's after their first date, to sleep over, he'd unknowingly made her cry then by not asking her out again, keeping her

82

and his other girlfriends in a dither. She turned off onto the twisty dirt road, a bobsled run between high snowbanks, and drove up the driveway looking down at the icy sheen of the lake.

She parked at the back of the Cape. Hadn't she intended to visit Julia before returning to school anyway?

There was a cloud of chickadees around the bird-feeder tray outside the kitchen-table window, and although a downy woodpecker flew off the suet feeder squeaking like a toy, the chickadees paid no attention to her as she got out of the car.

The barn's small door at one side of the two big doors opened, and Fred stepped out, wearing work pants and a plaid wool jacket, a wrench in his hand. Inside the barn you could see, beyond the 1956 blue Mercury, the Jeep he was constantly tinkering with. He might work at Gunthwaite Savings, but in his heart he wasn't a man in a gray flannel suit, and he loved to drive his Jeep to town every day, not just when the dirt road demanded four-wheel drive, mortifying Bev who felt that a limousine would definitely be more her style. He said, "Snowy! Home for the weekend? Julia's out in the woods but she should be back soon. Can you wait?"

"I could try to catch up with her if I could borrow your snowshoes."

"Of course." Fred went into the barn and lifted them down off the wall.

"Thank you." She laid them on the driveway. She'd always used these snowshoes to accompany Julia in winter to their favorite spot year-round, the bog, but the harnesses hadn't got any easier to adjust to fit her boots, the leather frozen, her hands mittened, and she thought that wrestling with them would be what finally started her crying.

Fred asked, "Need help?"

"Thanks, no." She yanked the last strap through a buckle and started up into the old orchard on the trail which Julia's daily snowshoeing had cut deep. Bev's opinion of snowshoeing was, "How arctic!", but in sixth grade and junior high she and Snowy had practiced skiing here every winter before venturing

83

onto the Recreation Area's slopes, enduring the sport for the sake of the boys and the clothes. In high school they had rejoiced to discover that you didn't have to ski to be popular; never again would they have to submit to the perils of the T-bar, the chair lift, and the downhill runs! Snowy did, however, like to go snowshoeing with Julia, who'd taught her how to read the snow. Deer tracks had been easy, and still were. Around the piles of dropped apples Julia gathered each autumn for the deer the snow was trampled with them, while clearer tracks stepped between, daintily high-heeled.

Julia's trail went into the woods under arched birches, re- minding Snowy today not of Robert Frost but of weddings, photographs of military weddings with the bride and groom leaving beneath crossed swords. All these woods had long ago been fields, and she squinted, trying to make the trees disappear so she could see the land logged off, the stone walls enclosing pastures and livestock, not second-growth trees. One man, Julia had told her, could build sixteen feet of stone wall in a day. It was as hard to imagine open fields as it was to realize, when she came to the bog, that this white silent bowl would soon be deafening with spring peepers whose hectic pulsing kept Bev awake way back at the house but soothed Snowy to sleep imme- diately.

In winter, you rarely even heard a chickadee here. The birds were smart enough to be down at the feeders. Snowy broke the silence. "Julia?" A voice replied from farther along the trail which began following a brook, looping back to the orchard, and she rushed forward. "It's me, Snowy!" The brook was a wide black stripe through the white snow, and under the thin sheet of ice the water swam like inky fish. Then ahead amid trees bright color flashed, the red of Julia's parka, and Snowy saw Julia bashing her snowshoes into a snowbank to make room to turn around.

"Snowy!" Julia exclaimed, always prepared for the worst. "You're home, what's wrong? Bev—you—your parents—"

"Nothing, nothing, Non-Resident Term is over, that's all."

"Oh, thank heavens. I talked with Bev yesterday, she forgot to tell me."

"No need for Bev to waste long-distance money on the end of NRT." Snowy took a deep breath. "I'm sorry I didn't write you to thank you for your letter and the clipping about—Ed. I didn't know how. I was ashamed. You were right, Tom dated Bev because of me. I stole him back and he asked me to get pinned. I declined."

"Ah, Snowy." Julia held out her arms. They embraced across snowshoes, Julia noting a muscle jumping wildly in Snowy's jaw, a sure sign she was upset.

Beneath the parka, Julia felt as gaunt as ever. Snowy said, "I'm sorry I hurt Bev."

"But in January she said things are all right between you again. Did you choose to go to Boston for your NRT in hopes of this reconciliation? I guessed that you had."

"Yes, that's why. Only we aren't going to Camden together, did Bev tell you? I'm working at Commonwealth this summer."

Julia thought of those two miserable years she had worked in Boston before marrying Richard Colby. She wasn't cut out for city life. And after the chicken farm she'd even had an aversion to living on Chestnut Street in a Gunthwaite neighborhood, but she'd had to sell the farm to save Bev from isolation—and to save herself from seeing shadows of Richard everywhere. She had been certain she would never return to the country, yet eventually she'd met Fred Miller who, like Richard, wanted a farm, though unlike Richard he didn't want to do any actual farming. Fred was also otherwise very different from Richard, dramatic red-headed Richard who had acted the role of farmer. She could vividly recall the expression on her mother's face when she'd described Fred by saying, "He's a simple man, with simple needs. He enjoys chopping wood." Her mother had said incredulously, "A *bank teller?*" Thus with Fred she had after all gone back to the life she loved. "Bev says you've decided that publishing is the career that'll support your poetry—Snowy, let's skedaddle to the house and warm you up, you're so white you look as if you've got frostbite." Julia turned and continued down the trail, asking over her shoulder, "Puddles is working 'on the floors,' is that the term?"

"Yes."

"I suppose she's the terror of the wards."

In the brook now there were stretches of open water where ice along the edges became stalactites, stalagmites. "She's having a field day."

"Good, but it's a damn shame that girls who ought to be doctors must settle for nursing."

"Trask's! He'll have to drop out of school and go to work at Trask's!"

"What?" Julia stopped. "Something *is* wrong."

"I saw him and Joanne coming out of the Congregational church, they got married this afternoon—"

"Tom?"

"—and she must be pregnant, why else get married at such a weird time, and his job at Rumford is washing pots and pans in the school kitchen, that won't support a wife and baby—" Suddenly Snowy remembered how, when she and Puddles and Bev were gazing through the maternity-ward window during their freshman year's Girl Scout nurse's aide project at the hospital, Puddles had declared, "I'm going to have six children. Three boys and three girls." Bev had said she would too, and let the nanny take care of them, while Snowy had got as close as she ever had to revealing her desire to be a twin and said, "I'm going to have twins, twin girls." Then when she and Tom began going steady, she had assumed he would be their father.

"Tom and Joanne," Julia said.

"He'll quit school and take a full-time job at some awful place, Trask's or somewhere, and it's Joanne's fault, it's the girl's responsibility, you can't let a guy get so carried away he forgets—" Shocked at referring to sex and Puddles's rule of responsibility in front of a grown-up, Snowy swayed off-balance and fell into a snowbank, seeing Tom carried away with Joanne in the cream-colored convertible.

86

"No," Julia said, reaching down to help her up. "Tom bears equal responsibility. Anyway, maybe Joanne isn't pregnant. I have a confession. There was an engagement announcement in the newspaper sometime in January, and I didn't send it to Bev and I hoped your folks wouldn't spot it and send it to you. I was afraid the news would stir things up, after you and Bev had made peace."

"Engagement."

"People don't dilly-dally around with engagements before a shotgun wedding. Get married quickly, that's the general idea."

Then Tom hadn't married Joanne because he'd knocked her up but because—he loved her. Snowy shouted, "Why get married in *March?* Joanne is a June bride if ever there was one!"

"And on Sunday," Julia said. "Unusual." Since Snowy wasn't brushing herself off, Julia did so, softly although Snowy's bruises were within. "Come on, let's go warm up, I'll make us a hot buttered rum."

Hurrying behind her, Snowy said, "Tom wouldn't care which day or month, he's never gone by the rules, but Joanne would want the wedding comme il faut to the nth power, the stupid bitch!"

Jealousy was probably better, Julia reflected, than the agonized concern for Tom that Snowy had blurted out first. She joined in, concocting cattiness, "Did Joanne at least have sense enough to buy a dress she can wear again, or did she succumb to tribal custom?"

"She went whole hog, white satin—I guess it was satin—and the bridesmaids in pink. Probably she even had a sixpence in her shoe."

Julia began shifting the subject. "Well, Fred and I are planning to move to the poorhouse whenever Bev gets married and stars in a big wedding. Can you imagine me the mother of a bride wearing a picture hat? Maybe I'll wear my gardening hat." There was a shriek of laughter and she glanced back, relieved by success.

But Snowy was both laughing and sobbing. "I know! I know

87

why! I'm sure Rumford Teachers' College doesn't allow married cheerleaders, so Joanne waited to get married until basketball season was over! What do you bet Rumford's last basketball game was last night? Isn't that a *riot?*"

ESTHER, A FRIEND of Snowy and Harriet's down the corridor, returned from NRT with a new nose.

Snowy gasped to Harriet, "An operation?"

"A nose job," Harriet said. "Snowy, where have you been all your life?"

"In front of mirrors hating my nose. I never dreamed—" Then and there Snowy resolved that someday when she could afford it, she would have her nose straightened.

Harriet herself returned with a wineskin and a bottle of red wine. "To get in the spirit of things," she explained. "We're reading *The Sun Also Rises* in my Lang-and-Lit next."

Snowy had read most of Hemingway on her own in high school, and she intoned, "It was a big bull."

"I've named the wineskin Scrotie. That's short for scrotum. Doesn't it look like one?"

Snowy whooped. "It was a big scrotum."

"We'll have to practice. In the movies everybody has great aim, but I know I'll squirt myself in the face."

Classes, assignments, and writing reports about their NRT's kept them too busy until Saturday afternoon. As they sat on the floor at the coffee table unsuccessfully practicing, passing the wineskin back and forth, Harriet pursued Snowy's news of the morning about last night's date, sensing something more. Oblique approach. "Are you sure you can't count it a milestone?"

"Eek!" Snowy said, holding the wineskin at arm's length and dousing her bangs. "Well, the time I was asked to get pinned before, it was only a local fraternity at a state teachers' college."

"There, this was your *national* milestone."

Whit Bennett's heart had grown even fonder during Snowy's absence, causing him not to break up with her, Tom's Girls'-State reaction, but to want to get pinned. And on the rebound Snowy had almost accepted. After she'd left Julia's and driven home, she had gone up to the attic where, atop the cartons of her dolls and childhood books, she saw the Tom carton in which, when he broke up with her, she'd packed her souvenirs of him and everything he'd given her except his letter sweater, disposing of that by mailing it to him at Rumford. Without opening the carton, she carried it down to the garbage cans in the garage and threw it away. But as she started into the house, she ran back and took out the carton and yanked open the flaps. A smell of Valentine chocolates from the pink heart-shaped box. Pressed corsages, a napkin she'd slipped into her jacket pocket at Hooper's Dairy Bar to commemorate their first date, the Parker pen he had given her on her sixteenth birthday, the "I Love You" charm she'd snapped off her charm bracelet, his framed yearbook photograph, the tassel from his mortarboard. And the wooden figure of Laurie he had carved, her seventeenth-birthday present. She ought to save the carving, she told herself, for Laurie's sake. So this was what she preserved, throwing the rest away once more, but she didn't bring the carving to Bennington; she stowed it in a drawer in her empty bureau at home.

Harriet said, "I guess I'd say no if a guy asked me to get pinned, even if I loved him. Too secure, too early in the game."

Snowy followed this tangent, a detour that might keep her from telling the other news that was dying to be told. "With Whit, I start feeling I'm not a separate person. Literally. Biting his own nails is bad enough, but when he's holding my hand at the movies he begins biting *mine,* nibbling—and if he scratches his ear with my hand, what if he had to scratch elsewhere? Speaking of such things, here, take Scrotie. I suppose that's the reason I said no. Becoming too close to someone is a mistake."

"But there's our art, which must be fueled by grand passions."

They laughed, and Snowy lit a Kent.

Harriet squirted her chin. "Shit. Do you ever write lyric poetry?"

"Um, yes. But I've got plenty of material, I don't need to be pinned."

"A person doesn't need to be pinned to sleep with a guy, either."

Inhaling, Snowy contemplated a fat nude. "That certainly is being close to someone." Like Siamese twins, as she'd said to Tom afterward.

Harriet said, "You can do it for physical purposes and stay separate from the neck up."

Which was exactly what Snowy had thought last night, parked in Whit's revived Studebaker, saying, "I'm sorry, I'm not ready in my freshman year to get engaged-to-be-engaged to anybody." Getting laid, though, she was ready for that now, and when he began trying to induce her to change her mind with kisses, she suddenly unzipped his fly and reached into the heat, into his Jockeys, and boing!, out shot an enthusiastic ramrod. Astounded but overjoyed, quick as a wink Whit whisked down her slacks and underpants, yet the pegged legs of the slacks impeded removal and she'd have started giggling at his being frustrated by fashion if she hadn't been extremely horny too. Kicking off her loafers, curling up her feet to aid his struggles, she tapped the glove compartment and asked, "Were you a Boy Scout?" "Huh?" he said thickly, then grabbed for the Trojans. She figured that it wouldn't hurt this time because she wasn't a virgin. She was wrong. Although urgent, Tom had pushed himself into her slowly. Whit thrust himself in, she clenched her fists and didn't yell—and he exploded and flopped panting onto her. Speedy Gonzales, Puddles would say. Furious, Snowy almost wept, but moments passed, he wasn't making an exit, he was swelling up again in there. Puddles had talked of doing it twice. Was this what she meant? Or were they getting stuck, the way

90

Puddles said dogs sometimes did? Would water have to be thrown on them? Despite this danger, Snowy's hips began to writhe involuntarily. He kissed her throat with such fervor she knew he was causing a hickey, and then he heaved himself up, pounding against her. Before she lost her wits, the possibility of spillage occurred to her. God! She groped for the Trojans he'd tossed on the dashboard. He got the hint, and she learned they weren't stuck. He didn't knot his used Trojan as Tom had, but he also threw it out the window, leaving in the woods the spoor of parkers. Back into her he went, and it wasn't hurting so much now. The problem was Tom; she couldn't stop thinking of Tom until her mind bloomed scarlet and she stopped thinking at all.

Harriet said, "Guys can screw without involvement, why can't we?"

"Mmm," said Snowy evasively, picking a froth of ash off her sweatshirt. She hadn't got pinned on the rebound, but she sure the hell had got laid. Today she was as lame as the first day of cheerleading practice, and she couldn't alleviate the pain cheer-leader-style by complaining loudly and proudly about being out of shape. She couldn't tell Harriet she had Gone All The Way with someone she didn't love. Or so she'd assumed. This after-noon, however, Harriet was sounding like she was trying to let Snowy know that she screwed her dates more guiltlessly than she stole sugar bowls. Snowy said, "In Gunthwaite, if a girl does it just to do it, she's called cheap; that's why I wondered if Whit would ask me out again after I let him last night."

At this, Harriet's jaw dropped, she clenched Scrotie, and the wine made a perfect arc.

"Bull's eye!" Snowy said. "Hooray! It was a big bull's eye."

"You what? You said no to his fraternity pin and then let him?"

"A consolation prize."

They laughed, Harriet thoroughly impressed.

Snowy took Scrotie and squeezed. The wine spurted past her shoulder to splash her hair. "With my aim, I'm going to end up with hair like Bev's, only it'll be really red, not auburn. Bev had

91

a carroty phase growing up, though, so *Anne of Green Gables* was her favorite." Snowy said to the fat woman on Harriet's easel, "Do you do it every time? Afterward, we were horsing around and he said he'd get some French ticklers for next time—" (Snowy had known what he was talking about thanks to Puddles, who knew of them just by hearsay.) "—and I informed him there wouldn't be a next time, I wouldn't take the risk again. Okay, guys can do it without involvement. Lucky them, they don't get pregnant."

"Did he make another date?"

"Uh-huh."

"He doesn't think you're cheap."

"He thinks if I did it once I'll do it again, no matter what I say. Hope springs eternal."

"You cynic!"

"Realist. He's a guy. I'd *like* to screw every time." Would she ever, now she was getting the hang of it! Or the hung of it, Puddles might remark. "But I'm not so brave as you."

Harriet lit a Kent and she too contemplated the easel. "You know Lewis?"

He was the boy Harriet had left behind, the one who wrote her, a freshman at some California college. "Yes," Snowy said, yanking a tangled leg of her Levi's. "Ouch!"

"Lame?"

"Crippled."

They laughed.

"Lewis and I finally Went All The Way the night before I flew back East last September." Harriet flicked ashes toward the ashtray; they fell on the table. "We were in love, we planned a lovers' farewell."

Snowy set Scrotie down and surreptitiously held the ashtray under the table's edge and brushed at the ashes.

"That is," Harriet said, "we started to screw, but in the midst of our thrashing around his elbow hit the gearshift-thing on his steering wheel and knocked it out of park into drive."

"The car was an automatic?" Snowy asked, in turn impressed, dusting her hands.

"And we started rolling down a steep hill. We always went parking near this romantic Japanese garden, and before Lewis could get the brake on we ran over a slew of dwarf trees and landed in an ornamental lake. After we climbed out and found a phone to call an all-night garage, and after the car was *winched* out—it still ran—we were no longer in the mood."

"I'll bet."

"We intended to make up for lost time during the holidays, but Lewis came back from school with crabs."

Snowy stared at Harriet. The day Snowy's grandfather had taken her to the ocean, she had brought home a crab shell she'd found on the beach, along with clam shells and a hank of seaweed, treasures her mother made her leave in the garage, yet—

"So," Harriet said, "the truth is, I haven't gone *All* The Way, and I've been trying to get up the guts to do it with one of my jocks."

"Crabs?" Snowy asked tentatively.

"Lice in your crotch. Lewis swore he'd remained faithful, he claimed everyone in the fraternity house got them, like trench mouth. Be that as it may, I wouldn't even permit a peck on the cheek, and I could've done without his progress reports on how his de-crabbing medication was working."

Puddles had never lectured about crabs. Snowy retched. "I definitely won't do it again."

"Oh, Whit would tell you if he had them, he's an expert on bugs, isn't he, or you'd hear they were going around."

"Nope, I won't." Snowy picked up Scrotie and tilted her head. Although she, the provincial, had Gone All The Way completely, three times, Harriet's experience continued to win the day.

But then Harriet asked, "What does it feel like when a guy shoots his load?"

"Bull's eye!"

A YEAR PASSED, but on a Sunday in May 1959 Snowy and Harriet were acting as if they had got younger, not older. As always when winter went and the blossoming trees frothed white, spring fever swept the campus. Girls lay daydreaming on lawns, the breeze idly flapping the pages of their books. And in front of McCullough, girls were leaping in under the swinging arc of a long jump rope which yesterday Snowy and Harriet, punchy, had driven into town to buy and now stood twirling, everybody remembering rhymes.

Fudge, fudge,
Tell the judge,
Mama had a baby,
Not a boy,
Not a girl,
Just a little baby!

Then Snowy saw Whit walking along the path. Surprised, she handed her end of the rope to Esther, smoothed her ratty old Bennington sweatshirt (still backward) and her Levi's chopped into short-shorts, and went to meet him. After their date last night, he hadn't said anything about visiting today.

"Hi," he said. "Second childhood?"

"It's amazing, nobody's forgotten how."

He took her hand. "Want to go for a walk?"

"Okay." They started back along the path toward Commons. So, she thought, he hadn't driven here in hopes of a repeat of last night's piece of ass, although he must have realized she had a tendency to break her vow of abstinence in the spring. Last year on May fifteenth, a Thursday, she had called him up and suggested a date that night, bewildering him because she normally wouldn't go out on weeknights, and the jerking-off compromise they'd reached was temporarily shelved and they did it again, Snowy imagining Joanne baking Tom a cake in a Rumford apartment kitchen. May fifteenth was Tom's birthday. The next day she had explained to Harriet, "I couldn't help myself, springtime madness." "Yes," Harriet replied, "isn't it heaven?" Spring fever had given Harriet the courage to put the All in All The Way with one of her jocks.

Bennington's school year went later than Williams's, almost to the end of June, and last year Snowy had broken her vow again when Whit left for the summer. He planned to spend his summer driving across the country—and should the Studebaker conk out for good, he'd junk it and buy another used car and drive onward. Carefree, the call of the open road! She was first astonished that he harbored this vagabond desire, then wistful, then envious, then angry; she could never undertake such an expedition alone because she was a girl, even if she didn't have to spend *her* summer earning a paycheck.

Whit had a trust fund, from his grandparents.

That summer, Snowy's room in the Beacon Street rooming house had been on the fourth floor, and she wondered if she would descend, during each stay here, down the flights of stairs closer and closer to the telephone and front door. A Boston summer. The hot sticky days. Her cotton dresses and skirts and blouses she starched and ironed so crisp went limp on her walk to Commonwealth Publishing, where the tall windows didn't cool the corner office, nor did the fans levitating papers, and her sweaty hands slipped off the typewriter keys and dripped onto rejected manuscripts.

On weekends she escaped her ovenlike room to sunbathe on the Esplanade, putting up with wolf whistles for the sake of her tan and the breeze off the Charles River. The river reminded her of home, provoking the same yearnings that had always tormented her when she sat on the riverbank below her house, and she was glad when Puddles could join her, because Puddles's retorts to wolves' advances squelched both the guys and her longings she'd never been able to define—well, partly longings for Tom, but she had sat on the Gunthwaite riverbank and wanted whatever it was years before she'd known Tom existed. Occasionally she and Puddles would seek coolness at the pond in the Public Garden, buying a ride on a swan boat. "Just like tourists," Puddles said. While they glided along and commiserated over how Bev was probably drinking gin-and-tonics on a yacht right now, Snowy watched the way the green water reflected the green trees, and here she felt content, safe in artificiality.

But Puddles had only every other weekend off, and usually she took the train and bus home to see Gene, who worked summers as the Fryolator cook at Riley's Drive-In Restaurant near the lake, a considerable responsibility since Riley's was famous for its fried onion rings.

At the end of that summer, home in Gunthwaite before heading back to Bennington, Snowy slept over at Bev's and learned about her Camden adventures, conquests ranging from busboys to playboys. "No marriage proposals," Bev reported, "just indecent proposals, and I can't imagine why but the only times I did it the entire summer were when Roger visited." Snowy said, "You're pure at heart!" Bev said, "Oh horrors, how boring."

Harriet's fat-lady period came to a close, and she had returned that fall in her sphere period, painting a single big bright orb on a canvas. Maybe, Snowy thought, gazing perplexedly at primary-colored circles, maybe it was a logical progression.

Snowy took Poetry Writing her sophomore year, and shaking, dry-mouthed, she read her poems aloud, determined that after graduation she would steer clear of groups of poets who did readings, despite any cost to her career.

Once again during NRT the triumvirate had gathered in Snowy's room, back up on the fifth floor though a different room. "Same view," Puddles pronounced, looking at rooftops. Bev said, shaking Side-Cars in the vase, "Consider it a penthouse with the elevator temporarily out of order." " 'Temporarily,' " Snowy said, "that's the problem; I'm a temp here as well as at work." But she was given a raise at Commonwealth, to fifty-five dollars a week, and it was assumed she would return this summer. Sipping coffee at her desk, Snowy had studied the cubicle.

Whit said, as they neared Commons, "Where I first saw you."

His approaching graduation was making him elegiac, she sensed. Would he suggest a nostalgic farewell at the Sleepytime Motor Lodge?

She said, "Gate-crashing Skits Night. It seems an eternity ago."

They started walking down Commons lawn toward the Cliff. Whit said, "Last year, you told me you weren't ready to get pinned. Engaged-to-be-engaged."

"Mmm," said Snowy abstractedly, thinking of Bev who was graduating too this spring. Puddles had recently written Snowy, "Bev has ants in her pants about what to do after she graduates. She KNEW she'd be the first of us to finish, but I suppose she forgot."

Whit said, "Let's cut out all the preliminaries. Let's get married."

Snowy stared at him, then sat plunk down on the stone wall at the edge of the Cliff's gentle descent to a field. Off across town, the good old Bennington Monument stood erect against the sky.

He sat down beside her. "I mean it."

Whit's plans after graduation were clear: He'd be going on to graduate school at the University of Michigan, to get his doctorate in bugs.

He continued, "We could rent an apartment in Ann Arbor."

An overwhelming urge possessed her to say yes, to give up. She had a vision of reading Agatha Christies all day instead of as carefully apportioned rewards for her exhausted brain after writing papers. She wouldn't have to write another paper in her life! She could write what she wanted to; she could write poems all day! Whit had that trust fund now and eventually would inherit his parents' dough. She would never have to worry about money again. How wise of Bev to want to marry a millionaire— what freedom that meant!

Whit said, "If you want to, we could start a family right away." He ran his hand up her thigh. "Like tonight."

> Fudge, fudge,
> Tell the judge—

She pictured the cosy apartment, the darling baby clothes. Say yes.

Snowy said, "You've forgotten one drawback. I'm still in school."

"Oh that," he said dismissively. "You don't have to finish school. Why bother? It's a waste of time for girls."

She couldn't believe her ears. "What?"

"Come on, no need to pretend. Everyone knows that girls only go to college to catch a husband."

She exploded, "No!" and thudded to her feet. "You bastard, the hell with you forever, *you've* been a waste of my time!"

Raging, she raced away from him across campus, back to McCullough where, predictably, childhood rhymes had been replaced by lit majors' suggestions, and under the jump rope she skipped, joining the chant:

> Sumer is icumen in,
> Lhude sing cuccu!
> Groweth sed, and bloweth med,
> And springeth the wide nu—
> Sing cuccu!

A marriage proposal was, however, a milestone.

THE NEXT EVENING Esther shouted, "Snowy, phone!"

It wouldn't be Whit. Snowy had posted a note in the phone booth requesting, "If it's for me, please ask who it is, and if it's Whit Bennett, please say I'm not in." Thus had she avoided a half-dozen calls from him. She hurried along the hall to the booth.

Esther whispered, "It's a Beverly Colby."

Bev was making her first call to Snowy at Bennington.

Snowy said into the receiver, "Bev!"

"I'm going to marry Roger." Bev burst into tears.

There was one big reason why Bev was crying after such an announcement. "Oh God," Snowy said, "do you—do you have to, are you pregnant?"

"No!"

Snowy leaned back against the wall of the booth.

Bev said, "I saw too many movies about dumb-blonde secretaries marrying their millionaire bosses. A real millionaire hires a secretary with experience, and experience takes years, and I want things decided *now.*"

While Bev blew her nose, Snowy tried a joke. "Skirt-hitching doesn't ever override experience?"

Bev didn't hear. "Roger came down to do some stuff at B.U.—did I tell you he's decided to go to law school there?"

"Nope."

"We got talking, and it just seems natural, we could rent a little apartment and I'd decorate it inexpensively but with flair—"

Bev, Snowy thought, had seen too many of another type of movie. Then she sampled her vision of life as Whit's wife, she reminded herself how bewitched she was by newlywed nests.

Buoyed up at the prospect of interior decorating, Bev continued, "And I'll get a job; he won't have to work part-time, he can concentrate on becoming a brilliant lawyer—and perhaps a millionaire!"

Bev and Roger. Puddles and Gene. Not Snowy and Tom. Snowy said, "You've loved him a long time."

99

But this renewed tears. Bev blubbered, "Where's the fun and adventure, it's so—*domestic!*"

"Have you called your mother?" Snowy knew that Julia had hoped Bev would someday marry Roger, if she didn't go to drama school.

"I'll phone her next."

"Remember playing Emily in *Our Town,* the wedding, and Dudley playing George Gibbs and your big clinch?"

"That wedding dress, from the Dramatics Club costume collection. I thought it was beautiful." Bev brightened, anticipating all the shopping ahead. Buying things made Bev feel pleased and defined. "How I wish you were here to go shopping with me, but I'll pick the perfect blue for your eyes. Besides you as maid of honor there'll be Puddles as a bridesmaid, of course, and my roommate, and a cousin, and Mother can find a flower girl, a granddaughter of some relatives."

Snowy remembered laughing with Julia at Joanne and Tom's wedding and the prospect of Bev's. Except during their rift, Snowy and Bev had taken it for granted that they would be each other's maid of honor ever since they had played Wedding in their childhood, but now Snowy realized she had grown up to find formal weddings silly. She herself would elope—no, that would kill her folks; she'd have the simplest ceremony possible. If she did get married, years and years hence.

And then the thought of money occurred to her. She couldn't afford a maid-of-honor gown. In her bank account, her meager savings all had to go for school. She could overcome philosophical objections to weddings for Bev's sake, but she couldn't surmount the financial impossibility. She sought an excuse. "When are you planning the wedding, right after you graduate? We let out so late, I wouldn't have time to come home for fittings or go to rehearsal."

"I could postpone—"

"But then I'll be at Commonwealth. I could come for the day, a regular guest."

"Snowy, I implore you—"

In a gulp of embarrassment, Snowy said, "I just plain can't afford the gown, Bev."

"I'll pay for it, Mother will!"

"No."

After a pause, Bev said, "Damn your pride. Oh hell and damn!"

"It's just as well, Bev, because what we didn't take into consideration when we used to play Wedding was that I'd bawl straight through yours. Bawling kids in the audience of *Hansel and Gretel* and *Alice in Wonderland* are okay, but a bawling maid of honor—"

"You've *got* to be part of it. I've decided to ask Mother if we can have it outdoors at the house—yes, I know, I always dreamed of sweeping down the aisle of the Unitarian church, but Roger says if his family sets foot in a Protestant church they'll be eternally damned or something. The guest book! You can be in charge of the guest book and bawl in the background."

Snowy walked slowly back to her room, where she lit a Kent and discussed with Harriet the presumptuousness of weddings in modern times, of inviting people to witness a ceremony so personal.

When Bev had played Emily, she had awed Snowy with her stateliness, and at her own wedding she didn't let the lack of a stage cramp her style. On her stepfather's arm, as she regally crossed the freshly mown lawn toward the justice of the peace, following the flower girl, the bridesmaids, and maid-of-honor Puddles suppressing self-conscious giggles, Bev deserved a standing ovation. Snowy did indeed bawl.

Bev and Roger had rented a basement apartment on the wrong side of Beacon Hill, and they returned to it after a honeymoon in Camden during which Bev relished being the waitee instead of the waitress. Bev began working in the secretarial pool of a bank, explaining her choice of jobs to Snowy by saying, "Because of Fred, I know about banks. Well, I know more about Jeeps, but skirt-hitching would be fatal in a garage." The apartment had only a tiny windowless kitchen and

101

bathroom and one other room, a living room with a pull-out sofa and a dining table at which Roger studied. Bev made it a city nest—scatter rugs on the tiled floors, opaque curtains in the high-up windows, her mother's woven placemats turned into wall hangings on the sallow walls; wedding presents that included a silver gravy boat and a silver candle snuffer and, more practical, the set of Bennington Potters coffee mugs Snowy had given her, and, most practical if startling, Puddles's present of an ominously large first-aid kit—but the apartment's size precluded the triumvirate's gathering there regularly, bothering Roger with laughter, so except for occasional Saturday lunches at Bev's, they continued to gab in Snowy's room, which was on the third floor that summer and the fourth floor again the next NRT.

Snowy's junior-year NRT started off glumly, a figurative first-aid kit needed in the fourth-floor room where she and Bev tried to mend Puddles's broken heart. At Christmas, Gene had asked Puddles for his pin back, having found at UNH a new bosom he wanted it to adorn. "All this time," Puddles seethed over and over, "he's been going out with other girls there, fucking other girls there, I can't *believe* how he lied to me! Gene Chabot, winner of the National Honor Society's Good Citizenship Award!" Snowy and Bev would say, "Men," and launch into pep talks to try to revive her ego.

But Puddles eventually healed herself, at the bedside of a new patient, Guy Cram, who was *thirty years old,* who had been too busy establishing a building-contractor business to get married, who lived in South Carolina, of all places, and who, in Boston to attend a trade show, had been rear-ended while driving a rented car, the accident landing him in Mass. General under Puddles's care. He invited her to fly back with him to spend a few days seeing Helmsdale, S.C., and in Snowy's room Puddles invented a stroke for her mother that would necessitate Puddles's taking a week off, saying, "Lying to the school isn't like Gene's lying to me, and anyway, Guy should have a nurse along." Bev said, "To minister to a neck brace?" "Imagine,"

Puddles said, unmindful, "South Carolina. He says the average temperature in February is around sixty degrees." Snowy started singing Tom Lehrer's song about such Dixie delights as whupping slaves and wearing sheets, but this didn't faze Puddles, and off she flew to Helmsdale, returning with a marriage proposal. While Snowy and Bev worried that Puddles had fallen in love on the rebound, Puddles fretted, "Can I marry a man named Guy Cram? Makes me want to cross my legs every time I say it." Bev said, "If you've really kept them crossed, I'll have your mother's stroke," and then Bev and Snowy immediately pictured torrid passion in a neck brace and they collapsed howling. "Well," Puddles said, giggling, "South Carolina is very romantic. And his accent—"

When Snowy visited Julia before returning to Bennington that March, Julia asked as they snowshoed to the bog, "You mentioned you and Dudley correspond?"

"He's behind by a letter, I haven't heard from him for a couple of months. Studies must've piled up."

"He's in Gunthwaite. Yesterday Fred heard that he's living at home and has gone to work for Turmelle's Sign Company."

"*Dudley?*"

"Maybe you should call him."

Snowy did, and Dudley said, uncharacteristically laconic, "Mono."

"What about your scholarship, will they keep it until you can go back?"

He ignored the question and said, "Got a job painting signs for Turmelle."

Then Snowy remembered how in geography and social studies classes he had drawn the best maps. Maps; signs; okay, but a job? With mono, weren't you supposed to rest? Fearing she'd ruin the friendship if she pressed him, she quashed more questions, pretended it was normal that the boy whose goal was to be President of the United States was working for Turmelle's Sign Company, and gave him all the gossip about Bev and Puddles and Boston.

Back at Bennington, on a Saturday night, March 19, 1960, Snowy's date took her out to dinner at the Paradise, an acclaimed restaurant downtown, where she drank her first legal-in-Vermont drink. She chose a grown-up martini: Today she was twenty-one.

Typing rejection letters at Commonwealth had discouraged Snowy from sending out her poems, but her spring fever this year became a spring flooding of the "little"-magazine market with these poems, and one day in her mailbox she found an acceptance letter: *Divergences* would publish "Sweetland"! That's what the letter said in plain English, but her brain couldn't comprehend it as she stood beside Harriet in Commons rereading over and over the words which seemed to shrink out of focus. From far away she saw the letter, Harriet, Commons, the Bennington campus.

Harriet glanced up from her own mail. "What's wrong? Bad news?"

"Good. So good I don't believe it."

But when Harriet grabbed the letter and shrieked with joy, Snowy began to believe.

Although the payment would only be two free copies of that issue of the magazine, she celebrated this milestone by splurging, treating herself and Harriet to the movies on a weeknight, a sci-fi flick, *Angry Red Planet,* and a George Montgomery western, with large popcorns and Cokes and many candy bars throughout.

The copies arrived. She read the poem holding her breath. No typographical errors. Printed, it looked—real. Still, her instinct was to hide the naked thing, and she balked at first at Harriet's exhortations of, "My God, are you mad, show your counselor, your lit teachers present and past, flaunt it, you fool!" Eventually persuaded, she burned and sweated during congratulations from these adults, writers of poetry and prose themselves, who appeared to take the publication as seriously as she privately did. Professional, she thought. I too am a published professional.

Harriet said, "Show Julia, for God's sake, and your parents and Bev and Puddles." "Well," Snowy said, inventing a rule that allowed her to show a poem to friends and relatives if it had been published. Shyly she sent one of the magazines to Julia, who wrote back: "Dear Snowy, After I read 'Sweetland,' I went to the bog, simply beaming. Love, Julia." By mail, she lent her parents the copy she would keep, suspecting that they would probably read her name more often than her poem. "Your father and I," her mother wrote, "are mighty proud. Your name looks so nice in print, like in the newspaper when you won things at school. Maybe *now* everybody will call you Henrietta?"

To Bev and Puddles she sent typed copies of the poem. She hesitated about sending one to Dudley, deciding against, afraid of dancing on a grave. Bev phoned and said, "Our Sweetland, immortalized! It's devastatingly wonderful, Snowy!", while Puddles, who was planning her wedding, wrote, "Congrats, thanks for swell poem," and continued, "Graduation isn't until September tenth. Who the hell gets married in September? I'm going to have the wedding before, the last Saturday in August and spend the—ha-ha—wedding night and Sunday at a motel on the lake, and we'll go on a real honeymoon after graduation. I know you can't afford a maid-of-honor gown—but I bet you didn't truly want to be Bev's maid of honor anyway. Bev's head may have been in the clouds but mine isn't, and you don't have to make any excuses to me. You've become a beatnik, Henrietta Snow. So you can just handle the guest book again and I'll ask Bev to be maid of honor. No—it's MATRON of honor, won't she hate that, it sounds FAT."

Thus at the wedding ceremony, once more Snowy was a spectator. Sitting in Gunthwaite's Congregational church, the church in which Tom had got married, Snowy wondered if Puddles would enter doing cartwheels down the aisle, but when Puddles appeared she was transformed by peau de soie, ethereal with solemnity, as distant as an angel. Snowy yanked out her hankie.

After the reception at the Gunthwaite Inn, Snowy joined Bev and Puddles's roommate and another nurse bridesmaid in Puddles's room at the Gowen Street house. While the bridesmaids tended to her wedding dress, Bev and Snowy helped Puddles change into a Jordan Marsh suit, and Puddles said, "Two down, Snowy, one to go. You."

"I didn't catch the bouquet."

"You didn't try, I sure the hell aimed it at you."

And Puddles was known to have wicked aim. She'd have mastered Scrotie in nothing flat. Hoping to sidetrack her, Snowy asked, "Where are you going on your real honeymoon?"

"I've told you a hundred times, the Virgin Islands."

"See?" Snowy said to Bev. "Every time she says it, she says Virgin Islands, when the specific island she's going to is St.—" Here Snowy stopped.

"Thomas," Puddles supplied. "No saint, he."

Snowy and Bev glanced at each other, laughed, and Snowy said, "My theory is that Puddles chose this place simply to be able to use the word virgin when discussing her honeymoon."

"It was Guy's idea," Puddles said. "He's been there before, he loves hot weather, he claims he hasn't recovered yet from Boston in February, he won't put a toe in Winnipesaukee— though he put more than a toe somewhere else last night."

Snowy shrieked, "The night before your wedding?"

Bev asked, "Is nothing sacred?"

Puddles said, her voice suddenly tremulous, "South Carolina. Like moving to the moon."

The triumvirate hugged.

❧

THROUGHOUT THE PAST year Snowy had scrimped and saved harder than ever, for the car she would need to do her thesis research. On the Monday after Puddles's wedding, Snowy's father spent his lunch hour from Trask's with her at Gunthwaite

Motors, where he supervised her purchase, a 1952 light-blue Ford, two hundred dollars.

She and the car got acquainted driving to and from Julia's, and the next day she set off for the seacoast, to Eastbourne, New Hampshire.

During her sophomore year she had decided to do her thesis on Ruhamah Reed, a nineteenth-century "minor" poet who had lived in Eastbourne. The subject was unconventional, one that hadn't been done before, the likes of Wallace Stevens and W.H. Auden more popular choices, but in her junior-year proposal she laid it on with a trowel, emphasizing Ruhamah Reed's "unique regional voice," and the proposal was accepted. While working on her bibliography, she'd written to the Eastbourne public library and learned that they had Ruhamah Reed's collected works, the Eastbourne Historical Society's privately published biography, a vertical file, and six cases of uncatalogued papers and memorabilia, left by a great-niece. The helpful librarian also told her that the house in which Ruhamah Reed had been born, had lived and died, still existed and was standing empty, having been bought up as part of a planned Old Eastbourne restoration project. If she wanted to go inside the house, she should get in touch with Mr. Samuel Eldridge, the person in charge of the project. This summer from Boston she'd written Mr. Eldridge asking for an appointment, and he'd answered that an assistant would take her to the house. An eleven A.M. appointment; after seeing the house, she would delve into the library treasure trove.

Gunthwaite played Eastbourne, but when Snowy had gone there on the cheerleaders' bus she hadn't really noticed the route and town, instead doing bumpy homework amid chatter and giggles, and what she remembered clearly about the place was the high-school gym. For all she'd seen of the ocean, Eastbourne could be a mountain fastness instead of a port. She did recall it was bigger than Gunthwaite, a city, but she had conquered a much bigger city, hadn't she?

She'd conquered Boston on foot. Although she managed not

107

to get lost driving to Eastbourne, driving in the city itself she got lost thrice in the hot hubbub of downtown traffic despite Mr. Eldridge's directions, and she wished she were walking on the narrow streets that reminded her of Boston. Amongst stores she glimpsed large square old houses with widow's walks. Was one of them Ruhamah Reed's?

Then finally she came upon her destination, the waterfront, where a mountain of white was piled on a dock, apparently deposited by the huge black ship being prodded out of the harbor by tugboats which looked like bathtub toys beside it. She turned and drove past dilapidated warehouses to a lone building newly painted cream. It didn't give the feeling of having been transported and set down there; it suggested a resurrection like a phoenix risen from the site where it belonged. A small creamy sign said: OLD EASTBOURNE.

Some cars were parked along the crooked sidewalk, and she parked behind the last, a rusty red Volkswagen. She got out, locking her door, dropping the keys in her white pocketbook, smoothing her blue seersucker shirtdress which she'd chosen for the drive because it hardly showed wrinkles. The ocean smell. This smell had been here when Ruhamah Reed had walked along the harbor, as Ruhamah Reed must have though she didn't write about the ocean so much as Celia Thaxter did. Ruhamah Reed, looking pert and impertinent in the frontispiece in Snowy's copy of her poems, made gossip her specialty.

Snowy went up the steps and opened the screen door into home-repair chaos and saw a young man sitting at the nearest desk amid a motley assortment of apparently begged-borrowed-stolen office equipment. He was what she and Bev and Puddles in their youth would have called a doll. Brown hair, cut collegiate; brown long-lidded eyes. He stood up. Tall. Button-down short-sleeved striped summer shirt; chinos. No wedding ring. Why the hell hadn't she checked her makeup in the car mirror and combed her hair?

"Hello," he said, his head held sideways, his expression delighted. "Welcome to Hopkins Tavern."

108

The walls were peeled down to the laths, the fireplace's pine paneling had been stripped of paint, leaving chalky remnants, and tripods displayed a map and an architect's drawing. "This is a tavern?"

"It was once, it will be again. May I help you?"

"I'm Henrietta Snow and I've—"

"The Ruhamah Reed House," he said. "How do you do. I'm Alan Sutherland. Your escort. Shall we take my car?"

His was the sorry Volkswagen. He opened the passenger door for her. After he'd folded himself behind the wheel, they looked at each other in this close little space. Moments passed.

Then she laughed. "An ignition key. It makes the car go vroom-vroom."

"Shit," he said. "That is—I—" He clambered out of the car, fished the key from his pants pocket, got back in. And looked at her. And leaned across and kissed her.

She blushed redder than the car.

He said, shocked, "Feel free to have me fired. I ought to be."

"An ignition key goes in the ignition." The dense sexual atmosphere transformed this comment into pornography. She laughed again, blushed again. He used English Leather after-shave lotion.

He started the car. "You've got no reason to believe me when I tell you I've never done that before."

"I believe you."

"Thank God." But he remained stunned. What had possessed him?

As they drove off, the Volkswagen wheezing and rattling, she took her Kents out of her pocketbook and sought a remark pure of innuendo. "That white mound, I haven't ever seen such a sight." Mound.

"It's salt." He pulled a lighter from his shirt pocket and flicked a flame for her, eyes on the street.

"Thank you. I love salt, but that's ridiculous." Love. "Or is it to salt winter roads, not meals?"

"Roads." He lit a Camel, inhaled, untensing, and continued,

109

"Ships bring the salt, and then it's delivered to towns by trucks."

"What's the Old Eastbourne project?"

"The city in its infinite wisdom was about to tear down history and replace it with urban renewal, so a group of people plus the Historical Society got together to start saving the houses. Over to your right, the brick warehouse, we've bought that too." Brick warehouse. Christ, would she hear a double-entendre? A shame that, cute though she was, she certainly wasn't built like one. He went on rapidly, "It's nineteenth-century. Eighteen-o-nine, to be exact. Some of the houses we're buying go back to the sixteen hundreds, and some we want are Victorian."

She saw a ramshackle building which wasn't deserted, its parking lot full of cars. The sign said: EASTBOURNE CANNERY. She asked, laughing, *"Cannery Row?"*

"Sardines," he said. And after a pause he added, "My father works there."

"Oh."

"I can get them for you wholesale. Plain? In mustard sauce? Tomato sauce?"

She laughed.

He pointed to another old building, empty. "Originally a ship chandler's. We've bought it."

"Are you a historian?"

"At this stage, I'm mainly helping to scrounge money wherever we can—government, business, private donations—though what I'm supposed to be working on is the selection of buildings to buy. I was a history major, art minor, some architecture credits. From UNH a year ago. Mr. Eldridge gave me your letter. I've heard of Bennington."

She should inform him that Bennington girls didn't start kissing within moments of meeting—or do anything else, though she wanted to postpone Ruhamah Reed and see his etchings instead. He was a year out of school, he must have an apartment. But had she gone crazy? She ground out her cigarette

110

in the full ashtray. Alan Sutherland wasn't car-proud, as Tom had been.

He asked, "What got you interested in doing your thesis on Ruhamah Reed?"

"She's a woman poet from New Hampshire. *The* woman poet from New Hampshire besides Celia Thaxter."

"I don't know anything about her except her name, and I was born and brought up in Eastbourne."

Could he possibly be living at home? Not someone who looked like him; he had to have an apartment. With a roommate? "My high-school texts didn't include her either, but her hometown teachers should have supplemented them, judiciously." Ruhamah Reed's poems could get too steamy for high-school English departments.

He put out his cigarette. "Maybe we did read her and I wasn't paying attention."

This reminded Snowy to pay attention to where she was. They had reached a slum of rickety apartment houses. She saw ahead a big square house that was in even worse shape than its neighbors, its clapboards weathered a rough brown, its windows boarded up. Only a suggestion of a wooden fence remained. But the house wore its widow's walk like a crown, and the doorway was beautiful. Nailed beside the door was another Old Eastbourne sign.

"The Ruhamah Reed House," Alan said, parking in front of it. "Federal."

"Federal?"

"The Federal style."

"I'm an ignoramus about architecture."

"And I am about Ruhamah Reed. Between the two of us . . ."

They smiled at each other, and Snowy began, " 'Jack Sprat could eat no fat, his wife could eat no lean—' " Wife. Eat. Lick. She started to open her door. Alan quickly extricated himself from the car, and she waited until he opened it. "Thank you," she said.

111

When she began to get out, cursing Volkswagens for being so undignified, he took her pocketbook-less hand, and he kept holding it as they crossed the sidewalk.

Was this really love at first sight? Or was she just uncontrollably horny? Since Whit, she had gamboled with many other guys who didn't look like Tom, but she hadn't Gone All The Way except twice, control lost, again choosing the best-looking guy whose major insured they had nothing in common. Geology. Danger: Alan Sutherland's work intrigued her. Danger: He was a stranger, in a strange city. She stopped, slid her hand out of his, groped in her pocketbook for her notebook and pencil. "Federal?" she asked, pencil poised as in her waitressing days ("Plain or toasted?").

He said, "About seventeen-ninety, I guess. I haven't done any research, we simply grabbed the place before the wrecking ball got it." Ball. "This whole area was due to be demolished. There's no money yet to restore the house. I'm trying."

She jotted. "It must have been some house. Her father was a wealthy merchant. I'm hoping there are privateers in her background, I'm heading for the library next." Not to any apartment.

He opened the gate, which staggered on its hinges. The lawn was dirt. "Beware of the steps," he said, not touching her as they tiptoed over broken boards. "That sill is rotten." He unlocked the door. "Careful indoors too."

Cautiously they entered the front hall. The ocean smell changed to dank mold. Mottled wallpaper had curled off in long tendrils. A spiral staircase swirled upward.

He said, "The staircase is pulling away from the wall and Mr. Eldridge gets nervous despite insurance, so I'm just supposed to show you the downstairs."

Snowy was trying to concentrate on the house. Why should even his habit of tilting his head seem sexy? "I wonder where she wrote. She lived alone after her parents died, but she had lots of company, her poems are full of people, and of course there were servants. Jane Austen wrote right in the midst of things, though

112

she'd slip her work under a cushion or someplace if company arrived. Maybe poetry can also be written that way."

"I know enough to know that Emily Dickinson hid." He opened a door into an empty room. "You said in your letter you're from Gunthwaite?" He ought to have made such small talk at the outset. What *had* possessed him? "We played Gunthwaite in high school, I've been to Gunthwaite to play basketball."

"You have?" She looked up at him. "And I was cheering for your opponents. Go, Gunthwaite, go! No—which class were you?"

"Class of '55."

This told her he was probably twenty-three, two years older than she, and he hadn't been in the service, he'd escaped the draft—at least up to now. She said, "Then I was a sophomore when you were a senior so I was a JV, not Varsity yet."

"You were a cheerleader?"

It inevitably got a reaction. "Um, yes. Did you play all through high school?"

"JV my freshman and sophomore years, then Varsity."

Gunthwaite's JV cheerleaders didn't travel to games as far away as Eastbourne, and thus she hadn't seen him play in his hometown gym, but when she was a seventh-grader, an eighth-grader, a freshman, a sophomore, she had seen him play basketball in the Gunthwaite gym, although she hadn't known it. They had been together in the same sweaty gym.

More introductions than that weren't necessary. Here, Snowy thought, is where we came in, and he bent down to kiss her.

A long kiss. Was Ruhamah Reed's ghost watching, amused?

Snowy's stomach growled.

He straightened up, laughing. "Hungry?"

She giggled, embarrassed. "I'm always hungry."

"Were you planning to have lunch before the library?"

"If I spotted a cheap place."

113

Cheap? From what he'd heard of her college, a Bennington girl could afford pheasant-under-glass.

She caught his surprise. "I'm on a scholarship. At Bennington they call it Reduced Tuition. My father works at that big factory en route to the high school; my mother works at the shoe factory." So you don't have to be ashamed of the cannery.

"Oh."

Another long kiss.

When they came up for air, he said, "May I play tour guide and guide you to cheap dining?"

"Thank you."

"As for guiding you here, the ell is this way—"

They walked through the downstairs hand-in-hand. Snowy saw it all in a haze of cobwebs, and upon entering the front hall again she didn't have the faintest idea where she'd been. She held out her notebook. "Would you draw me a floor plan, please?"

In the time it would have taken her to decide how to set the house, he had dashed off a professional sketch. He could probably do his own etchings.

"There," he said. "Downstairs. I'm glad about that staircase, it means you'll have to come back when it's fixed and see the upstairs."

What if she told him she'd just bought a car primarily to be able to travel back and forth to Eastbourne, for research? She took the notebook. "Many thanks."

"I'll draw you a better one at the office and send it to you."

She wanted to suggest he deliver it in person.

He said, "Or I could deliver it in person. Your letter had a Boston address. Are you still there?"

Hooray! Should she invite him to Gunthwaite? No, she must hold her horses and wait to present herself for a date at Bennington, independent, a college senior, with her hometown, her parents, and her cheerleading firmly in the background. "I'm between places, I'll be at school the weekend after next."

"I think I can manage to find Bennington, Vermont."

114

They smiled, and his stomach growled.

Opening the front door, he said, "We're a symphony."

Now on the broken steps he held her hand and hovered in a gentlemanly fashion though she could have tap-danced down to the rhythm of a Ruhamah Reed poem. She took a deep breath of the ocean air Ruhamah Reed had inhaled while descending these steps. "Living here, do you get so you don't smell the ocean?"

"I suppose."

"I doubt I ever would."

In the car, he lit her cigarette and his. They drove away, and he wondered if he dared. He'd already suggested an implied date; they had declared a future. "Tips for the Traveler," he announced. "The most inexpensive place to dine in Eastbourne is the Sutherland Club, where there's a refrigerator to raid and the beer is cold and plentiful."

His apartment? "Sounds lovely," she said demurely.

A silence fell as they left the slum behind.

He asked, "What were you doing in Boston?"

"I was working at Commonwealth Publishing, I've worked there the past three summers and NRT's—that's the Non-Resident Term which Bennington has in the winter."

"Will you work there after you graduate?"

"If I'm offered a job." She stubbed out her cigarette. "Last summer I filled in for the secretary to the assistant to an editor when she was on vacation, and this summer I filled in for the assistant, who's beginning to itch to move on to New York. So I'm hoping."

They were approaching downtown's lunch-hour traffic, and he showed himself a true hometown boy by suddenly darting down side streets.

He said, "In school, I used to go to Boston to see shows and paint it red, but nowadays I go on duller missions, to get proposals from construction outfits and try to convince banks to cough up loans."

"Were you there this summer?"

115

"Last month."

They thought about this.

He glanced at her. "You've got quite a tan for Boston."

She'd never outgrown being embarrassed by personal comments and she murmured, "Sunbathing on the Esplanade," and changed the subject. "Why did you decide to work for Old Eastbourne?"

"I was planning on teaching history at some college, but when the time came to apply for graduate school I couldn't stand the idea of more school, and I'd heard about this restoration project that was starting up, so I applied there instead, figuring the pay couldn't be worse than teaching and I wouldn't have *any more classrooms* in my life. Well, we've bought a schoolhouse, but that's as close as I've—aha!" He pounced on a parking space in front of a little watch-repair shop and climbed out of the car and walked around and opened her door.

As he helped her out, Snowy thought of what an academic day she had expected when she set forth this morning.

He didn't keep holding her hand. They walked down the street past a photography studio, Snowy getting scared. They neared a store window wherein dwelt a vision wearing white glossiness—a bride mannequin, with bridesmaids dressed in the colors of pastel autumn leaves. Despite Puddles's opinion, people did marry in September. Married. Alan *could* be married, free of a ring though he was. This apartment might be a love nest. He could be engaged. He could be Jack the Ripper. When he stopped and opened a door between this store and an antique shop which would have fit right in on Charles Street, she attempted a joke. "Do you live over the bridal shop or the antique shop?"

"The bridal."

"Kind of an unnerving location?"

"Kind of," he said, jittery, regretting the invitation.

Without speaking, they went up a dim flight of stairs, and on the first landing he unlocked his door. They stepped into the living room.

116

She was alone with a man in an apartment. A milestone.

He cleared his throat. "Welcome to the Sutherland Club."

Despite the open windows, the apartment felt sultry. A fuzzy smell of Camels floated over exhaust fumes and ocean. The sofa looked discarded. The one chair was a green vinyl recliner, its wounds bandaged with plastic tape; she'd bet it had once lived in his fraternity-house room. There were books piled on the end table and the coffee table that had both seen better days, there was a large elderly TV with a tiny yellowed screen, but there were no posters or beer mugs, no junk, no evidence of a room-mate or a girlfriend. The single distinctive item was—

She asked, "Is this a drafting table?" and touched it, then pulled her hand back, afraid he would think she was checking for dust.

He'd noticed her hand trembling. A muscle was leaping in her jaw. "Yes."

"They use them at Commonwealth. The artwork people."

He put his arm around her and said, "This way to the bar." He could feel her relax slightly as he led her into the kitchen. "You don't have to have beer. The Club also has gin-and-tonic and rum-and-Coke."

"Beer's fine." Windowless like Bev's, the kitchen wasn't so small as Bev's and he'd been able to wedge in a narrow old dinette set, yet it was much too small for him. Even the toaster on the counter was small.

"Voilà!" With a flourish he took two beers from the aged refrigerator which had its motor on top.

"Your toaster," she said, laughing. "I never knew they made toasters that toast just one slice." He was opening a cupboard for glasses. "I can drink out of the bottle."

"Not when you're dining at the Sutherland Club."

The glasses were tall and slim and modern. They must be Swedish, bought by a girlfriend.

He poured Schlitz, tipping perfect heads of foam. "My sister gave me the toaster, she said it was symbolic of my nature."

One slice; a loner, a confirmed bachelor.

He added, "She also gave me these glasses."

"More symbolism?"

"No, she was sick of drinking out of peanut-butter jars. Here you go."

She took the glass. "Thank you."

He clinked his glass against hers. "To Ruhamah Reed."

"Ruhamah Reed."

They drank. He again opened the refrigerator, and she said fast, to get the embarrassment over with, "May I borrow your bathroom to freshen up?"

Without looking around, as if this was an ordinary request, he said, "It's the door to the left off the living room."

She set her beer beside the toaster and retreated carrying her pocketbook.

In the bathroom, she turned on the washbasin's cold-water tap and let water splash down the worn blue channel all the time she was there, a trick for those wanting to converse unheard by bugging devices, and she hoped to God it covered the roar of the toilet flushing. The tub, standing on claws, had a shower nozzle, and as she washed her hands at the basin she pictured him behind the plain white shower curtain, naked, soaping. Dial soap. After she had combed her hair and reapplied lipstick and eaten some of his Colgate toothpaste, she eased open the medicine cabinet. Band-Aids, aspirin, deodorant, nail clippers, razor. English Leather shaving cream and aftershave. Any Trojans? Nope.

She went back to the living room. The other door must be his bedroom door. She looked in. A metal bedstead. Size: double. The brown chenille bedspread would match his long-lidded eyes. No photographs on the bureau. Oh, what the hell. She slunk in and pulled out the drawer of the bedside table. Trojans.

Wearing a halo of innocence, she strolled into the kitchen, where to her joy she saw that Alan took food seriously.

"Lobster?" she said.

"Leftover." On a chopping board he was cutting the tail meat into chunks.

"Really? I didn't know anybody had leftover lobster."

"Friends with traps keep you supplied enough so you're apt to have leftovers. Don't worry about food poisoning, it's only from last night."

In a flash she imagined the scene: Last night he'd entertained a girlfriend here, but passion had engulfed them before they could finish their feast. If he did that sort of carousing on a weeknight, what revels were there on weekends? Jealous of the girlfriend, feeling lots more than two years younger than Alan Sutherland, she reached into her pocketbook for her Kents.

He paused to light her cigarette. "I can make you a lobster omelette, my mother's recipe, but I figured you'd prefer a lobster roll in this weather."

She leaned against the refrigerator. Emphasize your ignorance. "I'm an ignoramous about the ocean, too. I've just had lobster a few times, Julia—my best friend's mother—buys it at the Gunthwaite fish market and she brought some back when she picked up my best friend in Camden—Bev, my best friend, waitressed there, and I almost did but I worked at Commonwealth instead."

Concerned, he looked up from the bowl into which he was scooping the chunks. "You do like lobster?"

"Oh, yes. May I help?"

"Sit down and recite me a Ruhamah Reed poem."

"How come you think I've memorized any?"

He grinned. "Male intuition."

She blushed. Wanting to tell him she was of the silent-reading school of thought, she sat down at the table and gulped her beer. She would so wow him with her smart-aleck intellect that he'd forget all about the broad he'd been bouncing on in that double bed last night, and she would also let him know she was no virgin. "Page one, believed to be amongst her earliest:

I saw my white life waiting
The prick of golden thread,

119

Of peacock blue and silver
And scrolls of royal red.

But now a simple cotton
On ancient cloth instead
Is all I see behind me
And all I see ahead.

"Of course," Snowy said bravely, "speaking of symbolism, that prick and cock business can't be ignored, but the most interesting aspect of this poem is that it's a batch of bullshit. Ruhamah Reed saying that her life is simple is like Walter Savage Landor saying, 'I strove with none, for none was worth my strife,' since he actually was an irascible bastard, his middle name is the right description. On the surface Ruhamah Reed's life might *seem* to be ordinary, but she could convolute the most mundane incidents into high drama, and a broken tea cup would mean to her that a mistress had been discovered. She was quite forthright, a nineteenth-century version of another friend of mine, so she didn't particularly disguise in her poems any of her speculations or information. Or any of her own goings-on. She might have been a spinster, but she had her flings, and she makes very thinly veiled references to fellatio and—" Snowy took another gulp of beer.

With a knife, Alan began peeling strings off a celery stalk. She'd never seen that done before.

He asked, "Why didn't she marry?"

"My guess is so she wouldn't die in childbirth. There are some heartbreaking poems about a sister and a friend who did." Snowy stopped again. Dying in childbirth wasn't exactly an appropriate topic during a seduction. But maybe he wasn't intending a seduction. Maybe what she was going to get, instead of a roll in the hay, was just a lobster roll. She said, her voice small enough to match the toaster, "Things were awfully dangerous then."

He looked over at her. He put the bowl and the celery in the

120

refrigerator. Washing his hands, he said, "I'm not dangerous, I'm scared."

She set her glass down. Would any other man admit being scared? Yes, one; Tom once had, about her absence.

Alan asked, "Is it love at first sight?"

"I think perhaps it is."

There were no necking preliminaries. Holding hands, hot hands, they rushed for the bedroom. Alan pulled the window shade but left the window open, so Snowy, standing in a stranger's bedroom, heard the traffic of the strange city as he unbuttoned her shirtdress fast, as she lifted her arms, surrendering her slip. She wasn't wearing nylons and a garter belt because of her tan. His fingers slowed now, unhooking her bra, pushing down her underpants, and she started unbuttoning his shirt, yet she couldn't wait and unbuckled his belt and he gasped and toppled with her onto the bed and she lay naked in the arms of this stranger who was getting all tangled up trying to clasp her and yank his pants and shirt off at the same time and she helped, tugging his T-shirt over his head. Both of them nearly forgot and he almost plunged in, but Snowy's knees snapped shut, he whipped on a Trojan, and then she felt the invasion of privacy she'd been wanting ever since she walked into Hopkins Tavern. The bedsprings squeaked something terrible. He kept meaning to oil them, and oh, he exulted, could he oil them now with homemade lubricant! She thought of prospective brides in the shop below listening to the wild wedding-night music above. She laughed and he laughed.

❧

SNOWY DID NOT, after all, hold her horses. Instead, a stampede.

That evening the phone rang on the end table beside the sofa, and she answered it. "Hello?"

A man's voice asked, "How did your research go?"

"Alan?" She sat down, delirious with relief. Ever since

121

they'd kissed goodbye at her car, she had feared she'd never see or hear from him again. Would he actually appear at Bennington? Despite his I-love-you's, had she just been an opportunity for a lunch-hour tryst? She would die! She must see him again, *tomorrow*. She had to return to the Eastbourne Library tomorrow anyway, but how could she brazenly drop in at Hopkins Tavern? What excuse could she dream up?

He said, "Sorry, yes, this is Alan Sutherland. I wondered if you'd got home safely—and if you'll have to come back to the library."

"I worked there until it closed, and I hardly made a dent."

"So you'll be returning? Otherwise I was thinking of a trip to Gunthwaite; Bennington seems a long time away."

"I'm returning tomorrow."

"Let me take you to lunch."

"Thank you," she said, prim and proper.

"I'll meet you at the library. Noon okay?"

"Okay."

Well, he might have been planning to take her to a real restaurant, but the moment they kissed in his car outside the library, they realized they'd better hie themselves to the Sutherland Club fast or they'd be screwing in public, and once there they only got as far as his sofa. And Snowy learned, during her daily trips which followed, that he had behaved with great formality that first lunchtime; it was remarkable he hadn't done it on the kitchen floor. Aside from basic bed antics, which soon included what she'd learned with Tom, his mouth between her legs, he enjoyed changes of scenery, making love in the shower, in the recliner, *over the drafting table!*

Then she was back at school, and when Alan drove to Bennington on Saturday she acted not too knowledgeable about places to go parking, yet soon they were busy in the back seat of his car, a Volkswagen demanding a contortionist's skills.

But she remained terrified of a Tom trap. She had a Williams date the next Friday night, and she supposed Alan wasn't sitting home alone either. Jealousy wrecked her evening. She raged at

Tom, who'd got her so mixed up, at Alan, who'd aroused her damped passion. Goddamn Alan, she had broken her rule and fallen in love again.

Nonetheless, as she'd arranged with him, that Saturday morning she signed out for an overnight, saying her destination was Gunthwaite, and she drove to Eastbourne praying no emergency would occur which would cause the school to phone her parents or her parents to phone the school. After her stint in the library, Alan gave her a tour of New Hampshire's short seacoast and took her out to dinner, where she had her first cherrystone clams and Coquilles Saint-Jacques.

Another milestone: her first whole night with a man. Awakening Sunday morning, she looked at the miracle of Alan asleep beside her and savored it until she came to her senses and sneaked off to brush her teeth, etc.

She had another Williams date the next Friday night and spent it imagining Alan fucking some Eastbourne girlfriend.

When Alan arrived Saturday, she got up the courage to say, "This round trip must be murder for you. I've heard of a motel that's cheap, could you afford to stay overnight tonight?" Eyes humorous, he replied, "Great minds think alike." She said, "Maybe I could watch some TV there, I miss TV." He said, "I miss *you.*" Off to the Sleepytime Motor Lodge!

A routine developed. She forced herself to be footloose and fancy-free with Williams dates on Friday nights. On some Saturdays, Alan drove to Bennington, picked her up and took her to the Sleepytime, and they'd spend the afternoon dallying, Snowy afraid that, no matter how casual this motel was, a policeman would barge into the room and arrest them in the midst of making love in bed, in the Pig-Pen shower, on the bedroom floor (using a blanket after the carpeting produced rug-burn, Alan's knees raw), *over the luggage rack!* Replete, they'd watch old movies on television. Snowy brought along books and did some studying, turning the motel room into the weekend combination of love nest and dorm which she'd denied herself and Tom; she brought her typewriter, too, and worked on her thesis or a paper

123

or her column, but she never brought her own poems, embarrassed. Although more had been published in "little" magazines, she kept her poetry a secret from Alan as she had, for a while, from Tom..

Because the Sleepytime didn't have ice buckets or even ice, the beers in Alan's six-pack grew warm before consumed, and eventually he and she would seek cold beer at the State Line or the Top Hat, a pizza, and at eleven he'd take her back to school. Then on Sunday mornings he would pick her up again and they'd have breakfast downtown at the Paradise. New Hampshire natives, they went sightseeing in Vermont. "Claustrophobic," Alan decided, "no ocean." "Softer than New Hampshire," said Snowy, accustomed to sharp mountain peaks, gawking at Vermont's round Green Mountains which looked like giant grazing buffalo. After, in Snowy's room, Alan and Harriet talked art, and then Harriet would obligingly go off to Commons or somewhere and Snowy would lock the door.

When he left, she cried and cried, finding no sweetness in the sorrow of parting. Alan hated the endings of their weekends just as much; he grew silent, depressed, enveloped in a thundercloud. Would he do a Tom and break up with her?

Other weekends, Snowy drove to Eastbourne, to the library and then to his apartment for the night. Looking at him asleep one Sunday morning, she realized his long-lidded eyes reminded her of movies about ships in which an engineer, invariably named Scotty, with the same eyelids, would go berserk at a crucial moment, shouting in a strangling burr, "Captain, we must slow down! We've got the pressure up! The boiler's about to blow!" Later, waiting for a second slice of toast to pop out of his confirmed-bachelor toaster, she asked Alan, "Is Sutherland a Scottish name?" and he said, "Aye, me lass," and she told him, "You have Scottish eyelids," and he asked, "Did you say Scottish or Scrotie?" He had met and conquered the wineskin.

As the time for her to leave drew near, his thundercloud of depression thickened, darkening the apartment. He lay on the sofa staring at the ceiling while she packed her overnight bag

124

and gathered up her books and notebooks. He wouldn't get up to see her to her car; he wouldn't even acknowledge her goodbye kiss. His lips were as cold as a corpse's. She always drove away from Eastbourne in a blur of tears.

Bev and Roger didn't have to say goodbye, nor did Puddles and Guy, though Puddles's letters were more about adapting to South Carolina than about marriage adjustments. The nearest Puddles had got to describing wedded bliss was, "I've finally toilet-trained Guy—I taught him to put the seat down." In her first letter, after grisly details of her work at the Helmsdale hospital, Puddles wrote, "I just went shopping and I saw a woman standing in a parking lot with a man who was pouring her a glass of champagne. She drank it while eating a peach! Life here is sure going to be different from Gunthwaite, N.H." Puddles subsequently reported that palm trees looked like cement posts, expressed more approval of live oaks dripping moss, and claimed that the squirrels there walked instead of leaping like northern squirrels—"I suppose they have accents, too. I can't understand ANYBODY here, not the whites or the Negroes, sometimes not even Guy, and they can't understand me." The Puddles entry in Snowy's address book began to shred with erasures; Puddles and Guy lived in the houses Guy built and had to move out to another when one sold. But then on her Christmas card Puddles wrote, "Guy has promised we'll stay in this latest house. Because it has the nicest patio. No, because I'm pregnant! PLANNED. I decided Guy is so old I'd better start having those six kids. Though nix that SIX. Guy's business is feast or famine, and I make the steady income but it wouldn't support a family. Merry Christmas, have a snowball fight with that Alan of yours for me. You two must look like Mutt and Jeff, how do you manage in bed?" Puddles pregnant. A milestone.

Wanting to spend every day of her Christmas vacation in Eastbourne ostensibly doing research, Snowy feared smothering Alan and instead played hard-to-get, saying she was too busy with yuletide obligations to drive down, yet this backfired, Alan

125

phoning to ask, "Would you have any spare time to see me if I drove up to Gunthwaite?" Home ground, her hometown, her parents. He himself hadn't yet suggested she meet his parents, though she gathered they lived somewhere near downtown, in a residential section like hers, not a long expedition from his apartment; she therefore had assumed he and she felt the same about parents, but here he was willing to meet hers. "Okay," she said, and then threw caution to the wind, inviting him to dinner on Christmas Eve. It was a Saturday this year, two days from now, which gave her time to do cookbook homework, choose an exotic recipe, buy the expensive ingredients with her own money, beef tenderloin, mushrooms, sour cream, and practice the beef Stroganoff twice on her parents who were agog with curiosity about the first young man to appear out of her college life, the first boyfriend she'd ever invited to supper— dinner. They had posed themselves in the living room when he arrived at the front door bearing a pot of poinsettias, disarming her mother and causing her father to break out his bottle of Four Roses, so Snowy had her first drink in this house. After the impressive main course and the anticlimactic but no-work fruit- cake borrowed from her mother's Christmas dinner tomorrow, she told her parents she was going to show Alan the Christmas lights decorating Gunthwaite, and they drove off in the Volks- wagen. Having admitted to possessing those parents in her background, she now had to admit to knowing places to go parking, which they did instead of sightseeing or a snowball fight.

How confusing, to be parked on the Cat Path with out-of- town Alan Sutherland instead of all the hometown boys she'd parked here with, notably Tom! Was Alan also sensing their presence? He only kissed her. Then he got out of the car and took from the trunk a large flat package, got back in, and placed it on her lap, unaware that she detested opening presents in front of anyone because her parents made such a production out of this, her mother as excited as a child.

"Oh my," Snowy breathed. A pen-and-ink sketch of the

Ruhamah Reed House, signed A.S. (Like herself, he didn't have a middle name; he was lucky, he'd told her, that his folks hadn't chosen one starting with S, their choice of his first initial being bad enough.) She'd expected he would bring a present, so she had in her pocketbook the paperback she'd wrapped in holly paper. "Just something silly," she said, "don't bother opening it here—" But he already was. A collection of Agatha Christie stories. She explained, "I'm trying to get you addicted too." And maybe he'd curl up with Agatha on Friday nights instead of with Eastbourne girls. Not bloody likely, as they'd say in Agatha's country.

"What's this?" he asked, extracting some folded typewriter paper.

"More silliness, don't bother reading them here. I'm out of cigs, may I bum a Camel?"

"Poems? Yours?"

"A slim homemade volume."

He didn't yawn or laugh. "Yours," he said, sounding awed. To stop him from reading any, silently or—God forbid— aloud, she unzipped his fly.

Driving home, he asked, "New Year's Eve? Would you want to drive down and go to some Eastbourne parties?"

She'd get to meet his friends, if not his parents. His girl-friends, too? Play hard-to-get! She lied, "I'm sorry, I already have a date."

For the first time he quizzed her. "Who? Hometown guy? Williams?"

She thought of Dudley, whose letters had resumed that se-mester, full of Gunthwaite gossip. Dudley never mentioned Yale, and he never suggested a date. She said, "An old friend, platonic."

Besides no middle name, Alan shared her ability to raise one eyebrow. He proceeded to do this. Then the black silence closed around him until they reached her house, when he arranged a date for her first Saturday in Boston.

Keep him guessing, Snowy thought later, crying on her bed.

A stupid ploy that meant he'd be seeing 1961 in with somebody else, while she watched TV with her folks.

The last NRT. At the rooming house, a room on the ground floor! At Commonwealth, though, a Barbara now mum about any further New York plans. And if Barbara did move on, why would they hire Snowy, wet behind the ears despite her NRT experience?

That Saturday at noon, Snowy stood in the cold on the top step of her rooming house to mark the location for Alan. Right on time, along Beacon Street came the red VW. She ran down the steps and hopped in, and he double-parked to kiss her. Then out of his pocket he took two rings. Snowy reeled.

"Woolworth's friendship rings," he said, sliding the smaller on her left ring finger. "They look enough like wedding bands to fool people, don't they?"

"Oh. What—why?"

"It fits, good guess. This is the Big Time, not the Sleepytime. I've rented a hotel room."

She acted nonchalant. "Does it have a TV? I only go to your rooms to watch TV."

He kissed her again, and horns blew.

As they drove off, she said, "Bev's invited us to lunch, is that okay? She's dying to meet you."

He had been intending room service. "Fine. Where to?"

She directed him over Beacon Hill. She'd agreed somewhat reluctantly to Bev's invitation; although Bev was supposedly settled down now, Snowy hadn't ever been able to imagine her staying married to one man. But besides lunch Bev had offered their apartment, saying she and Roger would get an urge to see a movie, adding, "We know far too well the frustrations of dating in Boston."

Alan said suddenly, " 'The subway like a porpoise / Taking air.' "

Never having heard a poem of hers quoted outside a class, for a moment Snowy didn't recognize it.

He said, "The poems, they're terrific."

128

Some other time, she reflected, she would clue him in about the silent-reading school of thought. "They aren't really," she said, "but thank you."

"Do you plan to try to publish them?"

Ah, such a lovely opportunity to brag. She said diffidently, "They already have been. In 'little' magazines."

"Published?"

"There, that's the building."

When introduced, Roger and Alan tried unsuccessfully to remember each other from Gunthwaite-Eastbourne basketball games, and behind their backs Bev made swooning faces before fetching four beers. After some general chitchat in the living room, Bev and Snowy left the guys and went into the kitchen to get lunch, and Bev whispered, "He's gorgeous!"

"You don't have to go to the movies. Look." Snowy displayed her left hand. "A friendship ring, a disguise, we're going to a *hotel.*"

"How illicit!"

"I just know we'll be caught by a house detective, rings or no rings."

Bev took two cans of Campbell's tomato soup out of the cupboard and a package of Kraft cheese and a loaf of Pepperidge Farm bread out of the refrigerator. "Did I remember pickles? Tell him you prefer our humble abode."

They'd learned to work together in this tiny kitchen, as they had in their mothers' kitchens. Opening the soup cans on the wedding-present can opener, Snowy said, "It'd be a milestone. I could stay overnight, too, the way I do at his apartment. I've got spoiled—the Cat Path last time, like kids!"

Bev switched on the wedding-present electric frying pan, wishing she and Roger had had the money for a hotel during their courtship and envisioning with what style she'd have carried off such an escapade, wasted on timid Snowy. "God, all the parking we've done, I'll be amazed if we don't spend the rest of our lives at a chiropractor's."

"And," Snowy said, "things get so horribly messy in a car.

129

When a—uh—romantic interlude ends in a bedroom, it's certainly undignified to clap your hand to your crotch and run for the bathroom, but I'd rather have a place to wash up than dignity."

Bev stopped assembling the grilled cheese sandwiches and stared at her.

Snowy turned the shade of the soup she was scooping into a saucepan.

Bev said wonderingly, "I've always thought I was the only person in the world who had to run for the bathroom afterwards. In books, people go to sleep or put their clothes back on."

Snowy giggled. "If Alan did, he'd stick to the sheet or his Jockeys."

"He washes? Roger does, and I was afraid that made him a sissy!"

No house detective discovered them, and during Alan's next visits he and Snowy continued posing as Mr. and Mrs. Alan Sutherland, Snowy still expecting to be arrested in flagrante delicto. She began thinking: Married, really married, I could relax.

Henrietta Snow Sutherland. Her initials would be a hiss. At the Boston Public Library she found books about Scottish clans, and she almost collapsed when, flipping through the first toward the Sutherland chapter, she saw a chapter on the Forbes clan. Tom was Scottish too! Did she have a penchant for Scots? She herself might also partly be one; both her parents were vague about their heritage, her father because he hated his poverty-stricken past, her mother because of dottiness. Whenever she'd asked, they had said, "From England, Ireland, over there." She hastened on to Sutherland. The Forbes and Sutherland tartans were both blue and green. How much alike *were* these two guys? Tom's austere bedroom. Like Alan's apartment. If Tom had graduated, he was a teacher. Alan had planned to teach. But then she noted that the Sutherland tartan did have some red. Alan *was* different.

Bev phoned and said, "Snowy, it's terrible, Mother sent a clipping, Jack O'Brien has died."

Charl's husband, famous for passing out. Big football-captain Jack, with whom Bev had once gone steady. In Bev and Roger's apartment, they and Snowy read and reread the newspaper clipping, shocked, trying to deduce between the lines the details which came a few days later in a letter from Dudley to Snowy. At a party at Brenda and Butch Knowles's house, Jack had apparently stepped out the back door to take a leak and had passed out in a snowbank. Earlier, he'd kept saying he could only stay a few minutes, he had to get home, so everyone assumed he'd left. And as the other guests themselves finally left, they didn't see him, the design of the Knowleses' little pink ranch house decreeing that you came and went by the side door through the garage, and nobody noticed his car parked down the street. The person who would have missed him wasn't there, because Charl had remained at home in their own little ranch house they'd bought recently, their latest child due. She had fallen asleep with a late movie, and when the other two children awakened her the next morning and Jack wasn't anywhere in the house, she figured he'd passed out at the Knowleses' and she phoned Brenda, who, groping her way into the kitchen through last night's party rubble and booze fumes, picked up the receiver and happened to squint toward the back window. Jack O'Brien had passed out for good.

The end of NRT drew near. One afternoon Snowy was summoned to the office of Mr. Palmquist, now a full-fledged editor, and Barbara winked at her as she left. That evening she phoned Alan and said, "The assistant job, I've been offered it after graduation. Complete with cubicle." She'd hoped that telling him would spark the elation she should be feeling; it didn't.

"Shit," Alan said.

"What?"

"The timing—I've been beating the bushes trying to get money to start work on restoring the Ruhamah Reed House this

131

summer. There'll be a perfect job here for you, you the Ruhamah Reed expert."

Dumbfounded, Snowy gaped at the phone.

Alan said lamely, "It was going to be a surprise."

"I don't know a damn thing about restoring houses. Except how my folks have done theirs."

"But you know all about Ruhamah Reed. You've got all the material in the library memorized. You're the best researcher for the project. Have you given a definite answer?"

"Well, unless I flunk out between now and June or whatever."

"Shit." He hung up.

Snowy ran into her room and burst into tears. Everything was haywire!

The phone began ringing. Alan. She dashed back to the hall and answered it and almost hung up on someone singing "I'm Getting Married in the Morning." An obscene phone call?

" '—get me to the church on time'—Snowy?"

"Dudley?" she asked. Dudley indeed, tight as a tick.

He said, "Hang onto your chapeau, guess who the bride is, I'll give you a hint. If you were at the ceremony, you'd think you were seeing double, which I am at the moment, now that I mention it."

"A—twin?"

"Bigamy? A harem?"

"Charl?"

"Bingo!" he said. "The wedding isn't really tomorrow, we'll wait 'a suitable interval,' but tonight she agreed to become Mrs. Dudley C. Washburn."

Snowy said, "That's—great," a little better than speechlessness though not much. After the joking they'd done about the twins! She couldn't remember that he'd ever dated either Charl or Darl in high school. He hadn't written about dating anybody since he dropped out of Yale. "That's great, Dudley."

He said, "Thanks for joining an early stag party. You and me and Jim Beam. Goodbye."

132

Immediately dialing Bev's number, Snowy marveled at what Dudley was taking on, a widow with three children.

"How heroic!" Bev said. "How inexplicable."

Snowy hesitated. Then instead of telling Bev about the assistant-job triumph and Alan's news, she said only, "One thing is clear, the twins are still working fast."

The next afternoon, the telephone on her office desk rang and Alan said, "I've got the dough! Come help restore your Ruhamah Reed! We can live in my apartment until her house is finished, when there'll be a caretaker's apartment in the ell."

"We could live in Ruhamah Reed's house?"

"Uh, if we get married."

And suddenly Snowy had no doubts about what she wanted. Him. Once again she would do the unconventional; she wouldn't work in a publishing house, she wouldn't marry a Williams boy. "Okay," she said.

They both gripped their receivers, stunned.

Snowy looked around the big corner office. Frances was typing away madly, but Snowy didn't hear any sound except the silence on the line.

Alan said, "You mean it?"

"Do you?" she said.

Another silence.

"Hell," he said, "I'll even buy a two-slice toaster."

"Unnecessary," she said. "Wedding presents mean an abundance of toasters."

He lowered his voice. "I love you."

She lowered hers. "I love you."

❦

"HOWEVER," SNOWY TOLD her parents when she came home from Boston for the break after NRT wearing a modest diamond, "we won't have a church wedding, Alan and I are atheists."

133

Her parents were Methodists, and her father blanched, although he and her mother never went to church themselves. Her mother wasn't listening, ooh-ing over the ring.

Snowy said, "It'll be a very small wedding, us and the Sutherlands and Julia and Fred and Bev and Roger, here in the living room."

"Our living room," her mother said, listening now.

"Puddles can't come," Snowy said. "Her baby will be almost due then, and Harriet can't either. She's leaving for Europe the minute we graduate." But Harriet had said, phoning with felicitations from New York in reply to Snowy's letter, "I could re-schedule the trip—" Snowy had said, "Over my dead body, you *know* we feel the same about weddings." "Sure you can't elope?" "Positive," Snowy had said, "especially since I met Alan's parents when I went to Eastbourne for my Old Eastbourne interview." Alan's mother pretty and doting; his long-lidded father argumentative about everything, provoking one of Alan's depressions. To her own parents Snowy continued, having done her homework as usual, "We should put an engagement announcement in the *Gunthwaite Herald,* I've typed one up. Personal invitations are suitable for a very small wedding. After the wedding, announcements are sent to relatives and friends who weren't invited, engraved, not printed."

"The living room," her mother said. "Your wedding here in our living room."

Snowy implored, "Don't go to any bother." She was well aware that this plea would be ignored.

Her parents did wait until she left for Bennington before launching into the project of dressing the house in wedding finery. Off came the four-year-old living-room wallpaper of Colonial eagles, and off came the dining-room wallpaper of blue grapes. The white ceilings, drab from cigarette smoke, were repainted, and so was the white woodwork. Up went "Floral Medley" on the living-room walls; up went "Golden Cornucopia" on the dining-room walls. The sofa got yet another new slipcover, new scatter pillows, and the good china in the maple

134

hutch became the everyday, the Currier and Ives scenes replaced by fleurs-de-lis. When Snowy opened the back door and entered the house after her graduation, which her parents took time out to attend, she saw that her mother had even purchased new rooster dishtowels.

Graduation. The wedding. She, who abhorred ceremonies, felt punch-drunk with ritual.

But she'd actually graduated!

Despite the smallness of the wedding, some presents had accumulated, stored in the spare room. The Saturday after Alan proposed, Bev had taken her under her wing, saying, "Socially accepted blatant greed, make the most of it!", and they'd gone to Jordan Marsh where Bev helped Snowy choose a china and a silverware pattern, the names of which Snowy registered at the jewelry store in Gunthwaite that also sold china and silverware. Snowy and Bev and Puddles had lingered often in front of this jewelry store's window, yearning over engagement rings, unable to believe they'd ever have one. Now she did, and in the spare room were two place settings of the pale blue Franciscanware china with a platinum band, bought by Alan's parents, and, from Julia along with an assortment of handwoven placemats, two place settings of Towle's Craftsman silverware. Snowy's mother had never possessed silverware, just stainless, and as she kept touching the new knives, forks, spoons, she would mention her own mother: "I wish your grandmother had lived to come to your wedding." Then she'd ask, "Don't you want some regular for everyday?" But Julia used silverware all the time, so of course Snowy would. Julia did use pottery for everyday, and besides these presents sent to Snowy's house, Julia and Fred's present had been a check sent to Snowy at Bennington with a note from Julia saying, "Have a spree at Bennington Potters." Snowy certainly had, choosing sophisticated black plates and mugs, bowls, platters. Meanwhile, Bev cashed a paycheck and prowled Jordan Marsh and, trying not to think of the groceries and the rent the money must stretch for, she almost bought a Corningware casserole dish, but macaroni-and-cheese was

135

dreadfully unromantic and she splurged on an honest-to-good-ness cocktail shaker. Puddles racked her brain for something distinctly Southern to send, and finally, in the Old Slave Market in Charleston, she spotted just the ticket, a Low Country basket made and sold by an old Negro woman. After buying it, she commanded Guy to drive through woods and get out and pick up a collection of the enormous pine cones that lay everywhere. At home, she filled the basket with them, knowing this would remind Snowy of the picnic-table centerpieces they'd foraged for on Girl Scout cookouts, and then she added a white satin bow, in honor of Snowy's virginity, hee-hee, found a carton, and mailed the basket north.

To the spare room Snowy brought Bennington presents. The pottery. A shower present from friends, a Marriage Mobile made of a dish drainer, measuring cups and spoons, a cork-screw, kitchen shears, wooden spoons, pot holders, vegetable and bottle and *toilet* brushes, and a recipe file containing each girl's favorite recipe, Harriet's with a special meaning: Coffee Cake. Harriet had also given her a portrait of Ruhamah Reed, having secretly copied the frontispiece, naming the portrait "The Matchmaker." "Oh," Snowy had said, much moved, "oh, thank you, oh God, where's a Kleenex?"

Snowy's mother wanted to display the presents. Snowy knew that Emily Post okayed this, but Julia thought it vulgar, although Bev had prevailed. So Snowy lied to her mother, "The custom isn't appropriate at small weddings."

Disappointed, her mother accepted Snowy as the etiquette authority, and then, refusing her help, began coming down the home stretch. Hardwood floors were waxed to an alarming sheen, the latest organdy curtains were washed and starched and rehung crisscrossed in the living-room and dining-room windows, furniture was polished, and on the day of the wedding there appeared vases of flowers, the flowers Snowy had ordered at the florist's after consulting Julia, bouquets of irises and pink azaleas, and snapdragons and baby's breath and marguerite daisies, and a white arrangement of white roses and white car-

136

nations and white sweet peas, and from Julia's garden some bouquets of roses, sweet William, peonies.

Just last week, she had been a student. Today she was a bride. A June bride. Conventional! But she was unconventional enough to have requested, Alan agreeing, that the justice of the peace omit "God" and "obey" and substitute "husband and wife" for "man and wife."

In the sunlit living room, Snowy and Alan stood before the justice of the peace, Alan wearing a tan summer suit, Snowy wearing a pale blue piqué suit with a corsage of pink rosebuds, her hair in a chignon. She was attempting to keep a straight face, remembering how Alan had remarked that she should get a discount from the bridal shop below his apartment. Around them stood his family, his mother tremulous, his father uneasy, his sister and brother-in-law assessing Snowy, his young niece fascinated, his young nephew fidgeting, and her parents beaming, Julia and Bev tearful, their husbands bored. The room smelled of perfume—Snowy's was White Shoulders lately—and of the bouquets and corsages, Snowy's mother's yellow tea roses and Mrs. Sutherland's violets. Mrs. Sutherland. Snowy blinked. These last months, her final work on her thesis had made the wedding ahead abstract. But once home, she ought to have confronted the impact of the ceremony. Had she been in a trance here, dazed by details? Had ritual buried reality? A few more moments of the justice of the peace's droning would mean another Mrs. Sutherland in this room. She would be Alan's wife, not a falsehood on a hotel register but the truth forever.

Then from out the open windows came the sound of the ducks in the river, and Snowy heard a stifled giggle. Bev.

"—honor and keep her," the justice of the peace was asking Alan, "in sickness and in health, and, forsaking all others, keep thee only unto her, so long as you both shall live?"

Quack!

"I will," Alan said faintly.

"Will you, Henrietta Snow, have this man to be your wedded husband, to love him, comfort him, honor and keep him, in

137

sickness and in health, and, forsaking all others, keep thee only unto him, so long as you both shall live?"

Quack-quack!

"I will," Snowy said.

Alan slid the wedding ring on her finger.

The justice of the peace said, "Please join right hands."

Snowy's hands suddenly poured sweat.

"—in accordance with the laws of the State of New Hampshire and powers encumbered upon me as justice of the peace, I do hereby pronounce you m- husband and wife."

Alan and Snowy quickly kissed, embarrassed in front of everyone. Then they stared at each other.

Quack-quack-quack!

Earlier that week, Snowy had phoned Julia and said, "Emergency. Mother was planning a fruit punch, but I'm insisting on champagne, plain champagne like at Bev's, not a champagne punch, but we don't need a caterer's supply of glasses, could I borrow your set, if any get broken I'll—" Julia said, "Of course, and I insist that you let the champagne be a present from us." Snowy protested, "You've done too much already," and Julia said, "Fred and I have had more experience in buying champagne, that's all." Fearing her mother's Velveeta on Ritz, Snowy had insisted upon ordering fancy hors d'oeuvres from a caterer. These and ice cream and the wedding cake from Vachon's Bakery, she tried to tell her mother, would be plenty, light and elegant, yet it was her mother's turn to do some insisting. "The Sutherlands," her mother said, "they'll think we're stingy. Besides, people like to eat at weddings." And her mother had baked a huge ham and made a ton of potato salad.

A good thing, because after the toasts and hors d'oeuvres, the guests lined up at the dining-room buffet and piled their plates high.

Snowy didn't. In shock, she had actually lost her appetite. She and Alan were married. She couldn't change her mind.

Bev whispered, "Thank heavens your mother isn't serving roast duckling."

138

Snowy laughed weakly. Across the room, Alan stood clutching his tulip-shaped champagne glass, listening to his brother-in-law who'd thrown a stag party last night in Eastbourne, but looking at Snowy, dumbstruck.

Bev asked, "Did you see Dr. Mitchell?"

"I will never comprehend how Puddles can be a nurse." Two days ago Snowy had entered the Gunthwaite Clinic for an appointment with a gynecologist and had emerged from the clinic pharmacy the owner of a diaphragm. A mortifying milestone. "It was enough to make me give up sex. Almost."

"Have you remembered to pack it? I forgot mine, Mother reminded me just before the rice-throwing."

Snowy hadn't mentioned the appointment to her mother; they hadn't discussed such subjects since her mother had told her the Facts of Life when she'd got her period. "I remembered."

Alan and Snowy had been unable to think where on earth to go on their honeymoon. In bed at the Sleepytime, the television muttering, Snowy had said, "Someplace where people won't point and snicker—newlyweds!" Alan said, "Niagara Falls? We'd blend in with the crowd." "Not Niagara Falls, conventional. Oh hell," Snowy said, "how about the nearest motel?" This idea distracted them a while, and then Alan said, "Nova Scotia!" "A foreign country?" Snowy said, overwhelmed. "No passports needed," he said. She asked, "But can we afford it?" He said, "My sister and brother-in-law went there last summer with their kids, a cruise to Yarmouth. They took their car and drove around for a week, Prince Edward Island included because the main thing was to show my niece the site of some girls' book she's crazy about, it was her birthday present." "*Anne of Green Gables*," Snowy said, reflecting that Howard, his brother-in-law, was a podiatrist who could afford a week of motels. "Anne lived on Prince Edward Island. Isn't a week too long? We've only got that week off, and we'll have the wedding presents to unpack in your apartment and settling in and—" "Our apartment," Alan corrected, saying, "I'll investigate.

139

There must be different deals." She said, "I've never been on the ocean." He said, "Bring Dramamine." She asked, "Will we look like newlyweds?" He said, "We'll masquerade as tourists."

At an Eastbourne travel agency, Alan selected a short package, an overnight cruise on the *Highland Fling* out of Portland, Maine, to Yarmouth, Nova Scotia, with an overnight stay there at the Hotel Balmoral, terra firma beneath Snowy's feet, then a day cruise back to Portland.

So, after the wedding cake and more toasts, Alan and Snowy drove off to Portland, both of them extremely quiet, chain-smoking. They reached the dock at dusk.

The *Highland Fling* resembled their wedding cake magnified a million times, its white tiers surely sugary.

They joined the waiting crowd, and Alan set down her suitcase and his, but Snowy, her new white pocketbook in one hand, held on with the other to her vanity case which contained her hard-earned diaphragm. The sight of the ship and the feel of excitement in the air awakened her from her petrified numbness; her terror changed to happy apprehension about the adventure ahead, she could talk again, and she whispered to Alan, her husband, "Some people don't have suitcases."

He said abruptly, "They're taking the round-trip cruise."

"Why?"

"Just to see the ocean, I guess. Or have an affair."

Snowy gasped, "An affair, really? Look, what's happening?"

The *Highland Fling* was opening her maw, and cars were arriving.

Alan said, "People bringing their cars to go touring. Like Howard and Margaret."

"Let's do that on our—oh, our twenty-fifth anniversary." Utter nonsense, since she couldn't imagine herself and Alan at such a great age, but a whistling-in-the-dark affirmation.

And finally he grinned.

"Okay," he said, panic and misgivings beginning to fade.

The cars were swallowed, and the passengers were signaled aboard. Stepping onto the ramp, Snowy regretted that passports

140

weren't necessary, added glamour. She wanted to halt on the deck to examine the first sensation of being on board a ship, yet everybody was going inside to a sort of lobby with slot machines, the first slot machines she had ever seen except in movies. Alan did what the other men were doing, picking up a key from the woman at the information desk.

"We're Cabin 411," he reported. "She says it's on the main deck, this way."

Snowy followed him down a very narrow corridor to number 411. As he unlocked the door, she remembered entering his apartment less than a year ago. The tiny cabin had two lower and two upper berths, the lower ones made up, the bedspreads orange. The walls were beige. Would the décor clash with her new peach-colored baby-doll nightgown?

"Bunk beds," Snowy said. "Fun!" But could she and he fit into one together?

Alan opened a door. "Private bathroom." He'd paid extra for this.

"It's beautiful, it's like a playhouse."

"So let's play." He seized her.

In the middle of their first private married kiss, the floor lifted.

"Eek!" Snowy said. "The earth moved!"

He laughed. "We're under way. Want to go watch?" He patted her bottom. "We've got all night."

During which she wouldn't worry about getting arrested.

They went on deck, Snowy walking carefully, wishing she'd changed to flats. Other people were here, but after the Portland lights disappeared the deck quickly emptied and Snowy and Alan were left standing alone.

She asked, "Is everybody going to bed already?"

"Let's find the lounge."

They went back inside to a deafening noise and discovered that the people had flung themselves on the slot machines. A Las Vegas scene from a movie!

141

"Jesus," he said. "It must be you can't gamble until the ship's out to sea. Want to try?"

"I never have."

"But these are occupied."

They roamed onward, up to the restaurant deck. The machines crammed along the corridors were loudly busy, the players attached in limpet fashion, holding paper cups of coins. A sign outside the restaurant told them that tonight's specialty was Digby scallops.

He asked, "Would you like supper? You only had cake."

She knew the package included a free breakfast buffet tomorrow and a dinner buffet on the cruise back. Not, apparently, this dinner. She said, "You only had cake too."

"Nerves."

They walked on past the duty-free shop which sparkled with glassware and jewelry and bottles of booze, and they came to a real casino with gaming tables and ranks of slot machines, all in use. As they went up the next wide flight of stairs, Snowy, clasping the gilt banister, felt a definite roll.

On the boat deck were more frantic slot machines, a snack bar with food-vending machines, another casino, and at last the lounge, the Lighthouse Lounge, a big open area of green plush seats and low round tables, a dim oasis of quietness, for it was empty, the man at the piano playing softly while nobody danced on the dance floor to "Our Love Is Here to Stay," the passengers preferring gambling to Gershwin.

Alan pulled out a green chair and Snowy sat down, and when he himself was seated, a waiter appeared. A Negro. Snowy had been friends with a Negro girl at Bennington, but neither she nor Alan had ever encountered a Negro waiter before in person, only in movies.

"What will your pleasure be?" the waiter asked, his voice lilting.

Alan looked at Snowy. "Gin-and-tonics?"

"Fine," she said. After the waiter left, she whispered, "He sounds like a Harry Belafonte song."

142

"Jamaican," Alan said and lit their cigarettes.

They looked around. Through an archway they could see into the casino. There were croupiers!

When the waiter brought the drinks, Alan realized how serious the tipping was here; no running up a tab; you paid and tipped each time.

"My thanks," said the waiter and did a little coin trick, flipping his tip off the tray into his hand, before leaving.

Snowy and Alan couldn't have been more embarrassed if he'd started tap-dancing for Massa. Subdued again, they sipped their drinks, which weren't tall highballs but squat and weak. The piano player had noodled on to " 'S Wonderful."

Alan laughed. "My brother-in-law! The purpose of that trip was a girls' book! The exemplary father! Bull! To think he and Margaret never once mentioned the gambling."

"Those people without suitcases, I guess their purpose isn't amour?"

"Nope, a different vice."

"Is it me or is the ship rolling?"

"Some. Well, I assume it has stabilizers, so it's pitching, not rolling."

Knowledgeable Alan, born and brought up in a port. If he hadn't managed to get deferments, he had planned to avoid the draft by joining the Navy. "Have we hit a storm?"

"Hell, no. I checked the weather report this morning, nothing. Go with the motion, don't fight it."

The waiter came over to them. "May I get you another?"

Such playhouse-size drinks. Snowy nodded when Alan looked at her. "Thank you." After the waiter was gone, she smiled at Alan. "A lot of milestones today."

"And we'll be losing our virginities soon—" He stopped. Jealous of the guys she'd dated before they met and the non-platonic guys she must've dated after, damn curious about who'd first got her to Go All The Way, which she'd certainly call a milestone, he'd never asked for details because that would invite questions about his own love life. Initiation: The summer he was sixteen and had a job delivering milk along a route of summer cottages, and the woman at the last cottage suggested he bring a bathing suit and go for a swim to cool off whenever he liked. An older woman, probably as ancient as twenty-five, with a baby, her husband in Boston during the week. Even though she was good-looking and went jouncing around in a skimpy bathing suit, he'd been so stupid that at the outset he had actually just gone swimming there, changing back into his milkman's uniform in her bathroom, thanking her politely and leaving, cases of empty milk bottles jingling in the rear of the truck. Then one afternoon, into the bathroom she walked, stark naked. He finally got the idea, and on a turquoise bathmat which smelled of salt and sand, he had become, as they say, a man. What a heaven-sent pussy-whipped summer that had been! She evidently thought the bedroom and the baby's room sacred, so they'd done it in every other room, on the guest-room bed, on the kitchen table, over the backs of living-room chairs. The chances she took! Maybe she'd taken too many the following winter, for she didn't return the next summer. After ball-busting disappointment, he'd felt relieved, a reprieve from more guilt. Christ, the memory of another woman was giving him a hard-on on his wedding day. Disgraceful. "It *is* pitching. Let's go look." He stood up and held out his hand to his bride.

Wondering who the girl had been with whom he'd lost his virginity, and when, Snowy was led across the lounge to the curve of black windows, where she grasped Alan's arm to keep her balance.

The piano player called, "It's getting rough!"

"Sure is." Alan said to Snowy, "See the bow down there? On boats, if you watch what the boat is doing you'll feel okay, and I assume the same goes for ships. Watch the bow."

Snowy dropped into a chair and looked out the window at the vague white V of the bow plunging up and down through the dark spray. She opened her pocketbook. "I remembered Dramamine."

144

The waiter, swaying, carried their drinks to their new table. "Like the view?"

Alan paid. "Does it usually get as rough as this?"

The waiter said, "Not when I'm up north, man," and departed without doing the coin trick.

Snowy lifted her glass. "Here's to Mother Nature's jokes." She swallowed a pill. "Too late?"

"Maybe we should go on deck. Fresh air."

"My God, Alan, we'd be washed overboard!"

"Maybe we ought to eat something. If you're going to throw up, you should have something to throw."

Very romantic. "I wouldn't dare eat a bite."

"Well, I'll pick up a couple of sandwiches at that snack bar on our way back to the cabin." He continued, his voice deliberately calm, "Maybe we'd better go now, it might get worse."

"Okay."

They'd never before left a paid-for drink undrunk. But they walked as if they'd drained every bottle in the lounge—and in the duty-free shop too. The seas were so rough now that at each staggering step they had to grab chairs, door jambs. The gamblers were clinging to their slot machines. From a vending machine Alan bought two sandwiches, choosing peanut-butter-and-jelly ("Soothing," he said), and then they reached the first flight of stairs to be survived. Gripping the banister, they descended a staircase which was going up. The second staircase went down, and down and down and down. At the foot, on the main deck, they clutched the gilt newel post until the deck started coming up again, and then they lurched hand-in-hand across the lobby to their corridor, grateful for its narrowness which held them upright to Cabin 411.

Snowy fell against him. "Made it!"

"I've been caught in lobster boats in a storm, but small boats don't do this wallowing. At least we're not smelling bait and gasoline." He hugged her.

"No more goodbyes."

"Goodbye to goodbyes."

145

"Guess what I'm about to do. I'm going to slip into something more comfortable."

"Aha." Alan hugged her again and snapped open his suitcase. "And guess what Fred gave me. Kind of warm now, I fear."

A bottle of the wedding champagne. Snowy said, "Champagne and peanut butter, a feast!"

He went into the bathroom. A champagne cork popped, and he came out with the fizzing bottle and two paper cups.

She said, "I'll only be a minute," and carried her vanity case into the bathroom. Having walls so close to grab was useful, though they meant she could hardly undo her hair and struggle out of her suit and underwear. She opened the pretty pink plastic case that daintily held her diaphragm. She applied gel and poised herself over the toilet. These past two days she had practiced and practiced until she'd got the routine down as pat as a cheer, but she hadn't practiced while squatting on a bucking broncho, which was what the bathroom floor was.

Alan called, "You okay?"

"Yes!" At last she poked it in. Elbows banging against walls, she pulled the peach nightgown over her head. Hairbrush wielded, toothbrush. She rescued the wedding suit from the toilet seat she'd folded it on, and paused. Ridiculous to be shy. She and Alan had been fucking for almost a year, they'd seen close-ups of each other's bodies they couldn't see themselves. But when she stepped out of the bathroom she was blushing.

"Wow," Alan said. He knew from their phone talk two evenings ago that there was an invisible wow, as well. Goodbye to Trojans also.

Snowy groped in the teeny-tiny closet, hanging up her suit while hanging onto the door jamb. He handed her a paper cup of champagne.

She asked, "What shall we toast this time?"

"To Ruhamah Reed," he said, his head tilted.

"To Ruhamah Reed."

At her first sip, Snowy's stomach rebelled. She spun around

146

and dived back into the bathroom and threw up her guts in the toilet.

"Snowy?"

"Don't come in!"

He came in and held her shoulders.

They spent their wedding night wedged into one berth, their virginities intact. Alan eventually slept, but Snowy lay awake in his arms listening to the wedding-cake ship and the sea. Were the ship and the sea their stand-ins tonight, gigantic? Great screeching, ferocious pounding, shuddering. She waited for them to be thrown from the berth, bashed against the bulkhead. She prayed she wouldn't barf again. The cramps in her stomach felt like menstrual cramps; she had carefully scheduled the wedding so she wouldn't have her period. Perfectionist! Toward morning, she drifted into a doze of gauzy grayness.

"YOUR FATHER," THIRTY-seven-year-old Snowy said to her daughter, five-year-old Ruhamah, crossing the parking lot to Eastbourne's busy Burger King on a Thursday afternoon in October 1976, fifteen years later, "your father ate both those peanut-butter-and-jelly sandwiches that night, and then—"

"—the next morning," Ruhamah recited, her voice a rich version of Snowy's, her speech a chortle, "Alan ate the free breakfast buffet, *all* of it, eggs, bacon, sausage, toast, even a chocolate doughnut, while you nibbled one single morsel of toast. The seas were still so rough that two *waiters* slipped and fell, not to mention some of the few passengers who braved breakfast—" She hauled open the door.

"Wise guy. The usual?" Rhetorical; Ruhamah always had the same meal here. She was such a fussy eater she should have been Puddles's daughter, Snowy often thought, but she obviously belonged to Snowy, looking just like her except for her denim eyes, which had Alan's eyelids, and her hair, which was pale blond, darkening from her towhead days. She wore her hair very short. Snowy, who'd courageously tried a Twiggy cut in the mid-Sixties, returning to the Bennington style in the late Sixties and early Seventies when long straight hair had become political, nowadays had a shag but was getting tired of it. They both were wearing jeans, jerseys, jackets, though Snowy would have died before buying any mother-and-daughter outfits. The line moved forward, Ruhamah watching the boisterous older kids, Snowy checking her list of errands: This afternoon she'd taken Ruhamah to the dentist, and while Ruhamah was suffering that ordeal she'd gone shopping for a fancy top to wear Saturday night when she and Alan were going out to dinner with Karen and John Beebe at a new restaurant they had waited to try until the tourists left, and then she'd visited Alan, Curator of Old Eastbourne, afterwards returning to collect Ruhamah. On the way home she would buy the odds and ends of groceries on the list. Ruhamah nudged her, and she said to the young woman behind the counter, "One hamburger and hold everything, please, one order of fries, one strawberry shake, one apple pie,

151

and I think I'll have—" Was a ham-and-cheese worth saying the word aloud? "—a Yumbo, and a Diet Pepsi." Amused by the tradition of rewarding Ruhamah with a cavity-causing treat after a trip to the dentist, by her own anticipation of a junk-food fix after virtuous weeks of whole foods, she put the list in her shoulder bag and took out her wallet, and the bright noisy room spun around. She was going to fall down, the way those waiters had.

Ruhamah whispered, "Snowy?"

Shaking and sweating, Snowy pulled out a ten-dollar bill. If she attempted to pick up the change, she'd scatter it all over the counter. She said to Ruhamah, "You get the change. And the tray."

Walking toward the booth was like walking on waves. The walls were pulsing. Snowy grabbed the table and collapsed onto the seat.

"What's wrong?" Ruhamah asked.

The Swine Flu. The government had decided to give the nation shots, and Snowy and Alan had been debating the pros and cons. Snowy said, "I guess I'm coming down with that flu," and leaned across and felt Ruhamah's cool forehead. "Are you feeling okay?"

"Fine." Oh, to have a mother who didn't fret!

Jerkily, Snowy lifted her Yumbo, then laid it back. If she took a bite, she'd choke to death, she would kick the bucket right here in public, in front of her daughter. She tried a sip of Diet Pepsi and let it slide back down the straw, her throat closed up.

"The Swine Flu?" Ruhamah peered under the bun, making sure everything except the hamburger had been held. "Is it like being seasick?"

But Snowy wasn't nauseated; she was hungry. During morning sickness, she had craved food and puked at the same time. She eyed the door, which seemed five miles away. She certainly couldn't be pregnant. "Why don't we pretend we bought take-out; you can eat yours en route home."

Ruhamah's eyelids vanished, and, wide-eyed, she asked with keen interest, "Are you going to throw up?"

Maybe this child *was* Puddles's daughter. "Hurry."

"Aren't you bringing yours?"

"No." Snowy stood, grasping the table.

"Waste not, want not. That's what you tell me."

Conquering a desire to throttle Ruhamah, Snowy picked up the Yumbo box and started toward the door. She had become Christ, she could walk on water—if her wobbly knees didn't sink her. Everybody must be staring. She reached the door, the parking lot, without falling. Her car, safe haven!

The dark green Volkswagen began to smell like a fast-food joint as Ruhamah resumed her early supper while Snowy drove away down the Miracle Mile past the shopping malls and carpet centers and McDonald's and Pizza Hut and Kentucky Fried Chicken and muffler shops and Dunkin' Donuts, all new since she'd moved to Eastbourne. She left the city behind, driving through foliage the color of faded tartans, to the ocean road. Pregnant? Impossible.

For ten years she had worked at Old Eastbourne, a general factotum doing research on buildings, composing brochures and contribution appeals, giving tours of the Ruhamah Reed House and telling herself she wasn't devoting her life to a house à la her parents, because her real work occurred in the evenings at her desk in the ell apartment's spare room. She and Alan kept postponing a decision about a baby, their discussions inconclusive until the time she said to Alan, who was drying the supper dishes she was washing, "Look, we've *got* to decide. We're getting too set in our ways, it's now or never. Do we or don't we have a baby?"

Her parents, eager to add grandchildren to their portrait of family life, had hinted strongly during the passing years, making her stubborn and confused. Alan's parents weren't even that subtle, especially his father, though they had Margaret and Howard's children to coddle. Alan replied with a question. "Just how much would a kid disrupt things?"

153

"A lot. You'd be the sole support, at least for a spell." Snowy could hope to keep earning money from her poems published in magazines (she was, however, still often paid only with free copies) and from advances on books (to date, Commonwealth had published her thesis and two collections of her poetry), but this would hardly keep a baby in diapers, much less pay for the nose job she'd promised herself long ago. True to her resolve, she hadn't done readings, and because she remained far removed from other poets, their groups, workshops, in-residences, she was amazed that any big magazines chose her poems and positive she wouldn't have had a book published without her NRT connection. Indeed, when she'd received the letter from Mr. Palmquist saying they would like to publish the thesis and collection of her college poems she'd submitted, her reaction had been that her doctor had told Alan she had an incurable disease and Alan had somehow talked Mr. Palmquist into this charade so she would go smiling.

The letter had arrived on moving day, in the midst of their shifting in carloads their belongings from Alan's apartment to the Ruhamah Reed House, and it was Alan who, shouting, reread the letter aloud—"*two* books, 'the biography and collection to be published simultaneously'!"—and jubilantly proclaimed a milestone celebration at an Eastbourne restaurant they couldn't afford, while she sat quiet on a carton of cooking utensils wondering in a detached fashion how much time she had left. But she went along with the game and wrote Mr. Palmquist back gratefully. He sent the contracts, then a check, causing her to doubt that Commonwealth would carry compassion to this extreme. When the mailman brought a package containing dangly strips of galley proofs to correct, she was convinced.

Besides, she had thought, holding at last the first finished copies, it didn't matter now if she did die, because her books really were published and thus would live forever. That night she and Alan and friends tried out a new Gay Nineties bar, where in the earsplitting razzle-dazzle of tenor banjos they drank mugs of beer and joined in the singing. "Oh, them golden slippers," she sang, purely happy, "Golden slippers I'm gonna wear to walk the golden street."

At the Eastbourne post office she had mailed autographed copies, and at the apartment mailbox she nervously awaited replies. Her counselor, who had written a blurb, responded kindly. Her mother wrote, "Your father and I are very proud, here's a clipping from the newspaper, but it upsets us you don't use your married name. Your father says some married authoresses use maiden names, but people will think you're not married and what about when you have children?" Bev wrote, "I loved both books! I can't rave enough! Even the photograph of you Alan took for the dust jackets, ocean behind you, is so *artistic!*" Puddles wrote, "Ruhamah Reed sure is hot stuff, ditto Henrietta Snow." And Julia wrote, "I've never doubted that hard work and talent would reap success. Congratulations are inadequate to express my joyous admiration." Luck, Snowy thought, feeling momentarily older than Julia. Hard work and talent and *luck*. But probably Julia knew that and had tactfully omitted it.

Her luck had held through the reviews of these books and the next collection. Writing poetry, working at Old Eastbourne, loving Alan, filled her life. A baby?

"Well," Alan said, putting away a Bennington Potters plate, "we could manage on my pay now, it wouldn't be like it used to."

In charge of their exchequer, she'd always endeavored to save her salary toward a down payment on a house, but she'd had to dip in fairly regularly. Throughout the lean years, her salary had bought, stick by antique stick, their furniture, and had rescued them in emergencies, such as when their cars broke down, which was often. God, how she had counted every penny, every slice of bread in the kitchen, every drop of milk, every wholesale sardine! She had invented a Night-Before-Payday Casserole based on whatever potatoes and onions were left in the larder. By now, though, Alan had become the assistant to the

155

curator; she could budget some luxuries, and last year they'd raided their savings for a trip to Britain. With a baby, would she be counting every spoonful of Gerber's? She said, "A decision about a baby means a decision about a house. It means—we're used to doing what we want to, when we want to, no obligations. Freedom. Heavens, we couldn't even fuck on the living-room rug anymore!" She flicked his dishtowel. "If you were in the mood, you couldn't parade around bollicky bare-assed pretending you're a towel rack. I don't know, I've never been able to picture myself a mother." Those twin babies had been fantasy. "Maybe I can't. My mother's history of miscarriages. Maybe you can't. Maybe we can't, decision unnecessary."

Suddenly randy, Alan said, "Let's find out," and swung her onto the kitchen's harvest table, pushed up her skirt, tugged off her underpants and pantyhose, and unzipped his fly.

Laughing, waving soapsuds, she said, "I took a Pill this morning!" A baby *would* inhibit him. Eek, more likely present a challenge. "I won't get pregnant tonight!" But when she lay back and toppled the pewter salt shaker and pepper mill, she threw salt over her left shoulder, spread her legs wide, and as he lifted her hips and entered her the act seemed so laden with consequence that she could believe she'd really get pregnant tonight.

The next day she stopped taking the Pill, and they began house-hunting, eventually buying an unused gray fish house across a road from the ocean in the nearby small town of Pevensay. They could afford it because it was a wreck, and after they moved in they spent busman's-holiday evenings and weekends fixing it up, saying, "This is the place for us, baby or no baby." There might not be one; Snowy wasn't getting pregnant, although she'd done her homework and they had seen their doctors and were trying ardently. She'd figured the procedure would become businesslike, what with charts, thermometers, appointments to screw at the proper time, yet she and Alan had instead returned to a love-at-first-sight passion despite their matter-of-fact purpose. Since they weren't sure they did want a

156

baby, desperation didn't afflict them. Then when they learned they'd started one, their passion increased—so did her waistline, and also her boobs. She said, "I'm finally blossoming!" Alan sighed, "Incredible," fondling and suckling every chance, Snowy wondering if nursing would feel this sexy and if it did would she be normal. Were she and Alan behaving normally? Had desperation struck, were they bidding farewell to their privacy, to their being Snowy-and-Alan? She worried about miscarrying and about the monstrousness of her unspoken hope for a miscarriage. During the last month, she wept as she came, his head where a baby's would emerge, and when he cautiously turned her over and knelt behind her and eased himself in, she wished his penis were a plug which would keep the baby inside forever.

The moment her obstetrician said, "You have a daughter!", Snowy's initial exhausted emotion was relief that it was a girl. She'd said she didn't care, girl or boy. Sheer sham. If she was capable of being a mother at all, she'd probably be luckier with a girl because at least she knew something about girls and this might help a terrified klutz who'd had no kid sister or brother to practice motherhood on. A daughter. She reached for the baby, real, and counted ten fingers, ten toes. She and the baby had survived the seven hours of labor she'd thought would kill them both.

Carrying flowers, Alan walked into her hospital room, kissed her, and asked, "How are you?" She said, "I'm wondering if there's a chance cheerleading will be abolished by the time she's old enough to try out." They laughed, and then he started crying. She had never seen him cry. She held him, as she had held the baby, too tired for tears herself. Were his tears of joy? No. But *she* was the person who was supposed to have postpartum depression, for Christ's sake!

The next day in the hospital she wrote on the note pad she'd brought:

> Now there is this baby
> And now all my days

157

Are not mine, and all my years
Are marked by another's birthday cakes.

The small clamorous creature invaded their house, and
Snowy and Alan soon agreed that one child would be plenty.
Snowy's doctor wasn't too thrilled about her taking the Pill until
menopause, and he vaguely suggested a vasectomy without
recommending a doctor who did them, so they were on their
own. In Eastbourne five years ago, searching for a doctor who'd
added vasectomies to his repertoire began to seem like a hunt for
an abortionist, but after it occurred to them to consult Alan's
podiatrist brother-in-law they were successful at last, the doctor
they found asking them to sign a paper in which they stated they
understood that the operation would render Alan sterile. That's
the whole idea, Snowy retorted silently as she signed firmly.
Friday, vasectomy-day, she insisted on accompanying him, leaving Ruhamah at his sister's, to drive him home afterwards.
Unfortunately, the doctor's office lacked soundproofing. In the
waiting room Snowy sat gripping a magazine, trying not to
envision the scene in the adjoining room, yet she couldn't ignore
the sounds.
Snip.
Snip.
Although she flinched for Alan, she had nary a second
thought.
Alan emerged from the room acting casual, and outdoors he
said resolutely that he would drive home. First he drove to a
drugstore, but when he started to get out, she said, "Enough
heroics," and took the prescription and went in and bought the
pain pills. Then he drove to Margaret and Howard's house;
Snowy went indoors and picked up Ruhamah, and Margaret
came out to the car with them and said to Alan, "I wish Howard
had your courage. How are you feeling?" "Foolish," Alan said.
At home, he refused to go to bed, so Snowy, after putting
Ruhamah in her crib, tried to be as efficient as nurse Puddles,
settling him in his wing chair in front of the television, bringing

158

him tea. She asked, "How do you feel now?" He said, "Like I've been kicked in the nuts." This got them laughing, and he said, "Maybe an ice pack would help," so she rooted around in the bathroom closet for it, filled it with ice cubes, and he spent the rest of the day sitting on the ice pack which she periodically replenished, tending to Alan's balls and Ruhamah's diapers, mentally inquiring, "Where hath romance flown?"

Yet she had been happy to have him sitting there recuperating, compared to the spells when he just sat in that chair brooding. The few times she had ventured to suggest he should see a doctor or psychiatrist about his depressions, he had blown up at her. "For Christ's sake," he shouted, "it's normal to be depressed when your job is wearing you down; it would be *abnormal* not to be depressed!" And he would list all the logical reasons, from the Old Eastbourne Board of Directors who were a bunch of idiots, to—sometimes he even blamed the weather. "This fog! Maybe we should move inland."

After the vasectomy, Alan had gone back to work that Monday, only one workday lost. She couldn't possibly be pregnant, but she was dizzy again, as dizzy as the first days she and Alan had quit smoking six years ago. The car was no longer a haven, and the road ahead was a tightrope she was going to fall off. She pulled over and stopped, sweating, palsied.

"In school this morning," Ruhamah said, twisting a French fry, "Michael threw up and there were pieces of carrots and—"

"*Ruhamah!*"

"For science, Snowy, as you always say."

"Michael threw up?" Snowy touched Ruhamah's forehead again.

"He doesn't have the flu. Wendy punched him in the stomach."

"Oh."

Across the road beyond the sea wall, the ocean looked so peaceful. At this time of year, it became hers once more, tourists and summer people gone. Snowy began counting the waves. The seventh wave, Alan had taught her and she'd taught Ruhamah, is the big one. And the counting calmed her down.

She drove on. Bev had had a hell of a surprise last year, a fourth child born nine years after the third. On the birth announcement Bev wrote, "You guessed it. I finally forgot. How typical! We call her Etta, and her hair is red. Did I write you that my hair went completely gray? Now it's white! I still refuse to kowtow to Clairol. Besides, it gets attention." A namesake: Henrietta Lambert, 7 lbs. 6 oz. Bev a mother again last year at thirty-six, white-haired like Julia. Snowy had assumed that a nannyless Bev wouldn't have six kids, and she'd been startled when Bev had a third. Roger was a lapsed Catholic, so the reason must be forgetfulness—or were people who were only children apt to have larger families? Then she'd been struck by the surmise that Bev had supplied a cast for the play which was her life down in Connecticut. When Roger had graduated, his best offer had come from a firm in Ninfield, Connecticut, and Bev had thrown herself into the role of wife to a brilliant young lawyer, beautiful mother of a bouquet of darling children: Julia Marie, nicknamed Mimi, whose middle name was Roger's mother's name; Richard William (red-headed), named after Bev's father, nicknamed Dick; and Leon Frederick, named after Roger's father and Bev's stepfather, no nickname. Snowy imagined Bev doing the stage sets too, redecorating the various suburban houses they'd bought. While Roger climbed the ladder of success, Bev climbed many a literal ladder, hanging wallpaper.

Such details were guesswork on Snowy's part, because during these past years when everybody was involved in new lives, the ties of the triumvirate had stretched thin. Except for notes about the publication of Snowy's books, they communicated by notes on Christmas cards (Bev and Puddles sent the children-photograph variety, not to Snowy's taste and more expensive, anyway) and birthday cards and birth announcements. Bulletins from the front, Snowy thought.

Bev may have sent out the most birth announcements, and, like Snowy, Puddles may have sent just one, but Puddles's announced—"TWINS!" Puddles scribbled, this news meriting a memo-pad letter shoved into the envelope, "twin GIRLS, and now I'll have to take back all those awful things I said about Charl and Darl! The doctor suspected—I refused to believe him, though Guy's mother remembered twin great-aunts twice removed or some such relatives, I cannot follow Southern genealogies. Guy wanted to name them Florence, as in Nightingale, and Clara, as in Barton, but I decided that was carrying a career a little far. And since my name is so plain—let's not even talk about my nickname—I wanted to give them something pretty. Guy came up with Melanie and Melissa, but the trouble with Melanie is that childbirth scene in *Gone with the Wind,* and I'd ruled out names that are alike. So we settled on these." Susan and Amy. "P.S. Speaking of childbirth scenes, I was very unprofessional and yelled my head off. Weird to be at the other end. I'll start work again as soon as they're in nursery school, maybe I can do night shifts before then. P.P.S. You'll be sending a present—yes, MY twins will wear clothes which DON'T MATCH."

Snowy had felt terribly guilty about not returning to Old Eastbourne after Ruhamah was born, yet she had immediately been spoiled by the free time to work on her poems during the day, while Ruhamah napped, instead of only in the evening. "And," she told Alan when they talked it over, "if I'm home, I can give her the help I never had except for Julia, get her reading early. You know my mother, she was home through junior high but her idea of help was pink curtains." Snowy also sought the fine mother-daughter balance Julia and Bev had achieved. Alan said, "Whatever you think." "I'll go back," she said, "when Ruhamah starts nursery school." Staying home, scrimping on one salary, isolated with poetry and Ruhamah, she had accumulated enough poems for another collection and taught Ruhamah so thoroughly that Ruhamah could read before she could talk. Then, at age two, Ruhamah started nursery school, and Snowy decided not to take a part-time job at Old Eastbourne until she saw how Ruhamah adjusted. Ruhamah was so tiny and

161

shy! But after a tearful week Ruhamah settled in—and Snowy had these entire mornings of solitude. I'll go back, Snowy thought, when Ruhamah starts kindergarten. Kindergarten arrived, and Snowy still didn't return to Old Eastbourne, working on poems in the mornings, picking up Ruhamah at the Pevensay kindergarten and playing with her and doing chores in the afternoons. Last month she had recognized that maybe she was imitating Julia's hermit life, transplanting it to the seacoast. Yet she remained part of society, throwing and going to parties, even performing the civic duty of petitioning the Pevensay school board to put seat belts in school buses, a crusade which seemed doomed to failure.

And as a civic duty and a favor to a friend, she had actually broken her rule and done a reading. Over the years Karen Beebe, the Pevensay librarian, had been cajoling, pleading, Snowy steadfastly refusing until, at Karen and John's house one evening recently, Karen had said, "We've got the go-ahead to start the fund-raising to build the library addition. Wouldn't you *please* lend us a hand and do a reading?" Sipping an ill-advised third gin-and-tonic, Snowy agreed. The reading had been last Saturday night. She couldn't work for days before, stewing and rehearsing and longing to be Bev. It was held in the library's basement meeting room, attended by maybe thirty people, local literati, teachers, retired folk, Friends of the Library, but not by Alan, whom she'd made stay home babysitting. Chin up, she stood at the lectern in front of them, she blushed, her heart pounded, her mouth went dry. Masturbating in public. She got through the ordeal, and during the coffee and cookies she tried her best to steer conversations away from poetry to school-bus seat belts. Afterwards, she couldn't work for several more days, her poems sullied. Never again.

She slowed at the grocery store where she usually bought supplies between supermarket expeditions. Whole-wheat English muffins, her list had said, orange juice, low-fat cottage cheese, and hot dogs, the last Alan's junk-food counterpart of their Burger King supper. Hers still uneaten. She glanced down at the carton of Yumbo. She didn't *have* to stop here, she could concoct Alan some other treat, she didn't *need* anything on the list.

Ruhamah asked, "We aren't stopping?"

"Nothing vital." Snowy drove past, on to the Pevensay Point Road. She clicked the directionals. She was nearly home, almost safe.

Ruhamah chortled, "With Swine Flu, you don't get sick as a dog, you get sick as a pig!"

Snowy had run this road this morning, the salt air heavy, the rising sun a silver disk behind a dull tin sheet of fog which hid the ocean, fog outlining in white the cobwebs suspended from twig to twig on the burnished trees and bushes. She'd been running here ever since Ruhamah was born, so she'd started jogging before it became such a fad. Unconventional, then. While Alan babysat, she had begun going for a walk in the evenings to supplement the exercises she was doing to fit back into non-maternity clothes, and one evening the walk became a run, escape, the rhythm of the ocean waves cheering her on. Soon she had bought a utilitarian sweatsuit; there weren't any running togs then, nor running shoes, only sneakers. And soon she switched to running in the mornings before Alan left for work, so all these years she'd been greeting sunrises, including the ones she called Puddles Sunrises because they were the cheap pink of rayon underpants, reminding her of the time when she and Puddles, sophomores, were browsing in Woolworth's and Puddles discovered an array of huge underpants and, declaring that they were exactly Snowy's size, chased Snowy around the store waving a pair at her until Snowy darted outdoors where Puddles couldn't follow without shoplifting.

The other gray fish houses across the road from the ocean had been bought and remodeled by summer people, and their windows and porches were boarded up now. Like the ocean, the road was hers again.

Jogging a couple of miles a day had brought her weight back down to a hundred and five pounds, so she now weighed the same as she had in high school and college, but she was a different shape. Cheerleading and gym and strolling the Bennington campus hadn't done to her what jogging did. Although Alan—and Tom—had always claimed she had great legs, in snapshots of her wearing her cheerleading uniform or shorts you couldn't see all that much space between her thighs. Nowadays, you could drive a Mack truck through.

Ruhamah asked, "May I have a half-birthday?"

"A half-birthday?"

"Michael has a birthday in June and a half-birthday next month, and his mother makes him a cake each time. Chocolate. His brother, he's in second grade, he has a half-birthday too."

"His mother ought to have her head examined. Don't repeat that!"

Ruhamah giggled, and Snowy pulled into the driveway of the last fish house, the old gray-shingled house with a deep screened front porch, yellow chrysanthemums sunny in window boxes. Across the road, waves foamed against a jetty of slick black rocks.

"Mad dash?" Ruhamah asked, gathering up her Burger King debris.

"I've recovered." Five years ago there wouldn't have been a bathroom to dash to, just an outhouse. Snowy got out of the car. Beyond the fish house lay a field of tall grasses, a contrasting playground to the rocky shoreline, and safer. Snowy had watched Ruhamah like a hawk when she began to crawl and walk; an ocean home was dangerous as well as picturesque, a warning Snowy still drummed into Ruhamah who nowadays chased the tide and scrambled around the jetty on her own, Snowy trying to heed Alan's remarks about apron strings. But Snowy couldn't be fatalistic, and she kept constant watch from windows and porch, missing the years of total control. She missed those years too when, wondering what Ruhamah was thinking, she remembered how it had been much simpler to see things the way Ruhamah did back when they played in the field and she would crouch down in the grass to Ruhamah's height

164

for her view of this world, a jungle of grass stems. The path they'd made was a green tunnel, and the earth seemed very close. Such tall grass ought to have been confining to a small child, but Ruhamah had trotted along without much trouble until she attempted to run, and then the tangle would trip her up. The waving grass dusted her with seeds, and the dew soaked her if they'd ventured out before the sun had dried it.

Snowy inhaled. As she'd predicted, she hadn't become blasé about the ocean smell. She unlocked the trunk and took out the azure box from Monique's Boutique. She was that person again, who'd walked briskly into Monique's, chosen some tops to try on, and bought the one which flattered her most and didn't demand a bra, since she only wore a bra while jogging, a sports model she'd named The Iron Maiden. She wasn't the person in the Burger King, who'd driven so shakily home, who couldn't go in the grocery store.

"Mew mew!" Ruhamah called to the sea gulls on the jetty, though sea gulls didn't just mew, they talked, making human sounds which scared you when you thought you were alone. "Mew mew!"

Snowy and Ruhamah crossed the backyard. At the Ruhamah Reed House, Snowy had grown flowers and herbs. Here, there was room for a vegetable garden, and she'd copied another part of Julia's life, well aware from Julia's example the work involved. This season was over, the garden harvested into the freezer and canning jars, only kale and parsley and Ruhamah's pumpkins remaining, but come spring—"Sometime," she reflected, "I should put together an exercise manual for gardeners. I'll begin with simple warm-ups like throwing a bowling ball overhand and carrying the sofa on your back up and down the stairs. Then I'll get to the tough stuff."

"Mew mew!" Ruhamah snatched Snowy's keys and ran ahead and unlocked the side door which always reminded her of Christmas carols because when she was little she had mistakenly heard "Oh, come let us adore him" as "Oh, come to the side door." Up out of the kitchen's Boston rocker stretched her

165

cat whom, when she'd been given the black kitten two years ago, she'd named Baa-Baa. Black sheep, she had explained to Snowy. Have you any wool?

Theoretically, Snowy didn't believe children should own pets, yet Ruhamah had wanted a kitten and Snowy knew how the warm fur of Kit used to comfort. Dead now, Kit and Laurie. Maybe Laurie would have lived longer if Snowy had been able to bring her to Eastbourne, but dogs weren't permitted in caretakers' apartments. Her parents hadn't consulted her either time about the decision to "put to sleep" *her* cat, *her* dog, "sparing" her, they said, and she had been wild with fury despite knowing it would be cruel to prolong the suffering of each aging ill pet. During spring cleaning and fall cleaning, she'd lift the carving of Laurie out of her bureau drawer.

Cleaning! Ah, the clarity of autumn light which allowed you to see every speck of dust! Not many specks, however. As Snowy tossed the Yumbo into the green—avocado—refrigerator, she ruefully admitted that perhaps she'd come a great distance from her parents' maple-furniture sets, but her tidiness gave her antiques a similar on-display air. She went into the bathroom, where the washing machine and dryer were kept so it was also the laundry room, and left the new top to wash for Saturday night, and back in the kitchen she told Ruhamah, "Brush your teeth," before she began making sure the house hadn't been burgled in her absence, a habit that drove Alan crazy even though there'd been robberies at other Pevensay homes, including a fish house on this road. He would say, "Those were summer cottages, closed-up. We're year-round." She would say, "Not all burglars discriminate." So she took attendance: pewter bowl of apples on the kitchen counter, present; pewter vase of dried grasses, ditto; small black-and-white TV, ditto; silverware in the utensils drawers, ditto. Nobody had stolen the pewter salt shaker and pepper mill on the harvest table, or the harvest table itself. Into the living room she went, checking first Alan's pen-and-ink sketch of the Ruhamah Reed House hanging over the fireplace, though probably a burglar wouldn't consider this priceless art, and Harriet's portrait of Ruhamah Reed over the Sheraton sofa. Where oh where was Harriet, who made Bev seem like Abigail Adams when it came to correspondence? After some postcards from Europe, silence. Eventually Snowy queried the alumnae office and they replied they had no address. Then, five years ago, forwarded by the Eastbourne post office, in Snowy's mailbox arrived a postcard from *India*. Evidently Harriet had done as thorough a job talking her father into that European trip after graduation as she had with the Jaguar purchase, and she'd just kept traveling. Harriet wrote tersely, mysteriously, "Am living in an ashram," but she did give the address. Snowy had to look up ashram in the dictionary: A place of religious retreat, in India. Harriet in a *retreat?* Nonetheless, Snowy joyfully wrote a long newsy letter, mailed the next day, but she didn't receive an answer. A year later she again asked the alumni office for help (alumni now, not alumnae, and Snowy hadn't yet resolved her feelings about Bennington's going coed); again they reported that Harriet Blumburg was "lost."

Nobody had backed up a moving van and stolen that sofa and the glass-fronted bookcases like Mr. Palmquist's, the thin oriental rugs, the tavern table, pedestal table, butterfly table, or the wing chair and the Martha Washington chair which faced the fireplace and the color television beside it, the fireplace blocked off and a Jøtul woodstove installed because of the energy crisis. Alan's chair and hers. Ruhamah watched TV lying on her stomach on the sofa, so she had to watch at an angle. Snowy had watched many a movie in high school at an angle, sitting fashionably on the end of her spine on the fashionable side of the Gunthwaite theater, where the wars on the screen were made in Hollywood. Ruhamah had watched a real war in this living room. Vietnam. Snowy had never got used to the sound of real gunfire, for it didn't seem authentic, not like the movies' barrages. Instead, it sounded like the movie theater's popcorn machine. The cheery noise would send Snowy fleeing the evening news to walk down the road or climb out on the jetty, listening to the waves and the bell buoy in tears.

Unlocking the door from the living room, she checked the front porch, big enough to hold her country-auction triumphs, an expandable oval golden oak dining table with golden oak chairs, a canvas glider, old wicker chairs, painted porch rockers, and here they ate supper, read, talked, and entertained, until cold weather. They always pushed the season, sometimes getting caught by storms before they capitulated and boarded the porch up against winter. Nobody had burgled the porch, or auctioned it off.

She wished Bev and Puddles could visit this place she loved; she wished the triumvirate could be sitting on the porch now, looking at that lobster boat sliding along the horizon. All three of them hadn't got together since Puddles's wedding. Usually she accepted the lingering death of the triumvirate, inevitable under the circumstances, telling herself she must go forward. Anyway, the time Puddles had visited the Ruhamah Reed House apartment, and Bev's visits, had been disasters.

When Bev and Roger were still in Boston during Roger's last year at B.U., they had come up a few times to spend the weekend, first at Alan's apartment (borrowed foldaway bed in the living room) and later the Ruhamah Reed apartment (the foldaway again, but in the spare room), and Snowy was so nervous about boring Roger and Alan with old-school-chum chat, not to mention Alan's falling for Bev, that she had jam-packed the visits with activities, a tour of Old Eastbourne, picnics, a sightseeing boat ride to the Isles of Shoals, lobster dinners, a maritime *museum,* and she and Bev only had a chance to talk privately in the kitchen, their conversations distracted as they hurried to finish making meals, fearing their husbands' small talk might trail off. Snowy said, "Would Roger be interested in seeing an old fort or—" Bev asked, "What on earth are you doing to the celery?" Snowy said, "It's called threading." Bev said, "I've never heard of such a thing. You never used to." Snowy said, "Alan's mother does." "Oh," said Bev.

Then when Bev and Roger moved to Connecticut and started having children, Julia and Fred went down there for holidays and Bev didn't return to Gunthwaite even for a summer visit. On Leon's birth announcement ten years ago, however, Bev wrote, "I'm determined that next summer we'll spend a week with Mother and Fred, and we'll come to Eastbourne. I'm dying to have a heart-to-heart, and the children must meet their almost-aunt. Have you noticed that all their names are above the line? I got extremely sick of writing the y's in Beverly Colby on my school papers." Snowy hadn't noticed and hadn't known, and Bev seemed farther away than ever. She hoped Bev would change her mind and leave the children (and Roger) with Julia and Fred or with Roger's parents to give herself and Bev a fighting chance at a reunion, but five Lamberts arrived at the Ruhamah Reed House, Snowy staring in disbelief as the family got out of the station wagon, so many of them, like a sight gag, Bev holding a baby—and Bev's auburn hair extinguished, turning gray! Did graying hair mean a mousy Bev, aged? Of course not! Bev was even more beautiful, she was striking. Snowy could hear Puddles saying, "It isn't *fair!*" From the beginning, Alan had only commented, "Yes, she's very pretty," yet Snowy knew he enjoyed looking at her; gray hair wouldn't alter that, though maybe all those kids might nip any envy he felt for Roger. Maybe.

Having a heart-to-heart amid three children was impossible, but Snowy and Bev tried during a few minutes alone in the kitchen making the old summer favorite, tuna fish sandwiches, for the throng. Bev said, spooning mayonnaise, "Well, when are you and Alan going to produce an infant I can be the almost-aunt of?" Snowy said, "We keep putting off a decision." Bev said, "Sometimes I look up and wonder what happened and who I am. I certainly wasn't ever the type to adore children, and—you're still threading celery." Snowy said, "I have to admit it stops contortions behind napkins, though it's a big pain in the ass." Bev glanced hastily over her shoulder to see if Mimi or Dick had sneaked into the kitchen, and Snowy warned herself to watch her language. Then Bev said, "Remember one of the summer-boy water-skiers I dated, the one who spent an entire evening flinging me onto his shoulders and around his hips to convince me I could be his partner in his water-skiing act?" "Mmm," Snowy said, remembering another one, Bev's first water-skiing boyfriend with whom Bev had cheated on Roger, causing a breakup. Had Bev forgotten him? Bev said, "All the time I was pregnant last summer, I kept remembering that evening." Snowy said, "Wistful for your waistline?" Bev said, "I don't know. Children. Roger and I ask each other, 'When does the fun part of being parents begin?' " Snowy couldn't think what to say, but Bev laughed and added, "Unlikely, me as a mother—and as a driver. I learned to drive, suburban life demanded it. Eek!"

That had been their final attempt at a reunion. Snowy's reunion with Puddles, also a flop, had occurred earlier, Puddles descending on the apartment in a tornado of twins, up from South Carolina to go to her grandmother's funeral in Portland, dragging reluctant Guy who had previously prevailed upon her to have family holiday gatherings down South and subsequently talked her parents into moving to Helmsdale, into a house he built, when her father retired. "Twins," Puddles said, rescuing Snowy's Staffordshire vases from four little hands, "if I'd known they were going to be such double-trouble, I would've stuffed them back in!"

The lobster boat disappeared, and Ruhamah and Baa-Baa appeared, crossing the road to the jetty. Perhaps this year Ruhamah would find a best friend. Perhaps Michael would become her Dudley. Snowy went back into the living room and climbed the stairs. Alan would inquire, "Are you going to look under the beds?" She did not look under their four-poster, but she did check her jewelry box, although it didn't contain diamonds and rubies, only costume jewelry, some gaudy chains left over from the Sixties and the peace-symbol dog tags she'd bought through an ad in the *New Republic,* a pearl necklace and earrings, and what she'd steal if she were a burglar, two of the three pairs of gold earrings she'd ordered from the catalog of a Bennington jewelry-maker, Ed Levin, when she had her ears pierced ten

170

years ago, pain endured for fashion's sake. The third pair she was wearing, loops. Whenever Ruhamah asked why she couldn't have pierced ears too, Snowy replied, "Because I say so," hearing herself sound just like a mother. She, a mother?

In the spare room, her office, with its wall of books, filing cabinet, pull-out sofa in case of company, and the mahogany veneer desk she'd had since junior high, she opened the fireproof box where she stored her work-in-progress. No poetry-loving thief had purloined the pages accumulated toward her fifth collection. Her fourth would be published next April. Out the window, Ruhamah was twirling a lariat of seaweed over Baa-Baa.

Going back along the hall, Snowy glanced into Ruhamah's room, knowing she shouldn't. Articles in magazines advised: Don't nag; keep your sanity by keeping your children's doors closed. How the hell could she have borne a daughter who, despite persuasive arguments and direct orders, instead of hanging up her clothes threw them on the floor? And soon a toy-animals annex would have to be built unless Ruhamah's grandparents ceased and desisted. In her youth she had also had a menagerie of toy animals, though not so many and not so exotic as the puffin and unicorn and koala bear and anteater which were the stars of Ruhamah's assortment—and hers had sat only on her bed, not all around the floor too, like a sit-in.

Spam. She went downstairs to the kitchen. Alan's father hated Spam, wouldn't allow it to be served in the Sutherland house, because he'd eaten a ton of it in the Army during the War; consequently, of course, to Alan it became a treat he got at friends' houses. A great delicacy! Nowadays putting up with Snowy's conversion to whole foods, he did ask if there could always be a can of Spam in the larder. Okay, tonight she would make the Spam-and-noodles casserole she used to make in her unenlightened days, and since Ruhamah had already eaten she could add onions. A daughter of hers loathed onions? The other day, Ruhamah's kindergarten teacher had reported that Ruhamah had said when confronted with a mid-morning snack of

171

apple crisp, "I don't like it, I've never had it." The teacher was amused, Snowy embarrassed. Ruhamah would *have* to be a changeling, if she hadn't inherited appearance and photographic memory.

Okay, the Yumbo, reheated and shared, their hors d'oeuvre, ham before Spam. My *batterie de cuisine,* Snowy thought, taking a kettle out of a cabinet, starting the supper routine, keeping an eye on Ruhamah out the windows. One child was too much responsibility for her; how did Dudley manage? His letters had stopped after he married Charl, but until recently Julia had sent clippings from the *Gunthwaite Herald* about his news, mainly children. A baby every two years. Horrified, Snowy wondered why glib Dudley hadn't convinced Charl that she wouldn't burn in hell if she shoved in a diaphragm or took the Pill. And why didn't the number of Charl's and Darl's offspring match? Julia had noted, on the clipping announcing the birth of a daughter (Arlene Lee), Charl's second child by Dudley who, added to Jack's three, brought the number to five, "Darl seems to have stopped at four. ???" Snowy wrote back, "Darl must have decided to risk damnation or is very lucky with Vatican Roulette or has become celibate. Celibate, married to Bill LeHoullier?" But Charl continued her population explosion, the total now ten. Charl had probably never read *Cheaper By the Dozen,* yet she'd seen the movie, every kid saw every movie which came to Gunthwaite, so was she aiming for that goal? The seams of the ranch house had earlier split; on the newspaper announcement of #4 (Dudley C. Washburn, Jr.), Julia had written, "Fred says Dudley and Charl have bought a big Victorian house upstream from your folks' house, a bargain in disrepair." Then Julia had sent a newspaper ad: Dudley had gone into business for himself, but how did Washburn's Custom Signs, Gold Leaf Our Specialty, put food on the table to fill so many mouths?

She heard Alan's car and looked out the sink window at the blue Volkswagen parking behind hers, which had formerly been his; she got Alan's hand-me-downs. Ruhamah ran across the road, and he lifted her up, kissed her, set her down, and she

172

skipped off. Was it only-child self-reliance or tact that always caused Ruhamah to make herself scarce a while after Alan got home, letting her parents be alone together? Ruhamah didn't otherwise hide in her room, the way Snowy had.

As Alan walked toward the house he looked weary, unknotting his tie almost feebly. He showed more temple than he had when she'd first stepped into Hopkins Tavern. He opened the side door and she did her Edith Bunker dash to him, shrieking, "How was your day, Archie?"

"Just get me a beer, Edith."

They hugged and kissed. She said, "It's been for*ever*." Two hours, actually, since she'd visited his office.

He stared at the counter. "Spam?"

"I had a touch of flu or something, so I didn't stop for hot dogs. I figured you'd prefer Spam anyway."

"Swine Flu?"

"Whatever it was, it's gone."

"Good."

While he went upstairs to change, she turned on the oven and mixed two gin-and-tonics. Pushing the season. Out the window, Ruhamah and Baa-Baa were stalking a sea gull, which lazily flew off. She plunked the Yumbo on a cookie sheet. The wall phone rang. Karen, she thought, about dinner Saturday night. Damn, some screw-up. She slid the cookie sheet into the oven. "Hello?"

"Henrietta?"

"Oh. Mother." A granddaughter had made her mother profligate with long-distance money, once only spent on emergencies. "How are you? I'll give Ruhamah a shout, she's outdoors—"

"We're in Hanover."

"You're where?" Snowy could think of no more incongruous place. Then, before she started laughing, she remembered that besides Dartmouth, Hanover also meant a hospital. Mary Hitchcock Hospital. Very carefully she turned off the oven.

173

"Your father," her mother said. "They're going to operate tomorrow, maybe you'd better come."

"Operate on what?"

Her mother paused to get the word right. "His pancreas."

Snowy had learned to cope with her panic over taking care of a child by seeking detailed information the pediatrician wouldn't supply, Ruhamah's illnesses sending her to the household medical handbook and the library, studying upper-respiratory infections, wishing she'd gone to Mass. General instead of Bennington. Pancreas? Insulin. Diabetes. You weren't operated on for diabetes, were you? "Does Daddy have diabetes?"

"He's been awful sick, Henrietta. He didn't want you to know until he got well."

"Has he been in the Gunthwaite hospital?"

"They couldn't do anything, they sent him here a week ago."

"A *week* ago? Why didn't you tell me?"

"Your father didn't want—"

"Are you staying in Hanover?" Snowy reached for the telephone notepad and pencil. Her hand was cool and steady, as dry as her eyes. "A rooming house? Is there a vacant room? Okay, reserve it for me, I'll pack and be on my way. What's the address?"

Alan came into the kitchen wearing jeans and a sweatshirt.

Jotting, Snowy said, "Try to rest, Mother. Goodbye."

He raised an eyebrow. "Your mother?" Next he raised his glass. "Confusion to our enemies, particularly bureaucrats, I am so tired of—"

"My father's at Mary Hitchcock, I'm going to Hanover, he's being operated on tomorrow, his pancreas. Where the hell is the pancreas?" Snowy ran into the living room, opened a bookcase, grabbed the medical handbook, but she didn't begin reading; she ran upstairs to her office and dropped the handbook on her desk, on which stood her address book along with a dictionary and thesaurus. C; Cram, Jean. She'd never used Puddles's phone number. Nurses worked odd hours. What hours did Puddles?

174

The twins, age fifteen now, would be home from school. She sat down and dialed. Busy. Out the window, waves sloshed up against the jetty. In its lee, Ruhamah was placing twigs into a cake of sand—playing half-birthday? Snowy took a pencil from her Bennington beer mug and found "pancreas" in the handbook's index. She dialed again. Still busy. *Teenagers.*

Alan tapped on the door jamb, hesitating. "Cancer?"

"That's what I'm thinking and Mother must be, though she won't say it. I bet neither of them has said it."

No muscle was jumping in her jaw. "Want me to go with you? Ruhamah could stay at my folks' or Margaret's."

Snowy dialed. "God, yes, except I don't know how long I'll have to be there. Can you take care of things here, pick Ruhamah up after kindergarten, leave her at your mother's for the afternoon?"

"Sure. You okay? Are you canceling Karen and John?"

"Calling Puddles. It's ringing." In South Carolina.

The nurse, he thought. Typically, Snowy was doing her homework. "Shall I dig you out a suitcase?"

She nodded, and he retreated. A young female voice said, "Hello?"

Of course Puddles's twins would have Southern accents, but Snowy was disconcerted. "Hello, is this Susan or Amy?"

"Susan," said the voice impatiently.

"I'm Snowy, an old friend of your mother's, is she home?"

"*MOM!*" Susan yelled.

Now Snowy's hands started to sweat. She hadn't heard Puddles's voice since that visit over a decade ago.

"I'll be goddamned," Puddles said. "Snowy, did the kid get it right?"

"She did—"

"This is *crazy,* I've been bursting to call *you!* Congratulate me, I just received my certification and I'm a nurse practitioner!"

"Congratulations, but what's a nurse practitioner?"

"Something new, I read an article and got all revved up and

175

took a leave of absence and enrolled, nine months like a baby—how come you're calling, are you going to visit at long last?"

"Puddles, you have a Southern accent!"

"I haven't!"

"Well, slight."

"I can't, I'm still being teased about my Yankee accent. If you'll visit, Guy will do one of his Low Country cookouts, he's planning one this weekend, it's fucking horrible, you'd love it."

"Low Country? Like my wedding-present basket?"

"A kettle of shrimp and corn and Polish sausages and some special seasoning all boiled up, and it has to be eaten off newspapers, he covers the table with newspapers, that's the tradition. My tradition is, I cook myself a hamburger. I'll cook Alan and Ruhamah anything they'd like."

"My father is being operated on tomorrow at Mary Hitchcock. His pancreas. Does that mean cancer?"

Snowy was trusting Puddles not to have developed a bedside manner.

Puddles hadn't. "Probably. The doctor hasn't told your folks?"

"If they've been told, they're playing ostrich. Can a surgeon—cut it all out, so to speak?"

"Depends on how advanced it is."

"I didn't even know he was sick until a few minutes ago when my mother called, my folks have been 'sparing' their paper doll."

Miles and miles away, Puddles heard the anger loud and clear beneath the light sarcasm. "Be glad they did, you may have a long ordeal ahead. Susan, I live in this house too; in fact, I pay the phone bills. Scram."

"If it can't be all removed, how long before he dies?"

"Crotches are my field. OB/GYN, I can give you your annual physical now, I can do just about everything except prescriptions and surgery. Pancreatic cancer, I'm no expert."

"You're almost a gynecologist?"

176

"Jean Cram, ARNP—that's Advanced Registered Nurse Practitioner."

"Male doctors. After all these years, I still dread it."

"I'm going to have my own practice at the Helmsdale Clinic, my own office, with posters of Paul Newman and Robert Redford, and I'm going to put that centerfold of Burt Reynolds on the ceiling over the examining table and nice warm striped socks on the stirrups!"

"Puddles, you'll get more clients than you can—er—handle."

"I'm hoping. It's been a lot of work. I didn't write you on your birthday card about the course in case I didn't make it. How old's your father?"

"Sixty-four. He retired from Trask's last year."

"Has he kept busy? My father's playing golf all day down here, you'd think it'd turn his brain into Jell-O but it's his dream come true."

"My father has devoted himself completely to that house. Scraping and painting shutters, I'd go mad." Yet this was precisely what she'd expected his retirement to consist of, though she'd hoped he might astonish everyone by taking up skydiving or something. "How's your mother, your brothers?"

"Mom's growing geraniums, per usual, and she's having a fit because Malcolm is getting his *second* divorce—can't imagine how he can afford to with what Guy pays him—and Bobby isn't married yet at all, out in Colorado bumming around. How are your mother and Alan and Ruhamah?"

"Fine. Mother is still at Cinderella Shoe, I guess she must've got an emergency leave. Guy, the twins?"

"Guy's on the verge of bankruptcy but that's nothing new. Susan's a cheerleader but Amy didn't try out, couldn't care less, so they aren't like Charl and Darl hogging two places, cute cute. I bet the coach was some pissed off!"

"Are they alike otherwise?"

"Amy wants to be a *doctor* when she grows up, and Susan

177

wants to work for Guy, she can already drive a bulldozer. Oh—do you hear from Bev?"

"Christmas cards and such."

"So do I. Did she write you last year about her folks moving to Florida? For Fred's arthritis?"

"I cannot picture Julia in a Florida bungalow."

"Me neither. And I can't picture having a one-year-old in the house."

"Bev wrote on my birthday card that she's joined the Ninfield Players, she's getting out of the house."

"Yes, she wrote me that too. From what I've seen of acting groups around here, she's hunting for hanky-panky."

"Puddles!"

"Well, did you think she'd stay married to Roger this long? Susan, I told you—"

Snowy said, "May I call you tomorrow evening?"

"I'll check with some people about the pancreas."

"Thank you—and again, congratulations!"

In the bedroom, Snowy found that Alan had opened on the bed her blue vanity case and overnight case, part of the luggage which had replaced her old Skyway for the trip to Britain. She'd donated that white Skyway, painstakingly chosen by her mother and father, to a rummage sale.

Her dizziness this afternoon couldn't have been a premonition.

A MONTH LATER, en route to Hanover the last time, Snowy stopped in Gunthwaite. She and her mother were going together, taking her parents' Ford because it was bigger, more comfortable, more a makeshift ambulance. The other times they'd driven separately, her mother returning home periodically to get a change of clothes, Snowy going home to Pevensay to do the same and to reassure herself that Alan and Ruhamah still existed. Puddles had been right. A long ordeal. And winter had started early, two snowstorms already.

But she'd been spared the flu, or whatever that dizzy spell had been, and she was not, by some crazy mischance, pregnant. At least there were those couple of things to be grateful for.

During their sessions in Hanover, when she and her mother weren't at the hospital Snowy went for walks, recalling Dartmouth boys foraging afield to Bennington, wryly realizing that she had no qualms about allowing women students here, whereas her reaction to a coed Bennington remained mixed. She invited her mother along, but her mother always said, "I'd just as soon stay in my room." Like a blind person, her mother had learned two new places, the rooming house and the hospital, and Snowy understood that she couldn't strain herself further. Her mother didn't actually stay in her bedroom; Snowy would come back to find her in the overstuffed living room watching the gigantic TV, yet the shows weren't a respite, soap-opera hospitals and bedsides.

Once when they were driving from the rooming house to the hospital, her mother briefly groped deeper into her surroundings by asking, "Years ago, you wrote that Bev went to a circus here?"

Snowy glanced over at the placid face, the mask hiding worries. "No, I don't think she ever—"

"Roger took her."

"Oh, *carnival*," Snowy said, surprised her mother had paid attention to news which hadn't involved her daughter. "Winter Carnival, she went twice."

That memory gave Snowy a topic to jabber about during that visit to her father, borrowing from storyteller Bev. During all the visits she talked incessantly, because her parents didn't say anything. Her mother didn't describe a purchase, and her father didn't ask about the house. She also talked because maybe, she hoped, if she kept up this wall of small talk, maybe she wouldn't see his eyes. But the wall was only glass, through

179

which her father looked with those helpless frightened eyes, witnessing finality.

The evening after the operation, Snowy had phoned Puddles and said, "They removed a third of his pancreas, the cancer's too advanced to do more."

"Six months at the most," Puddles said. "According to my sources."

"Six months?"

"That's the guess. I suppose they'll send him home when he's recovered from the operation, you and your mother will need help. There must be a community health agency in Gunthwaite nowadays, make arrangements to have a nurse stop in. Will you have to take care of him alone? Is your mother going back to work?"

"She's got an indefinite emergency leave, without pay. Should I tell my folks how long?"

"If they ask."

"The doctor has said cancer to me and Mother, I assume he has to my father, but I doubt if they'll say it. Or ask."

"Communication is a problem. Try to get them talking."

So Snowy talked, but they just listened, and she knew she didn't want them to shatter the glass. Eating with her mother in the hospital cafeteria, sitting with her in the rooming house watching television before bed, Snowy lapsed into exhausted silence and her mother did occasionally start a conversation, yet she spoke of what was on their plates and the TV screen, not what was on their minds.

And now Snowy drove down the driveway of the Emery Street house in her parents' car, her mother in the passenger seat. Mission: Bring your father home from the hospital. After she was born, he had brought her home from the Gunthwaite hospital, in her mother's arms; when they had brought her home after her tonsillectomy, she had sat in the back wearing the new dress whose purchase her parents were recounting.

Usually the evolution of her hometown upset her, but she was racking her brain for subjects to fill the trip back, so as she drove along Main Street she saw impassively the Princess Beauty Academy now occupying Puddles's A&P, and the Gunthwaite Savings Bank's drive-up window where the demolished Sweetland once stood. The movie theater had been remodeled into three theaters to compete with Cinemas I, I, III on the Miracle Mile. In high school, the theater had gone downhill since its original rococo splendor, but enchantment had lingered.

Hooper's Dairy Bar was flourishing, despite the fast-food chains, and it showed this off with a big new wing of booths, a barn-board exterior, and credit card signs.

Outside of downtown, you could be in Eastbourne or anyplace, the same restaurants and stores, from Arby's to Zayre's, except the malls had different names, the Gunthwaite Mall, the Abnaki Mall, the Lakeside Outlet Mall. There were turnpikes now connecting parts of Gunthwaite, and past the Kentucky Fried Chicken establishment Snowy got on an entrance ramp and swooped over housing developments once woods and farmland. Dudley had said in high school, when they were parking at his special spot on a dirt road beyond a new housing development, "Civilization is encroaching, and where will people go parking twenty years from now?" She took the exit ramp to the road through Leicester, the sports rival town, which led to the interstate.

Her mother said suddenly, "We'll have Thanksgiving."

Oh God.

"Same as usual."

"Mother, are you sure? Daddy's got to be on a diabetic diet." Snowy had been studying the materials about food exchanges the doctor had given them, but she hadn't seen her mother open even the simplest pamphlet.

"Same as usual," her mother said.

Snowy turned on the radio, moving the dial to Public Radio's classical music.

In his hospital room, her father sat in the chair beside the bed, dressed, waiting to go home to die.

During the return trip, Snowy regaled her parents with Ruhamah-reminiscences, not caring if they'd heard them before and not looking into the rear-view mirror at her father's face. "The summer Ruhamah was two," she said, "a desire possessed her to fill the house with bouquets of flowers. She picked every wildflower in our field and put them in vases and glasses everywhere, me close behind with coasters. Each morning she did the wet chore of changing their water, and when Alan came upon her standing on a chair at the sink he decided to give a demonstration, to instruct her unformed mind. He filled the sink with water and held up the sponge and said, 'Let's find out, will it float or will it sink?' Ruhamah grabbed the sponge and threw it in the sink and announced, 'It will exsorb!' "

No reaction. Dementedly, she wanted to stop talking and start singing at the top of her lungs. She turned on the radio.

Then, as they were almost home, dizziness struck. The car was going to shoot off the turnpike; she was going to kill her parents, her father wouldn't die of cancer, he'd die in a car accident. She slowed and took the next exit.

Her mother said, "Henrietta, this isn't ours, the fried-chicken one."

"I'm sorry, I still get mixed up on the new roads."

Down into Gunthwaite she drove, and the streets she'd known all her life steadied her though she drove past familiar sights altered or just plain gone. The junior-senior high school had become only a senior high school, the baby boom having demanded a school of its own, a new junior high across town. The long lawn had been reduced for more parking spaces, but the two brick buildings had grown and were so fat now with additions that they'd swelled onto the practice field. Because of the energy crisis, the tall windows had been shortened, insulated panels and thermoglass installed, and the effect was tinted, as if the school were wearing sunglasses. The school day had ended, and kids swarmed across the lawn, lighting cigarettes. When she was in school here, you would have been hauled off to the principal's office if you *stepped* on the lawn; you'd've probably been drawn and quartered if caught smoking on school grounds.

182

The girls wore jeans. Pea green with envy, she still couldn't get over that, wherever and whenever she saw schoolgirls.

Varney's had become self-service, the station torn down and replaced by outer-space architecture, the old rounded gas pumps now square. It wasn't a hangout anymore. Customers, not boys and jalopies.

How many times had she walked along this street with Bev and Puddles, giggling, gossiping, groaning about homework?

The Congregational church had built a new modern church outside town, where there was plenty of parking, and the Salvation Army had bought the old building. This must amuse Tom, unless living with Joanne had cost him his sense of humor. The grocery store next to it was a pizza joint now.

Inadvertently, Snowy glanced up at the rear-view mirror. Her father was looking at Trask's, the factory in which he had worked forty-five years.

That evening she phoned Alan and reported, "I got him home. They're already in bed. Together. I thought Mother would move into the spare room. He wouldn't eat any supper."

"How are you?"

She was standing in the living room. The telephone was new since her youth, ivory to match the background of the latest wallpaper, Country Heritage, but it sat on the end table beside the sofa where the old black one had always been. She'd done homework over the black phone, yattering away with Bev and Puddles, she'd even phoned a boy—Tom; phoning Dudley to discuss homework didn't qualify as a milestone. And on it she had received Alan's first phone call.

"I'm okay," she said. "Well, actually, I had a dizzy spell, like when I thought I had the flu last month."

"Stressed-out."

"How are you and Ruhamah?"

"Lonesome. You'll be back tomorrow?"

"After I meet the nurse. Oh—Mother's determined to make Thanksgiving dinner."

"Jesus."

183

"I should've expected it, the way they behave about holidays, birthdays, sacred traditions. She'll do the whole works."

"Christmas too?"

"God help us. We'll have to prepare Ruhamah, he looks like hell."

"You sound like hell. Hoarse again."

"They still aren't 'communicating.' I miss you, I love you," she said, touching the sofa on which she and Tom used to neck so feverishly. Umpteen new slipcovers might have been bought for it in the intervening years, but underneath it was the old make-out sofa. She laughed.

"What?" Alan said.

"Getting punchy. Until tomorrow, kiss kiss."

"Kiss kiss."

They hung up, and she tiptoed upstairs to her bedroom which remained the one room her parents hadn't redecorated. The absence of her desk was the only change. When, after her marriage, the desk had gone to Alan's apartment lashed to the roof of her car, her mother hadn't rearranged the bedroom furniture to fill in the gap and Snowy felt there should be an "On Loan" card, a velvet rope across. Her parents had bought the desk at her request when Bev mentioned that Julia and Fred were giving Bev a grown-up desk that junior-high Christmas—"In hopes it'll improve my grades, wasting money I could have spent on clothes!" Her parents had bought the exact duplicate, secretly consulting Julia and then with relish revealing the intrigue upon the unveiling.

Although nowadays this was Ruhamah's room when they happened to stay overnight, Snowy and Alan sleeping in the double bed in the spare room, her parents still called it "Henrietta's room," and her mother had made up this bed for her tonight.

Tears prickled. "Don't," she told herself. She took her address book out of her shoulder bag and went downstairs intending to ward off emotion with a strong dose of Puddles, but she leafed past the C's to the L's and impulsively dialed Bev's num-

184

ber. In Ninfield, Connecticut. On a Christmas card after Bev and Roger had moved there, Bev had described the town as "so tasteful that it's impossible to find places like the post office and the drugstore." The phone rang in Bev and Roger's newest house, which, Bev wrote on a birthday card five years ago, "we intend to be permanent." Reading that, Snowy had remembered Bev's once saying, "What's so great about permanence?", referring to boys. The Pevensay house; Puddles's house; Bev's house; the triumvirate had settled down permanently. And she, Snowy, who probably would have been voted the girl Most Likely to Succeed if their yearbook staff hadn't decided against Superlatives, she was the member who had stayed in New Hampshire, a hick.

"Hello?" Bev's voice. Not heard since the Eastbourne visit nine years ago. Low, cautious.

"I'm sorry, is it too late, I forgot the baby—"

"Is this—Snowy?"

"With laryngitis."

Bev squealed, *"Snowy!"*

"I have a burning question. Did you keep your desk?"

"My desk?"

"You know, our identical desks, like twins."

"Oh horrors, those desks! You're calling about *them?*"

"Not really. What does your house look like? You wrote it's a white Colonial? Does it look like my folks' house?"

"Yes, only more . . ."

"Only more so?"

"Can you imagine, I've gone from Danish modern to collecting pine cupboards. I've just bought my sixth, a jelly cupboard! A mania!" Amongst these cupboards, in the big kitchen of the stupefyingly expensive house, Bev looked out the window where in daylight she would see the swimming pool she hadn't told Snowy about on a Christmas or birthday card. It had been installed a year ago, supposedly for the children but she used it most, pretending to be Esther Williams as she had in the lake when a girl. A swimming pool! They had reached this pinnacle after owning three other houses, the first the one she sometimes perversely found herself missing, a new ranch house, all fresh and hopeful, their neighbors in the development either newly-weds or new parents. Then had come the bigger and bigger houses, each with its particular interior-decorating challenges such as hideous paneling to hide and shocking-pink bathrooms fixtures to mute. And now this—estate, almost! "That desk—I'm trying to remember. It never was my favorite piece of furni-ture, of course, and I guess it must have been part of the things Mother and Fred sold when they moved to Florida. Did you keep yours?"

"Out of necessity at first, and now out of sentiment. How are Julia and Fred?"

"You write your poems there, then? Those desks. Nineteen-fifties veneer. Latin, algebra, *Silas Marner!* Fred isn't well, I'm so afraid Mother's going to be a widow again."

"Damn."

"Roger's father died, his mother is living with a sister in Quebec, she sold the Gunthwaite house. How are your folks?"

"Tell Roger I'm sorry about his father. My father—I'm calling from their house, my mother and I just brought him home from Mary Hitchcock. What are the Ninfield Players doing?"

"We're rehearsing a festival of Christmas plays, and even though I'm the newest member I got the lead in *The Gift of the Magi,* a one-act, I've given in and had my hair dyed to match the wig, she—Della—has her long hair cut in the story—well, I'm certain you remember the story." Bev was babbling, and she wanted to rush on and tell Snowy about Brad, her leading man, just the thought of whom made her tingle between her legs, though this was only flirtation, but flirting at cocktail and din-ner parties never aroused such a sensation, simply reassurance. Roger tolerated the party flirting and joked about it because, she realized, he knew her of old—old!—and because he knew that afterwards in bed she'd be as contented as a cat who'd lapped up a saucer of flattery, feeling sleek and languorous, letting him

186

take his time, children and chores forgotten. But the men at those parties were bores, other lawyers, corporate executives. Brad sold birdhouses! Swanky ones, to be sure, for suburban birds, yet in comparison this made him a romantic. And he was the handsomest man she'd met here. These qualities, however, hadn't kept his wife from divorcing him: "She took wing," as he put it ruefully, "to find herself." So he needed his self-confidence restored, and it was all harmless fun, his phone calls to confer about their roles, the touching during rehearsals, the stage kiss now almost a French kiss. She imagined sleeping with him, she dreamed of it. But in reality she slept only with Roger—and more often, for besides bolstering Brad's morale, the flirtation benefited Roger; if she was a cat after a party, she was a tiger after rehearsals. Roger commented, "Why, it's true, women want it more as they get older." Having given in to Clairol temporarily, she quoted a Clairol ad as an alibi, "I'm not getting older, I'm getting better." Now she asked Snowy, "What's wrong with your father?"

"Cancer of the pancreas. I phoned Puddles when I learned a month ago, and she says maybe six months."

"Oh, Snowy."

"I figured the Eighties would be the decade of death, parents in their seventies, not this soon. Anyway, Puddles sounds great, she's become a nurse practitioner. She says she's going to have that Burt Reynolds centerfold over the examining table, and when I told Alan I asked him if he ever would have posed naked for *Cosmopolitan* holding his hand discreetly, and he said his hand wasn't big enough to be a fig leaf for *him*. Male egos!"

They laughed and laughed, Snowy muffling mirth from upstairs ears.

Thus the triumvirate began to reunite, rallying around Snowy during her vigil, Bev and Puddles phoning her in Pevensay or Gunthwaite, Snowy phoning them. She and Puddles put their phone bills out of their minds for the time being; Roger paid all the bills in Bev's household but she hadn't had to worry about his complaints about her extravagance in years.

Not even with Puddles did Snowy discuss her father, after answering each conversation's initial inquiries. And she didn't consult Puddles about the dizzy spells, which were increasing, for fear Puddles would diagnose a brain tumor. She listened to Puddles lambaste doctors skeptical of nurse practitioners, she speculated about Bev's just perfunctorily mentioning her leading man when telling stories of rehearsals, and she described the latest changes in their hometown. Bev cried, "An outlet mall? How Filene's Basement!" Puddles fumed, "The *Salvation Army?* You mean the place I got married in is full of secondhand clothes?"

But one time Bev said, "I've realized I was too self-centered back then to get to know your father."

"I never did," Snowy said.

Thanksgiving and Christmas. These occasions in her parents' house always appeared to Snowy as such a Norman Rockwell pretense that this year's celebrations turned out not to be so macabre as she'd expected, and when she saw her father watching Ruhamah, the look was gone from his eyes. At Thanksgiving he sat gaunt at the head of the table, his dinner untasted, but he ate his dessert, a piece of pumpkin pie made by Snowy and Ruhamah out of one of Ruhamah's pumpkins. Both he and her mother were ignoring the diabetic diet, and for everyday meals all he wanted was a blueberry muffin; during her visits, Snowy spelled her mother with the Duncan Hines packages, suspecting that her mother wasn't eating much else either and only stocking the refrigerator before her arrival. At Christmastime, he directed the purchase of the best toy animal her mother could find in Gunthwaite for Ruhamah, deciding upon, when her mother brought him the list of choices, a Galápagos turtle. Snowy went to the liquor store and bought his annual Four Roses and then helped her mother make the annual Velveeta on Ritz. He sipped a drink, left the hors d'oeuvres uneaten. At Christmas dinner, he ate half his slice of fruitcake.

Snowy asked Bev, "How did the play go?"

"Wonderful, but I forgot to check with you about managing

long hair, my wig was like a third person on stage, it practically needed stage directions."

"Oh, mine isn't long anymore."

"It isn't? When I last saw you, it was longer than your miniskirt. And in the photo on your last book."

"A shag now, growing out."

"Snowy, this sounds awfully high school, but could you send me a snapshot of you? The pictures on your books *are* you, but they fill me with awe. A snapshot of you, and Alan and Ruhamah?"

"You too. I know the kids from your Christmas cards but not you and Roger."

"Roger has a *mustache*," Bev said, wanting to send Snowy a picture of Brad. "Would you like to see a picture of me in that wig? I'll send you a publicity photo of me and Brad that'll slay you! We pulled it off, though, playing fifteen years younger. Rouge tricks, like when you played the Crybaby in *Hansel and Gretel*."

"If I recall 'The Gift of the Magi' story correctly," said Snowy, who in fact had reread the story since Bev's news, "there's at least one clinch, when he comforts her about the mix-up. A kiss on stage—for me, that'd be impossible. Remember my wedding, how Alan and I scarcely pecked?" Hint, hint.

"It's all just part of acting," Bev said, though it certainly hadn't been. And during the cast party after the festival's last performance, a Christmas party held, at Bev's suggestion, at her house, Bev deciding this was the best strategy of innocence (also more exciting, titillating), Brad had come into the kitchen while she was replenishing a tray of Christmas canapés garnished with green-pepper Christmas trees and wreaths, and he had taken her in his arms for an unrehearsed kiss, a thorough French kiss, holding her so tight that she could feel the erection of this other man pressed against her, perfidy beside a pine pie cupboard. His hand slid onto her breast. High-school flirtation was abruptly adult. Adulterous. Bev had gasped, "The guests—" and escaped with the tray, and now she changed the subject, saying to

Snowy, "Did I ever tell you I have to hide Roger's presents more carefully than the children's? A neighbor keeps them. Way back, Roger told me he always knew what his parents would give him because he'd discovered where his mother hid the presents, in his parents' bedroom closet—not exactly inspired—and when his father was at work and his mother was shopping and his brothers and sisters were somewhere, he'd take his presents out and undo them. He said it was like defusing a bomb in a movie. He would do them up again so well and he'd be so surprised on Christmas Day that nobody ever guessed."

After the second Christmas of her marriage, Snowy had recognized that she was falling into the trap of her background, giving Alan spectacular presents to equal his. As she gushed over these presents he gave her, she remembered how she always had feared she didn't thank her parents profusely enough, and she resolved henceforth to keep hers and Alan's present-giving light-hearted. The next year she said, "We can't afford big-deal presents, let's be realistic, small fun stuff, agreed?" They began exchanging magazine subscriptions, books, records, food treats like canned artichoke hearts, and continued the practice with Ruhamah. No chance of a "Magi" mix-up here. She asked Bev, "What did you give Roger this Christmas?"

"A tennis outfit, another one. I love to buy clothes so much, I even love buying sweatbands!"

"Roger plays tennis?"

"We belong to a tennis club. Haven't I mentioned that?"

"*You* play tennis?"

"Isn't it amazing? You and I in school, detesting gym and sports. I still do, except for tennis—and I don't like tennis when I'm playing with Roger, he's too competitive. Mostly I play with three women friends—we took lessons together—and I've got quite good. Every once in a while in the middle of a game my inner voice says, 'What are you doing here, you can't hit that ball, you're dreadful at sports!' But I ignore it, and I actually win a lot of games."

"Incredible. You own one of those little white tennis outfits?"

"Snowy, I'd have to go to my closet and count how many little white tennis outfits I own."

Outfits. After Christmas, Snowy's father stopped getting dressed. He stayed in bed, coming downstairs only for meals. Wearing his pajamas and bathrobe, he ate his blueberry muffin at the dining room table. His eyes had become larger as he grew thinner.

In addition to being early, this winter was hard. Snowy organized her trips to Gunthwaite around weather reports, dodging snowstorms, yet sometimes she was caught there, enraging Alan who would say when she phoned, "Doesn't your mother have *any*body else to help, just you and a visiting nurse? Hasn't your mother *any* friends?" She'd remind him that her parents had enough friends to have supplied wedding-present booty, china, silver, two-slice toasters. But some of these friends had since moved to Florida, and besides, her parents had been so involved in each other and her and the house that more than token friendships had seemed unnecessary to their vision of their life, so now her mother had none close, literally and figuratively, to sustain her.

One time after Puddles asked how her father was doing, Snowy didn't say briefly, "Okay." She said, "The radio. He's never listened to the radio except for the weather, but he's staying in bed and lately he's got the transistor on the bedside table and he listens to one of those stations that play music that all sounds the same, syrupy violins. Ed, Ed used to listen to the radio in that hospital bed in his folks' apartment, but at least he looked at magazines while he did. And my father is smoking in bed, against his strictest rules. Cigarettes and the radio are keeping him company."

"It's too bad your folks don't have a downstairs bathroom, you could rent a hospital bed for the living room and save your mother the climbs upstairs."

"I don't think she goes up that much, even when I'm not

there. Except at night; she still sleeps with him. When I'm there, I work on a clipboard in my old room part of the day, and occasionally I hear her come up, but they don't talk. Now and then I bring him coffee he doesn't touch and I prattle on about this and that, only I get the impression I'm interrupting his radio, and she must feel the same."

"He's withdrawing."

"He's done that from the beginning." Snowy took a breath; while she was at it, she might as well unburden herself a bit more. "The whole ordeal seems to be affecting my equilibrium. Physically. Sometimes I get dizzy when I'm driving or my legs go shaky when I'm walking. Rooms start spinning."

But Puddles's diagnosis was the same as Alan's. "Stress does funny things."

"Yes. Actually, it started before I knew my father was dying. Weird. Anyway, how're things at the clinic?"

"In my mail today was a catalogue you wouldn't believe, thank *God* it was sent to the clinic instead of home where the girls might've seen it first—how I ever landed on such a mailing list, I wonder if that male chauvinist pig Dr. Redmond put me on it—I've smuggled it into the house to show Guy, I have it here, get a load of these ads: Mr. Terrific, Rotates Wildly With Thrills Galore! Orgy Gel! Erogenous Zone Shampoo! Oriental Sex Doll Eager To Do Your Bidding With Her Pulsating Battery-operated Vagina!"

"Puddles!"

Alan's patience wore thinner, and every time Snowy left for Gunthwaite she could sense the black thundercloud enveloping him; his misery accompanied her.

Bev phoned and exclaimed, "I got the lead in *Same Time, Next Year!*"

"Congratulations! It's a Broadway hit?"

"Yes. Um, Brad and I seem to have the right 'chemistry,' so the director says, and he got the male lead."

Chemistry? Snowy recalled the Christmas festival publicity

192

photo she'd studied with a raised eyebrow. This Brad was a very good-looking man.

Bev dropped her voice to a whisper. "I can't tell anybody in the world except you, please don't even tell Puddles." A pact from the past, to which she added, "Or Alan."

Snowy hesitated over the second reservation, for she told Alan almost everything. If he'd asked about the guys before him, she'd have told him about Tom, wouldn't she? Well, only a précis. Guessing what Bev was on the brink of revealing, she said, "Of course."

"To celebrate, Brad and I went out to lunch in Hartford at a romantic French restaurant but it was a business lunch, professional, a further discussion of our roles, and then Brad suggested going to a motel to get the mood in a real setting—the play takes place in a bed-sitting room in an inn's cottage. We'd just sit and read some of the script aloud."

"Bev."

"Yes, if you were Puddles you'd be saying there's a nice bridge in Brooklyn I could buy. I *knew* what might happen. Have I mentioned he's divorced?"

"You haven't."

Bev fell silent.

Despite her guess, despite being a well-read thirty-seven-year-old woman, Snowy felt as uncomprehending as a child. Inanely she asked, "What does he do for work?"

"He sells birdhouses."

"Huh?"

"It's a very elegant shop, a little gold mine, birdhouses and bird feeders and a range of items from extremely expensive bird books to jeweled hummingbird earrings. The shop is named For The Birds—go ahead and groan."

"Is he a whatchamacallit, an ornithologist?"

"Amateur. His father wanted to set him up in a business and he chose this, not the sort of business his father had in mind, but Brad's a free spirit." Bev plunged on, "We'd driven to Hartford in separate cars, we drove to the motel in separate cars," and she stopped again.

Snowy still couldn't picture Bev behind a wheel. "What kind of car do you have?"

"With this gang, what else but station wagon after station wagon. Roger has the flashy car, a Porsche."

"Wow."

"Roger. I love him, Snowy, but I've known him so long!"

"What kind of car does—Brad have?"

"A BMW. I followed him to the motel, and I'd only had two glasses of wine at lunch but I felt like I'd had a dozen. And then we parked in the parking lot and Brad got out of his car and walked over to mine and opened my door for me just as a woman came out of the restaurant section of the place and she'd obviously drunk that dozen. She looked at us and said, 'Shack-ups!' And Brad and I looked at each other, guilty as sin, and I switched on the ignition and he ran back and jumped in his car."

Snowy began laughing. "I'm sorry, but—"

"We were laughing too before we were out of the parking lot, and I kept laughing until I got near home, and then I was so sick with guilt I drove past and went on a shopping spree and bought clothes for the children and Roger and nothing for me. I was going to do it, I really was. Uh, have you ever—"

"No."

"Not even in fantasies?"

Snowy confessed, "The only person I have erotic dreams about is Alan, my *husband* of all people."

Therefore Bev didn't confide that her own fantasies included Brad and Paul Newman—and Tom Forbes.

Snowy asked, "Are you quitting the Players?"

"Good heavens, no!"

"But the temptation—"

"We've proved we can withstand it," said Bev.

Back and forth from Pevensay to Gunthwaite, back and forth past snowdrifts swirled like ocean waves. Caught once again one day in Gunthwaite by a snowstorm, Snowy phoned

Alan at his office to tell him she wouldn't be home, and later that night she phoned him again after her parents were asleep and said, "Promise me that if we go through this ourselves someday, we'll talk and talk and eat lobster and drink champagne."

"And fuck."

"We would, on our deathbeds." But she thought of her mother upstairs lying beside that skeletal man. "I love you."

"I love you. Goddamnit, I wish you were home!"

The snow turned to rain during the night, and the next morning the icy world was blinding. Beset by river longings, she started to take a slippery walk down the street along the riverbank, the iced-up trees overhead melting in the sun, ice sliding off branches with great crashes as if a hundred chandeliers were breaking.

Then her balance went haywire, and she had to turn back to the security of the house she hated, walking as unsteadily as she had on the *Highland Fling* during that honeymoon storm.

One evening Puddles phoned and said, "Guess what Guy and I did last night when the girls were out on dates."

"Okay, what?"

"We played with a vibrator."

"Puddles!"

"That catalog I got, couldn't resist."

"But Guy—"

"Oh, he isn't jealous, he says that at age forty-seven he could use some help. The trouble with the contraption is, it makes such a racket. It sounds like a dentist's drill!"

"Open wider," Snowy said.

Puddles howled.

Snowy's father stopped coming downstairs entirely. But during a visit in March, when she brought his blueberry muffin to him he said more than his usual "Thank you." Over the radio—violins were playing "Rock around the Clock," for God's sake—he said, "I'll come downstairs for your birthday dinner."

"Please—"

195

"Your latest book, it'll be published this spring?"

"The publication date is April eighteenth."

"Do you have an extra carbon copy or photocopy of your manuscript?"

"I'll bring it next time."

Out in the hall, Snowy looked at the gallery of her school pictures. Her parents had started a new row, with Ruhamah's nursery-school and kindergarten pictures.

In between the lines her father had said he might not live to read this collection, and she had acknowledged it.

And she and Alan and Ruhamah would come here on—let's see, her birthday was on a Saturday this year, and as always they would eat the traditional meal, the menu unchanged since childhood: roast beef and gravy, pan-roasted potatoes, and her favorite vegetable, broccoli, and then chocolate cake with white seven-minute frosting in which her mother wouldn't put a tactful few candles but the entire thirty-eight, thirty-eight pink candles. What would she wish for as she blew out that conflagration?

But when Snowy returned home from this visit, the next morning her mother phoned and said, "He's in a coma. The hospital just called. I'm going there now."

"The hospital?"

"He fell last night. He was getting up to go to the bathroom, I phoned an ambulance, he told me to, and he told me not to call you and wake you up. I'm leaving now."

"So am I. Mother—"

Her mother had hung up. Snowy dialed Alan's number and said, "This is it, he's in a coma. I'm off. How's your schedule, can you come back here and pack some stuff for yourself and Ruhamah, ask your mother to pick Ruhamah up after school, call Ruhamah at school and explain what's happened, and drive to Gunthwaite?"

"Yes, are you okay?"

"I think so."

She didn't pause to change out of her Levi's and sweatshirt.

196

She threw slacks and sweaters and underwear into her suitcase. This morning she'd intended to phone Warren Palmquist (whom she still thought of as Mr. Palmquist) and ask him to send her a set of bound galleys for her father. She ran into her office, dug beneath her work-in-progress in the fireproof box and yanked out the folder containing the photocopy of her latest collection and shoved it in her briefcase. What an idiotic gesture.

She drove the Pevensay-Gunthwaite route faster than she ever had. Not yet, she kept chanting, not yet, I'm not ready, I thought I was but I'm not, not yet not yet. Be practical, she told herself. Her mother would want as fancy a funeral as the Methodist church allowed, and that would cost a fortune; how to talk her into investigating the North Country Coffins business up in Newburgh, which she'd seen advertising pine coffins in the *New Hampshire Times?* Maybe her mother would let her and Alan handle arrangements. After the funeral? Her mother would want to stay in that house, there'd be no question of moving to an apartment.

Not yet, not yet. She flew past a grove of maples tapped the newfangled way with plastic hose. Sap running, spring coming, and her father wouldn't be taking off the storm windows and storm doors this spring.

She reached Gunthwaite without being assailed by dizzy spells. Had her speed kept them at bay?

Since she'd last been to the Gunthwaite hospital to visit paralyzed Ed, some of its Little Canada neighborhood had been bought up and torn down to make room for new wings and parking lots, and the place was unrecognizable. It was also packed; she wasted maybe five minutes trying to find a parking space. When she did, she next couldn't find the old entrance, and, clutching the narrow black leather briefcase, she raced around the building and finally came to the new one. Indoors she slowed, but her voice was high as she asked at the desk, "Henry Snow's room number?"

"You're his daughter?"

197

"Yes."

"Two-twelve. Follow the blue."

She followed the blue stripe on the corridor floor to her father's room. The door was slightly ajar. Her heart thundered. She would open it and see her father's dead body.

She nudged the door, and there was her father sitting up in bed smoking a cigarette. Her mother sat in the chair, her face completely expressionless.

"Henrietta," her father said.

She bent and kissed his hollowed cheek. He must hear her heart.

He said, "That's a fine briefcase. I didn't know you had a briefcase. Did you, Charlotte?"

"No," her mother said.

He asked, "Did Alan give it to you?"

"I bought it in London, I was accumulating so many notes and everything."

"London. Imagine, Charlotte."

Snowy set the briefcase on the bedside table, snapped it open, and laid the folder on the bed.

"Thank you," he said. "Charlotte, Henrietta's latest collection."

Her mother suddenly stood up. "He wants his radio. We'll go home and have lunch and get the radio."

"All right," Snowy said, and to her father she said, "See you this afternoon."

He picked up the folder.

Her mother walked rapidly out of the hospital, and outdoors Snowy asked, "What happened?"

"They revived him. The nurses gave him a needle and brought him back."

"You shouldn't drive. Leave your car, mine's around the other side."

"They brought him back."

Driving home, Snowy chattered, "I wondered if he had a—"

Go ahead, say the word, say death. "—a 'near-death experience,' evidently it isn't painful, it's pleasurable, people report a tunnel and a light and a feeling of peace. Maybe Daddy would like to talk about it; he was talking more just now, did you notice?"

"Tomato soup? Or chicken noodle?"

"Please don't bother feeding me." Snowy drove up the driveway nowadays cleared by a hired kid using her father's snowblower.

"Tomato, I think."

In the kitchen, with robot motions her mother heated a can of soup and made two peanut-butter sandwiches. Snowy phoned Alan's office to tell him it wasn't necessary to come, but he'd already left, and she didn't catch him at their house or his parents' either. In the dining room, she and her mother sat opposite each other, the chair at the head of the table empty.

Snowy said, "Alan will be coming this afternoon, to visit Daddy."

"Ruhamah?"

"She shouldn't miss her nap. She'll stay with the Sutherlands." Snowy lifted a triangle of sandwich, and her throat closed up. Her spoon clattered in her Currier and Ives bowl; she'd spill. Was this what Harriet had gone through in front of guys and had she ever conquered it?

Her mother said, "You took him your poems?"

"He asked."

"A grandson. He was always asking, not out loud."

Snowy looked at her.

Her mother said, "I could only have you. You didn't try."

"Mother, my God—" Snowy jumped up, grabbed her shoulder bag and jacket, and ran out of this terrible house.

In her car, she sped along Emery Street, Chestnut Street, State Avenue, Main Street. The dizziness struck on the Miracle Mile. She braked past an Agway and a Bonanza and saw ahead the sign that advertised signs.

199

WASHBURN'S CUSTOM SIGNS
PAINTED, MAGNETIC, CARVED, PLASTIC, ELECTRIC
BILLBOARDS
GOLD LEAF OUR SPECIALTY

Before, she'd always driven past. Now she crept into the squarely plowed parking lot and stopped beside the other vehicle here, a flatbed truck whose doors repeated the sign. The building was the type she thought of as a modern Quonset hut. Tech-Bilt or some such name. Beige, neat, but not the White House to which Dudley had aspired.

If she got out, would she stand or fall?

She stood, and although the ground tilted she walked, wobbly, heart pounding, into a big room of long tables and benches where a tall balding man was lettering the door of a van: KATY'S CAT

He glanced up. "May I help—*Snowy!*"

"Katy's Cat?"

"Katy's Cathouse."

She laughed, as she had always laughed with Dudley, and they hugged and hugged.

He said, "I've been keeping track of you in the *Herald,* I've got a row of Henrietta Snows on my bookshelf, our Belle of Gunthwaite!" He glanced beyond her out the window. "So you're the VW I've noticed at your folks'."

"My father is dying."

No, she couldn't at last have cried about this when she was alone, could she, or with Alan, or even over the phone with Bev or Puddles. No, she had to break down here, where a customer might walk in at any moment, with someone she hadn't seen in twenty years. And she couldn't cry daintily. Screams, screams, "God*damn*it, god*damn*it!", fists clenched, tears and snot pouring down her face off her chin. Dudley held her.

As she tapered to hiccuppy heaves, he said, "I'm sorry."

"*I'm* sorry. Do you have a bathroom?"

"That door there."

It was plainly a men's room, maintained by a man, but it did have a little mirror, in which she saw a swollen blotchy scarlet reflection with mascara like smeared clown tears. After she found Kleenex in her shoulder bag and blew her nose, she made compresses out of wet paper towels and cooled her face down. Then she cleaned off the mascara. In her shoulder bag was the Ziploc bag containing her emergency cosmetics, and she tremblingly reapplied Revlon makeup, Cover Girl mascara and eyeliner pencil, Cover Girl lipstick.

Repairs done, she gazed helplessly at her reflection. She'd never had that big repair made, the nose job, because by the time she could afford the operation she'd grown resigned to her appearance, and besides, Alan was horrified at the idea. He liked her nose; retroussé, he called it, not a ski jump.

If only she could stay in here. She opened the door and said to Dudley, "I *am* sorry, I didn't mean to go to pieces on you. How is Charl? And your children?"

"The teeming multitude? Our own Little League?"

"Bev's mother sent birth announcements from the *Herald,* I think I've kept up."

"Are you in touch with Bev too?" He patted a bench. "Sit. Unless my Snowy has drastically changed, food would help, but I've had lunch, my lunch box is empty, and though what I'm lettering is 'Katy's Catering Service,' Katy's van's cupboard is bare. Ah—I know." He went to a desk in a corner, pulled out the bottom drawer, and produced a fifth of Jim Beam. "Just like a newspaperman in the movies. Or a private detective." He went into the bathroom, saying, "Tell me about Bev and Puddles and why none of you has been to any of our class reunions."

Snowy said, "I've got to take my mother back to the hospital," but she sat down. "Well, Puddles is too far away, still in South Carolina, and Bev's kind of far too, in Connecticut, and she's busy with her children—she has four."

"*Bev?*" Dudley said from the bathroom. "The mother of four?"

"Including a baby," Snowy said, remembering that when the subject of class reunions had come up during one of their phone calls, Bev had retched and said, "The very thought makes my gorge rise."

Dudley emerged carrying two Dixie cups. "And why haven't you, the vice-president of our senior class, ever attended?"

"Alan—my husband—hates reunions, he's never made me go to any of his." She had, however, met the old pals and a couple of old girlfriends who hadn't left Eastbourne, the girlfriends acting as if they must've somersaulted into a back seat with Alan quicker than you could say Trojan. Who wouldn't? He was Alan. Now *hers*. "So I don't want to inflict a reunion of mine on him." The other reason was that she felt if she went she might as well walk in wearing a sign, gold-leafed by Dudley, that said UNFULFILLED PROMISE. She'd be asked why she wasn't so famous as Rod McKuen, and nobody would understand about the miracle of getting published at all. (But maybe the new collection would win a prize. The Pulitzer, maybe. Sure.) "Thank you," she said, taking a cup. Her father was waiting for his radio. "What are the reunions like, when was the last, the fifteenth?"

Pretending not to see how her hand shook, Dudley sat down beside her. "There almost wasn't a fifteenth. Charl and Darl got into a fight over where to have it." He lifted his cup. "To our reunion."

"Our reunion. Charl and Darl fighting? They never fought, only squabbled." She reminded herself: He's Charl's husband now, no jokes.

"They fought, and I had a ringside seat. Darl wanted the reunion held at the country club as usual, but Charl had a brainstorm and thought it would be wonderful to hold it in the high-school cafeteria."

"The cafeteria?" Snowy could hear Puddles's description of the colors of the cafeteria's cement walls, puke green and baby-shit brown. Probably, though, they'd been repainted in fifteen years.

202

"Other people agreed the cafeteria was a brilliant idea—what nostalgia!—and others thought it was stupid, and everyone lined up on either side, and Charl and Darl stopped speaking."

"They didn't."

"It was like the Great Schism!"

Snowy choked on bourbon and tap water.

"Then," Dudley said, "something occurred to me, me the president, which should have occurred to me sooner, and I checked with the principal who said liquor couldn't be served in the cafeteria. So the country-club faction won."

"Poor Charl. Did she and Darl start speaking again?"

"Not until I began conducting shuttle diplomacy. They'd always worn matching clothes to reunions—"

"They don't otherwise?"

"They used to confer every morning on the phone, I gather, but while Charl was wearing black after Jack died they got out of the habit of matching. Afterwards, church and parties and special occasions only. So I figured the question of clothes would cause a breakthrough. They did indeed start speaking via me and gradually to each other, enough to go shopping together, but at the early phase of the bash Charl was still licking her wounds and Darl was still gloating. Luckily, a few screwdrivers worked wonders, and by the time the evening was over they were singing the school song in each other's arms."

And when Snowy left Washburn's Custom Signs, she was laughing almost as wildly as she'd wept.

The dizziness gone, she drove home to the house on the river, and there in the driveway was Alan's car. Indoors, he stood alone in the kitchen looking baffled.

He said, "Where were you?"

She ran to him. A long kiss; she didn't give a damn if her mother discovered them.

"Ruhamah?" she said. "You explained?"

"She took it matter-of-factly. What's up? Your mother

203

asked me to drive her to the hospital, she's upstairs getting a radio. A radio in a coma?"

"They revived him. I phoned you but—"

"*Revived* him?"

Her mother had washed the lunch dishes and stacked them in the dish drainer.

Alan said, "You've been crying. You went back to the hospital by yourself?"

"Oh, Alan, Mother said my work should be having babies instead of, you know, so I bugged out, I saw an old friend from school, Dudley, remember Julia's sending clippings—"

"She said that? Honest to God, I'll—"

"Shh, she's coming downstairs, fuck it, we're all at the end of our tethers. Better go in my car, I'm parked behind you."

"Muffins," her mother said, opening the refrigerator. "Two, his supper and breakfast, they're the ones you made yesterday; he likes yours best."

Snowy gave a laugh and reached into a cupboard for Saran Wrap. "Duncan Hines is Duncan Hines."

Alan drove, her mother in the passenger seat, Snowy in the back.

At the hospital, they followed the blue stripe to the closed door of her father's room, and her mother didn't knock, being a wife, and they stepped into a commotion of nurses, one of whom said, "Mrs. Snow. We tried phoning you. It just happened again, but he'll be—"

"No," her mother said. "No."

"Mrs. Snow—"

"*Let him die.*"

Snowy had never dreamed her mother possessed such courage. She stared at her father's shrunken body, she who in high school hadn't taken biology because she was afraid of dead things, she who had to ask Alan to clear smashed animals off her jogging road, she who shut her eyes against photographs in news magazines and scenes on the evening news.

Alan said, "Charlotte, is this what you want?"

204

Her mother looked at Snowy.

Snowy lifted the folder off the bedside table and nodded.

"Yes," her mother said.

A nurse said, "We'll call the doctor. Please wait outside."

Her mother set the radio and muffins on the bedside table. "I'll wait here. Henrietta, Alan, you wait in the waiting room."

"I'm staying," Snowy said, taking her mother's hand.

Alan could see the muscle jumping in Snowy's jaw. He put his arm around her shoulders.

So Snowy and Alan stayed, listening to the doctor's arguments, protecting her mother's determination, watching eleven minutes while her father died.

Be practical, she kept telling herself. Think ahead, plan the procedure.

First on the agenda, as they left the hospital, was her mother's car.

Alan asked Snowy, "Are you up to driving your mother home? I'm going to stop off at another doctor's, Dr. Green."

The old name for New Hampshire's state liquor stores, back when they had green fronts.

"I can drive," her mother said. "You go with him, Henrietta." She placed the radio and muffins in her car.

"I'll go with you, Mother."

Her mother drove them home, Snowy holding the folder. It was over. The words never to be said or deeds done. The image of her father lying there.

At the house, she faltered, "Can you try to rest, and later we'll talk about arrangements?"

"Supper," her mother said, putting the muffins in the refrigerator. "I should have gone to the supermarket." She opened a cupboard and took out a can of corned beef hash. "Does Alan like this?"

"Spam, you've got Spam." Snowy scrabbled in the cupboard, urgent with the need to cook. "Noodles, I'll make a casserole he loves. Can't you try to nap?"

Her mother found a package of chocolate pudding. "I'll make dessert."

Alan returned after they'd commenced cooking, and he poured three scotch-on-the-rocks, and then into the driveway drove yet another car, a black car in the dusk, and a man wearing a gray overcoat climbed out and walked along the snow-blower path for the mailman to the front door and knocked.

Her mother said, "The front door?"

"I'll get it." Alan went into the living room.

Snowy knew. She knew what her father must have done. She switched off the stove, remembering a similar gesture in the Pevensay kitchen six months ago when her mother phoned from Hanover.

Alan came back. "Charlotte. It's an undertaker."

Her mother said, "I don't understand."

Snowy followed her mother and Alan to the living room, where the man introduced himself. "I'm Timothy Higley of the Higley Funeral Home. Mrs. Snow, my deepest sympathy."

"How did you—"

"The hospital telephoned me. Several months ago, your husband consulted me. May I sit down?"

Everyone sat, Snowy and Alan on the sofa, her mother in her rocker, the undertaker in the armchair in which her father had sat years of evenings, reading the Manchester *Union* and *Reader's Digest Condensed Books*. While the undertaker enumerated details, Snowy saw her father going to the Higley Funeral Home, ill, alone, sparing her mother these decisions. Cremation—a surprise. Ashes buried in the Birchwood Cemetery; that same day he had bought two plots, only two, she supposed, because he assumed his daughter would want to be buried beside her husband, unaware that their wills stated their ashes be disposed of by the crematorium. No memorial service; the undertaker obviously disapproved.

At last she glanced at her mother. To have your husband do this alone.

Her mother said, "He was a thoughtful man," and tears sprang.

⁂

THE LEFT-FIELD Theory. She'd forgotten that, Snowy realized numbly, hanging up the phone in the Pevensay kitchen a week later. It was her name for troubles-don't-come-singly. The Gunthwaite hospital had just phoned to tell her that her mother had died of a heart attack. Massive, the person said.

SETTLED PERMANENTLY IN Pevensay? Henrietta Snow, poet, living the rest of her life on Ruhamah Reed's seacoast? Ha! At five-thirty Sunday morning, May 3, 1987, as she had every Sunday the past two years, forty-eight-year-old Snowy parked her white Subaru behind Alan's brown Chevy van at the far end of the gravel parking lot beside a white building over which hung a white sign painted by Dudley, the black letters reading WOODCOMBE GENERAL STORE and, discreetly, *Alan Sutherland, Prop.*

In their vehicles, Snowy and Alan had driven three miles from their new home, Hurricane Farm, along a dirt road to the main road through a babble of birdcalls into the center of Woodcombe, the village she and Harriet had visited on their sightseeing tour, whose white houses hadn't changed since Harriet sketched them thirty years ago. This store had been here too; she and Harriet had bought Cokes and Devil Dogs from that Prop.

Alan walked over to the car. "Okay?"

"Uh-huh." She wiped her hands on her light green corduroy jeans. According to the porch thermometer when they left the house, the temperature was freezing, but her hands were as slippery sweaty as if there were a heat wave. There had been a *blizzard* last week—"Naturally," Ruhamah had chortled, "it's my spring vacation, isn't it?"—and though now the foot of snow had mostly melted, dollops remained in the woods. She got out of the car.

On Sunday mornings she invariably had the sensation of attending an *Our Town* production, the scenery real, not imaginary. At any moment in this sleeping village, its main street lined with budding maples, its green lawns sprouting daffodils, a rooster would crow and the Stage Manager would appear and begin to speak.

"Well," Alan said, regarding the bundles of Sunday newspapers dumped on the store's long screened front porch on which sat a deacon's bench, "goodbye to another ten fucking acres of forest."

211

Near the porch stood the gas pumps, which could or couldn't be self-service, depending upon the customer's inclination. Two years ago the store's customers had taken almost all their trade, gasoline and groceries, elsewhere because the store had deteriorated, the old ailing owner having lost the energy to keep up with repairs or even stock, letting supplies dwindle to practically only bread and beer.

When Snowy bent to pick up a bundle of newspapers, Alan noticed that her lean jogger's ass was encased in corduroys. "You'll get newsprint on you," he said, unlocking the front door. "Why didn't you wear Levi's as usual?" Under her jacket a yellow Oxford cloth shirt, instead of a sweatshirt.

"These looked like spring." And last night she had silently made a hesitant springtime resolution: She would try to stay after the store opened at seven.

Lugging in the first bundle, she set it down on the worn wooden floor, switched off the night light, turned up the thermostat, because they stopped using the potbellied stove come May despite the weather, and went outdoors for a second bundle. Although Alan had escaped Old Eastbourne, the store was another example of his rescuing a building from ruin, from the sorry state it had been in when they bought it. He'd set out to lure customers back by having the exterior done first, a new coat of paint, new porch floor and screens, the friendly bench, and townspeople had begun stopping in to meet him and pick up a quart of milk; then gradually they had become regulars. The store, like the white post office next door, was a gathering place once more. Customers did still go to Gunthwaite's big supermarkets to do their major shopping, and Snowy couldn't blame them because the prices *were* lower, the selection far greater. Indeed, because of lack of variety, because the store's wholesale price was apt to be higher than the supermarket's retail, Alan himself shopped at a supermarket whenever he went to the Gunthwaite Mall, saying he should don a disguise. Unable to go into a supermarket herself anymore, or a mall, she would give him a shopping list, advising thrift, for they were on a strict budget again after this move to Woodcombe, though she hadn't yet had to resort to Night-Before-Payday Casserole. She remembered the glory of supermarkets' unbelievable bounty, wondering what a Russian resigned to waiting in line for hours to buy a rotten cabbage might think if dropped into such a place.

No rotten cabbages in the Woodcombe General Store, where fresh vegetables were as much a staple as milk and eggs. She prided the store on this but knew Alan considered the meat its specialty, having improved on the basic meat-cutting lessons he'd got from the old owner by studying books about butchery. Another specialty was cheese: Every country store must feature a wheel of Cheddar, and Alan had Brie and Havarti and blue, too. Wine could be sold in New Hampshire's grocery stores now, so one shelf held bottles at New Hampshire's low-low prices, which were as much a tourist attraction as the lakes and mountains. Also necessary for the summer people was the correct country-store décor, including the potbellied stove. Overhead an array of boots dangled from the ceiling, even though most of the customers bought theirs at L.L. Bean; above the soft-drinks cooler a pair of snowshoes was heraldic on a wall; dill pickles floated in a wooden barrel; impulse shelves near the cash register offered jugs of local maple syrup, jars of local honey, Saran-Wrapped fudge and cookies homemade by Irene, Alan's helper; behind the cash register, clamps holding slips, hung the antique rack for charge sales with which he'd replaced the regular rack when he found this discarded in the storeroom and had it repaired and refinished; beside the door a bulletin board announced grange and garden-club meetings, baby-sitting services (including Ruhamah's), lost-and-found pets, food and rummage sales. A final touch was the glimpse of the antique rolltop desk in the back room, Alan's office.

Alan carried in two bundles and took scissors and pencils from behind the counter. "Can you?"

Sometimes she could cut the plastic straps binding the bundles and write the names of customers on the newspapers, and sometimes she started shaking. Alan, she thought, lived with a

handicapped person. She tossed her jacket over the bread rack.
"Yes."

And she did cut these straps and those of the other bundles
he brought in. He locked the door, and they arranged the reserved newspapers on the counter and began writing. So-and-so
got the *Boston Globe,* So-and-so got the *New York Times,* and
a depressingly large number of people got the Loeb paper, the
New Hampshire Sunday News, the Sunday paper her father had
always bought. On one wall were pigeonholes for reserved daily
newspapers, but the compartments were too small for Sunday's
behemoths. Doing the Sunday newspapers reminded her of the
Smoke Signal, Gunthwaite's monthly school newspaper. Before
homeroom on publication day, the staff would line up along the
chest-high auditorium stage and fold the twelve hundred copies
and deliver them to the homerooms in the junior and senior
high; as editor, she had overseen this procedure. Without shaking.

Thank God for the *Donahue* show. It was run at midday,
and one lunchtime in Pevensay she'd been half-reading a magazine and half-watching the kitchen television, when she realized
they were discussing her problem, which had worsened over the
years. There were other people like her! She wasn't crazy! The
problem had a name: agoraphobia.

She'd phoned her doctor, who prescribed Valium. Ah yes,
male doctors doping high-strung female patients. She phoned
Karen at the Pevensay library and hedged, "I saw a *Donahue*
that made me think maybe Emily Dickinson was an agoraphobic, I might try an article—" Karen said, "An agora-what?"
"Agoraphobic," Snowy said, "have you anything on agoraphobia, could you get me stuff from the State Library, what's in
Subject Guide to Books in Print?" She did her homework, studying the involuntary nervous system, the fight-flight response,
"sensitization" and "desensitization," pondering the various
theories about the causes of agoraphobia. Opinions also varied
about therapies, but most involved a shrink. She checked the
phone book and found seven psychiatrists and psychologists in

214

Eastbourne, some advertising Biofeedback and Stress Management, terms that got her laughing. Then—oh shit, they were all men. Men: With the knowledge she wasn't insane, she'd been able to tell Bev and Puddles more about the panic attacks, yet she hadn't really described their extent to Alan, pretending her hermit's life was still a choice, making excuses about not driving, not shopping alone, asking him to pick up groceries on his way home. Too busy, her work, the housework, the gardening. After they moved to Woodcombe, she opened the area phone book to the yellow pages; five shrinks in Gunthwaite, male. Well, she couldn't afford one of either sex now, though Puddles kept upbraiding her because she didn't call the Department of Mental Health to ask about local agencies and support groups.

Mid-life crisis was the name given to what had happened to Alan two years ago last month. Old Eastbourne had been frantically organizing its summertime tours, exhibits, demonstrations, lectures, symposiums, and one night Alan had said while they sat on the fish house porch after Ruhamah had gone to bed, "I can't bear another summer. Dragging my ass, going through the motions."

He'd been saying this every spring for many a year. She hated to see his despondent face when he came home, she dreaded an evening of griping, a summer of misery. If she suggested therapy or antidepressant medication, she provoked his same old wrathful response of "It's normal to be depressed!", and who was she to argue when she was behaving like an ostrich about her own problem? So thus that evening she had sipped her gin-and-tonic and only said, "Mmm," and listened to the waves against the jetty.

Then he began to cry. He had never cried—at least in her presence—since Ruhamah was born. He stood up, turning away from her, but she jumped up and flung her arms around him. His whole body was quaking, his gritted sobs seemingly wrenched from his feet. He didn't know how to cry, to yowl it out, which was just as well so he wouldn't wake Ruhamah, but she thought he was going to choke to death.

215

She said, "It's okay. It's okay."

"We've got the money."

She could hardly understand his words. "Money?"

"Buy a business. Be free of committees, boards of directors, bosses, jerks. A new life."

They'd sat up late on the porch talking about the invested money from her parents' house now a law office, about what they could get for a winterized house on the ocean, about small businesses. Snowy said, "Anything except a restaurant," remembering her Sweetland days. That night Alan slept like a log, while she rubbed his back to continue comforting him even asleep; during their courtship she'd discovered he liked best having his bottom rubbed, but he was too tall, she'd smother under the covers, so she only rubbed his bottom at the start of their bedtime and then scooched up to concentrate on his back, laughing at this man who, if he went to a massage parlor, would actually be seeking a massage. She rubbed, listening to the waves. She couldn't move away from her ocean, her waves. Yet maybe a move would prove shock treatment for agoraphobia.

The search began, evenings, weekends, Snowy going with Alan and realtors when she felt capable of not disgracing herself by falling ("jelly-legs" was how the books put it) or bolting or having a heart attack, otherwise inventing excuses. Ruhamah sometimes accompanied them, alternately excited and resentful. Snowy did hope they'd find something on the seacoast, but prices were steep and the search ranged inland, and eventually there came the trip to investigate a general store up in Woodcombe. After the tour of the store section, while Alan and the realtor explored the downstairs stockroom and upstairs storeroom, Snowy hurried giddily outdoors and stood on the rickety porch, beside a post in case the floor or her balance collapsed. Doing deep-breathing exercises, she looked at the pretty village, seeing herself and Harriet.

"Possibilities," Alan said, joining her.

She said, "Gunthwaite. The nearest city."

"Hometown a difficulty?"

216

Its memories.

The realtor said, "As for a place to live—" and drove them out of the village along a lake, onto a dirt road. "Hold tight, everybody calls this the Roller Coaster Road, but the real name is Thorne Road, named after the Thorne family, been in Woodcombe generations, still here, Cleora and Isaac, she was a Woodcombe Sawyer, in their seventies now. The Thornes' is the only other farm on the road, couple of miles farther. Now this," he said, turning at a mailbox that read HURRICANE FARM, "this is Hurricane Farm, so named because it survived the hurricane of seventeen-eighty-eight that caused a lot of damage—"

Snowy stopped listening. They were driving up a long driveway to Julia's place. Although there was no lake view and behind the farm rose a mountain topped by a fire tower, although this old white shutterless Cape had an ell with a side screened porch that made it bigger than Julia's and its barn had white clapboards instead of gray shingles, she was reminded exactly, and when the realtor parked in front of the barn and Snowy saw an old orchard beyond the backyard and, tuned in again, clearly heard the realtor start apologizing because previous owners had sold off all but fifteen acres to a logging company and some of the remaining land was being consumed by a beaver swamp—a bog!, she recognized kismet.

That evening, as they sat together at the kitchen table in Pevensay with paper and pencil, Alan's pocket calculator tap-tapping like a chickadee cracking a sunflower seed, she realized that handling the finances of a business was too complicated for her; she couldn't help him with this, but damnit, by dint of sheer willpower and all the tricks she'd learned from books and tapes, the relaxation breathing, meditation, self-hypnosis—not to mention the cautious use of Valium—she would be his partner in every other way, working side by side in Mom-and-Pop companionship, whatever business he chose. Tap-tap-tap went the calculator, and Alan said, "If we can get the store for a hundred thousand and the farm for a hundred and twenty-five, it'll be tight but we can swing it." So she would be living near

Gunthwaite, in a meticulously restored version of Julia's farm.

Now at the store Snowy wrote "Wilcox" on the last *New York Times*. "There, finis." She took out her list and did her week's grocery shopping.

Alan said, "Careful driving home."

"Well." She left the bags beside the cash register and wandered over to the produce counter. In the summer, she gave him her extra vegetables to sell. Vegetables and helping with the Sunday newspapers were her sole contributions. On the official opening day of the store, when a second customer had come in while he was waiting on the first, she had panicked and fled into the stockroom and hidden behind an island of cases of soft drinks. Soon Alan followed her in. "I'm sorry," she said, "I'm either going to explode or faint." He said, "It's *that bad?*" "Yes," she said, trembling. He took the keys to the van out of his pocket and said, "Go home and calm down." They had driven here together in his van. Bought after they bought the store, the van was standard shift, and she could barely drive the automatic Subaru a short distance. "I'll walk," she said. He said, "The blackflies will eat you alive—" She said, "The fly dope on the counter, could you bring me some?" So she had walked home in a cloud of fly dope and hovering blackflies, the road undulating, the woods wavering.

When he had got home that evening he found her in the garden hoeing furiously, and just as furiously he asked, "What the hell is wrong with you?"

Although she knew Ruhamah was in her room doing homework, Snowy glanced around to make sure they were alone. "Agoraphobia. I've told you."

"You didn't tell me you were a fucking basket case."

And because she hadn't told him this, she'd allowed him to buy a business without complete information. Tears dropped straight off her face onto the earth. "I'm sorry," she said. "I'll try again tomorrow."

"What caused it all to start, way back?"

She hacked at weeds with the hoe. "I think maybe it was

218

triggered by that poetry reading I did for Karen, and my folks' death exacerbated it, and it's kept getting worse. But nobody really knows the reasons."

"You have dizzy spells. What else?"

"They're panic attacks. I feel like I'm going to lose my balance, fly apart, have a heart attack."

"Shouldn't you see a shrink?"

She looked up at him. "Shouldn't you?"

They stared at each other. Stubborn, she thought, both of them. Independent; determined to handle their problems by themselves, logically, rationally. Protecting their pride.

He turned and strode back to the house.

She'd spent the rest of that week going to the store with him each morning, then dashing into the stockroom when customers arrived, then walking home in tears. Alan hired Irene Mason, a plump and earnest local woman who worked every day except, being a devout Methodist, Sunday mornings (Alan closed the store Sunday afternoons). Two years later, Snowy was nearly a shut-in.

The store's door rattled.

Alan said, "Customer."

"It's okay."

He glanced at her, flipped the CLOSED sign to OPEN, and unlocked the door. A man came in, unrepentantly bought a *New Hampshire Sunday News* from Alan, and left. Next, a woman came in for her *Boston Globe* and the leg of lamb she'd ordered. While the woman and Alan were discussing the leg at the meat case, Snowy examined mushrooms although she'd already selected a pound, a luxury she squeezed into her budget. Then the door opened again.

An elderly man rushed in, snatched up a *New York Times,* and glared at Alan impatiently.

Snowy walked toward the man and went behind the counter to the cash register. Impossible that a person's heart could thud so hard and not cause a heart attack. The books claimed that agoraphobics never did have heart attacks during panic attacks, but she was certain she'd be the exception. Massive, like her mother's. The newspaper the man held was marked "Barlow." Alan brought gossip and descriptions of customers home to Snowy, and she remembered his saying, "Cedric Barlow— retired widower, rich, grumpy, and when he buys a dozen eggs, he counts them."

Grumpy Cedric Barlow said, "Always too much to do in May."

And Snowy recalled that on a Sunday-afternoon drive Alan had pointed out the Barlow place, joyous with flowerbeds. *Mirabile dictu,* he had the correct change! He put the dollar and a quarter in her wet outstretched hand and bustled away, while the store spun around and around.

"Snowy?" Alan stood beside her.

She set the money on the cash register. "One *New York Times.* I'll be going home now."

She drove off gripping the steering wheel, but she was rejoicing: I waited on a customer!

The morning had warmed up. She drove past the post office, the town hall, the high-steepled Federated church, the library, the historical society, and the old white school building which housed both the junior and senior high schools, where Ruhamah was now a sophomore. Worrying about Ruhamah's transferring here two years ago, Snowy had hoped such a small school wouldn't be intimidating to a newcomer. Yet maybe the opposite was true. In any case, Ruhamah might mention a Jennifer and a Kim, but she never brought them home or stayed overnight at their houses; in Pevensay too, Ruhamah hadn't found a Bev and Puddles. Whose fault? Mine, Snowy feared. Ruhamah was embarrassed by her handicapped mother.

As for boyfriends, Ruhamah didn't even mention any. Were boys still scared off by A-student girls? Ruhamah, unlike Snowy, *thrived* on exams. There were dances and parties, to which Ruhamah and Jennifer and Kim went without escorts, and whatever pairing up that took place during the evening apparently didn't last. Snowy had thought things would change as

Ruhamah's sophomore year progressed and more and more kids turned sixteen and got their driver's licenses, but she guessed Ruhamah hadn't yet gone parking. Ruhamah herself had got her license last month. Sweet sixteen and never been—? When Snowy consulted Bev over the phone about teenagers' social life, Bev said, "Kids nowadays don't seem to date steadily as early as we did, thank heavens." Snowy said, "On the news, teenage pregnancy—" Bev said, "Well, maybe they have intercourse, but they don't go steady." "Eek!" Snowy said. Bev added, "Etta has reached the crush stage, she's worshiping her riding instructor from afar. Mercifully, she continues to worship her horse too. The agonies of youth! With Dick and Leon, age sixteen brought the end of maturity, but Mimi handled it better—girls seem to. Don't worry about Ruhamah."

Snowy did, however, and at the conclusion of phone calls Puddles now asked, "Has Ruhamah decided to try out for cheerleading?" Snowy's wish after Ruhamah's birth that cheerleading would be abolished hadn't come true, though she gathered it wasn't so important anymore, girls' sports gaining prestige, but Ruhamah and field hockey? Definitely not girls' basketball, Ruhamah having grown only two inches taller than Snowy, who studied all the photographs of the Woodcombe High School cheerleading squad in the *Gunthwaite Herald*. Six girls; Gunthwaite still had eight. When she'd casually asked Ruhamah about the WHS squad, Ruhamah didn't act particularly interested but had acquired every detail. There wasn't a JV squad, Ruhamah said, only Varsity, and since Woodcombe was too small for football, they just cheered for the Varsity basketball team "which," Ruhamah said, "has quite a good record in its division." Snowy asked, "How's its record in other indoor sports?" Ruhamah said, "Mother!", a name she only used to discipline Snowy. Girls couldn't try out until the June of their sophomore year. Ruhamah's June was a month away, but she hadn't indicated any ambition.

Since their move here, Ruhamah had started staying in her room a lot. This is normal, Snowy told herself and Alan.

221

She left the village center behind. What she called the Monet season was beginning, buds a green haze. Ferns were unfurling. She drove along Woodcombe Lake, where on their way to the store today she and Alan had seen a pair of loons emphatically black in the mist, swimming across the silent satiny stretch of lake pale beneath the pastel mountains.

Onto the Roller Coaster Road she turned, driving so slowly the car didn't bounce over the renowned bumps. Beside the road, wild apple trees had begun to blossom, pink-tinged white. Some apple trees were invisible, hiding in the woods, but when she jogged from her house to the Thornes' farm she smelled the perfume and she would say, "I know you're in there."

She couldn't jog Sundays, because of the newspapers. Next Sunday she would attempt to wait on two customers. Salt, perhaps that was part of the answer. She had quit salt at long last, figuring in her lifetime she must've consumed more than any ship ever unloaded on the Eastbourne docks, and her innards felt a difference, a lessening of tension. No agoraphobia book she'd read had suggested a salt-free diet. Then she saw her sweaty hands clutching the steering wheel, she remembered the whirling store.

At the mailbox she drove up the driveway along which, the first autumn here, she'd planted daffodil bulbs. These masses of daffodils had bloomed right through last week's blizzard, provoking a poem. She ought to break her rule about showing unpublished poems and send it to Julia.

This winter Bev had phoned and said, "I'm sorry but I've got to tell—Mother says all Florida doctors are quacks stealing Medicare, but she's had stomach pains and finally went to one, and they operated today. I telephoned the hospital a few minutes ago and talked to the doctor. Snowy, he told me she's just packed with cancer." Although Bev's voice faltered, it was Snowy who started to cry. Bev went on, "When she's able to go home, I'll fly down and drive her to her bungalow."

Yes. Bev would have to take care of Julia alone, Fred having died of a heart attack nine years ago. Snowy had hoped Julia

222

would return north, but Julia had said wryly, on the phone to Bev, "I've become spoiled by the climate."

Bev said, "I'll stay with Mother two weeks, I think that's the longest Roger can cope."

Roger's mother couldn't come help run the household; she too had died. Mimi, who'd be twenty-five in November, had graduated from Rhode Island School of Design and was busy working. Dick, age twenty-three, was at Yale Law. Etta, age twelve, was still living at home, a reasonable situation for her but not for Leon, who would be twenty-one in September. Snowy knew Bev's distress about Leon's refusing to go to college, while Roger, Bev had said, wanted to toss him out—a son of his backsliding into a factory-worker heritage! Bev had prevented expulsion, and since high school Leon had done odd jobs in the area, apparently feeling no desire to leave the nest despite his father's displeasure.

Two weeks later Bev phoned and said, "I'm home, but midway between Florida and here I wanted to parachute out of the plane and vanish."

"What?"

"I expected that being with Mother would be hard, but it was easy compared with Roger's phone calls. He called me every night, in a fit over disaster after disaster. The major ones were, the water heater sprung a leak, a stove burner caught on fire, and Leon threw a party that made the neighbors call the police. Roger didn't cope at all! I do not understand how a man who advises corporate presidents can't handle one young adult and one child and a house for two weeks!"

"How is Julia?"

"She weighed ninety-nine pounds when I arrived. She weighs a hundred and four now, and she can drive, visit friends, though she isn't up to weaving. She's started chemotherapy—absolute hell. She sends thanks for your letter and the flowers. Have you seen Mimi since I've been away?"

Snowy was still disconcerted by the strangeness of seeing Mimi occasionally, not having seen Bev in two decades. Unlike

223

Bev, Mimi had inherited more than height from Julia; she had also inherited Julia's gawkiness, and her talent. Mimi was a weaver. As Julia had, she wove for the New Hampshire League of Arts and Crafts, which had changed its name to the League of New Hampshire Craftsmen. She lived nearby in Leicester with Lloyd Quinn, whom she'd met at RISD. He came from Nashua, New Hampshire, and when Mimi had gone home with him to meet his parents, she and Lloyd had driven to Pevensay to visit Snowy and Alan and Ruhamah after driving to Gunthwaite so Mimi could give him a tour of her mother's hometown. Then, when they graduated, Lloyd had taken a job doing graphics for a printer in Leicester, the very printing company to which Snowy used to drive back and forth getting the *Smoke Signal* printed. Taller than Mimi and as skinny, but serene, Lloyd had frizzy black hair that wouldn't fit into a bushel basket and an equally rampant beard. Mimi wore her brown hair in a long braid. They looked a throwback to the Sixties.

Snowy said, "Mimi visited one afternoon and she was fine; she'd finished a placemat order." Mimi worked on Julia's looms, which Julia had given her upon moving to Florida, keeping only the smallest.

Usually Bev's inquiries included, "Did she say anything about getting married?" and Snowy would reply, "No," wishing Bev wasn't so bourgeois, but this time Bev continued, "Snowy, you'll never guess what I've done. When I was picking up the newspapers they'd spread on the cellar floor because of the water-heater leak, I noticed a course advertised. Real estate, a ten-week course. It's held in the high school, seven to ten o'clock every Wednesday night. I phoned and enrolled."

"*Real estate?*"

"Houses are something I know about; we've owned four. And it's less drastic than vanishing."

"Your acting," Snowy said, "the Ninfield Players, I figured that was enough—"

"Since Brad remarried and left Ninfield, being on stage is my only thrill, but I'm an amateur. Nine years it's been since he

224

remarried. Nine years." Bev saw the strong curve from Brad's neck to his shoulder, felt the smoothness of his skin there, and her eyes were tight with tears. "Do you believe people who say they wouldn't change anything if they could live their lives over?"

"Well, I envy them."

"A two-year flirtation. Not an affair."

"You didn't dare risk the children."

"The children, the children. If I had an affair with Brad, Roger might find out and get a divorce and the children. If I accepted Brad's marriage proposals—and was he proposing just to lure me into bed because I wouldn't any other way or was it really true love?—if I accepted and asked for a divorce, Roger would find out about him and say I'd been having an affair and get the children. Divorcing a lawyer is disastrous. Besides the children," Bev said bitterly, "I would've risked losing this house, *and* the swimming pool, *and* my pine cupboards!"

"Brad wasn't exactly a pauper."

"I chose security! Me! And I loved him!" Although she'd known Brad must not be going without sex so she must have rivals, when he told her at the cast party after *Come Back, Little Sheba* that he was marrying a woman he'd met bird-watching, Bev was devastated, shocked, betrayed. He and his new (young) bride had moved to Oregon, and For The Birds was now a gourmet fast-food shop where she sometimes masochistically bought supper, trying to recapture rapture as she waited for her ground-sirloin hamburgers with avocado. Other male Players flirted, many seriously, but—Bev looked at herself in the kitchen mirror, mouthing Della's *Magi* line: "Please God, make him think I'm still pretty." Make whom? She *was*. She whipped a Kleenex out of the decorator dispenser and said to Snowy, "Anyway, I'm an amateur in a local acting group. Would writing poems that never see the light of day be enough for you? You and Puddles are professionals. I want to be a professional something, un-secretarial, and I'm too old to go to New York to casting calls. It will take all my courage just to face those classes.

225

I haven't set foot in a classroom in twenty-eight years except for the children."

Driving past daffodils into the barn where barn swallows were nesting on the rafters above the hayloft, Snowy tried out a phrase: the fragility of our forties. She still did her daily stint at her desk, but she was too ashamed to tell Bev—or Puddles or Alan's family or anyone except Alan and Ruhamah—the truth about her work's *not* seeing the light of day. Commonwealth Publishing had been bought up by a conglomerate five years ago, and its poetry department had been razed as completely as Sweetland. In the massacre of editors, Warren Palmquist was a victim who now edited an airline company's magazine. She had sent out her next collection to other publishers; they rejected it. Her latest collection was now making the rounds. Whenever Bev or anybody asked when another collection would be published, she said, "Oh, in my old age I work more slowly." Alan's fury about the situation upset her further, but, always efficient, she wept in the shower so he and Ruhamah wouldn't know. Hating to talk about it, nonetheless as she had retired the rejected collection she had felt she must try to explain to Ruhamah, then age twelve, who might be embarrassed by her agoraphobia but had been proud of the books, had helped with the correcting of galleys, had been writing her own poems, emulating a career, and who hadn't yet referred to this death in the family. Acting philosophical, Snowy had said, "Luck runs out," acting optimistic, adding, "But luck can change." On her face mute misery, Ruhamah asked flippantly, "How can it do both?" If Ruhamah had written more poems since Snowy's collections ceased, she kept them to herself. Snowy continued submitting poetry to magazines, dreading Alan's insistence on celebrating any acceptance by going out to dinner, which, thanks to her handicap, meant take-out. Sham festivities, cold pizza.

She parked below the hayloft. Plastic stapled to the joists overhead protected vehicles from bird shit; the realtor had said that Mr. Penrose, the previous owner, had installed this. Fastidious, the Penroses. Because Mr. Penrose had died and Mrs. Penrose had moved to Arizona before Snowy and Alan were shown the place, they had had to deduce Penrose traits. She opened her door and got out. The barn hadn't been a working barn for years, but an aroma lingered which pleased her despite the images the smell conjured up of doing milking in thirty-below weather, shivering, fingers cracked, the way Cleora Thorne still had to. A combination toolshed and workshop had been built into the end of the barn by Mr. Penrose, who must have had considerable time on his hands for he'd actually painted black silhouettes of tools on the walls, from scythe to pliers. Whenever Snowy hung a rake or a hoe back up against its silhouette, she thought of Peter Pan's shadow. "Boy," she would say, "why are you crying?"

As she stepped out of the barn carrying the groceries, above the rush of the brook beyond the orchard she heard spring peepers yelling their heads off in the swamp. She missed the sound of the ocean, but in the spring there was this, just like at Julia's, and if the wind was right you could hear in the Thornes' pasture a cow bell tolling like a bell buoy.

The telescoping of time! She had lived here two years and it seemed a wink, whereas the years of high school and college had been as long as the Paleolithic Age.

In the herb garden beside the ell porch, a chipmunk was sitting in the chives, looking up at her anxiously yet tame enough not to dart away. It had no cat to worry about or any dog; after Baa-Baa had been killed by a summer-people's German shepherd roaming free down the Pevensay Point Road, Ruhamah had never wanted a pet again. When the chives bloomed, their blossoms would match the nearby lilac bush whose buds were ready to burst.

She went up the porch steps, marveling at the astonishing assortment of boots which country living required. She'd thought they had plenty in Pevensay, but they had accumulated even more in Woodcombe, and on the porch she walked past her old dirt-encrusted resoled Maine Hunting Shoes into the big low-ceilinged kitchen where, if she opened the coat closet, she would see other Maine Hunting Shoes, Woodsman boots, Sorels, Wellingtons, Ruhamah's ski boots, plus dressy boots. And in her youth she'd deemed boots inconvenient, unromantic! The house felt empty, Ruhamah going through a phase of sleeping until noon on weekends. Before this, you couldn't have pried her out of bed Sundays early enough to help with the newspapers anyway, but Ruhamah did work for Alan occasionally Saturday afternoons and had worked for him last summer.

The phone rang. While Snowy had broken her habit of checking the house upon her return to make sure it hadn't been robbed, Alan had developed the habit of checking to make sure she got home safely. She said, "Hello?" The phone was on the wall beside a window facing the barn, and on the nearest countertop was her mother's rooster memo pad; she had amazed herself by keeping the rooster collection she'd despised all her life, though the memo pad was the only item she used, the rest of the roosters packed away in the attic.

Alan said, "You got home okay?"

"At my snail's pace."

He paused. Responsibility; guilt. He'd heard of an A.A. term, "enabler," and he feared he enabled Snowy to remain agoraphobic by not demanding she seek help, by doing the things she couldn't, but it was just plain easier. Should he make a big deal out of her effort at the store? "Thank you for waiting on Barlow."

Embarrassed, she asked, "What was the result of the leg-of-lamb conference?"

"The leg is now partly a roast and partly shish-kebab material."

"Food—how about a picnic at the swamp? If the bugs are too bad, we can move back to the porch."

"Okay."

"Thank you for calling, sweetheart."

They hung up, and she put the groceries away. She loved this ell kitchen with its familiar things, her *batterie de cuisine*, the

228

houseplants, the clamshells and sand dollars on the windowsill over the sink, its furnishings from the Ruhamah Reed House apartment and the fish house—and from her parents' house: Under the harvest table was the rug braided by her grandmother that had lain under the maple dining room table, the one rug her parents hadn't replaced when they bought new ones. She'd sold the maple table at which she'd done so much time. There were Woodcombe additions to these possessions, the black wood-stove beside the door to the woodshed, the new (it's been *two* years) yellow gingham tab curtains she'd bought by mail. She did love this nice big kitchen, and she wished she could use it properly, making food for cocktail parties, dinner parties—they had a dining room here! Making, with Ruhamah, cookies for pajama parties. She asked aloud, "Who were you back then in Eastbourne, you who could make spaghetti for a whole bunch of people while now you fret about the perfection of sandwiches for three? You who in Pevensay, for five years before the onset, carried to the table a tray of lobsters held *high above shoulder,* Bev-style, to wow your company? You who in Boston didn't care if the chafing-dish fudge was a flop?"

Her poems were clues, yet she hated rereading herself, so she avoided the printed page. Impossible, though, to avoid rereading the pages in her photographic memory.

"Who were you when—"

The phone interrupted.

"It never fails," Bev said. "This time when I was in Florida, Leon threw another party, the washing machine broke down, and Etta's horse fell in the swimming pool!"

"God. How is Julia?"

Bev looked out a kitchen window at the swimming pool's torn blue lining. "The chemotherapy is wearing her out more and more. She's decided to give it up."

Not yet, Snowy thought, not yet.

"She wouldn't come back with me," Bev said. "I don't know how I drove away from that bungalow in that rented car, Mother waving. She's—dauntless. She insisted I go home for my last class and the exam. She helped me study while I was down there."

"Exam?"

"The real estate exam."

"You're actually—"

"I'm terrified, I assumed the course would be about houses, but it's about how to pass the exam; it's about *fiduciaries* which I can't even spell. Mother gave me pep talks, but I'm sure I'll flunk—and she's so proud of me for taking the course. Roger just laughs at me."

"When's the exam? How long have you got to study?"

"The sixteenth. If only we could swap and you'd take the exam for me, the way Charl and Darl used to fool teachers."

Why, Snowy wondered, hadn't Bev ever completely comprehended that she also had been terrified of exams, had also hated school?

Bev said, "I want desperately to get my real estate sales license. One afternoon before this trip to Florida, I took a break from those ghastly books and when I was browsing in a dress shop for real estate outfits—professional!—I overheard at the lingerie counter a woman with a traumatic emergency, she'd bought a dress to wear somewhere that night but she'd discovered when she got it home that it was cut so low in back that all her bras showed, and she had brought in a bra pinned to mark how low the bra she was hunting for should be, so the clerk started pulling out bra after bra, and another clerk joined them and they finally found one that would do but it was white and she wanted beige, and I was snickering away until all at once I realized she could be me. I've done similar things so often! Fiduciaries made me feel superior. Have you seen Mimi?"

"She phoned on Ruhamah's birthday, she and Ruhamah talked and then we had a chat. Have you phoned her since you got back? Does she know Julia's decision?"

"I'm calling her next. Did she say anything about getting married?"

"No. We talked about mountain-climbing, she and Lloyd

230

are climbing Mt. Pascataquac some weekend—that's the mountain behind this place—and she invited us along."

"Sometimes I can't believe she's my daughter, she *adores* the outdoors. Remember whenever we had to climb a mountain in Girl Scouts, we'd never have reached the top except for Puddles nipping at our heels? Did our troop climb Mt. Pascataquac?"

"In eighth grade, but you and I got out of going because we had colds. Puddles was very suspicious. Alan and Ruhamah have climbed it a few times; they say our barn roof can be seen from the top."

"Will you go with Mimi and Lloyd?"

Snowy had told Mimi maybe, planning to beg off and ask Alan and Ruhamah to go or just Ruhamah, in whom Mimi took an interest which was more aunt-like than cousin-like because of the age difference. Snowy said, "I'm out straight, planting," and quoted Cedric Barlow, "There's always too much to do in May."

Excuses, Bev thought, bending a thumb backward.

Snowy said quickly, "Guess what I found in the mailbox the other day, an invitation to a Fifties party next Saturday night."

"A Fifties party?"

"A 'Fabulous Fifties' party, have you ever been to one?"

"Oh horrors, no!"

"What do I *wear?*"

"You mean you can go? Your attacks."

"It's the Fletchers, we've been to their house before."

"Familiarity breeds confidence?"

"Sometimes. And we can leave early, the town knows we have to get up at an ungodly hour—pun!—on Sundays. I didn't save any of my Fifties clothes, did you?" When Snowy had cleaned out the Emery Street house, she'd taken a carload of clothes, her parents' from their closets, hers from their attic, to the Salvation Army in which Puddles (and Tom) had been married.

Bev said, "I've forgotten, I suppose whatever clothes were in Mother's attic went the way of my Fifties desk. Roger saved

231

some stuff, his letter sweater. Did Alan save his letter sweater? You could wear that, going steady for how many years next month?"

"Twenty-six." And last year they hadn't celebrated their twenty-fifth anniversary with a trip to Nova Scotia, as they'd pledged on their honeymoon; they couldn't afford to, Alan said. Besides, there was the matter of her handicap. Snowy said, "That makes you and Roger twenty-eight years next month." She would have bet Tom's letter sweater that Bev wouldn't have stayed married to Roger for twenty-eight *months*. "Alan didn't save anything. A curator—an ex-curator—ought to want to save every stick and stitch, but at home he's a great believer in throwing things out, I keep accusing him of liking a trip to the dump better than sex."

They laughed, and Bev said, "A gray sweatshirt! Have you got a gray sweatshirt and a white blouse and jeans—Levi's—what did we call them back then?"

"Dungarees."

"Turn up your collar and roll up your dungarees. Isn't it funny to see turned-up collars back in fashion?"

"Gray sweatshirt, yes, and Alan's got one, and Levi's too, and when I threw out my own letter sweater, I kept a couple of the letters, the cheerleading letter, a relic, and the G.A.A. letter to prove I survived the Girls' Athletic Association."

"Us, goalies! How barbaric!"

"I'll sew the cheerleading one on my sweatshirt and the G.A.A. one on Alan's, we didn't do that then but it'll be a letter-sweater gesture—my hair, my hair's all wrong."

"Mine's wronger," said Bev, looking in the mirror at her white helmet.

With her free hand, Snowy lifted her hair. Once every six weeks, after school, she would walk into the village and meet Ruhamah at the Village Beauty Salon in Marge Ames's ell, where she and Ruhamah would have their similar hair cut *differently*, Ruhamah's an intentionally disheveled mane, Snowy's shorter but shoulder-length, defying the law that said women over forty should be shorn. The presence of Ruhamah usually kept Marge's room from spinning, the floor from tugging, and they joked about how Ruhamah had more money than Snowy so she paid, and then she and Ruhamah would either walk home or, if it was too dark and cold, go to the store and Snowy would read in Alan's office and Ruhamah would do homework or help Alan, until he closed up and they drove home with him. All this to get a haircut. Now that Ruhamah had her license, she could chauffeur them to Marge's. "Well," Snowy judged, "I can manage a ponytail shorter than in high school."

"A Shetland-ponytail! I'll phone next Sunday, I want to hear everything."

"You'll be talking with Julia this week? Give her my love. I'll write her today. I'd phone her, but I'd cry."

"She sends her love to you. Damn, *I'm* going to cry. One of my big acting talents, weeping at will. Since I left her there, I can't will myself not to cry. I must, I've got to put this household to rights. A broken washing machine and no clean towels! They had to call the fire department to rescue Prancer from the swimming pool, and they used every towel in the house to dry him off. Goodbye until Sunday."

"Goodbye, Bev." Hanging up, Snowy heard a sound like distant dogs barking, but she recognized what it really was and ran outdoors. A chain of geese flew overhead. To be capable of flight, she thought, of just getting on a plane to fly to Florida. Nowadays the word for Julia would probably be mentor. This didn't exactly sum things up.

Who had she been when she'd flown to England?

Indoors, she made a mug of chamomile tea, which Ruhamah had dubbed Peter Rabbit tea, and carried it into the main house, walking through the dining room past the new (antique, bought by Alan at an auction two years ago) cherry dining table and chairs into the living room arranged as much as possible like the Pevensay living room to ease the jolt of moving for Ruhamah, the television set beside the Jøtul installed in the shallow brick fireplace. Off the center hallway was their bedroom and the

233

downstairs bathroom; she climbed the stairs to the second floor: another bathroom, her office, and Ruhamah's room overlooking the side hill they'd named Violet Hill because of the profusion of violets each springtime, beginning now to bloom. Behind Ruhamah's closed door would be more stuffed toy animals, still given by Alan's folks, and one Ruhamah had bought for herself, a baby seal.

Typewriter clatter had never disturbed Ruhamah, but Snowy's typewriter stayed quiet a long time before Snowy finally wrote, tears trickling, "Dear Julia: Bev has phoned. A brave decision." Paragraph, and she hammered out news about Ruhamah's school and Alan's store, and then she typed up a copy of the daffodils poem and enclosed it.

Sliding a fresh piece of paper in, she next typed, "The fragility of our forties," and spent the rest of the morning staring at these words, at the walls of books, at her view of woods out of which had stepped last fall twin fawns. Twins! They'd been an excuse to blow the telephone budget and call Puddles. Fragility? Puddles had always only looked fragile. Did she nowadays, as the triumvirate neared age fifty? Puddles's news during the fawns phone call was that some evenings, after her practitioner work, she was giving lectures on menopause. And this winter Puddles had phoned to announce she'd just learned from her daughter Susan, who was Guy's foreman—"Foreperson?" Snowy asked—and who'd got married a year ago, that a baby was due in May, one baby, a son, not twin girls. Menopause; grandmotherhood imminent.

At noon Snowy left her office. Ruhamah, she could hear, had got up, was showering. She herself had never slept late when she was a kid, and she'd gone crazy at pajama parties when everybody snoozed forever while she was starving for breakfast. She went downstairs, and in the kitchen she put the mug into the dishwasher, opened the refrigerator and took out a head of leaf lettuce and washed and spun some leaves, opened a cupboard and took out a can of low-salt tuna fish.

"Hi," Ruhamah said, strolling in wearing jeans and a

234

T-shirt which was a gaudy tangerine because she was still rebel-
ling against *Color Me Beautiful*'s decree that she and Snowy
were the type who should wear soft pastels. She carried a package of Kraft Macaroni & Cheese Dinner.

Snowy said, "Alan and I are going to picnic at the swamp.
Want to have a little cereal now and come eat lunch with us?"

"Thanks, I guess not."

"Pretty soon the bugs will be so bad there'll be no more
picnics."

"I've got homework."

"Oh."

Ruhamah began boiling a saucepan of water for the macaroni, and Snowy, adding onion to the tuna fish since Ruhamah
wasn't partaking, mentally shut her eyes. Ruhamah's midday
weekend breakfasts consisted of this salty glop that Snowy refused to stock in her cupboards so Ruhamah brought it home
from the store and kept it in her room. Weekday breakfasts
weren't much better; Ruhamah spurned the Erewhon cereals
available, the whole-wheat bread, but did eat an English muffin—with a scoop of black raspberry ice cream, also personally
acquired at the store, on top. Snowy sighed, reminding herself
of the time she and Puddles were sleeping over at Bev's and the
next morning they discovered only one heel of bread in the
breadbox so Bev and Snowy let Puddles have this for toast while
they themselves investigated the refrigerator and breakfasted on
the remains of the gingerbread they'd made last night, accompanied by Julia's leftover anchovies, Puddles retching.

"Sneakers," Snowy said. "We don't own any white sneakers, just running shoes."

"What?"

"For the Fifties party. Are plain white sneakers even sold
anymore?"

"Tennis shoes, Snowy."

"Oh yes, and Bev must have a closetful, but Alan and I—eu-
reka, we'll take off our shoes when we get there and pretend it's
a sock hop."

"The seniors had a sock hop."

"They did?"

"To earn money for graduation."

"I'm surprised they knew what one was—is."

"Probably somebody's mother's idea."

"An elderly mother," Snowy said, carefully packing lettuce and tuna fish into pita bread. "Was this one of the dances you went to?"

"Nope."

The isolation booth of adolescence!

They heard the van, and Ruhamah said, "Alan's home."

Out of the refrigerator Snowy took a bottle of Miller Lite which she almost didn't allow in the house because of the way it was spelled, and as Alan came into the kitchen she did her Edith Bunker dash. "Here's your beer, Archie."

"Just put it there, Edith."

Ruhamah said, "Honestly, Mother, you're so *dated*."

Snowy said, "To think I spent seven hours in labor to produce such insolence."

"I've read," Ruhamah said, "that you should masturbate during labor."

Snowy saw Alan almost drop the beer he'd picked up. "Why?" she asked, for science.

Alan scrammed, into the main house.

Ruhamah said, enjoying her bombshell, "It cuts down the labor pains or something."

"Oh," Snowy said. She put green pepper strips into a Baggie. "That would have caused a commotion in a hospital sixteen years ago. Where'd you read this?"

"One of those books you're always giving me."

Which Snowy didn't always read first, just skimmed. "Oh," she said again. Ruhamah drained the macaroni and stirred in butter and milk and the powdered cheese that smelled like Friday lunch in the Gunthwaite High School cafeteria. Snowy glanced away, out the sink window. What in the world, she thought, is a jackass doing in our yard?

236

It stood looking at her over the daffodils. A blimp of a body on knobby-kneed stilts. Not a jackass.

"Ruhamah," she whispered. "In the yard. A moose. Our first." Alan, she summoned telepathically, get back here, don't hide from the womenfolk.

Ruhamah hurried to the window, and Alan came into the kitchen deliberately introducing another subject, "When do you want me to go buy tomato plants and—"

"Shh," Ruhamah whispered, "a moose."

He joined them at the window. "No antlers."

The moose stood immobile, enormous and eerie, grotesquely beautiful.

Snowy returned to reality enough to fear huge hooves clumping through daffodils, demolishing the peas in the vegetable garden. But when the moose did move, it moseyed directly through the orchard to the woods.

Alan said, "Terrific, New Hampshire's going to copy Maine and have a moose-hunting season. Like shooting the Thornes' cows."

He sounded exhausted. Even before the arrival of summer people, Sunday mornings were busy, the newspaper customers, churchgoers, and he had to work alone. Her fault. Snowy said, "Our picnic, do we dare go in the woods?"

"Of course," he said.

Ruhamah said to Snowy, "That's the only place you *do* dare go," and dished up her defiant breakfast.

Snowy looked at her, then Baggied four sodium-free cholesterol-free fructose-sweetened chocolate chip cookies, and took two more beers out of the refrigerator and rolled them in sheets of newspaper to keep them cold. Into Ruhamah's rucksack she put a clean trash can liner, napkins, the beers, and the rest of lunch, and armed herself with a container of Deep Woods Off, nonaerosol. "Ready?" she asked Alan.

He chugalugged, adjusted the straps, and lifted the rucksack.

"Have fun," Ruhamah said, as if she were sending the children out to play.

Examining hoofprints big as dessert plates, Snowy and Alan crossed the backyard past the picnic table beneath the pines, the vegetable garden in the sun, listening to the frantic splashing of the brook, the subdued midday throb of spring peepers.

Snowy said, "A female moose, or male? Males must shed antlers like male deer, new growth in spring."

"I don't know."

"I'll see what the library has and do some reading up." The village library was open four afternoons and one evening a week; on those evenings Snowy asked Alan for a lift, and after she selected the books, he handled things, gossiping while the librarian stamped them out, Snowy staying in the stacks supposedly browsing.

He said, "Ruhamah has been doing some reading up."

"Shouldn't give her the satisfaction of a reaction."

"She's a little wise guy."

"That's better than the other way around. My mother— when I first got my period, I would've thought I was bleeding to death if I hadn't been prepared by Bev, who'd been prepared by Julia, and even then we were horrified. Oh, Alan, Julia—"

But she didn't tell him about the chemotherapy because they'd skirted the orchard and reached the brook which was now so loud she'd have to shout. It wasn't simply splashing; the golden-brown water was thumping, thudding, galloping, it was a family of moose! She handed Alan the fly dope, today's chilly start not having discouraged the blackflies, and they walked alongside the brook up the old logging road into the woods.

Bright green cornucopias, Solomon's seal, had punctured the woods floor. Here, where you had to step over a mossy green log in leaf mold moldering, she had seen a coyote last month as it came around a bend. A dog, she had thought, no, fox, no. It was gone in a blink, and a moment later she remembered a newspaper article about how coyotes had appeared in New Hampshire in recent years. She hadn't seen the coyote again, though Alan said that when he'd mentioned her adventure to customers a few had reported sightings, and then both she and he had begun hearing howling on Pascataquac at dawn and dusk. Brushing bugs away from her face, she took back the fly dope and sprayed.

The brook quieted, spreading out past the long dam into the bowl of the beaver swamp, sleek brown water glinting, the logging road flooded, dead end. Stumps protruded. Trees lay felled or stood gnawed at beaver-height into hour-glass shapes. As Snowy and Alan approached, the spring peepers shut up entirely. Snowy was moving stealthily now, out of force of habit because she usually came here in the evening when the beavers were awake and working instead of sleeping the day away.

This swamp was even better than Julia's bog, thanks to these beavers. Snowy had begun to try getting acquainted with them her first autumn here. Remembering Julia's apples for deer, she had filled a paper bag with dropped apples, Ruhamah enthusiastically helping, and together in the evenings at sunset they had walked up to the banking on tiptoe, but invariably they stepped on twigs that crackled and out in the swamp there would be the indignant smack of a beaver's tail. Despite the lure of the apples tossed into the water, the beavers never resurfaced. Ruhamah, impatient, gave up and stayed home. You had to be patient, Snowy kept exhorting herself. (You also had to ignore Alan's comments—out of Ruhamah's earshot—about wide-open beaver.) Evening after evening she lugged a bag of apples into the woods and crept up to stand on the banking and impersonate a tree. The inevitable tail-slap made her smile, it sounded so deep, like a boulder dropped into the water. Then one magical evening it was apparently only a token slap, for soon a brown hummock appeared. Absolutely silent swimming, gliding, peeling the water away. The beaver came so close that Snowy had a pang of misgiving over its intentions and large teeth, but it veered away. When she tossed the first apple in slow motion, the beaver didn't slap and dive; it swam over to nudge the floating apple with its head, maneuvering to bite in, where-upon it climbed up onto a rock and, hunched, began eating, the sound of munching like the grating of a carrot. After it finished,

239

off it swam. In search of a second helping? She tossed more. Soon other beavers were silently swimming forth from the lodge, a dome of sticks on the far side of the swamp. She continued tossing; they swam and ate. Dusk darkening. Alone with these creatures bobbing for apples.

During subsequent evenings she had started sorting out different sizes and personalities. There were the adolescent apple addicts, devouring singlemindedly and making hands-off noises when any other beaver came near; there were the cautious babies; there were the big parents, who dined quickly and went to work stripping logs or towing branches. Come winter, she had snowshoed across the swamp, once plunging through up to one hip when she got too close to the lodge where the ice was warmed by their snug presence. In the springtime, her evening vigils began again, and the silence of beavers swimming in the limpid glowing pond would be brushed by a thrum of wings overhead as ducks slanted down to land with a whisper, plash plash plash.

"Last night," she told Alan, "I heard twigs snapping over there and saw a dark form that lengthened out into a deer stopping by for a drink."

Alan balanced the rucksack on the picnic seat, a fallen white birch, its protuberances of gray fungus as solid as stone and two of them level, shelves to rest beer bottles on. "Maybe a moose this afternoon."

Unzipping the rucksack, Snowy took out the trash can liner, the tarpaulin she'd improvised for picnics, and draped it over the birch to protect her good pants. "Listen."

In the lodge, the babies, kits, were awake and squeaking like a basket of puppies.

Alan said, "You love it here."

She glanced at him. He stood gazing across the swamp, his shoulders slumped, his face so tired. He worked six and a half days a week. Her fault. She said, "Yes, I love it here. The swamp, Hurricane Farm, the whole place."

240

"Maybe I should've stayed at Old Eastbourne for the security. Steady income."

"My God, Alan, Old Eastbourne was killing you! You'd've had a heart attack if we stayed! We're managing fine here on our budget, aren't we?" But as she spoke, she thought that the stress of being his own boss could cause that heart attack. "Even though you're working too hard, don't *you* love it here, aren't you happier?" Then she thought: It's never been in his nature to be happy; I have to be the Merry Sunshine for both of us.

"Ah," Alan said, "who wouldn't be happy, with all this beaver presence," and he kissed her, a sudden kiss like the long-ago kiss in his Volkswagen outside the Old Eastbourne office, but now he didn't apologize. He began to unbutton her shirt.

Snowy said, *"Alan!* The bugs—Ruhamah—"

He twitched the tarp off the birch onto the ground and pulled her down, kissing her so greedily she shed her worries faster than her clothes. And his. No time for blackflies to bite that hard-on, right into her he went, she was his Deep Woods Off, and he was protecting her breasts with his mouth, back and forth, and then he began to groan and shudder, and she shrieked, and a flock of blue jays flew up screaming out of some treetops.

Blackflies didn't permit any lingering cuddling. She said, "Can you reach the rucksack? Napkins. And where's the fly dope!"

After their picnic, as they walked out of the woods away from the roaring brook, she asked, "Have I got a silly smile on my face too?"

"Shit-eating grin."

"We must compose ourselves for Ruhamah, in case she isn't in her room."

"Is that the dinner bell?"

They stopped, and Snowy heard the big antique brass dinner bell she'd bought in those years when she was able to go to auctions.

"God," she said, "something's happened—Ruhamah—"
She ran.

Ruhamah stood on the porch, bell raised. "Puddles!" she shouted.

Alan panted, "Puddles?"

"I told her you were at the swamp and should be home soon if she wanted to call back, but she remembered how I've rung for you, Snowy, in the garden, and she asked me to ring so I gave it a try. Did you see the moose again?"

Snowy went into the kitchen. "What can be so urgent—oh Jesus H. Christ, is Puddles a grandmother? Hello?"

Puddles said, "Bev phoned about her mother stopping chemotherapy. You need sheer iron will to face those treatments."

"And to stop them."

"The quality of life. When people blab about the quality of time they give their kids versus the quantity, I want to throttle them, they're just fucking relieved they've found that cliché, but with this it's different, quality of life, quantity of life."

"Did Bev ask you how long?"

"She didn't, but are you?"

"Yes."

"I'll check."

"Has Susan—"

"She's big enough for twins, though she still swears it's one boy, and she'd deliver in her bulldozer if I let her, but I told her I'd have Guy fire her if she didn't quit work at least a week before the baby's due. He may have to fire everyone, including my brother, the business is on the skids again, mortgage rates going up. Did you ever think I'd be paying attention to mortgage rates?"

"How's Amy?" Snowy asked. Amy was an intern now.

"She's bringing a new boyfriend to one of Guy's god-awful cookouts this afternoon, let's hope he's an improvement over her usual losers—she's got all these fellow doctors to choose from and she brings home dropouts. But if he has a hamburger

242

with me, I'll declare him a future son-in-law. Have you got an audience?"

"Huh?"

"Kitchen phone or office?"

"Kitchen."

"Could you go upstairs?"

"Okay. Alan?" Snowy handed Alan the receiver. "I'll get out of the way upstairs, say hi to Puddles." She wanted to detour to a bathroom, but she went up into her office.

"—Low-Country cookout," Puddles was saying.

"Yum," Snowy said. "I'm here."

Alan said to Puddles, "Good to talk with you," and hung up.

Puddles asked, "How's the flow?"

"Under control," Snowy said, regretting that she'd told Puddles that once while Ruhamah was at school she had picked her way across the mess in Ruhamah's room to the bookcases and, thanks to the indexes of some of "those books," found information which assured her she wasn't dying when occasionally ten Tampaxes and a dozen Kotexes weren't enough to feel so-called safe.

Yet this afternoon she didn't get a long-distance menopause lecture. Puddles said, "My menopause classes *are* popular, and Guy believes I've had to expand them from two nights a week to five, but as a matter of fact the other three nights from seven to nine I've been, well, I've been having an affair."

"*You?*"

"Have you ever?"

"Me?"

"Even a housebound person can have an affair. Or before your agoraphobia—why the hell won't you phone the Mental Health—"

"*You're* having an *affair?*"

"I bet Bev has had many, and I almost asked her except the timing didn't seem right, she was so upset about her mother."

It was like fumbling through fog, Snowy thought. Were

243

Bev's real estate classes not legitimate? Bev hadn't mentioned any other man since that Brad remarried. If Bev was planning to take the exam, she must be taking the course—or wasn't the course required? No. Bev wouldn't lie to her. Snowy said, "Who's the guy you're—I mean—"

"He isn't a Guy, he's Calvin Merrill. Calvin owns a little mattress factory that does custom work, and a month ago at long last I got around to going there to order a new mattress for the cradle that's been in the Cram family for generations, Guy's mother made me use it, rotating the twins, I'm passing it down to Susan. Well, Calvin's clerk was out sick, and Calvin waited on me himself in this roomful of mattresses and pretty soon we were on one in the workroom, and that's where I am now from seven to nine Monday, Wednesday, Friday, and Calvin's telling his wife he's working late on a big order."

"He's married?" Another new thought struck Snowy. Was Roger, not Bev, unfaithful?

"Calvin's a doll, Snowy, and he's thirty-five years old, and I'm almost a grandmother with a husband who's pushing sixty. I didn't realize how hot to trot I was—and wouldn't you know I'd wait to have an affair during AIDS."

"Oh my God, Puddles!"

"After the first time, we've used skins. Calvin is certainly hetero, but that's no guarantee, and he claims he's been faithful and so has his wife, they've been married ten years, but ever since Gene—Being in love means taking the risk. Skins, it's like going parking again!"

Puddles, Snowy reminded herself, always was crazy. "Are you thinking of—divorce?"

"I'm not thinking of anything except when I'll see Calvin next. Tomorrow night. Two hours is so short! We don't just fuck, we talk and talk. I had to tell you, I want to say his name every other word, I want to tell *Guy* how happy I am!"

"Does Guy suspect?"

"I'm keeping him happy too. Nowadays he's getting lazy, likes blow jobs all the time. Are you mainly vaginal or clitoral?"

"Puddles!" Blushing, Snowy answered, "The latter," remembering being vaginal on a trash can liner rather recently.

"I'm more vaginal, so Calvin is filling my void."

They began laughing.

Puddles asked, "Ruhamah decided about cheerleading?"

"I gather she hasn't."

"Off to the cookout. Take care. Calvin Calvin Calvin." Puddles hung up.

Feeling as much a prude as *John* Calvin, Snowy sat at her desk looking at her Bennington beer mug holding pencils, a souvenir of years of parking and Trojans.

There was a tap on her door, and Alan opened it and leaned in, carrying the wastebasket from Ruhamah's room. "Call over? Wastebasket collection. Got anything?"

His Sunday afternoon dump trip. Snowy stood up, saw beyond him that Ruhamah's door was closed, and tipped her wastebasket into Ruhamah's. Puddles hadn't asked her not to tell anybody and evidently would be telling Bev. She went downstairs with him and in the kitchen said, "Puddles is having an affair."

"That's dumber than ever since AIDS." He emptied the wastebasket into the big kitchen wastebasket. "Anything else you want to get rid of?"

She laughed. "And you're having an orgy today, aren't you."

He grinned, kissed her, and said, "Back in a while."

She watched him cross the side yard into the barn and load the van with trash bags. He honked and drove off, and she went into the bathroom, returned to the kitchen. She would now proceed to create more junk for him to cart away next Sunday and for herself to put on the compost pile. Routine, habit. Taking out her crêpe pan, she recited William James: "Habit is the enormous flywheel of society." The Thornes' cows reminded her of that whenever she saw them plodding home from the pasture at milking time. Her Sunday-night suppers were always some sort of crêpes, and as she mixed the batter, making

245

the crêpes up ahead, as Alan came home with his emptied van and she read on the porch while he puttered in the barn, as she stirred their gin-and-(no-salt)-seltzers, as she filled the crêpes with spinach and mushrooms and baked them, as she and Alan and Ruhamah ate on the porch at the golden oak table, and later, dishes washed and put away, as they watched a rerun of *Upstairs, Downstairs*, a favorite episode about the King's coming to dinner, Snowy savored an unaccustomed sense of peace, strangely caused by Puddles. Then Ruhamah went upstairs to bed. Alan had once said, commenting on the end of the evening they had to themselves, "When we sit together and watch the tube and don't say anything much, it's—well, I suppose it could be improved upon, but I think it's the best time of day."

❧

SNOWY REMINDED ALAN, "Remember to take off your shoes indoors."

Parking the Subaru behind the last car in the line in front of the Fletchers' farmhouse, he said, "Got a hole in my sock."

"You haven't." During his shower this evening, she had laid out their clothes: their Levi's, her white blouse, his gray sweatshirt on which she'd sewn the G.A.A. plain green G, her gray sweatshirt with the green G shouting into a megaphone, his Jockey shorts and T-shirt, her underpants, and their newest white socks. She doubted these socks would get irreparably dirty on Patsy Fletcher's floors.

He said, "It isn't really a hop, is it?"

Since agoraphobia, she had been glad he hated to dance. She said, patting her ponytail to make sure it remained secure, a gesture from thirty years ago, "I'm assuming it's a Woodcombe party. Sooner or later everybody will start talking about his septic system." She got out of the car. Wearing sweatshirts and Levi's, they were going to a party formal enough for written invitations! This was as confusing as the Fletchers' house, which, she'd learned when she and Alan had come to a barbecue in the Fletchers' backyard last summer, was one of Woodcombe's split-personality houses, its front adorned in Sunday-best white paint, its back doing chores in barn-red. Certain thrifty old Yankees had pinched pennies where it didn't show, and the summer people and retired people who bought and restored the houses kept up the custom, agonizing over choosing the right red paint, the most authentic shade. Whenever she and Alan found themselves in the midst of such a discussion, they would exchange an Old Eastbourne look.

Alan asked, "You okay?"

"Mmm." Valium: 2 mg.

They went up the walk, the front door's outside light showing a clump of daffodils at the foot of the front-yard maple. A car pulled in behind the Subaru as Alan rang the bell, and three car-pooling couples got out, the women wearing cotton circle skirts which hung limp.

Snowy said, "They didn't have petticoats in their attics. Damn, we're going to be the most under-costumed guests."

"Who gives a fuck?" Alan said.

The couples greeted him familiarly and Snowy vaguely, and to Snowy's relief she was hidden in a bunch of people when the door opened. A record player yelled, "Shake, rattle, and roll!"

"Come in!" cried Patsy in a pale pink strapless gown, a pale pink crinoline stole snapped into the bodice, its skirt with a netting overskirt and ruches lifted by a froth of crinoline petticoats.

Like my junior prom gown, Snowy thought, without the stole. Taken to a Salvation Army fate.

In the hallway the two other women were exclaiming, "Patsy, is it your junior prom gown? You showoff, you can still fit into it! Crinolines, you saved your petticoats too!"

Patsy laughed. "Nelson calls me a pack rat. Snowy, you were a cheerleader, I just knew you were!"

"Um, yes."

"So was I!"

Snowy had guessed this at their first meeting. A few years ago Puddles had sent Snowy an Erma Bombeck column about rejected cheerleaders, women who had never recovered from not making cheerleader, Erma declaring that you always could tell who *had* been a cheerleader.

"Come see the gym," Patsy said, leading them into the living room. "Nobody's started to dance, they're all in the kitchen as usual."

One of the men said incredulously, "You even saved your record player?"

In the empty room, the Fifties record player accompanied only phantom jitterbugging on the floor bare of rugs. Chairs stood around the edges like chaperons, and rainbow-colored paper bunting crisscrossed the low ceiling, making Alan duck.

Patsy said to him, "I bet you played basketball."

"I didn't want to, but I got dragooned."

"And Snowy, you cheered for him?"

"We were enemies; we went to different schools." Snowy realized that the sight of Patsy's junior prom gown had caused her to forget to take off her shoes, and as Patsy said, "Let's get you people some drinks," and led them back through the hallway, Snowy whispered to Alan, "Our shoes," and they untied and left them beside the umbrella stand.

In the dining room, Patsy said, "The Malt Shoppe!"

The Malt Shoppe was also empty, although there was food here, grown-up cocktail fare on the dining table folded into a counter. The Fletchers, Snowy decided, must have borrowed card tables and chairs from every neighbor; these were set up all over the room, with paper napkins and salt and pepper shakers and a bottle of catsup on each table. The effect wasn't Hooper's Dairy Bar, but Patsy and Nelson were from Utica, New York, and who knew what places Utica kids had hung out in.

From the kitchen came a din of voices. The doorbell rang, and Patsy said, "Excuse me," hurrying off to the front door, crinolines bouncing.

On into the kitchen. Thank God, in the noisy throng were

248

other people wearing sweatshirts, the women with or without blouses beneath, and rolled-up jeans. Some of the women in jeans wore men's white shirts, tails out, collars up; one brave soul had enhanced this basic outfit by wearing slanty horn-rimmed glasses and her hair in pincurls wrapped in a kerchief sling. Other women were wearing fancier clothes, a quilted skirt, a poodle skirt of felt, a rickrack-decorated felt skirt, more cotton circle skirts, but all lacking crinolines. Hadn't anybody except Patsy saved crinolines, because they took up too much space? Snowy had thrown hers out as they'd worn out. Remembering the project of starching those crinolines in gelatin and how her felt skirts always got horribly wrinkled from sitting, she was surprised that the other guests' clothes were the same as hers had been, for she and Alan were usually the only New Hampshire natives at a Woodcombe party and she had expected Massachusetts and New York fads to vary. Television hadn't homogenized everybody by then, had it? Had movies, *Life* magazine? *Seventeen* magazine? Look, a pair of white sneakers! The woman wearing them had painted them into saddle shoes. Another woman wore a straight skirt with a cardigan backward, buttoned up the back, a fashion Puddles and her boobs had favored. The men here weren't so adventurous as the women, and those not clad in jeans and sweatshirts were wearing the chinos and button-down Oxford cloth shirts that were part of their present-day wardrobes.

"Welcome!" Nelson said, standing behind the kitchen-table bar. "What'll it be?" He was decked out to complement Patsy in a white dinner jacket, black trousers, maroon cummerbund, but his shirt was too frilly for the Fifties. He had retired early from some Utica company, and he and Patsy had moved permanently to this summer home of theirs, where in the barn he built canoes.

Alan asked Snowy, "Gin-and-seltzer?"

She nodded. Making an effort, she said to Nelson, "Did you save your junior prom clothes?"

"Nope, mine were rented then and these are rented now.

249

Had a hell of a time getting something plain. They kept pushing purple with velvet." Nelson was pouring Gilbey's as he spoke. Back when she and Alan gave parties, she'd always kidded Alan because, unlike most hosts, he couldn't mix drinks and talk at the same time; he would become interested in the conversation, talking with a bottle in one hand and a glass in the other while the poor guests grew parched.

Alan asked Nelson, "Have you and Patsy been feeling nostalgic lately?"

Nelson confided, "It's Patsy's fiftieth birthday, that gave her the idea, the fiftieth and the Fifties. It's supposed to be a secret so people wouldn't bother with gifts, but I've got a surprise birthday cake."

Snowy glanced at Alan, whose fiftieth birthday was fast approaching, in July. A milestone. When Guy had turned fifty, Puddles phoned and said, "My brainstorm for Guy's birthday party went over like a lead balloon, Susan and Amy and I draped the house in black, and he sure the hell didn't find it the riot we did."

"Here you go," Nelson said, "a chocolate malted, two straws."

"Thank you," Snowy said, taking the highball glass and holding it tightly. Nelson's first name, she realized, was the last name of the Gunthwaite High School shop teacher who had suggested that Tom go to Rumford Teachers' College. Mr. Nelson. She hadn't thought of him in thirty years. This party! She asked Nelson, "Did you really drink malteds back then?" In Gunthwaite, malteds weren't drunk by the townsfolk, only by summer people. There had been a rusty can of malt on a shelf in Sweetland, but if a summer person ordered a malt from Bev, sometimes Bev would say they didn't have any, practicing her acting skills and adding drama to the waitressing grind.

Nelson said, "What I remember best was a Spanish Tango, a hot fudge sundae with whipped cream and Spanish peanuts. We're having hamburgers and French fries a little later. We know you've got to leave early, but we hope you can stay until then."

"Try to," Alan said, his eyes assuring Snowy that in case they didn't leave before, he would surreptitiously consume her portion.

Somebody behind them said, "Strawberry milkshake, please," and they moved away, Alan saying, "Food."

Hunger was making other people begin to leave the kitchen and wander into the Malt Shoppe, people who, after greeting Alan, said to Snowy things like, "He been keeping you under lock and key?" and "So he's finally let you out of the house again."

Snowy laughed, always at a loss about how to reply. And she worried she would offend by not knowing people's names, shyness mistaken for rudeness. From the record player in the living room, Paul Anka asked her to put her head on his shoulder; how she and Harriet had scorned him, and Frankie Avalon! Juvenile! She looked wistfully at the Eighties goodies on the dining table, a scooped-out loaf of pumpernickel filled with dip for its cubed insides surrounding it, crackers and Brie (Alan's cheese or a Gunthwaite supermarket's?), marinated scallops, electric warmers of Swedish meatballs and stuffed mushrooms and Italian sausages and liver wrapped in bacon, and the big bowl of shrimp toward which everyone made a beeline first, Alan included. Alan Sutherland, Prop., was her prop at parties, and he gave her a stage prop, a toothpick-speared shrimp cupped in a cocktail napkin. He hadn't dunked the shrimp into the cocktail sauce so it would be tidy to hold, knowing she liked to have both hands full as an excuse during introductions not to shake hands sweatily. The shrimp he sold were smaller, peeled and frozen in bags; these were from a Gunthwaite supermarket or the Gunthwaite fish market.

"Thank you," Snowy said. "Did your hangout serve Spanish Tangos? Hooper's didn't, or Sweetland."

"The specialty at Akerman's Drugstore was fudge cake with chocolate ice cream and hot fudge sauce."

251

"My complexion! Are the card tables and chairs pretending to be booths? Sweetland had booths."

Yet people weren't sitting down, they were standing in cocktail-party stances, and they weren't gossiping about who-was-going-out-with-whom—well, yes, they were. In the talk eddying around her, Snowy heard a discussion of Gary Hart's speech yesterday withdrawing from the Democratic presidential primary race. That, and the Iran-Contra hearings, but mostly the weather, chilly again this morning—

"Hi," said a man and woman who were maybe thirty, so they would have been wearing diapers in the Fifties instead of their sweatshirts and rolled-up jeans. The woman said to Alan, "Finally getting that leach field put in. Harry's Septics is doing the job, just the leach field because when he pumped out the septic tank he said it looks good for ten years."

The man added, "To make conversation, I asked him how business was. He said, 'Oh, the same old shit.' "

Alan and Snowy laughed, Snowy trying to recall their names and if they were married or living together. Or divorced, because when Woodcombe couples broke up, both halves were apt to stay in Woodcombe, and they kept running into each other. Alan reported interesting encounters in the store, when sometimes there were conferences about the sump pump or who had the food processor and sometimes the ex's presence was completely ignored while grabbing a quart of milk. The children might be perplexed, but they didn't have to travel far from parent to parent.

In the living room, the Everly Brothers sang, "Bye, bye, love—"

"At our place," said another thirty-year-old man, wearing a sleeveless sweater over his button-down shirt and looking fairly dapper, though he was one of the ones, Snowy was pretty sure, you saw in daytime wearing painter's coveralls so stiff with paint they could walk by themselves, "Harry took a look at our backyard and said, 'In Woodcombe, there ain't enough topsoil to bury a dead cat.' "

"The Granite State," said the woman with him, wearing a sacque dress. Her mother's? "Remember the civil defense guy who came here to give a talk about how we can save our lives during a nuclear war if we dig a hole and jump in it? I asked him, 'Have you ever tried to dig a hole in New Hampshire?' He hadn't."

"Civil defense?" Alan said, head tilted. "When was this?"

The first woman said, "Before you moved here, wish you already had so you could've helped our little band of liberals pack the audience in—"

The whole town, Snowy thought, must know that she and Alan were registered Democrats, a minority in Woodcombe and in New Hampshire.

"—the town hall auditorium. The civil defense director showed a 'Duck and Cover' movie throughout which our gang hooted, and when the lights came on he was red-faced but he climbed up on the stage and told us that in the event of nuclear war our county would be designated a 'host area' and one hundred and seventy thousand people from 'risk areas' in Massachusetts and Rhode Island would come here. These thousands, he said, would be allowed to bring food and tents and flashlights, but no firearms. This caused rolling in the aisles."

As everyone laughed, Snowy heard Rosemary Clooney begin singing, "Hey there, you with the stars in your eyes . . ." My God, that was from way back in—1954? She had danced to that record with Ed Cormier.

The doorbell rang, latecomers arrived, and there were more cries of "Patsy, you showoff, you can still fit into it!"

"Refill-time," Alan said.

Carrying her full glass (Valium and booze don't mix, even if she dared attempt to swallow), Snowy followed him into the kitchen so she wouldn't have to contribute to a conversation alone. Such a fund of fascinating chitchat she was: She could tell how their first rose-breasted grosbeak of the season had arrived at the bird feeder Thursday precisely on schedule; she could mention her dismay when she was jogging this morning and realized that the sunrise looked like those paintings you see decorating the rear window of pickup trucks' cabs.

Nelson said, "Mind helping yourselves?" He'd removed his dinner jacket, rolled up the sleeves of his frilly shirt, donned an apron that read I ♡ WHITE WATER, and on the stove he was arranging frying pans. On a countertop were plastic sacks of hamburger buns, not the two brands Alan carried. "Patsy didn't think people would really want hamburgers and French fries, but I said you've got to have hamburgers and French fries at a Fifties party."

"Of course," Alan replied and reached for the Gilbey's.

Hamb., Fr. fr., that had been her waitress-shorthand. Snowy saw no deep-fat fryer in the kitchen; cookie sheets were set out, though, indicating the French fries would be the frozen kind, baked, a compromise.

"Well, now," a man said, coming in with an empty glass, his concession to costume a bow tie, "have you heard this one? What goes over rice?"

Nelson said, "Gravy?"

Snowy wanted to whisper to Alan that the woman in the news was named Donna Rice.

Alan said, "Chop suey?"

Out popped Snowy, "Gary Hart."

The man looked as taken aback as she felt. So did Alan, and so did Nelson, who laughed.

"Right," the man said, pouring Johnnie Walker, and to Alan and Nelson he said, "Our goddamned septic system, trouble every spring when the water table's high. Though it's better than the system the place had when we bought it. A pipe into a brook."

Alan sipped. "The good old days."

More people were coming in to get refills, and with second drinks the mood of the party shifted to what Patsy and Nelson had wanted. People at last began dancing in the gym, Patti Page singing "The Tennessee Waltz," Bobby Darin "Mack the Knife," Gogi Grant "The Wayward Wind," Elvis "Don't Be

254

Cruel," The Crew Cuts "Sh-Boom," the McGuire Sisters "Sincerely," Nat "King" Cole "Too Young," Kay Starr "Wheel of Fortune," Bill Haley and the Comets "Rock Around the Clock," Theresa Brewer "Music, Music, Music," and some of the people in the Malt Shoppe at last sat down in the mock booths. Snowy stood with Alan amid a group, listening to their talk and the records, until from a booth the woman wearing the poodle skirt called, "The Sutherlands!"

"The Rollinses!" Alan responded, advising Snowy sotto voce, "Fay and Martin, he's semi-retired from a computer company outside Boston, does consulting, comes in the store more than she does, she works full-time, owns a bakery in Gunthwaite—"

"Join us!" invited the baker.

Alan said, "Thank you," pulling out a chair for Snowy.

Sitting down, she clutched both the shrimp and her glass, hands full.

"My wife," Alan said, "Henrietta."

"But called Snowy," Fay said. "At least, so Jennifer has mentioned. I see you were a cheerleader, do you have any inkling if our daughters have made the big decision?"

"Jennifer?" Snowy said. In the living room, Elvis sang, "Down at the end of Lonely Street . . ."

"Our youngest. Isn't this party fun, and isn't Patsy something? I know for a fact she didn't have to let out that gown, mother of two though she is, while I had to let out this skirt three children and two bakeries later." Fay inhaled a deep breath, and Snowy wondered if she was doing relaxation breathing or lessening the strain on her waistband. The latter; Fay did not seem the sort who needed the former. Snowy looked at the other women in the Malt Shoppe, envying them from behind the bars of her prison.

Alan asked, "You have two bakeries?"

"No mouse!" Fay said.

Martin said, "Fay, I smell hamburgers, people are going to be eating—"

255

"That's the point," Fay said, "you can smell only hamburgers. A mouse," she told Snowy and Alan, "died in that wall over there, and Patsy and Nelson have been going crazy hoping it would fade before the party; they've been debating canceling or tearing the wall down, but apparently the mouse cooperated. I haven't yet caught a whiff, have you?"

A mouse, Snowy thought, or a pack rat?

Fay said, "Not two bakeries at once. I had one down in Massachusetts, an outgrowth of making cakes for friends, and when we moved here, well, I was in the habit and there was one for sale in Gunthwaite. Your book jackets mention you were born and grew up in Gunthwaite?"

Snowy blushed and nodded, bracing herself. Fay would ask when the next collection was coming out—or say she herself wrote poems as a hobby.

Fay said, "Then you knew Vachon's Bakery."

Remembering how shocked her mother had been to learn Julia *bought* Bev's birthday cakes, at Vachon's, Snowy said, "Yes," and as the Rollinses looked at her expectantly she cudgeled her brains and went on, "When my best friend and I worked the morning shift at a downtown restaurant that's gone now, we were sent down the street to Vachon's to pick up the day's doughnuts and pies, and one morning we were walking along and talking and without thinking we both automatically went into the dress shop next door instead. We were so used to making that turn, to browse in Yvonne's Apparel. We stopped stock-still, feeling like idiots—white uniforms and little aprons, out of place—and then we hightailed it, giggling. An education in the power of habit."

Alan smiled, but Fay said, "Oh, the bakery isn't downtown anymore, we're Indulgences, in the Abnaki Mall."

Snowy said, "It's been ages since I've been downtown."

"And you're not alone," Fay said, "that's why we moved to a mall. Doing very well, if I do say so myself."

Alan lifted his glass. "Congratulations."

Jo Stafford was singing "You Belong to Me."

256

"We've branched out to catering," Fay said, "and tonight I've catered a secret birthday cake, Patsy doesn't—oops."

From the kitchen came Patsy and two women guests bearing trays. They should've changed their costumes for those white nylon uniforms of yore, Snowy thought nervously, as Alan took her shrimp and ate it. Patsy said to the Rollins-Sutherland table, "I hope you saved room, this is Nelson's idea, he's even got Cokes if you'd like, regular and cherry."

"Thanks," Martin said, helping himself and Fay to paper plates of hamburgers and French fries, "but I'll stay in the Eighties for my beverage. How about you, Fay?"

"Yes, to think cherry Cokes are back, the children groaned when I told them we used to get cherry Cokes made from scratch by a soda jerk in a drugstore instead of out of a can."

Alan glanced at his watch and at Snowy and stood up. "Ten. I'm sorry, Patsy, but we have to be leaving."

Snowy rose outwardly reluctantly, inwardly leaping. "Thanks so much. Fun!"

Patsy asked, "Can you still remember all your cheers?"

"Like yesterday."

"So can I!" Patsy said and moved on to another table, and Fay said, "It's good to meet you, Snowy, we all must get together," and Mark asked, "What did a Fifties hamburger cost, a quarter?"

Snowy said, "A cheeseburger five cents extra."

She and Alan went into the kitchen, where more hamburgers spluttered in frying pans and Nelson was conducting with his spatula The Platters' "Great Pretender."

"Our curfew," Alan said. "Thanks for—"

"Wait." Nelson dropped the spatula and grabbed his highball glass. "We'll have a toast now, before you leave. Pour yourself a short one, Alan; drink up, Snowy." In the doorway he announced, "A toast! A toast!"

The Malt Shoppe hushed, but in the living room the record player kept singing.

Nelson said, "To the Fabulous Fifties!"

257

The Malt Shoppe chorused, "The Fabulous Fifties!"

When, Snowy said to herself, roles were defined and accepted by the Silent Generation. She sipped and swallowed.

Alan muttered, "Was the Korean War so fabulous? Joseph McCarthy?"

Patti Page inquired, "How Much Is That Doggie in the Window?" and Nelson turned back to the kitchen and said, "A doggie bag for the Sutherlands!"

Walking through the Malt Shoppe, Alan carrying the doggie bag, Snowy heard people talking about reunions. Dudley phoned her occasionally with Gunthwaite news, Snowy suspecting that these long-distance calls and Jim Beam might be his only luxuries, although the production of children had stopped when Charl turned forty, the total a dozen, the older ones now married and producing grandchildren. During his latest call he'd said that Charl and Darl were organizing a thirtieth reunion in August, the first since the twenty-fifth, "and," he continued, "now you're just a half hour away, leave that reunion-resisting husband at home and come by yourself, stop at our house and go with us." Then he'd made his only reference ever to dropping out of Yale, saying, "If I can face our classmates, you certainly can. I'll have Charl add you to the list of reservations, send twenty bucks." She had sent a check, telling Alan, "It's worth it to placate Dudley; I'll get the flu." She told Bev, who said, "Wild horses couldn't drag me."

While Kitty Kallen began singing "Little Things Mean a Lot," Snowy and Alan brushed off their socks, put on their shoes, and left, and in the car Snowy leaned back as they drove off, the sound of spring peepers in invisible nighttime ponds and swamps shrilling in her ears. She had survived the party; she hadn't fainted, she hadn't started screaming, she hadn't had a heart attack, she hadn't done anything embarrassing or fatal.

"I hope," she said, "Fay's 'get together' was just a social reflex. Awkward, owing the Fletchers, et al."

"People know we can't throw a blast on Saturday nights."

"There are other possibilities. Oh, well. What was the dip in the pumpernickel?"

"Something like a Reuben."

"Salt!"

They came to the village center and drove past the glow of the night light in the store and took the lake road. On the black lake, a breeze was making glittering fish scales. They rode the Roller Coaster Road until the darkness of the woods thinned to the haze of a field and he drove up their driveway into the barn.

She ran her finger along his forearm. "A suitable ending to this evening would be to climb into the back seat."

"How would you explain our delay?"

"Ruhamah's gone to bed, no outside light." Jittery about leaving Ruhamah without a baby-sitter though Ruhamah *was* a baby-sitter, Snowy always instructed her to turn on an outside light only after she heard their car, so she wouldn't advertise being alone, and not to turn it on at all if she went to bed. Excess caution, in Alan's opinion. Snowy took a flashlight out of the glove compartment and opened her door. "But maybe she's still awake, alas."

In the kitchen, Alan asked, "Two?"

"Thanks." Okay to have a drink here. He mixed them as Snowy fetched plates and unwrapped the hamburgers and French fries. She said, "It's the Fifties, we don't know about cholesterol yet. You go ahead, I'll eat mine while I get ready for bed."

She went into the dining room and opened the bathroom door, put her plate and glass on the washing machine, and left by the other door into the bedroom, switching on the bedside lamp. The four-poster was like a feather bed now, high with the flowery down comforter they'd given themselves three Christmases ago, the shop owner giving them the present of a new word by calling the comforter a duvet. "In the Fifties," she told it, "you were a puff." On Alan's bureau stood framed snapshots of her and Ruhamah; on hers, snapshots of him and Ruhamah, Ruhamah's school photographs (not quite a hallway gallery), and Bev's last year's Christmas card of Etta looking exactly like Bev age eleven, the red-headed playmate from Snowy's past.

She tiptoed upstairs and listened at Ruhamah's door, then peeked in. Ruhamah lay safely asleep amongst a pajama party of toy animals.

Back downstairs in the bedroom, collecting her nightgown and slippers, she went into the bathroom, took off her Fifties clothes, put them in the hamper. As she removed her Eighties makeup, she wondered at her makeup rituals through the decades. Who had she been in the late Sixties, early Seventies, drawing a brushload of eyeliner above her lashes? She sipped the drink, ate the hamburger and French fries, patting on Night of Olay cream, thinking of the layers of Noxzema she'd smeared on in her youth. She undid the ponytail, brushed her hair, brushed her teeth. When she opened the bathroom door into the dining room, she heard the television tuned low and went to the living room. "It's all yours."

He was sitting in his wing chair, his hamburger half-eaten. "I guess I'll stay up a bit."

Because of the Sunday newspapers, they didn't usually have their end-of-day sit after a Saturday night party. "What's on? Shall I stay up? Eating so soon before bedtime—" She yawned. "Better hit the sack." In the kitchen she rinsed her glass and plate, put them in the dishwasher, and on her way through the living room she said, knowing she sounded like a wife, "Shouldn't you come to bed? Sundays tire you out."

"I'll be along."

"I don't know why *I'm* tired, I only planted six hundred onion sets today." She kissed him. "Tomorrow I'm going to try to stay at the store again. Wait on two customers at least."

"Good."

In bed, she thought with satisfaction of the onions which would supply her and Alan through the winter and be given to his parents and Margaret and Howard for Christmas.

The clock radio's alarm woke her at four-thirty, its buzz almost lost in the noise of spring peepers. After she snapped it off, she rolled over to snuggle Alan awake. He wasn't there, he must be in the bathroom, but as she sat up she saw that the bathroom door was open, the night light still on, unnecessary at daybreak. He must be in the kitchen, getting some juice. She climbed out of bed, toed her slippers out from underneath, went into the bathroom, brushed her teeth and hair, and padded through the dining room to the kitchen. He wasn't here either. The morning felt warmer, and she glanced at the porch thermometer in the window beside the phone, a reflex action. Fifty degrees! Had he fallen asleep in his wing chair? Then she noticed the barn door, open. The van was gone. Somebody had stolen the van. Or Ruhamah—Ruhamah had run away.

Racing into the living room, empty, and up the stairs, she told herself that this was one of those nightmares in which you knew you'd awakened but really hadn't. She leaned into Ruhamah's room. The sight of her daughter asleep with toy animals didn't evaporate the nightmare. The way she used to check for burglaries, she checked the house for Alan, room by room, even going down to the cellar, circling back to their bedroom, staring at the smooth pillow on his side of the bed. She opened the closet. On his hook behind the door were his beige pajamas and white terry-cloth bathrobe.

There had been an emergency. After she'd gone to bed, he had got a phone call; something had happened at the store, a burglary, a fire. But he'd have wakened her or scribbled a bedside note before taking off. Nonetheless, she ran to the kitchen phone and dialed the store's number. The ringing and ringing became a scream.

Ask Ruhamah to drive? Don't worry her. Snowy ran into the bedroom. Heart slamming against her chest, she kicked off her slippers, pulled off her nightgown, but her hands quaked so violently she almost couldn't put on underpants, Levi's, a sweatshirt, socks, and she couldn't tie her shoes. She shoved her feet into an old pair with Velcro tabs, seized her shoulder bag.

Outdoors, the ground swayed as she stumbled across the yard to the barn. On the third try she fitted the key into the

261

Subaru's ignition, and, incapable of speeding, maddened by her slowness, she drove down the Roller Coaster Road and the lake road, her goal the next telephone pole ahead. Spring was filling out; trees were fluffy, green upon green.

The village awaited the Stage Manager, lilac bushes in front yards blooming, lawns polka-dotted with dandelions. The store hadn't burned down. It looked normal, bundles of Sunday newspapers delivered. But no van.

Her key chain: Car keys, house keys, and her spare key to the store. Inside, she switched off the night light. Near the cash register were pots of flowering cyclamens and gloxinias, reminding her that today was Mother's Day, a holiday she had commanded Alan and Ruhamah from the very beginning not to observe on her account, but Alan would dutifully phone his mother.

"Alan?"

His office served as a broom closet too, so in the corner beside the safe there was a domestic still life, broom, dustpan, mop, bucket, a box of Spic and Span. The safe was locked, uncracked. Once, after he and she had made the same comment about something in the same breath, as they often did, he'd remarked, "If you knew the combination of a safe, I could probably open it." She should be able to sense where he was, and why. In the rolltop desk's pigeonholes, papers were neat, business as usual. The desktop was clear, anonymous except for a framed snapshot; he'd chosen one he'd taken of her climbing along the Pevensay jetty carrying young Ruhamah. Pre-agoraphobia. Checking the empty office bathroom, she heard a knock on the front door.

She walked back into the main room and saw through the door window a man wearing a black uniform. Out the big storefront window she saw the police cruiser parked, a black Jeep Wagoneer. She and Alan had laughed about the necessity of four-wheel drive to maintain law and order up here. The man tried the door and stepped inside. He began to blur, the walls caving in.

262

"Mrs. Sutherland. I'm Chief Danforth. I noticed your car.
I'm afraid I have bad news. You'd better sit down. Shall we go
in the office?"

"He's dead."

"I'm sorry."

"How?"

"Wouldn't you prefer to— He drowned, Mrs. Sutherland.
I'll phone for a friend of yours to come."

"Where is his body?"

"Being taken to the Gunthwaite hospital."

"Why?"

"There'll have to be an autopsy."

"An autopsy?"

"It looks suspicious."

"What does 'suspicious' mean?"

"He was fully clothed."

"He fell in the lake?"

Chief Danforth paused. "His van was parked in Murray
Cove, with a half-empty half gallon of gin and an empty bottle
of Valium, the prescription made out to you. Let me phone for
a friend."

"Who found him? When?"

"A fisherman, approximately twenty minutes ago."

"Could you drive me home?"

"Your daughter's there?"

"Yes."

"You'll need an adult."

"All my friends are long-distance. What should I do about
the newspapers?"

"Leave them on the porch. Honor system."

He held her elbow as she went down the porch stairs and got
into the Wagoneer's front seat. There was a wire grid between
the front and back seats.

He said, "Your car keys? I'll lock it up and have it brought
to you."

"Oh."

263

When they drove off, the CLOSED sign still in the store window, she now seemed to be seeing the village on this warm morning from a very high balcony. The Wagoneer's two-way radio crackled. They came to the lake.

She said, "I don't know where Murray Cove is."

He looked over at her, then said, "Four miles farther on, Tolman Road, goes in to a shallow inlet. Mrs. Sutherland, was your husband depressed lately?"

She nodded, shook her head, nodded. "It's part of his nature."

"Business troubles?"

"Getting the store back on its feet. But."

"When did you realize he was missing?"

"I woke up and he wasn't there. He hadn't come to bed."

They turned onto the Roller Coaster Road.

"Cleora," Chief Danforth said, sounding relieved by the inspiration, "we'll get Cleora Thorne."

So they drove past Hurricane Farm, along the road she'd jogged yesterday morning, the sunrise at her back making her shadow run ahead of her on stilts and during the run home dazzling her eyes.

A rash of robins had broken out in the dooryard of the Thornes' old farmhouse. Up the robins flew to burble in treetops, and Chief Danforth parked behind the Thornes' rattletrap pickup and rusting Ford sedan and walked to the kitchen door. A man in a black uniform, his revolver in his holster, standing on a granite doorstep near a big clump of rhubarb.

Snowy opened her shoulder bag and located her emergency bottle of Valium. The other bottle had been in the medicine chest. Chief Danforth went indoors.

Beyond the farmhouse sagged the barn, held upright, Alan said, only by the manure piles against its sides. Just yesterday she had jogged on to the pasture which the Thornes' herd of five Guernseys was now sharing with more robins. At the gate bar, she'd always stop and enjoy these cows grazing beneath Mt. Pascataquac, and then she'd jog home, to shower and make her and Alan's breakfast. Their first year here, when she passed the barn she would meet Isaac Thorne coming out, his walk typical of the New Hampshire farmer he was, loose-jointed, stooped, his head slightly preceding him. When he heard her running footsteps and acknowledged her wave, he had the same air of impassive curiosity as his cows did, but she suspected his look masked considerable amusement at her activity. This year, however, Isaac had begun to fail and she didn't see him outdoors anymore. Cleora had assumed his chores in addition to her own, for all the Thorne children had fled from farming ages ago. Cleora, spare and very arthritic, tended the cows now as well as her chickens, and Snowy, meeting her during her laborious morning progress across the barnyard, would run in place, feeling frivolous, ridiculous, while Cleora talked about the weather and the garden and this and that, concluding every conversation by saying, "If it was up to me, I'd get rid of them cows in a minute."

The Thornes' pickup lacked headlights and windshield wipers. One rainy evening in Pevensay, she and Alan were en route to a party when their windshield wipers ceased working; Alan found some rope in the trunk and tied it to the wipers, and thus they proceeded on to the party hanging out the windows operating the wipers manually, laughing uproariously. Their hostess happened to be at the door and witnessed their arrival, startling them with her reaction: "Your marriage survived that? Then it can survive anything." Soon after, hostess and host got divorced.

Cleora came hobbling outside on Chief Danforth's arm, wearing one of her faded housedresses and threadbare aprons, carrying a pie in a tin pie plate. "Drat these legs of mine!"

Snowy remembered her manners and climbed out and got into the back seat, to give the older woman the front. As Chief Danforth helped Cleora up, Cleora glanced over her shoulder and said through the grid, "Warmer this morning."

Snowy said, "Fifty degrees at our house."

Nobody spoke again until they reached Hurricane Farm,

265

where in the kitchen Chief Danforth said, "Sunday, but we'll get hold of your doctor. Dr. Shelton in Gunthwaite, I understand."

On the Valium bottle.

He asked, "Did your husband go to him too?"

"Yes." For gynecological physicals, Snowy nowadays went to a Puddles-equivalent, who'd opened a practice in Gunthwaite. "Would anyone like a cup of coffee? Tea?"

Cleora said, "I'll make coffee, Snowy, you go lie down, I'll find my way around here. Ruhamah asleep?"

"She sleeps until noon. Usually."

"Let her sleep."

"I didn't shower. If you'll excuse me, I'll do that."

Chief Danforth said, "I have to leave, tend to things, but I'll be back for—details. And when you feel up to it, could you look for a note?"

"A note? Oh. Yes."

The phone began ringing. He said, "Cleora will handle the calls. Do you want people to visit yet?"

"No, *no*."

As Snowy left the kitchen, she heard him say to Cleora, "News travels fast in Woodcombe."

"Don't it. Even before them CB's."

In the bathroom, Snowy vomited the Fabulous Fifties hamburger and French fries into the toilet. Then she brushed her teeth, opened the medicine chest Alan had opened and took out Scope to gargle, undressed, and got into the shower. She was lathering her hair when she skidded out onto the bathmat and dumped the hamper on the floor and pawed through it. She'd done a wash Friday, so of his clothes there were only the sportshirt and chinos and underwear he'd worn to work yesterday, but she snatched them up and smelled them, snuffling big breaths. A hamper smell.

Shampoo suds dripped. She must get back into water, under water, and rinse her hair, wash and rinse her live flesh. Pig-Pen.

Afterward, drying herself and getting dressed, what she smelled was coffee brewing in the kitchen.

266

She began the hunt for a note, going upstairs to her office. Lots of paper to write on here. But on her desktop lay no why. The phone rang, was answered. Her desk drawers were undisturbed, and the fireproof box.

Downstairs, she continued the hunt, more protracted than her previous circling. In their bedroom she opened his bureau drawers, examining every layer of stacked underwear, jerseys, summer sweaters. Each article of clothing she had washed and folded and put away; they were as familiar as her own, which she next checked. She opened the closet and felt in pockets. In the farthest corner stood his .22, for woodchucks.

The living room. The wing chair where last night she had kissed him goodnight. She lifted the cushion, replaced it, shook the magazines and newspapers on his table. The dining room. She looked under his placemat, hers, Ruhamah's, woven by Mimi, bought wholesale.

Cleora sat drinking coffee in the kitchen, watching a religious program never before seen on this little black-and-white TV screen. "Have some pie and coffee, I could only find decaf, this and instant."

"I'm sorry, that's all we've got. No, thank you." On the rooster memo pad was today's shopping list. The pages underneath were blank. Snowy opened a cupboard. There would be a note propped against the can of Spam, and it would all be a joke, a dream. There wasn't.

"You ought to eat some pie. The first rhubarb. Irene called, she wants to know if you want her to run the store tomorrow."

Snowy was investigating other cupboards. "What? Yes, I suppose."

"She said it wouldn't be suitable today. Besides, she'll be at church praying. Me, I watch these shows, better than a circus. The minister, he phoned after Irene—" The phone rang, and Cleora stiffly got up. "Hello?"

Snowy opened the dishwasher. While Cleora made affirmative noises and said, "She's holding up fine but she ain't ready to have company, I'll tell her you called," and said to Snowy,

"That was Joan Edgerly," a name Snowy didn't recognize, Snowy looked at his glass and plate. As the phone rang again and Cleora turned to answer it, she grabbed the plate and licked a stripe.

"Cleora here, she can't come to the phone—who's this, ain't you heard? Snowy, it's a Beverly Lambert, should I—"

"Thank you, I'll take it." Snowy slid the plate into the rack and walked across to the phone. "Hello, Bev."

"That accent! Not since our neighbors in Gunthwaite—was that your neighbor? I can call back. I must hear everything about the party and how your costumes went over and *every*thing."

"Alan's dead."

"Today is Mother's Day, it isn't April Fool's."

"He drowned. Don't come here, I'd fall apart if you did. I'll call you later." Snowy hung up and opened the screen door.

Cleora asked sharply, "Where're you going?"

"To look for the note."

She searched the porch, under the placemats on the golden oak table, under cushions, in magazines, then ran to the barn. Barn swallows flew in and out as she searched the toolshed-workshop, getting desperate. He'd written a note, changed his mind, thrown it away. She yanked off the lids of the garbage cans, pulled up the trash bags he would take to the dump this afternoon, and groped amongst the contents organized for recycling. She ran back into the kitchen, where Cleora was saying on the phone "—ain't ready—", and upended the kitchen wastebasket onto the floor, cascading unorganized paper-towel balls, a mayonnaise jar, a flattened box of Kraft Macaroni & Cheese Dinner. In the downstairs bathroom she emptied the wastebasket of Kleenex, a curled toothpaste tube, and ran through the bedroom and started up the stairs.

She saw Ruhamah come out of her bedroom, looking sleepy and cross, wearing a knee-length electric-pink nightshirt.

"Honest to God," Ruhamah said, "are you and Bev and Puddles trying for a milestone in telephone calls?"

The urge to protect hurled Snowy the rest of the way upstairs. She hugged Ruhamah tight, wishing she were still taller.

"Ow," Ruhamah said. "Mother, I have to tinkle!"

"Sorry."

The toilet flushed and the shower spurted while Snowy smoothed out every crumpled piece of paper in her office wastebasket. Now she was angry, furious at Alan, and when a turquoise-bathrobed Ruhamah finally emerged from the bathroom she charged past her to the wastebasket there, spilled Ruhamah's Kotexes wrapped in toilet paper—

"Mother, for heaven's sake, my privacy!"

"Yes, you go through the wastebasket in your room—no, I should." Snowy rushed into Ruhamah's room.

"Is this a raid?"

Snowy halted. Out the side window sloped Violet Hill, which Alan would never see blossom again. She walked back to Ruhamah and held her, and below they heard slow lame footsteps enter the hallway, then retreat.

Ruhamah whispered, "Who's here?"

Rocking, Snowy said, "Remember one suppertime in Pevensay, you'd been reading Sylvia Plath and thinking over her death and you said you'd rather take sleeping pills and I said I would only if I was dying in pain." She had known that Ruhamah was testing her, frightened about poets and suicide; she'd thought of the iodine and razor-blade episodes in her youth and she had been frightened about Ruhamah. "Remember? Alan said he would swim out until he couldn't swim anymore."

"Snowy?"

"We kidded around, and you and I said we'd build him a funeral pyre on the beach, like Byron and some friends did for Shelley."

The phone rang in Snowy's office.

Ruhamah said, "Shelley was an accident."

The phone stopped ringing. Snowy held Ruhamah, rocking, rocking, she'd be a rock for Ruhamah. "This is going to be terribly difficult, but you and I—Cleora's here answering the phone."

269

"Goddamn you!"

Ruhamah pushed her, shoved her out of the room so hard she banged her head against the opposite wall of the hall. The door crashed shut.

Snowy touched her skull; she couldn't feel a thing. She hung onto the banister as she went down the stairs to stand gazing at the wing chair. Then brakes screeched and a car came zooming up the driveway, the red Volkswagen Rabbit which always reminded her of Alan's old red VW Bug. The person at the wheel always reminded her of Julia.

Goddamn *Bev!*

In the kitchen, Cleora switched off gossip at her approach. "—they say gin—I'll tell her you called."

Snowy opened the door and stepped onto the porch. Mimi, not a petite and dainty coquette about whom Maurice Chevalier would croon, leapt out of the car, her long braid flying, her tall form wearing lengthy overalls as faded as Cleora's clothes. Funny, Cleora the farmwife did chores in a dress; Mimi and Snowy herself were the ones who owned overalls.

"You okay?" Mimi was saying, picking up the car keys she'd dropped. "Mother phoned, she isn't sure she heard right but she told me to—I saw the store was closed and people there, police—"

The bumper stickers on the Rabbit seemed to be babbling even faster than distraught Mimi: ABOLISH APARTHEID; STOP ACID RAIN; NO NUKES; SAVE THE WHALES; ABORTION—A PERSONAL DECISION; YOUR ENVIRONMENT: LOVE IT OR LOSE IT. Yet the infamous New Hampshire state motto on its license plates, LIVE FREE OR DIE, was mute, having been gagged with masking tape.

Mimi ran up onto the porch. "Would you like to come to our apartment? Where's Ruhamah? Does she know?"

"Isn't the day getting hot?"

Mimi put her arms around Snowy.

Snowy said, "I have to call Alan's parents."

"No problem, I will, I'll tell them the doctor gave you

270

something and you're asleep. Has he?" Mimi led her into the house. "Hi, I'm Mimi Lambert, Snowy's best friend's daughter."

"Cleora Thorne," Cleora said, "from down the road. Want some pie and coffee?"

Snowy's stomach lurched. "Excuse me," she said and started toward the bathroom. She wasn't out of earshot when Cleora said to Mimi, "Stay here. Leave them alone. Don't talk about it until they're ready to talk—that's best for widows."

❧

A VOICE SAID, " 'We must cultivate our garden.' "

Crouched in the garden, Snowy saw through the twilight a man striding into the backyard, tall as Alan but very balding. Dudley.

He added, "I almost had to show my birth certificate to get past that Mimi."

"I'm sorry, this planting to do—" Today was Monday. The news probably had been in today's *Gunthwaite Herald*. How had he found Hurricane Farm? The post office and town hall were closed by now, and the store. Had he just stopped at some house and asked? She didn't have time for speculation; she went back to planting lettuce, duck-walking along the row, following the white string stretched taut from stake to stake.

He came down the path of lawn down the middle of the garden. "It's practically dark, Snowy." Her face was dim, but he'd bet there was a muscle jumping in her jaw. Her overalls, tucked into boots, had muddy knees. A flat wicker basket contained seed packets and a flashlight. Did she intend to plant throughout the entire night?

She said wildly, "The lawyer, the accountant, here all day, they delayed planting." They'd actually made a house call to discuss the situation in *her* office; Mimi evidently had informed them she was handicapped. "Less buggy at night anyway, the

271

blackflies go under the forest duff. I've got the garlic in, and the first radishes, Julia used to tell how her husband, Bev's father, laughed at her because she'd planted a whole row of radishes in her beginner's garden, they're only supposed to mark rows but she liked radishes, and then she noticed they were disappearing from the garden and when she complained about rabbits or chipmunks, he confessed he was the culprit, he'd found he liked them more than he realized. I've planted the first Buttercrunch, our favorite lettuce, and Salad Bowl, and this is Red Salad Bowl, my experiment, Julia said you should have at least one experiment every year, my luck's been awful with other kinds of red lettuce, and there's Slobolt to plant, spelled S-l-o, so I wouldn't plant it except it does what its name promises, and spinach and Swiss chard and kale, the early stuff—"

"Let me help."

"Do you know how?"

"You and I were always fast learners."

She demonstrated how to cover and tamp the Red Salad Bowl seeds, and while he did, she lined up the next row with stakes and string, drew a furrow with the handle-tip of her hoe, and sowed Slobolt. Not even Puddles on the phone, after hearing the news from Bev, had got past Mimi's barricade, though no doubt Puddles in person would have succeeded. They worked silently, but Snowy's mind was chittering like a furious squirrel. She'd already bought these seeds and this year's supply of mulch hay, she hadn't yet bought tomato plants, and green pepper and eggplant, and broccoli and cauliflower and Brussels sprouts, and now she couldn't afford them.

Dudley said, "Reminds me of our sandbox days."

"How is Charl? Your children?"

"Charl and Darl are praying for you—and him."

Snowy laughed and measured off the next row.

"That time he came in to have the store sign painted, I could understand why he won your hand."

"You can cover the Slobolt."

Dudley said, "My junior year at Yale, I was going with a

272

Catholic girl and we were using the rhythm method. She was from town, and I had talked her out of her virginity by vowing she'd be a First Lady someday, even if she was only a typist now. She got pregnant. A future President couldn't quit school and get a job at Trask's to support a wife and baby, could he, so I withdrew my savings and she agreed to have an abortion for the sake of my career. I brought her back to her apartment afterward, and she started hemorrhaging and I couldn't stop it and—I should have called an ambulance. She bled to death right there on her bed. And I ran like hell. I don't know who found her. I kept waiting for someone to hunt me down. Nothing happened. She didn't have a roommate; she'd wanted a place to herself after growing up sharing a room with her sister. She and her sister weren't friends, so I guess she hadn't told her about me or told her parents or anybody at the office, at least by name."

"Her name, what was it?"

"Mary. Mary Callaghan. Some of the guys knew I was going out with a townie—for what I could get, they assumed, and I was, but I loved her."

Snowy stepped across the string and touched his arm. He had quit school, punishing himself because nobody else would. His eyes looked puffy.

He said, "I've never even told Charl. She thought the mono was an excuse to leave school and earn some money, which made sense to her."

"It wasn't your fault. It was illegal butchery back then."

He hugged her. "How are you doing?"

"Okay." She hugged him. "Let's cover the Slobolt and go get a drink."

Again they worked silently, but as they walked toward the house he asked, "Do you have rituals? The newspaper didn't mention any funeral plans. When Jack—well, naturally Charl had rituals."

"We hate funerals." Alan's parents would have put up a fight about no funeral if his death wasn't a suicide, a disgrace. Mimi had called them yesterday. When his mother phoned today, Snowy had said to Mimi, "I must, sooner or later," and had taken the receiver, saying to his mother, "I don't know why, I'm so sorry, so dreadfully sorry, it's not necessary to come here, Ruhamah and I will visit after everyone feels more stable," and then his mother had broken down and his sister had got on the phone in tears, asking, "*Why?*" and Snowy had repeated, "I don't know, I'm so sorry," certain that Alan's family was blaming her. If she'd been a better wife . . . They were correct.

Dudley asked, "How's your daughter?"

Also blaming her. "In shock."

"Do you have a school psychologist?"

"The area one. Mimi said she phoned today and offered to come to the house, but Ruhamah said she'd be going to school tomorrow." Mimi reported too, when the lawyer and accountant had left, that she and Ruhamah hadn't talked much during their drive to Leicester to pick up some clothes for Mimi this morning but that this afternoon Ruhamah had taken phone calls from a Jennifer and a Kim, half-hour calls during which Mimi eavesdropped enough to learn she'd mostly listened. These were the only times Ruhamah had emerged from her room, Mimi bringing her meals, and now as Snowy and Dudley went into the kitchen and heard the living-room television and Mimi's laughter, Snowy hoped Ruhamah hadn't been lured out by any sitcoms, for more than ever Snowy couldn't face her.

Although they hadn't entertained in years, Snowy kept an assortment of booze on a cupboard shelf, a pretense. The bourbon was Jim Beam. She stood holding the bottle where Alan had stood and reached in and picked up the half gallon of Gilbey's gin the last time.

Dudley took over. "Tell me where the glasses are, what'll you have? This is a very nice place, Snowy."

Tap-tap-tap went the calculator, and Alan said, "It'll be tight but we can swing it," and today in her office the accountant had said, "Overextended." Alan didn't need to leave a note because the accountant would provide the why.

"Vodka-and-seltzer," Snowy said.

Mimi came in. "Mother phoned again, and Puddles. They were glad you're here, Dudley, they send their love, and Puddles wants to know why Darl didn't have a dozen kids too. I'm not sure what that means, but you have *twelve?*"

"Believe me, it isn't cheaper by the dozen. Sheer economics is the reason Darl is risking her immortal soul with birth control. We couldn't afford a big family either, but Charl wouldn't dare risk hers— We've made do."

And Snowy now also knew this why. Mary Callaghan. "Thank you," she said, taking the glass Dudley gave her. She asked Mimi, "Has Ruhamah come downstairs for TV?"

"No, and I'm sorry to be laughing, but it's *Charley's Aunt.*"

"PBS?" Dudley said. "I read it's a good production."

Mimi looked from him to Snowy. "Want to come in and watch?"

Snowy said, "I'll change out of this mud."

When she had, she went into the living room and saw that Dudley had avoided the obvious wing chair and chosen the Windsor rocker. Mimi was sprawled on the sofa on which she had slept last night and would sleep tonight, where Snowy would have slept instead of on the pull-out sofa in her office if Mimi hadn't refused the office sofa, insisting Snowy sleep in some sort of real bed, making no reference to the bed in the bedroom. Snowy sat down in the Martha Washington chair. After condolences, the lawyer had said, "Sit down," as Chief Danforth had suggested in the store yesterday, and at the end of the session the lawyer had said, "Think things over a few days and then we'll sit down again."

And now Mimi and Dudley were baby-sitting her. She looked at the TV screen. There was little insurance; there were lots of debts. For a second time she had forgotten her Left-Field Theory.

She fell asleep in the chair and awoke to find herself covered with an afghan. The sick realization. Alan. The mantel clock told her she'd slept late, six-thirty. It didn't matter if she'd snored and drooled in front of Dudley and Mimi. So what?

275

Across the room Mimi lay on the sofa sound asleep despite legs dangling.

The morning was rainy, dark, miserable. She couldn't run, she couldn't plant. She could finish the spring cleaning. After her shower, she put on her oldest Levi's and took out of her bureau a yellowing white T-shirt whose silk-screened green broccoli had almost completely crackled off. Her favorite vegetable. A birthday present from Alan. Yes, every moment of every day would now be filled with such ambushes, minefields, trapdoors, camouflaged pits awaiting prey: memories.

She tugged the T-shirt over her head and went into the kitchen. First, clean the refrigerator. She opened the refrigerator and gaped. Mimi had said that while she was in her office yesterday Cleora had stopped by with food which people had dropped off at her house, and now she saw that the fridge was crammed, the casseroles and cakes as unreal as the make-believe eggs and pies in the white tin toy refrigerator her parents had given her one Christmas.

She'd have to postpone cleaning the fridge until it was somewhat emptied. Instead, clean the oven.

Ruhamah came in wearing this spring's latest fashion, a big sweatshirt, scarlet, and a pair of men's boxer shorts, fly stitched up. These shorts weren't Alan's; since he wore Jockeys, Ruhamah wasn't able to swipe any pairs of her father's, as she'd said other girls did, and she'd had to buy them in the Gunthwaite Mall. Still, Snowy wanted to demand she go upstairs and change.

"Breakfast?" Snowy said.

"Get something at school."

"Your raincoat—"

Ruhamah dashed through the rain to the barn, opened the door, slid into the car without, Snowy judged, a glance at the van, and backed it out. They'd given her a set of keys when she got her license, but until this morning she had continued riding the school bus. Snowy turned on the TV to the *Today Show* tuned to a murmur.

By the time Mimi had awakened and showered and come into the kitchen, the air reeked of oven cleaner and the harvest table was filled with stacks of china, pottery, groups of glasses. Snowy knelt leaning into a cabinet as if into a lion's mouth. A TV game show shrieked faintly.

Mimi said, "Are you sure that doctor didn't prescribe diet pills instead of tranquilizers?" She switched on the burner under the teakettle. "But you did go out like a light last night; we figured it was best not to wake you to move you. Stiff neck?"

Snowy straightened up and felt her neck. "Oh. So it is. Thank you for seeing to Dudley. Cereal? Toast, English muffin?"

Mimi spooned instant Decaf. "Have you eaten anything at all yet? I thought I'd pick up the groceries on your list. There're the offerings people have sent, but we're low on milk and veg."

Panic. "You're leaving?"

"I'll take the phone off the hook like when I was away yesterday. I'm not going to a mall, just to the village."

"You're going to the store?"

Mimi pointed out a window. "Hey!"

At the plastic globe of red fluid hanging from a cord under the eaves, a hummingbird hovered, iridescent in the rain.

Snowy said, "The first of the season."

Mimi patted her shoulder, gulped coffee, took the phone off the hook, and left.

When Mimi returned, Snowy said, cutting shelving paper, "I forgot to give you any money." She had been mentally counting money, the emergency twenty in her wallet, the forty-six dollars and twenty-three cents in Alan's "effects," the two hundred fifty-one dollars and ninety-three cents in their personal checking account, and Ruhamah's trust fund for college, which couldn't and mustn't be touched. The money in the store accounts was owed to creditors. The accountant had kept saying "Chapter Eleven," and at last she'd realized he wasn't talking about a book but bankruptcy.

As well as a paper bag, Mimi was carrying a maroon backpack decorated with proficient-looking patches, most of which showed silhouettes of mountain peaks. "Irene put the groceries on a tab." She replaced the phone receiver.

"Thank you, Mimi. How was Irene?"

Stowing milk, yogurt, lettuce, celery in the refrigerator, Mimi said, "She says she has to pay on delivery for beer and gasoline, and I told her your accountant would be handling things, right? Have you noticed, the weather's clearing. Guess what else I got? Italian grinders. We're going on a picnic."

Alan purchased these plastic-wrapped grinders and sandwiches from a Gunthwaite deli, temptation he sometimes brought home, a treat. Snowy said, "I have to finish this spring cleaning while the garden dries out—"

"Potato chips and beer, we're climbing Pascataquac." Mimi stuffed them into the backpack, and out of the kitchen closet she took Snowy's jacket. "Come on, let's go, change into your boots."

Ordered around by a twenty-four-year-old. "How much has Bev explained to you about my—affliction? I can't climb mountains."

"I need you to. I need your help with our wedding."

"*Wedding?* Your mother—"

"Boots. Yup, I finally announced it when she called last night. She was, well, she was crying again over you and Grandmother, so I thought it would cheer her up, but it made her so happy she cried some more. Come on."

Outdoors, Snowy got into the Rabbit's passenger seat and sat, obedient, as Mimi backed up and sped down the driveway, jouncing onto the dirt road which, drenched from the morning rain, smelled like mud pies, like childhood.

Mimi said, "Even though Pascataquac is right above your house, Irene says Pascataquac Road is off Center Road out of the village."

"You're getting married. Here. In New Hampshire. Not Connecticut."

"And you and Mother can have a reunion! Of course she had to ask if I was pregnant. I'm not."

If Mimi was, she wouldn't be for long, the way she drove the Roller Coaster Road. Snowy asked, banging into her seat belt, "Then why are you getting married?"

"I don't know."

They reached the lake road and drove toward the village, Snowy looking straight ahead.

"Nostalgia," Mimi said. "That's as close as I can figure."

In the village, some people were going into and coming out of the store, and others stood talking on the porch.

"Lloyd and I," Mimi said, swerving onto Center Road, "we've been checking out mountaintops for wedding sites, and we haven't got to Pascataquac because it hardly qualifies as a mountain, the book says it's only two thousand and ninety feet, an hour up, an hour down, but that does mean it'd be an easy climb for guests who aren't into mountains."

"Didn't mountaintop weddings end when flower children started to dress for success?"

"I know, formal weddings are in, and we ought to be having one like Mother's white satin album photos. The thing is, if I have a wedding at home, it'll become Mother's, not ours, Lloyd's and mine. Don't tell her. She can't help it."

Could, however, Mt. Pascataquac upstage Bev?

Mimi said, "Mother and I didn't discuss the problem of Grandmother, whether she'll feel up to coming. She wouldn't have to climb a mountain, needless to say, just come to the reception."

Snowy said gently, "She's very ill."

"While I work at her looms, I— Oops, Pascataquac Road."

On the corner, in the yard of his white Cape, Cedric Barlow was scowling at his daffodils which, like Snowy's, were beginning to die, their season over. He glanced up, recognized Snowy, lifted a hand to wave, hesitated.

Snowy waved and asked Mimi, "When is the wedding?"

"June sixth. Lloyd arranged to have his vacation start then,

279

before the summer-people invasion. We're hiking in the Adirondacks on our honeymoon. Not much time between now and the sixth, but that's the idea. We wanted to wait until the last minute to invite people so Mother would be too busy with her studying and exam to turn it into a gala event. Incredible, Mother a realtor! She's serious. Dad's just beginning to grasp that."

June sixth. The date rang two bells: D day, and the day Robert Kennedy died. Let Mimi remain oblivious. "Who marries people in mountaintop ceremonies?"

"Joe Fowler, a hiking friend who's a justice of the peace."

They drove past other white houses, through woods, and then a small brown-stained wooden sign appeared at the side of the road. MT. PASCATAQUAC. Quac. Like the ducks at the wedding in the house on the river.

Mimi parked in the clearing. "We've decided to invite eighteen people: my family including Grandmother, Lloyd's parents and brother and sister-in-law, and Kristin—my roommate, and Barry—Lloyd's roommate—and his wife, and a New Hampshire reunion, we're inviting Puddles and Guy and you and Alan and—oh shit, I *knew* I'd do this!"

"It's okay."

Mimi jumped out of the car. "Four cars, we figured, and Lloyd's pickup. There's plenty of room here for parking, don't you think? Come on, get out."

"The bugs, we didn't bring fly dope." So they'd have to go home.

Mimi opened the trunk and took out the backpack and two beautiful walking sticks. She unzipped a side pocket of the pack and produced a little bottle of Cutter's. "Fly dope!"

Snowy slowly got out.

Locking the car, Mimi said, "Lloyd claims my bumper stickers are just asking for vandalism. He won't put any on his pickup. Chicken!" She handed Snowy the fly dope and a walking stick and swung the pack onto her back.

Snowy anointed herself as they went into the woods up the

steep trail Alan had climbed with Ruhamah. You can always turn back; it's only a walk in the woods, an uphill walk. And the woods hid the elevation while she and Mimi climbed up and up, but she wished Mimi would provide some distraction by talking. If talking was against Mimi's hiking rules, the hell with those rules. She said, "These sticks are lovely."

"Lloyd made them, you have to find the right saplings—the handles are the roots, see? I'm trying to get him to make a batch and sell them at the League. Extra bucks. A married couple should be saving for a house, not live forever in an apartment over a ski shop, but at least that's better than the apartments in the likes of Leicester Terrace."

An apartment over a bridal shop. "You and Lloyd aren't Yuppies."

Mimi whooped.

On they climbed. Eventually Snowy commented, "Climbing must use different muscles than jogging."

Mimi got the hint. "Cellar hole," she said, stopping.

Snowy wouldn't have noticed it, the old granite blocks were so lost in moss and leaves and the trunks of the white birches growing out of it. She smelled an unseen apple tree. There had been a house and barn here, an orchard, pastures, a family. Had Alan spotted this cellar hole? She said, "Cleora remembers sheep grazing on Pascataquac when she was a child."

"Once Lloyd and I were hiking with some people from the Midwest, and one of the guys asked us why these stone walls had been built through the woods."

They smiled, and then Mimi said, "People my age, we have sex first and get acquainted second. Or we did before AIDS. Don't tell Mother. With Lloyd—"

"He and I did that. Alan and I."

"Really?"

"We called it love at first sight."

"With Lloyd, we were friends first. Did Mother and Dad sleep together first?"

"Have you asked your mother?"

281

"That's what almost-aunts are for." Mimi shifted the weight of the pack and they climbed onward. After a while Mimi stopped again, pointing. "Bear tree."

Claw marks six feet up a balsam, the bark slashed and sticky sap running out. "Eek," Snowy said. "Like a cat sharpening its claws?"

"Sometimes they're climbing the tree, sometimes marking the boundary posts of their territory."

Snowy prickled all over with goosebumps. Now she couldn't turn back; she couldn't confront a bear alone, wielding a walking stick. When Mimi started climbing again, she stayed close.

Mimi said, "Mother only says she and Dad dated off and on since she was a sophomore in high school. How sexually active was dating in the Fifties?"

Sexually active! Snowy began laughing, and she was still laughing as they walked out of the woods into blue. They were on a rock pinnacle in the sky. Ahead, a log cabin seemed a Lincoln-Logs project, with more logs piled in front near the unfinished porch, a plaything beside the fire tower which rose like a science-fiction monster on metal legs. Beyond lay a zigzag view of mountain ranges above gleaming lakes.

"What do you think?" Mimi said. "Seems perfect, unless there's a sheer drop. I don't want to exchange vows worrying about somebody falling over a cliff." She set down her pack.

The cabin door opened and onto the porch stepped Santa Claus.

"Hi," he said, welcoming them to the North Pole. He was in off-season clothes, faded jeans and chambray shirt, but his curly hair and beard were white, and gold spectacles circled his eyes.

"Hi," Mimi said, taking a pair of binoculars out of the pack.

"The tower's open," he said.

Snowy began backing up toward the woods. The summit wasn't actually the head of a pin in space; it spread into a plateau. She knew, however, that unless she lashed herself to a tree, she'd plunge over the edge.

Mimi said, "Plenty big enough for a wedding, don't you think?" She walked away to the brink. "Hooray," she called, "no cliffs, just slopes."

The man hadn't moved. He stared at Snowy.

She blushed. "Heights."

He said, "Snowy?"

Mimi returned. "Are you the fire warden? Would there be any objection to holding a wedding here?"

He was out of focus. Snowy saw him as if through Mimi's binoculars unadjusted. She blinked, and his disguise of years disappeared. "Tom."

Her stomach growled.

"It's Snowy all right," he said, remembering the fortune he'd spent in Hooper's Dairy Bar on her appetite. Snowy!

She blurted, "This is Bev's daughter." That took his gaze off her for a moment. Tom Forbes. He wasn't a true Santa Claus, though he was heavier than he'd been; his beard and mustache were trimmed to a sea captain's. His curls! Ringlets instead of his high-school crewcut, his short collegiate cut. Impossible!

Mimi said to Tom, "You know my mother? Neat, then you'll have to let us have the wedding here, and you're invited." She hoisted the pack. "Snowy, got to get some food into you. Over there's a good place to picnic."

Away Mimi went again.

In wonderment, Tom asked Snowy, "How many years?" Answering himself, he said, "Thirty."

Twenty-nine, she mentally corrected before realizing she was counting from that last glimpse on his wedding day, while he was counting from their last night in the cream-colored convertible.

He said, "And you're not a day older."

"Ah," she said, "as Bev's mother once remarked of you, 'He's a charmer.'"

"She did?" He hopped down off the platform. Nearer, Snowy wasn't the woman who'd come out of the woods laughing. The lack of makeup might be a feminist statement, but the deep washed-out weariness, the bags under her eyes?

Mimi waved a grinder. "Over here!"

Snowy blushed again. "I can't, Mimi. It's too far."

Tom asked, "Want to go indoors, would walls help?"

"You live in this cabin?"

"When I'm on duty."

Snowy didn't see any signs of Joanne.

Mimi loped back. "No problem." She plunked the pack down and handed Snowy a grinder and a bottle of beer and a bottle opener. "Eat. Per order of Mother."

Tom grinned. "Snowy doesn't have to be persuaded to eat."

"Well." Sitting down, Mimi leaned against a tree trunk and ripped open a bag of potato chips. "Snowy, did you know you can see your barn roof from here?"

Tom asked Snowy, "You live in Woodcombe?"

Snowy put her chin up. She said, her tone distant, "My husband and daughter and I have lived here two years."

"Oh." It had taken him a long time to learn that her haughtiness was really shyness. He watched her sit down abruptly, as though hamstrung. He asked, "May I?" and sat down on the other side of Mimi. If Mimi and Snowy were friends, Bev and Snowy must not have become enemies because of him. Snowy had a daughter too. Amazing. She had a husband. Of course.

Mimi said to him, "Sorry I can't offer you a beer, only got a couple, though I suppose you aren't allowed to drink on the job anyway. Some potato chips? Being a fire warden must be a fun job."

"It's a change." He saw Snowy fumbling sweatily with the bottle opener against the silver-foiled cap, so he reached around Mimi and took the bottle opener and the bottle. Unmechanical Snowy.

Snowy thought that he could have reached *through* Mimi, for all at once Mimi seemed invisible, a person who hadn't existed back when Snowy and Tom were swigging beer Tom bought illegally, underage. "Thank you," she said as he presented her with the opened bottle. To give Mimi substance again, she said, "Beck's Beer, imported. Mimi, this is Yuppie beer. Vaa!"

Tom laughed. That "vaa" was an admonishing noise used by French Canadians, picked up by other Gunthwaite kids, and he hadn't heard it in years.

"Our secret vice," Mimi said, "Lloyd's and mine." She asked Tom, "If I ever wanted a fire-warden job, how'd I go about getting one?"

"Helps if your college roommate is now a state senator." He ate a potato chip. "Do you live in Woodcombe too?"

Alan sat at the dining room table last month, telling Snowy and Ruhamah during supper that the fire tower on Pascataquac had been reopened and he'd met the new fire warden who came in for some groceries, a nice guy.

Snowy said, "I forgot introductions. Tom, this is Julia Marie Lambert."

Mimi cried, "Mimi for short!"

"Lambert," Tom said. "I read that Bev and Roger got married." Joanne's friend Adele had sent her a clipping about the big wedding. But no clipping had ever arrived about Snowy's wedding. Had Adele exercised tact? Or had Snowy eloped? Probably Adele just hadn't bothered, the importance of people from high-school days dwindling unless they stayed in town. Where had Snowy lived before Woodcombe?

"Mimi lives in Leicester," Snowy said. Tom's glasses had bifocal teardrops with a line: *tri*focals. "Bev and Roger live in Connecticut. Mimi, this is Tom Forbes. We all went to school together."

Mimi asked, "What's the fire-warden schedule like?"

"April to November," Tom said. "Nine to five, three days on, two days off, three on, two off, then nine days on and two off, the schedules overlapping so all the areas are always covered." He knew he should return to the tower in case a raging fire had broken out while he was dazedly talking to an old

285

girlfriend—and another old girlfriend's daughter. "I guess I ought to get back to work."

As he stood up, Mimi scrambled to her feet saying, "I'll come along. Snowy?"

"No, thanks." She looked up at Tom. Under ordinary circumstances she would have forced herself to make a social gesture, not invite him to dinner—panic attack!—but at least invite him for a drink, to meet Alan and Ruhamah. All grown-up, civilized, relying on Alan to carry the conversation.

He waited. Would she suggest a visit, to meet her family? Friends again, platonic, thirty years after she'd dumped him? To think that if he hadn't come down from the tower to take a piss, he'd never have recognized her, since she was apparently incapable of climbing the tower. She used to climb towers, he remembered; Puddles had talked their gang of girls into joining the Ground Observer Corps, and Thursday nights were Snowy and Bev's turn to climb the abandoned Gunthwaite fire tower to do their homework, supposedly on the alert for enemy planes. She had even climbed the Washington Monument.

Snowy said, "Small world."

Dismissal. "Small state, New Hampshire," he said, "but I never expected you to be still living in it." He followed Mimi to the tower and up the metal stairs, noticing regretfully that Mimi hadn't inherited Bev's walk, which back in high school caused guys to fall down and gnaw the floor.

Snowy repeated Tom's words. Did they mean Unfulfilled Promise? Had he become the type to make such a dig? You're oversensitive, she told herself, covertly plucking the grinder to bits and skimming them into the woods, junk food for birds and animals, and then emptying the beer bottle into the pine needles behind her as if tipping a drink into a potted palm.

In the tower's crow's-nest room, known officially as a cab, Tom asked Mimi, "How are your mother and father?"

"Fine," Mimi said, lifting binoculars, scanning the mountains out the windows. "They'll be at the wedding."

"Any brothers or sisters?"

"Two brothers, one sister."

Good God. Bev was the last person he could picture a mother. No, next to last after Snowy. "And Snowy has—?"

Mimi was reading maps now. "The one daughter."

"How old?"

"Sixteen."

He remembered Snowy's sixteenth birthday. "What does Snowy's husband do?"

Mimi looked up. "Huh? Oh, the Woodcombe store."

"Snowy's husband owns the general store in Woodcombe?"

"Um, yes."

You're shitting me, Tom thought. Since he got here last month he'd been buying provisions at that store, from an older woman and a tall guy with whom he'd discussed the weather and the reopening of some of New Hampshire's fire towers, joking about the hazards of packing in eggs to the cabin.

Mimi said, "You haven't heard."

"What?"

"Nothing." Mimi went to the door. "I'm positive Pascataquac's the site for the wedding, but I'll be bringing Lloyd—my friend—up to see if he agrees."

"Look forward to meeting him," Tom said.

As Mimi and Snowy walked down the mountain, Mimi talked about how maybe she'd wear some kind of wedding dress and maybe she could change out of hiking clothes in that cabin, and then she said, "Before, before—Lloyd and I were thinking that if we liked Pascataquac, there's this swell place below it to hold a reception."

Snowy was listing jobs that could be done at home, taking in typing, taking in laundry (Alan's unlaundered clothes hoarded in the trash can liner they'd last made love on), stuffing envelopes. "Reception?"

"At Hurricane Farm. We would handle everything, the food and decorations, the housework, the yard work, everything. But now since—"

287

Foreclosure, the accountant had said. The bottom line, he'd said that a lot.

"—not seemly," Mimi said. "The conventions, proprieties."

Harriet! She should call the Bennington alumni office and try to locate Harriet, a rich fairy godmother. But she couldn't borrow money from Harriet or anyone because she couldn't pay it back. She had to hang onto Hurricane Farm on her own. "The hell with seemliness," she said. "Have the reception there."

"We may?"

"What are almost-aunts for? And if it rains, have the wedding there too." She was saying this, she who found weddings presumptuous and silly.

Mimi gave her a hug.

When they reached the cellar hole, Snowy asked, "Did you tell him?"

"No."

"Thank you."

"Surprise, Snowy. You've climbed a mountain."

LATE THE NEXT afternoon, having mowed the front lawn, Mimi shouted to Snowy in the garden, "I brought in the mail and there's a letter from Grandmother, I didn't snoop, it was on the bottom and stuck out. You sure you'll be okay?"

"I'm fine."

The Rabbit hurtled away, Mimi going to Leicester to tend her apartment. After work, Lloyd would follow her here in his pickup and they'd climb Pascataquac for a picnic supper.

Snowy went into the empty house. Ruhamah hadn't come home yesterday; she had phoned and told Mimi she was staying at Jennifer's a few days, and to Mimi's wedding news and invitation she'd said only, "Oh." When Mimi asked if she wanted to talk to Snowy, Ruhamah said no, but Snowy had steeled herself and phoned her back at the Rollins house, which Snowy had never seen so she couldn't picture the setting as Jennifer answered the phone and said, "I'm sorry, Ruhamah is in the bathroom," but she *could* picture Ruhamah making "Get-rid-of-her" faces to Jennifer. Snowy asked Jennifer, "Is your mother there, could I speak with her?" Jennifer said, "She's at work." So Snowy had looked up the phone number of Fay's bakery and tremblingly dialed. "Fay, this is Henrietta Sutherland—"

Fay said, "Snowy? I was going to call you tonight. Martin and I are so sorry. How are you doing?"

"Ruhamah—she's staying with you?"

"If it's all right with you."

"The imposition—"

"No trouble. We're so very sorry—"

"Do you know if she saw the school psychologist?"

"Yes, Jennifer and Kim convinced her—Kim Parker, who saw the psychologist herself during her parents' divorce."

"Well. Thank you."

After hanging up, Snowy had realized she'd forgotten that Ruhamah would need clothes. The hell with it; Ruhamah had decided to stay at the Rollinses', and she could decide what to do about clothes. Probably she would borrow Jennifer's.

Then Snowy had phoned the school psychologist, a Carolyn McDonald, who said, "Ruhamah isn't reacting in an unusual way, Ms. Sutherland. She's temporarily escaping from associations while she works through her grief."

"What should I do?"

"Be there for her when she's ready to come back. If she wants you to join our talks, please do. Ms. Sutherland—I hope you yourself are getting help?"

"Oh, yes," Snowy had lied.

Now, on the kitchen counter beneath a stack of little white envelopes, sympathy notes, Snowy saw Julia's weak handwriting on a regular-size envelope. She opened it.

Dear Snowy:
There are phases you'll go through, and you'll never

stop missing him. With Richard and the War, I tried to
practice stoicism, tried to convince myself that
mourning, viewed objectively and perhaps
psychologically, was a form of self-pity, although
inevitably human and unavoidable. With Fred, I
surrendered myself to grief. "Give sorrow words . . ."
Now I'll write you about our turtles down here.

Snowy looked up. She was sixteen, the evening before the Varsity tryouts, and Julia had phoned to attempt to calm her, telling
her about seeing deer in the orchard at dusk. Thirty-two years
later, Snowy stood in the kitchen of this house that had reminded her so much of Julia's and listened to the country noises
outdoors which were the same ones she had learned at Julia's,
spring peepers, chipmunks, brook, the bird-feeder sounds of
wings whirring, rose-breasted grosbeaks clicking open sunflower seeds.

There are nests of turtle eggs on the beach and
tracks where at night mothers climbed up the beach,
dug the nests, laid the eggs, covered them, and then
went back to the sea. Certain people think this private
act is a tourist attraction and they bring cameras and
flashlights. Raccoons are a problem too, plundering the
nests.
Yet when I reflect on all the alligators and cranes
and egrets and herons and pelicans and buzzards and
hawks and armadillos and God knows what else I've
seen in my years here, I am astonished that so many
have somehow adapted to the concrete chaos Florida
has become. Today an enormous blue land crab went
scuttling across the yard.
My love and sympathy to you and Ruhamah—

Julia

The ground shook. An earthquake? Hooray, she welcomed it,
she hoped the lawn would crack into a canyon and the house

290

tumble in, with her inside. Then she heard a bell clanging and ran to the porch.

Five Guernseys galloped up the driveway, a seismic stampede. Jesus Christ, the Thornes' cows were loose!

"Stop!" She rushed down the steps. You forgot how *big* cows were up close, and these weren't placidly watching her from behind a gate bar, these were fugitives on a rampage. "Halt!"

They skylarked in the daffodils, their huge udders swinging between their legs.

"Nancy Belle!" Cleora came limping down the road brandishing a broom. "Nancy Belle! Look out—head her off!"

Snowy dodged a wall of brown hide as Nancy Belle thundered onward to the backyard, great hooves kicking up divots of lawn and the cowbell resounding deafeningly.

An old green Jeep braked at the mailbox.

Cleora yelled, "Keep them away from your garden!"

"*How?*" Snowy yelled. The herd was following Nancy Belle, and Snowy jumped aside again before she got trampled, then raced after them. They were aiming straight for her garden rows and the bales of precious mulch hay she'd been spreading. "You fuckers, *no!*" Nancy Belle stopped to investigate the wheelbarrow, so the other cows took a break too, munching the lawn.

Somebody behind her said, "If we can grab the one with the bell—"

Tom. He began sidling toward Nancy Belle, and Snowy copied him.

Cleora called, "Careful!" Hobbling past the house, she waved her broom. "Nancy Belle, you come here—oh, drat these legs of mine!"

Nancy Belle considered her. She considered the stealthy approach of Tom and Snowy.

"Careful!" Cleora said.

The bell clanged, and the cows romped forward across the garden.

Cleora cried, "Keep them out of the woods!"

291

The cows sailed over the stone wall as if it were the moon.

Swatting blackflies, Tom asked Snowy, "I don't suppose she has lots of strapping 4-H kids still at home?"

"No."

"Have you ever done this before?"

"No."

"Me neither."

They sprinted around the garden and clambered over the stone wall into the woods. The cows were crashing on ahead, the bell pealing jubilantly. Snowy had never *run* through woods, and this wasn't a tidy German forest; the second-growth trees had tangles of underbrush to trip you up, branches of saplings to slap you in the face, spiky twigs of dead pine boughs to blind you—Tom's glasses protected him from that fate, but either he or she was bound to break a leg as they leapt logs and slipped on the pale parchment of leaves and pine needles, squashing Solomon's seal.

She panted, "The brook, does water stop them? If they veer left, they'll hit the brook, and maybe we could turn them and drive them back down the logging road."

He thought how she sounded like characters in the many many westerns they had gone to together, and he would have made a joke, but for what he'd learned when he went to the store just now, his ostensible mission a pack of Trident gum, his actual one a new look at the owner. "Listen." The cowbell rang from the left.

On they ran, and suddenly the cowbell was close, and as they pushed through bushes onto the logging road, they saw the hind ends of the cows moving not in the direction of home, naturally, but farther up the road.

She lowered her voice under the noise of the brook and the bell. "There's a beaver swamp up there flooding the road, maybe that'll stop them."

"Maybe milking-time will."

She hadn't thought she would ever return to the swamp. They found the cows milling around here, bemused.

Tom said, "That's some dam—half a football field?"

Alan never measured in terms of basketball courts. She couldn't help glancing at the picnic birch log.

"If," Tom said, "we tiptoe to the other side of them—"

"Okay." She walked past the log, stepping on the ground where she and Alan had lain. Had he known it would be the last time, had he decided by then? She followed Tom into the woods and partway around the curve of the swamp. "Now what?"

"Make like a banshee."

They exploded out of the woods hollering. Nancy Belle didn't seem impressed.

Tom said, "So much for that brainstorm."

"Wait, look."

Nancy Belle lumbered off down the road, leading the others.

Snowy said, "*Got* to keep them from another chance at the garden," and she and Tom jogged after them as the pace picked up, Snowy wanting to do more yelling, screaming, lamenting, keening. Give sorrow wails. How had Tom learned where she lived? Had Mimi pointed out the barn roof and he'd figured directions? Or had he stopped at the store to ask directions?

Beneath the roar of the brook he said, "My daughter's a forestry major, but I doubt if she'll have to take a course in chasing cows through woods."

"Your daughter?"

"Libby, she's an Elizabeth after, well, after Joanne's grandmother, she's a sophomore at UNH."

"Where do you live when you're not in the sky?"

"Newburgh."

"Newburgh, New Hampshire?"

"North of here."

"Yes." She and Alan and Ruhamah had detoured to Newburgh on one of their trips to the White Mountains because she had been curious; in books about the mountains she'd read of this old farming town. Like Gunthwaite, Newburgh lay in a river valley, but its history was north-country-rowdy, for during the time of the long log drives the Main Street had been raucous with saloons and dance halls and men rushing out of the woods with five hundred dollars or more of winter wages burning a hole in their pockets. She had found that nowadays Main Street was a quiet place of two churches, a post office, a grocery store, a hardware store, a Sit 'n' Snack Luncheonette, a small lumber mill, and an old building with a newer sign saying: NORTH COUNTRY COFFINS. Alan and Ruhamah had been amused by that, while she remembered the ads she had seen; hadn't she considered it for her father's funeral? And Alan had admired the Victorian school building on a hilltop above the river, a wooden edifice of gables and turrets, with an ugly cinderblock addition about which he'd tsk-tsked.

Had Tom become a teacher? That must have been his school. Snowy said, "If I lived in a town named Newburgh, I'd always be hungry."

Tom said, "I recall that you're always hungry anyway."

They jogged along, brushing away bugs.

He said, "Newburgh plays Woodcombe. Joanne and I would drive down for basketball games when our kids were playing." Newburgh was too small for football, thank God; he disagreed with Joanne that autumn and football were as intertwined as spring and the Junior Prom. He didn't even watch football on TV, telling friends that he was a football widower. He was glad that Joanne stayed glued to the tube for football games, because early in their Newburgh years he had started hiking, and he preferred hiking alone. Joanne never missed him when there was a game on. Sports! Newburgh made up for its football deprivation with its passion for basketball, and the Victorian school building's cinderblock elementary-school wing had recently been balanced by an equal eyesore, a new gymnasium that wrapped itself around the other end like a flow of lava. The worthy citizens of Newburgh, he thought; they'll pay higher property taxes to get a new gym, but they'll scream bloody murder over buying new textbooks. And here he was still pissing and moaning about that, although he'd got free of school eleven years ago.

294

He asked Snowy, "Does your daughter play basketball?"

"Not on a team, just gym."

"Cheerleading?"

"She hasn't decided whether or not to try out."

"Libby didn't."

Snowy imagined and Tom recalled Joanne's reaction to this. He asked, "What's your daughter's name?"

"Ruhamah. After Ruhamah Reed."

"I used to teach Ruhamah Reed, what I could get away with in a high school."

She registered that he evidently wasn't aware of her biography. "Are you on sabbatical? How come you're working at the tower while school's in session? Damn, how far ahead are the cows—eek!"

She still eeked. One of the cows had taken a copious crap in the middle of the road. As they skirted it and ran on, he said, "You could collect it for your garden."

"I collect at the Thornes' farm when the stuff is well-aged, like fine wine. They let us use their truck to haul it."

The Snowy he had known in high school would never have dreamed she'd someday be standing on a manure pile, pitchforking shit. He said, "While I'm loading manure, I always think about Aldous Huxley and elephant shit in that 'Jaipur' essay, when he was riding an elephant who left a magnificent pile and an old woman ran out of her hut and thanked him."

Huxley had been startled, she remembered, and then he realized the pile meant a week's fuel to the woman, a thought which depressed him, but, mulling over the event, he also realized that no animal other than man had had the wit to do more than manufacture dung, and he had tried to take pride in this achievement. She quoted, " 'In spite of the consolations of philosophy, I remained pensive.' " She asked, "So you have a garden?" Thirty years ago, they would never have been discussing manure.

"Until this spring." She still had that trick memory.

Apparently, Snowy gathered, he did the gardening, not

Joanne. Snowy and Tom gardeners, residential kids whose mothers had dished up Bird's-Eye. The Tom she had known in high school wouldn't have had any more idea who Aldous Huxley was than Nancy Belle did.

They reached the resolutely moving cows, and when they emerged from the woods, Cleora stood on sentry duty beside the garden, broom ready. "Nancy Belle, *home!*"

Milking-time due, Nancy Belle obeyed, and Cleora went after the cows down the driveway, calling back, "Thank you."

Tom righted a pea fence.

Snowy asked, "Do I replant in the hoof craters or wait to see what comes up?"

They both remembered a high-school joke. Boy to girl: Why don't you sit on my lap and we'll talk about the first thing that comes up.

Tom said hastily, "I'd wait, less work." He looked at Pascataquac and the tower above Snowy's home.

With a shift in the breeze, from the orchard floated the aching scent of apple blossoms, heavier and warmer than that of the wild apple trees on her morning run. She should offer him a drink to thank him; on the porch they would continue catching up on each other's lives, the way the triumvirate had over the phone. But catching up was decidedly different with Tom. And she would have to tell him what had happened. The backyard began twirling, she was going to lose her balance, make a fool of herself, collapse. "Thanks for the help with the roundup. I'd better go with Cleora in case Nancy Belle takes another notion."

Dismissal again, he knew, but he ran on beside Snowy past the house, down the driveway.

Damn Tom, why didn't he leave? She would trip and fall.

Around a bend they came upon Cleora and the cows, and Snowy explained, "Just in case."

"I'm sorry about your garden," Cleora said, eyeing Tom.

Cleora must be thinking what Snowy had thought long ago about Charl: Fast worker. Snowy said, "Cleora, this is Tom

296

Forbes, an old friend. He's the fire warden on Pascataquac. Tom, Cleora Thorne."

Tom said, "How do you do?"

"Not as well as I used to."

They walked along, Snowy and Tom taking short steps to slow themselves to Cleora's painful steps and swiping at bugs with second-nature gestures that resembled some strange tribal dance, Snowy maintaining her balance by watching the massive bulk of the cows filling the road ahead. Tails swished; the cowbell clanked peacefully.

Bugs didn't bother Cleora, who said, "At least you hadn't set out your plants."

"Yes," Snowy said, adding politely, "Last year a deer walked through the broccoli."

Tom said, "Of course it chose your favorite vegetable."

He remembered. Her T-shirt yesterday with only a vestige of a green pattern left couldn't have reminded him. She said, "Last week I was worrying about a moose in our yard." Alan beside her at the window. "It spared us."

"Do woodchucks?" he asked.

"Oh lord, a constant battle. You too?"

Cleora told Snowy, "You need a dog. I never had no trouble until Zeke died."

Died.

"The pasture fence," Cleora said. "Pete'll say he'll be over this evening and then I'll have to phone him day in day out before he'll put in an appearance."

Tom asked, "Pete?"

"A boy we hire sometimes, now my husband ain't able."

Tom said, "I can fix the fence."

Cleora glanced at him. "You got cows?"

"No, but I'm handy."

The farm came into view, and the cows broke into a ponderous trot, Snowy fearing they were inspired to run away again. Instead, deceptively docile, they entered the barnyard and clumped up the ramp into the barn.

297

Cleora said, her grudging tone not quite masking gratitude, "There's probably some fenceposts in the shed. Isaac might never find a use for something, but he'd never throw it away." She hobbled after the cows, saying, "If it was up to me, I'd get rid of them cows in a minute."

Tom ducked into the swaybacked little shed, while Snowy looked at the fire tower. Fires: lightning, campfires, cigarettes. Tom didn't have a pack of cigarettes in his shirt pocket and he hadn't yesterday. Lucky Strikes, that's what he'd smoked. Fires: cremation.

Out of the shed Tom carried a peeled fencepost, a sledgehammer, and a large pair of pliers. "Fencing tool," he said, feinting with the pliers, "not a fencing sword."

"This is very kind of you. It isn't keeping you from the tower?"

"I'm off until Saturday. I got off early."

Why wasn't he driving up to Newburgh, then? She said, "Let me carry something."

He gave her the fencing tool. "Thanks."

Self-conscious, they walked along the road, scrutinizing the pasture's barbed-wire fence.

He said, "There."

It wasn't a break in the fence; Nancy Belle & Company had simply trodden the fence down. "Oh God," Snowy said, "they could do this every day—my garden—it's a wonder this hasn't happened a million times!"

"Maybe an extra-bad case of spring fever."

He pulled staples from the knocked-over fencepost. Swatting bugs, she remembered that his birthday was the fifteenth, Friday. He must have given himself the gift of arranging to quit work early.

She said, "Your parents?" A sign of age, interest in relatives. During high school, she'd wanted his family as nonexistent as she had wanted her own.

"My mother's in Florida, my father's—dead."

"I'm sorry."

He slammed in staples to hold the barbed wire. "Yours?"

"Both dead."

He looked up. "They are? I'm sorry."

She said, "Your older brother was in the Army? What did your little brother do?"

"George is retired from the Army, he's living in Massachusetts, doing TV repair. Doug went in too, he got out last year, he's also in Mass., starting an upholstery business. My older son decided on the Army. It's beyond me how they can stand it, even with the prospect of retirement and a pension in twenty years."

"Were you drafted?"

"I scraped by."

Older son, he had said. "You have two sons? How old?"

"David's twenty-two, Brandon twenty-seven in July."

Joanne must have chosen the name Brandon, Tom's middle name which had embarrassed him. A gap between these sons, though not so much as between him and Doug.

He drove in the final staple. "Let's hope that gives them pause."

They walked back to the shed, Snowy counting. Brandon would have been born in 1960. Two years after Tom and Joanne got married. This proved definitely that Tom hadn't had to marry her; he had married Joanne because he loved her.

"Yoo-hoo!" Cleora shouted from the doorway of the barn. "Snowy! There's pies on the kitchen table, take one."

"Oh no, thank you—"

"I know you got plenty of food, take one for him. I always make too many, habit."

Cleora disappeared back into the barn's gloom, Tom went into the shed, and Snowy stepped indoors, wary. She'd never been in the farmhouse before. The kitchen, bleakly shabby, had a genuine farmhouse smell of tracked-in manure mingling with the smell of baking. The old rocker beside the woodstove was unrefinished, its arms worn bare; the crushed pillow on its seat probably covered broken wicker. Snowy saw her own kitchen shriveled by poverty but she wouldn't care if she could just keep

299

the house, keep paying the mortgage. There were four pies on the scrubbed wooden table, and she gingerly touched a tin plate. Cool. Had Mimi returned Sunday's pie plate to Cleora? She'd lost control of her household.

Outdoors, Tom waited, looking at the barn. "Only sheer orneriness is holding that barn up. Want me to carry?"

"Thank you."

Up and down along the Roller Coaster Road they walked, Tom trying to think what shape he'd be in if Joanne had just killed herself. A drunken stupor, probably. The doctor must have Snowy on something.

He asked, "How did you like Bennington?"

"Bennington?"

"I drove over there once, the fall of your freshman year."

"You *did?*"

"To be able to picture where you were." Nice campus, he had thought; nice girls walking along the paths but he hadn't spotted her. And when he'd driven back to Rumford, he had phoned Joanne's dorm. Until the past April, he had been dating only Joanne and Bev, but that final encounter with Snowy, when she dumped him after they'd at last made love, had reminded him never to get too involved with a woman, so he returned to playing the field, from which Joanne eliminated herself, chastely faithful to Coast Guard Chris to whom she was pinned. But when Joanne answered the dorm phone he asked her, "Would you consider swapping a Kappa pin for an Alpha?" Joanne wrote a Dear Chris letter, and Tom's guilt over the whole situation was assuaged by steady tail again with the gorgeous Joanne.

Snowy was thinking: Tom at Bennington. What if I'd seen him there, what would I have done?

Tom said, "So you named your daughter after a poet." To be a poet had been Snowy's ambition.

"Yes."

"Did you ever get any of your poems published?"

300

"Some magazines, and a few collections." Snowy swiftly changed subjects. "Cleora is always—"

"Holy Christ," Tom said. "You can tell how well-read this ex-English teacher is."

"They aren't exactly famous works. Cleora's always threatening to sell the cows—when Isaac dies, implied. Even after the cows' havoc today, I'd be sorry, though I'm not the person doing the work."

"Another failed farm. Newburgh has a lot of them, but some farms there have been able to withstand the pressures of bulk milk production. These farm kids still bring the aroma of morning chores to school, like their ancestors did. Every time other teachers moved on to better-paying towns and asked me why I stayed in Newburgh, I would reply, 'Because it's probably the last school in the state that smells of manure.'"

This almost got a smile out of Snowy.

Tom said, "We bought a failed farm, unrestored."

"You restored it?"

"Well, I fixed it up. Back when I was graduating and we went to interviews at various schools, we decided on Newburgh because the principal—he was desperate, Newburgh being too far away from civilization to attract many prospects—he actually drove us around town to show us places to live, saying we could afford to rent a house there, not just an apartment. We chose the cheapest place, this run-down farm, for thirty-five dollars a month, and eight years later we could afford to buy it."

Snowy was imagining his farm when she realized that he had said, "*I* was graduating." He and Joanne were in the same class, so shouldn't he have used the plural? She asked, "Does Joanne teach?"

"Second grade."

"God, she deserves a purple heart."

Tom didn't reply that Joanne had one, a lavender Valentine chocolate box on the bedroom wall. It was part of Joanne's vast collection, which he'd first seen when, home from Rumford, they had gone out on a date—an Alumni-Varsity basketball

301

game and a New Year's Eve party welcoming 1958—and had returned to her house; her parents were still out at another party, so they had the place to themselves, a house much like his own, both their fathers machine operators at Trask's and earning, he supposed, about the same. He hadn't been upstairs before, and although he knew that Joanne loved Valentine's Day, because last February he'd got the strong hint he should give her a box of chocolates, he hadn't expected the sight of a wall in her bedroom almost completely covered with heart-shaped boxes, red, pink, blue, white, satiny and beribboned, and as he and she fucked frenziedly on her frilly white bedspread amid a faint scent of chocolates and almond flavoring, he found himself remembering the only other box of chocolates he'd ever bought, un-primed, for Snowy, whose flabbergasted expression he suddenly saw more clearly than Joanne's flushed face below him. Goddamn Snowy, he thought. Exorcism! Lying beside Joanne, panting, cupping his sticky Trojan off the mass of ruffles, he said, "Let's get married." After a while Joanne said, "I'd have to quit cheerleading. But—"

Snowy was saying, "Mimi and her Lloyd are going to climb Pascataquac later this afternoon, but you'll be in Newburgh."

"I'll be back Saturday. I've got a phone at the tower, if they want to arrange the wedding date."

"Okay."

They'd reached the mailbox. He asked, "Why's it called Hurricane Farm?"

"A hurricane in seventeen-eighty-eight."

"Oh."

Walking up the driveway, she took a breath and said, "Would you like a drink or a beer?"

"Thanks, I should be on my way." He'd be late enough as it was: Joanne had wanted him home early to get a head start on the spring chores he'd been neglecting, to perk up the house for his birthday bash Friday night. "I'll give you the cabin's phone number. Can't you use this pie?"

"No."

He set the pie in the Jeep, planning to dispose of it along the roadside to circumvent having to explain why he'd bought a pie at, say, a food sale, when Joanne would be making the usual enormous chocolate cake.

Snowy glanced into the Jeep. A laundry bag. He was taking his laundry home to Joanne, like a college kid. "Remember how Bev hated riding in her stepfather's Jeep?"

Instead, he remembered Snowy's last mention of Bev that April night thirty years ago. Snowy had said, "She was my best friend." Past tense. He asked, "You and Bev visit often?"

"Not for twenty years."

In the kitchen, looking around, he recited the phone number which she began writing on a rooster memo pad he recognized. And hadn't the braided rug been one of the many in her folks' house? He had assumed she had married an Ivy League guy and was living in a grand suburban house outside New York, Boston, someplace; no matter where her husband had gone to school and they'd lived before, she now lived in an expensively restored farmhouse an hour and a half's drive from Newburgh. Then he saw that her handwriting was shooting crazily over the pad. He said, "Snowy, I stopped at the store this afternoon. I know. How can I help?"

Snowy dropped the pencil.

He thought: She's going to faint. He gripped her by the shoulders.

"*You?*" she screamed. "He did what you did, only worse! He left me, left me, left me! Get out of here!"

"Where's your daughter? Is anybody staying with you?"

"Get the fucking hell out of here!"

He went.

❦

SHE'D GONE UPSTAIRS to her office then, to bed, semi-hibernation, dragging herself up just to go to the bathroom, blearily noting on her desk the bottles of vitamins brought from the kitchen, the trays of meals which were taken away uneaten, a succession of suppers, breakfasts, lunches—

Inside Saran Wrap, marshmallow fluff oozed, sticking to the plastic as she peeled it off. Marshmallow fluff and raspberry jam, a winter sandwich. She gobbled it. The sandwich was fresh but she smelled stale, so she went downstairs to her bedroom and bathroom, showered, and got dressed, an old shirt and a pair of painter's pants.

In the living room, two sleeping bags and pads lay rolled beside the fireplace. In the kitchen, she looked at the clock, the calendar, the thermometer, more little white envelopes stacked on the counter. The late afternoon was sunny. She opened the screen door and saw Mimi sitting in a wicker chair, feet up on the porch railing, writing in a notebook, sipping a Yuppie beer.

"Hi," Mimi said. "Did that sandwich whet your appetite? Mother hoped it might. Feeling rested? Puddles and your doctor told me to let you sleep, so when your lawyer called I put him off until Monday afternoon."

"Where's Ruhamah?"

"She's still staying at that Jennifer's."

"Has she stopped by for clothes?"

"She's borrowing Jennifer's."

"What day is today?"

"Saturday. Irene at the store called and said she's got a nephew to run the place tomorrow morning. Other people have called, Alan's sister and—the messages are on the memo pad. How about some early supper?"

"Your weekend. Lloyd."

"He's working overtime, he'll be here later, he spent the last three nights, we've been going over these plans, he agrees Pascataquac is perfect. The fire warden wasn't there when we went up Wednesday; we'll have to let him know the date and time. Does 3 P.M. seem right to you? People can have lunch and arrive here by quarter of two and we'll drive over, hike up, ceremony, hike down, reception."

"Mimi, your own work. Orders to fill."

"I'm not taking on any new ones until after the honeymoon—and, incidentally, the honeymoon plans have changed. When I told Mother about the Adirondacks, she said, 'How provincial!', which would usually make me dig in my heels but she got Dad to fork out for hiking in *Europe*."

Mt. Pascataquac, Snowy thought, didn't stand a chance at upstaging Bev. She said, "Your weekend, though. Don't you and Lloyd go somewhere special on Saturday nights?"

"Pizza."

"Please spend the rest of the weekend in Leicester, having fun."

"Are you sure?"

"Yes. Is Bev okay? What's the latest about Julia?"

"Mother hasn't phoned today, she's taking the exam, but when she phoned last night she was kind of off the wall, she was at a motel in Hartford—"

Not again, Snowy thought.

"—so she wouldn't have the drive from Ninfield to distract her this morning before the exam. She said she was studying her eyes out, cramming. Mother, of all people. You're really sure?"

"Really."

As Mimi sped down the driveway, the phone rang.

"Hello?"

"Snowy," Puddles said, "you're up. How do you feel?"

"Fine, how are you? Has Susan had the baby yet?"

"At least you're 'fine' enough to come to the phone. The baby's overdue now, got me on the edge of my chair, unprofessional. Mimi says you aren't eating; okay, but remember your vitamin pills. That Mimi, I don't know, nice of her to invite us, but my patients—and Guy detesting the North—and the baby—and mostly Calvin, his wife's begun to wonder about the big order for mattresses keeping him late at the factory. No dummy she, like me and Gene Chabot. If I leave for a few days, will it be like you going to Girls' State and Tom breaking up?"

"Good God, Puddles, that was high school."

"Dress rehearsal, as Bev would say. The reception—can you handle the strain so soon? Have you learned why? Was Alan ill? Cancer? You should be looking into grief therapy and support groups—and will this finally make you go to a phobia class? Get someone to drive you—"

Snowy hung up.

She had never hung up on anyone before. Immediately the phone rang. She picked up the receiver, anticipating the power of hanging up on Puddles again. "Hello?"

Bev cried, "I've flunked! I tried to be utterly calm and cool and collected, but the moment I saw the exam I forgot everything I'd learned!"

"They've already corrected the exams?"

"No, they mail the results—oh, Snowy, I shouldn't be carrying on like this. How are *you*, you're up, is Mimi with you?"

"Can you retake the exam?"

"Yes, but why bother, I'll flunk. I was so upset I nearly had ten collisions driving home, and I'm longing to collapse, but we have to go out; we're going to a chichi restaurant with one of Roger's important clients and his wife. *How* can I make small talk? Roger wanted to arrange it for last night, but I put my foot down and spent all yesterday and last night studying holed up in a motel—and I flunked. And I would have been *wonderful* at selling real estate, I know I would, once fiduciaries were behind me. I even jumped the gun and bought some real-estate clothes—*damn*, I haven't the slightest idea what I'm wearing tonight. Must go. Love to you, Ruhamah, Mimi, goodbye—"

"Wait. How is Julia?"

"In pain. I'll phone you tomorrow, bye." Replacing the receiver, Bev realized she and her mother now concluded their phone conversations with, "Until tomorrow," and she tried to remember when they had started avoiding goodbyes.

Saturday night, Snowy thought. A week ago, after supper, she had laid out their costumes for the Fabulous Fifties party.

She took her key chain out of her pocketbook and went to the barn, to the only vehicle here, the van. In the driver's seat

306

where he had last sat, she practiced stepping on the clutch and shifting. Tom had taught her to drive. She backed out and, bucking and jerking and stalling like a neophyte, she drove down the Roller Coaster Road and turned in the opposite direction from the village. Whenever an impatient car appeared in the rear-view mirror, she pulled over onto the banking above the shore, at last looking at the lake.

During their Sunday drives, she hadn't noticed the Tolman Road sign. She drove in first gear past old-fashioned summer cottages still closed up and came to a small cove where narrow docks splayed out into the smooth gray water. At nighttime, his headlights would have been a garish intrusion; he had clicked them off. Intimacy. Going parking with death.

Feeling rested indeed, she walked down to the scoop of beach and took off her shoes and socks. Virginia Woolf put stones in the pockets of her jacket.

The water was glacial. She grabbed up those shoes and socks and ran back to the van. Driving barefoot, Harriet-style, she made her way into the village, seeing people on the store porch glance over, then stare, when she stalled turning onto Center Road. He had been part of the community, and they had sent casseroles and cakes. She, who didn't belong to the community, would have to thank them, to read their sympathy notes and reply.

At the corner of Pascataquac Road, Cedric Barlow, surveying his garden, signaled her to stop so imperiously that she did, stalling.

He said, "I'm very sorry."

"Thank you."

"Is the store on the market yet?"

"On the market?"

"That's what people are saying, you'll be selling the store. My son would like to retire to Woodcombe, and he's young enough to need more than gardens to occupy him. If you haven't yet put it in the hands of a realtor, I can make you a direct offer from him. Why throw away money on a commission?"

307

"I haven't—I'll be discussing things with my lawyer Monday."

"My son is looking for a house as well as a business."

"No, no, I won't sell the house." She started the van.

"I'll give you a call Monday."

She drove on to the clearing, where she parked beside the lone green Jeep. Pulling on her socks and shoes, she wished she could also don a suit of armor for protection against black-flies—and bears. Were you supposed to run or stand stock-still if you met a bear, shout or shut up? As she began climbing the trail, she felt herself ballooning red with blood pressure; she could lift off and fly to the top of the mountain. Had her mother felt like this before her heart attack? She picked up a branch, a makeshift walking stick, and she didn't stop for breath at the cellar hole or bear tree.

The view from the summit seemed as blank as her mind. She was a bystander, watching to see what Snowy would do. Snowy crossed the plateau to the cabin, went up the porch steps which had been built since Tuesday, knocked on the door, and, when nobody opened it, she walked over to the tower and climbed. The metal stairs were a helicopter's ladder swinging into space.

Tom sat writing something at a long table in front of windows. He turned and said, "Welcome to—Jesus Christ."

The laundry Joanne must have sent back probably included the plaid flannel shirt and Levi's Tom was wearing. Snowy said, "Mimi says Lloyd agrees, and the wedding is 3 P.M., June sixth."

Tom jumped up. "She could've called."

"He didn't leave me. I killed him. Ruhamah knows that but she doesn't know how. I'm an Agatha Christie murderer because the store is going bankrupt because I couldn't do my share. Mimi wondered if she could change into her wedding dress in the cabin. The water is so cold. Remember when you told me you used to go swimming for the first time each year on your birthday when you were younger but then it got too cold as you got older?"

308

"Is your daughter home alone?"

"Ruhamah won't live under the same roof with a murderer, she's at a friend's. You were a lifeguard the summer before we started dating."

"The cabin's pretty rudimentary, let's go down and I'll show you."

"Quitting time? Yesterday was your birthday, you didn't have to work on your birthday, that's good."

He put his arm around her. "Don't look down."

At the foot of the stairs, she said, "Uncle Tom's cabin."

As they walked toward it, he took his arm away. "Great-uncle Tom."

"Are you a grandfather too?"

"Spared, so far."

"Dudley is. Puddles is nearly a grandmother."

"Washburn? Puddles? You hear from them?"

"You're building the porch? You were always building things. Remember when your shop class had to build all those picnic tables for the town?"

"Vividly. Careful, no railings yet." He opened the cabin door. "And there's no running water, could Mimi tolerate that?"

The log walls made the interior dark and corrugated. This room was a combination kitchen and living room, with an axe behind the door, pots and pans and dishes and canned goods on pine shelves, a hot plate, water jugs beside the small refrigerator, a wooden-slab table, some folding chairs, a tussocky old sofa, and two photographs on the mantel over the fieldstone fireplace.

"No running water," Tom repeated. "An outhouse out back."

"Mimi's a hiker, a backpacker; an outhouse would be a luxury."

He opened a door into a little bedroom furnished with two bunk beds. "The place doesn't feature a dressing room, but she—and her bridesmaid?—could take over the whole cabin. Would it serve?"

309

"It's fine," Snowy said absently, going to the fireplace, and while he filled and heated a dented teakettle, she gazed at a photograph of two young men and a young woman, all good-looking but, as luck in the genes lottery so often went, the males were the ones who'd inherited Joanne's cheekbones. At least Libby had got Tom's curls—or did she have a perm? Snowy asked, "What does David do?"

"David? He works with me. Decaf tea?"

"Thank you." She'd saved the other photograph for last: an enlarged snapshot of Joanne wearing a long hostess skirt. Even in her days of entertaining, Snowy had never owned a hostess skirt. She bet Bev did, more than one. Joanne wore a frothy red blouse (décolleté) and the green (Gunthwaite green) velvet hostess skirt; her glossy brown (Clairol?) hair was pulled back and held with holly, and she was hanging a snowman ornament on an earnestly trimmed Christmas tree. Mrs. Claus? Nope. Plunk a crown on her head and she'd still be Queen of the Junior Prom. "David works here?"

"In Newburgh, I've got a business there. Milk, sugar?"

Suddenly Snowy saw a pile of magazines and books next to the sofa. The books, she knew at a glance, were her collections.

Tom said, "I went to the village library."

Alan had insisted she come out of the closet enough to donate these copies, a goodwill gesture. "What kind of business?"

He handed her a mug, took a bottle of scotch off a shelf, and poured himself a belt. "Coffins."

"Coffins? Oh, are *you* North Country Coffins?"

He had been afraid to say the word.

She asked, "You're not teaching?"

"That was my first mid-life crisis."

"His mid-life crisis, we bought the store."

Tom said, "Come sit down."

But Snowy walked straight into him, and tea sloshed scalding on his shirt.

She said, "Everybody's been telling me to sit down."

He set her mug on the table and held her in both arms. He'd forgotten just how small she was, though he remembered her rounder, not sinewy.

She said, "You used to wear aftershave. Old Spice."

"You used to wear perfume. Lilacs."

"White Lilac. Why did you fall in love with me back then?"

He tried to think. "It had to do with laughing. We made each other laugh. And sex."

She lifted her face. His beard scratched softly.

He kissed her.

How warm he was. Bulky as a bear, cuddly as a teddy bear she wanted to take to bed to warm her, and she stumbled backward onto the sofa to lie under his heavy warmth, warming up the old sofa mildewed from winter.

He rolled over onto his feet. He would escort her down the trail, follow her home, make sure someone was with her. This morning when he'd detoured past Hurricane Farm en route here, there had been a VW Rabbit in the driveway, and when he'd stopped at the Thornes' to return the pie plate, Cleora had said, standing in the kitchen doorway, "The car is her best friend's daughter's. Mimi is staying with Snowy. Far as I know, Snowy ain't seen anybody else except me—and you," she added without intonation.

"Convertibles," Snowy said. "Is this a convertible sofa?"

"No."

"Did you keep your Chevy convertible?"

"Yes." For years he had driven it, the well-preserved cream-colored convertible known in high school by the guys as the Cunt-Wagon. Finally it threw a rod; he couldn't afford to put a new engine in it but he couldn't bear to sell it either, so he'd stored it in the barn cellar, protected with tarps from barn swallows. He had reluctantly offered it to Brandon, who said, "That old junker? Jesus, Dad."

Snowy said, "I suppose it's an antique now."

They laughed, shakily.

She watched him lock the door, close the windows, pull the

shades, and hang his glasses over a lampshade, the way he used to over the sun visor. On the sofa, the front seat of the cream-colored convertible, she touched him with little pats, getting reacquainted as they kissed. No bra to unhook one-handed these days. He kissed her breasts. He had taught her to drive, he had taught her this, clothing drifting to the floor. His chest hair was white but his pubic wasn't, interesting. She leaned down to his hard-on, feeling him leap in a spasm as she sucked it into her mouth, the Cat Path, the sandpit. Pulling her back, he kissed her between her legs until she was shrieking in a concussion of stars, and then he slid into her here and now, and as he commenced thrusting, tears began pouring down her face, but she gripped his shoulders, listening to his gasps rising to a shout.

When he regained his other senses, he realized she was crying. He kissed her wet face.

She asked, "What was that classic in our youth, that song, 'I've Got Tears in My Ears from Lying on My Back in My Bed as I Cry over You'?" Her stomach growled.

"Supper," he said, withdrawing himself.

The last time they had thus separated, he'd thrown a Trojan out the window. She cupped semen off the sofa. " 'Safe sex.' We had safer in days of yore. And weren't Trojans called 'safes' as well as 'skins'?"

"I'm safe."

Meaning he'd been faithful to Joanne. Tom, Most Flirtatious; Tom, who had not played by the rules? "Me too."

"Doubly, a vasectomy."

"Did you sit around on an ice pack? Alan did. Now for the least dignified part of an undignified act." With one hand she gathered her clothes before she ran out the door, to the out-house.

Tom put on his clothes and, adjusting himself stickily in his Jockeys, he contemplated the contents of the refrigerator. Joanne hadn't sent back with him much of any leftovers from his birthday party, trying to control his weight miles away. Since he stopped smoking last year, he'd been putting on pounds.

There was a Tupperware box of cut-up supermarket vegetables, *crûdités,* which of course all guests in their right minds had dismissed in favor of potato chips. Some slices of ham. A Tupperware box of macaroni salad. One piece of chocolate cake. There had been no piece of ass, he'd been too drunk. He opened the tiny freezer compartment.

On the toilet seat in the outhouse, Snowy mopped up fast with toilet paper, tears and crotch. She was starving. Dressed, she went back into the cabin asking, "You said that quitting teaching was your first mid-life crisis—what was your second?"

"Macaroni salad and ham? Frozen fish sticks? Canned anything?"

"Do you have canned corned beef hash and canned peas?"

"Sure." He took a can-opener off a shelf and opened them.

"I'll get supper," she said. "A Fifties supper."

"Okay." He went outdoors to the outhouse.

Above the kitchen sink hung a shaving mirror. Shaving? Yes, his neck was shaved. Surprised, she saw her face without makeup. She looked like the wrath of God, and she hadn't brought her shoulder bag with its Ziploc emergency cosmetics. Had she not worn makeup since last Saturday? She started crying again, which would have been a waste of mascara anyway. Below the mirror was a paper-towel dispenser. Blotting her eyes, she set a cast-iron frying pan on the hot plate and then investigated the refrigerator and pine shelves, amused to find low-fat yogurt, unsalted brown rice cakes, and out of these she made hors d'oeuvres, eating three ravenously, crunching and crumbling, in case she couldn't in front of him when he reappeared. She scraped a lump of Fleischmann's margarine into the frying pan; as she squashed the hash around in the pan with an old wooden-handled spatula, she remembered her parents' kitchen, the kitchens in the Beacon Street rooming house and Alan's apartment and the Ruhamah Reed House, and the cans of corned beef hash she'd cooked there.

"Eighties hors d'oeuvres," she said when Tom did reappear. "Your roommate helped you get this job?"

313

"It was the only tower still available this spring. Scotch? Hiking, I've visited a lot of towers. They were closed for a while, and then some were reopened and I gave my roommate a call, figuring it was a pipe dream, a kid's dream like living in a lighthouse."

"Celia Thaxter," she said. "What about your coffin business?"

He mixed two scotches. "I wanted to do custom work, but it developed into mainly selling wholesale to—crematories. Got boring. David's running things by himself until I'm through here in November."

"Too bad there wasn't a tower nearer Newburgh."

He handed her a drink, and they sipped.

She swallowed; she was able to swallow. "Did you and Joanne graduate together?"

He turned away from her and began arranging kindling in the fireplace. "At Rumford, legend had it that no couple ever left the married students' barracks without being blessed with a baby. We were determined to be the exception." Those barracks were supposed to have been torn down after the post-War invasion of married guys with the G.I. Bill, but they had still stood, sort of, a mile from campus, set in a field, two long sagging buildings, gray and shutterless, containing twelve apartments each. Chain-link fences bordered the barracks, enclosing a pair of narrow lawns where grass grew sparsely, crossed by cracked cement walks to the downstairs and upstairs door-stoops. His and Joanne's apartment was downstairs, an end apartment that always seemed one-sided, as if it had a limp. Some of their windows looked out onto the clothesyard between the buildings, the clotheslines often totally filled with fluttering diapers, a reminder of the legend.

Snowy started setting the table.

Tom said, "We weren't the exception."

At the barracks, spur-of-the-moment B.Y.O.B. parties enlivened every weekend. Some people, Tom had observed, were party-giving types and some were party-goers; because Joanne was the former, their apartment became a student version of Gatsby's mansion. One Saturday night in November their junior year, there had been a typical barracks party, loud talk drowning out the Kingston Trio on Joanne's record player, poverty hors d'oeuvres which Joanne made and other wives contributed, Lipton Onion Soup Dip, potato chips, pretzels, someone playing the bongos to the wrong rhythm. People were saying: "He tried to put *Catcher in the Rye* on the book list and—" "Anybody got a cigarette?" "—this hellhole called an institution of higher learning—" "Be right back, gotta check Susie, she's got a runny nose." "In Ed Psych I had to observe homogenous grouping at the junior high, ten groups in a class, Rapid One through Medium One to Medium Slow One to Slow Three or something, it's like the Alphas and Betas in *Brave New World,* for God's sake!" "—and the second question was 'How does the relationship between the Lord Chamberlain and his son compare with the relationship between Hamlet and his father?' " "Eight dollars in tips on an off-night—" "*Any*body got a cigarette?" "—graduation, the principal you go to work for is probably the type of guy who does the vocabulary test in the *Reader's Digest.*" "Where's the church key?" "You can earn more money pumping gas in a filling station than being a teacher; what are we doing here?" "Extrinsic motivation—" "The principal will be the type of guy who says a book is about man's inhumanity to man, if he's ever read a book—" "In my Tests and Measurements class—" "The last question was really cute: 'What *is* the matter with Hamlet?' " "One car, my job and his classes, it's like a relay race—" Because they too had only one car, Tom and Joanne had decided to student-teach different semesters, the student teacher taking the car, the other hitching rides with barracks neighbors; Joanne's schedule happened to make next semester better, so Tom was student teaching at Rumford High School this semester, two classes of freshman English and a class of social studies, his minor, and he explained to a stray townie, "Student teaching has no relation to regular teaching, you teach three classes under teachers who tell you exactly what and how

315

to teach, and the head of the Student Teaching Department comes in and stares at you about four times during the semester and then gives you a mark—"

And so it had progressed, somebody leaving a bowl of pretzels on the floor, somebody else knocking it over, everybody tracking pretzels across the hemp rug, until the beer ran out, the euphoria waned, and people left. Alone, Joanne and Tom vacuumed up pretzels, dumped ashtrays, located empty beer cans in odd places, and Joanne went to bed but Tom, as he often did, settled into a basket chair with a final beer he'd saved, squeezing in some sleepy studying. Tonight he opened his grammar book, because after Thanksgiving vacation next week he would start teaching the grammar unit that covered lie and lay, necessitating fancy footwork to outsmart the class clowns. Snowy had taught him the difference, when at the drive-in theater one night he'd asked her, "Are you laying on me that way accidentally on purpose?" and she'd finally corrected him, giving a grammar lesson atop him. The memory began causing a hell of a hard-on. No doubt she would be going home for Thanksgiving vacation, and they were going for the day, to dinner at Joanne's; he could think up some errand and drive past her house and she'd be walking Laurie and he'd pull up beside her—Tom stubbed out his cigarette, threw the grammar book down, and went into the bedroom. In the shadows from the living-room lamp he could see the walls covered with the valentine boxes Joanne had brought from home, the collection to which he would be adding every year the rest of his life. She hadn't brought her frilly bedspread; it was twin-size, and she'd bought a valentine-red quilted bedspread for their secondhand double bed. When he bumped into the bureau, he realized how much beer he'd drunk. He steered onward to the bed, carefully hooked his glasses over the bedside-lamp's shade. Joanne slept on her back, without a pillow, because she'd heard that pillows gave you a double chin. Gorgeous Joanne. He kicked off his Hush Puppies, dropped his chinos, his Jockeys, drew back the bedclothes, knelt above her, slid her nightgown up to her hips. "Asleep?" he asked, stroking

316

the fine curls in her crotch. She didn't answer. She was sound asleep; she had had a few beers too. He lifted her, parted her, and eased himself in. Over in Vermont right now, probably some Ivy League guy was doing this to Snowy. Lie, lay. He began slamming into Joanne furiously. She woke up and whispered, "Tom, wait, stop!" The walls were thin. He held her shoulders down and kept riding the crest, and despite the walls she screamed, "Stop!" He clapped his hand over her mouth and flooded her.

No diaphragm. He'd forgotten about that. He rolled off and slept.

The next morning, he awoke to remember rape.

Joanne and the car were gone. His head thick with hangover headache, he pushed aside the closet curtain and saw that her clothes were still here, so she hadn't left him—or had she not taken the clothes because they also were contaminated by him? In the bathroom, her douche bag hung over the shower nozzle. She couldn't possibly get pregnant the one and only time they'd done it without birth control. In the living room, he grabbed the grammar book and hurled it against the wall, and the baby in the next apartment began to wail.

When they'd got married, Tom had switched from his pots-and-pans job in the college kitchen to a better-paying job at a newsstand downtown. He was due there now. He showered, hitched a ride, and spent the Sunday selling newspapers, serving coffee and doughnuts, dazed, shaken, terrified. He had ruined everything.

Walking home at six o'clock, as he neared the barracks he saw the cream-colored convertible amongst that line of parked cars in the barracks parking area which looked as if it were a used-car lot lacking banners. His heartbeat raced. *He* raced. Then he slowed back to a walk, dreading confrontation. He could hot-wire the car and take off. Then he began running again.

The apartment smelled like meatloaf, like marriage. Joanne was wearing a wedding-shower apron over her sweater and slacks, and she was setting the Danish modern blond wooden dining table she'd bought mail-order from Montgomery Ward.

"Hi," she said, not looking at him, dealing out onto the two straw placemats stainless spoons, knives, forks. "Supper's almost ready. Meatloaf, baked potatoes, carrots."

"Sounds swell," he said. She was giving him a chance to pretend it hadn't occurred. Aghast, he felt tears fill his eyes, roll down against his glasses. He made a choking noise.

She glanced up. She rushed across the room and hugged him, her own tears streaming.

He said, "I'm so goddamned sorry."

"Too many beers. That's what I decided while I was driving around. I've known you since first grade, until last night. It wasn't your fault, it was the beer."

"My fault for drinking them. I'm sorry. I love you."

He rarely said that.

Joanne said, "I love you," and the oven timer buzzed.

And here in the mountaintop cabin Snowy finished setting this table and prodded the hash. She said, "You weren't the exception to the legend, but you both managed to graduate?"

Tom lit the fire. "It wasn't easy."

A month after the rape, he'd come home from work at midnight to find Joanne in bed sobbing. He said, "Joanne?"

"I'm pregnant."

He felt as if he'd been clobbered. The worry had disappeared when weeks passed and she didn't say anything. He gathered her up against him. Rules: The Rumford Teachers' College Student Teaching Department wouldn't let a girl student-teach if she was pregnant. Rumford got picky: If a girl became pregnant while student teaching she had to quit if there were more than nine weeks left before the semester ended. He'd heard stories, maybe apocryphal, about girls getting around this second rule by wearing baggy clothes. But Joanne had a full semester ahead.

He asked, "When's it due?"

"Late July."

In a cold sweat, he counted back to last month. They had made love as usual during November; just one time had they done it without a diaphragm, the time that couldn't be called making love. It was his fault that Joanne wouldn't graduate.

She said, "The doctor says I'm very healthy, I could teach right to the last day of school. He told me he'd put it in writing if that would help. I told him it wouldn't."

"No, get it in writing and we'll go see Fogarty, try to convince him."

"Wasted effort."

"I'll go alone."

"You'll lose your temper. We'll go together." Joanne began crying again.

Mr. Fogarty, the head of the Student Teaching Department, was a dry pinched man, a former school superintendent. Tom didn't really think he'd give a damn about Joanne, and he didn't. Sitting smugly in his office in the administration building, Fogarty skimmed the doctor's letter and said, "I'm sorry, but rules are rules."

Joanne said, "My record, excellent marks—"

"Mrs. Forbes," Fogarty said, enjoying himself, "if I let you student-teach, I'd have to let every other girl who is—expecting."

Tom said, "Every pregnant girl who wants to student-teach *should* be allowed to. What's *wrong* with that?"

Fogarty said, "It's upsetting and distracting to the students."

Tom said, "Having a baby is the most normal thing in the world."

Fogarty said, "Rules are rules. You're both aware of them. You should have taken more—precautions. This problem is one of the reasons we don't approve of our students' being married."

Joanne said quickly, knowing Tom was about to commit murder, "Thank you for your time," and dragged Tom out before he wrecked his own career.

Tom raged, "That sonofabitching bastard, I'd like to shove

319

his goddamn rule book up his goddamn ass!" And as they drove away from the administration building, he vowed, "You'll graduate. You'll graduate."

Joanne said, "You're thinking of an abortion, aren't you. I have, and I don't know how we'd find out who would do one, and how could we afford it, we couldn't ask our folks and probably they don't have enough money to pay for one, and anyway, I'd be too scared."

So would Tom.

The past two summers Joanne had worked in the office of Rumford Textiles; during her high-school summers and the summer after her Rumford freshman year, she'd waitressed at the Gunthwaite Inn. She said, "I'll quit and go to work at Rumford Textiles or a restaurant or a supermarket or something, like most of the other wives. I've felt guilty, you working, me not, but both of us going to school."

Guilty! His guilt was ferocious. "The housework is work."

"We'll need the extra money to buy baby stuff."

An idea formed. "They *won't* win. You'll finish this semester and just take next semester off, and when I graduate, we'll find a town that needs an elementary student teacher as well as an English teacher, you'll do your student teaching there and graduate only one semester late."

"How can I student-teach with a baby?"

"We'll hire a baby-sitter."

He'd hit upon an answer. Inside Joanne's head erupted a cheering like a crowd at a game, but she said, "Teachers' starting pay is usually four thousand, a lot to us here living on a shoestring, nothing in the real world. How can we afford a full-time baby-sitter with one paycheck?"

"I'll work nights and weekends if necessary."

"You'll have preparations to do. Look what you're doing now, just student teaching."

"I'll manage. You'll graduate."

She stroked his taut knuckles on the steering wheel and finally referred to their unspoken assumption. "Maybe it wasn't

320

that time, we could've got unlucky anytime. Don't hate the baby. Promise?"

He reached over and pulled her to him and drove home with his arm around her shoulders, the way they had when they were teenagers. But they were going to be parents.

Tom told Snowy, "Another reason we decided on Newburgh was that Joanne could do her student teaching there after Brandon was born and they promised she'd be hired as a regular teacher when she graduated."

Snowy dished up the hash and peas. "Day-care center?"

"None back then, we had to hire a baby-sitter."

"Expensive."

"I moonlighted at a lumber mill." As he held a chair out for Snowy at the table, he saw that old wooden building with sheds which seemed to have been added on by whim and rum. He'd begun working Saturdays there the first year in Newburgh, to pay for the baby-sitter, and he'd continued running a molding machine summers to eke out their paychecks after Joanne graduated and started teaching; he'd put in some hours while grimly going to summer classes to get his master's degree down at Plymouth State College (once Plymouth Teachers' College, Rumford also having eliminated its normal-school past from its name); the lumber mill had again supplemented his lone teacher's pay while Joanne had David and Libby. Then he had announced to Joanne, "The only good things about teaching are July and August, and I'd finally like to enjoy them." Although Joanne had welcomed the extra money, she had always wished he could find a more dignified summer job, and she asked, "Maybe you could do some tutoring?" "I'd like to do more hiking," he had said, "overnights, and—" Wily, Machiavellian! "—and," he'd continued, "I'll take Brandon along when he wants to come, take him off your hands." "Well," Joanne had said.

Snowy said, "Alan planned to teach history, then changed his mind."

Eating, Tom said, "Wise of him. At the outset, I decided that if I was going to make a career of teaching I didn't want to do so for the wrong reasons. I didn't want to delude myself into believing that teaching was somehow more rewarding than my meager salary. If anybody found teaching rewarding, it should be the students. I would present, to the best of my ability, the information the school demanded and whatever else I deemed relevant. The students could take it or leave it. Over the years, this philosophy got pretty threadbare. What did he do instead, go right into storekeeping?"

"Oh, no." Snowy put her fork down, plate clean. "He got involved in the Old Eastbourne restoration. How did you change from teaching to coffins?"

"One autumn day, after sixteen years, I stopped in at the hardware store after school to buy some weather-stripping. The clerk was new, a kid in his twenties, an out-of-towner I didn't recognize. When I went to pay him, he asked me, 'Do you want the discount, sir?' I asked him if there was a sale, and he said no, only the discount. I looked blank, and he said, 'It's Thursday, sir. Senior Citizen Discount Day.' "

Snowy giggled.

"Fucking *kid*," Tom said. "And when I drove off down Main Street, I saw the old empty building beyond the lumber mill. It had once been a coffin factory long ago. Appropriate, I thought, with that kid assuming I'd soon be dead and buried. And then I thought of my day in school and wondered if maybe I already was dead, the walking dead, zombie. I got out of the car to investigate the place, just curious, I'd never been inside, but the padlock held so I could only look in a broken window. There were racks for storing lumber overhead, and hardware bins along one wall, and a workbench across the back. On two sawhorses sat an unfinished child's coffin."

Appalled, he realized what a heartless account this must be to Snowy, so recently widowed.

But she nodded. "Your first love, woodworking. You would see that poignant little coffin as a work of art."

"I did."

322

"You've got a can of fruit cocktail, how about that for dessert?"

He stood up and opened it. "After I drove away from the factory, I started wondering about buying it. Working for myself. No more bullshit from dopes in administration. The crap I'd suffered from principals who'd come and gone, superintendents! Being my own boss."

Alan's words echoing, crashing around in her head. Snowy spooned fruit cocktail into two cereal bowls and said, "I'll take the cherries. As Puddles used to say, a girl can't have too many."

Tom laughed.

Snowy asked, "What did Joanne think of your idea?"

They sat back down. Tom said, "She threw a fit." Had Joanne always counted on his guilt to keep him in line? It sure the hell had for many years. But, as with his hiking, he had prevailed with his plan to buy the coffin factory. This year when he told her about his fire-tower plan, she hadn't thrown any fit—and had she seemed relieved by the distance?

"Alone," Snowy said suddenly. Her dessert was untouched. "My father went to an undertaker alone. Last Saturday night Alan went to Murray Cove alone."

Tom took her hand.

She said, "We promised. When my father was dying, my folks didn't 'communicate.' We promised we would. If one of us was dying, we promised, we would talk and talk and eat lobster and drink champagne and fuck."

Into the silence came a primeval high-pitched yelping, howling.

"Coyotes," Tom said. "Singing."

"I've never heard them so close."

"Don't worry, I'll walk you down the trail."

"Could I stay here tonight?"

CEDRIC BARLOW WAS in his front yard the next morning, weeding, and he looked up startled as she drove past. She waved. By noon, she presumed, the entire town would know that she had driven out Pascataquac Road yesterday afternoon and had driven back at sunrise.

The coyotes had been singing again when Tom walked her down the mountain. He'd said, "Remember how your dog used to bark her head off when I walked you to your door?" She said, "I still have the carving of Laurie you made." "I'll be damned," he said, and at the van he kissed her, the way he used to kiss her at that back door.

In the village, no car was parked in the store's parking lot, and the stacks of newspapers awaited Irene's nephew. Driving on, she saw herself driving to the store a week ago, searching for Alan. Last evening, while she and Tom did the dishes, Tom said, "They claim that most businesses fail in the first couple of years. If I'd paid attention to all the dire warnings I got, I'd never have started mine. It wasn't your fault." She said, "You *started* a business. We bought an established one—gone downhill, granted, but it would have succeeded if I'd helped, paid attention, known what was going on, talked about it, if he hadn't had to hire help. I was absorbed in my agoraphobia, but he was having one long panic attack." Besides, she thought, you could survive on Joanne's steady income.

"Tell me," Tom said, "about Bennington and Old Eastbourne and everything."

As she talked, they finished the dishes and sat on the sofa in front of the fire, and on the mantel Joanne posed with her Christmas tree. Exhausted, they both dozed off. Snowy snapped awake and saw him in the bedroom carrying sheets and a blanket. She said, "Bunks." Like the *Highland Fling*'s berths. "Heights," he said. "I'll move up to the top, you take the lower—" He looked at her and asked, "Or do you want to squeeze in?" His warmth. She went into the bedroom and partly undressed. Wearing her shirt and underpants, lying pressed tight against his back, she felt not seasick but heartsick. Then in his

324

sleep he began to tremble and whimper. Chasing rabbits was what she had called it when Laurie did this—and Alan. She rubbed Tom's shoulders under his T-shirt, the small of his back, his bottom under his Jockeys. "It's okay," she soothed, "it's okay." And he grew lulled.

She had awakened first this morning, at the sink washing her face and brushing her teeth with paper towels, borrowing only his comb. Over tea and toast, neither of them said anything about last night or another meeting; they talked gardening, vaguely.

The coyotes had caused the personal comments, the kiss.

Snowy braked, turning around in the driveway of somebody who liked tulips more than she did. She'd intended to go home and shower and change and work in the garden until a civilized hour at which to phone Dudley to ask if he knew a business or person in Gunthwaite who needed typing done at home.

But damnit, before she did that she could try to help organize the newspapers. As she drove back to the store and parked, she saw Bev on stage in the Gunthwaite High School auditorium speaking a line from *Our Town*: " 'Oh, earth, you're too wonderful for anybody to realize you!' " At fifteen, she had thought these were the saddest words ever, and when she unlocked the door and lugged in the first stack, she almost started crying again. Make it be two Sundays ago.

She could cut the plastic straps; she could write. She set to work so furiously that she forgot she was just supposed to help out. She herself was the important person in the auditorium at the moment, the month's *Smoke Signals* her responsibility.

A knock on the door. Outside, Cedric Barlow pointed to his watch. Time to open, and she hadn't finished and Irene's nephew hadn't shown up. Another person appeared behind Cedric Barlow, then another. Soon there would be a mob out there wanting their Sunday papers. As she walked toward the door, the floor dissolved into water and the walls were fluid, ebbing and flowing. She would scream and run past the customers and hide in the van.

"Bright and early," Cedric Barlow said meaningfully when she unlocked the door. "It's turned cloudy, though, the summit must be in clouds."

"Mrs. Sutherland," said a man, and an older woman said, "Such a tragedy, how are you, I'll get the roast myself, I called Irene yesterday and she said she'd leave it wrapped in the meat counter—"

Snowy said, "I haven't finished the newspapers."

"Don't you bother," the woman said. "My dear, we'll find our newspapers, we'll find whatever we need."

Cedric Barlow gave her the correct change and said, "I'll phone Monday." Snowy stood at the cash register and took the other man's five-dollar bill for a ninety-cent *New Hampshire Sunday News*. The headwaitress at Sweetland was teaching her and Bev how to make change ("Arithmetic wastes time, just count backward"), and she gave him his change, and the woman seemed ready to stay to chat but more customers began coming in, uncomfortable and sympathetic. Snowy presided at the cash register wearing no makeup and not her good clothes of two Sundays ago but rags and unclean underwear.

A guy came running in. "Sorry, I overslept!"

"That's okay."

"Aunt Irene will kill me."

"I'd better go home, I think."

On her way out, she leaned into the ice-cream freezer to cool her fiery face.

She'd been drained of her driving courage, so the trip once again consisted of getting from one telephone pole to the next.

At the house, she went into the bedroom, enfolded herself in Alan's bathrobe, and climbed into bed, edging over to his side. *The Song of Songs. By night on my bed I sought him whom my soul loveth: I sought him, but I found him not.*

She fell asleep.

"Muslin," Mimi said, driving them down Gunthwaite's Main Street Monday afternoon, "a simple white muslin dress, even that didn't get a reaction out of Mother when I told her

326

what I'd designed to wear, she didn't push for silk or satin. All she can think of is how she screwed up the exam. Things are working out just like we hoped—only we didn't want her to flunk. After I stopped laughing at the prospect, I knew she'd make a good realtor, it's acting—State Avenue. Then the first right, according to directions."

And onto Chestnut Street Mimi turned.

Snowy asked, "The law office is here?"

"Hey, isn't this Mother's old neighborhood? She drove us around to see it one time when we were little."

"That's her house, the yellow house. Where are we going?"

"Emery Street."

The warehouses across the river had been razed, and a sign on a new low building courageously announced competition for the Miracle Mile:

MAIN STREET MINI-MALL

THE VIDEO NOOK
MALIBU TANNING SALON
FAR HORIZONS SPORTSWEAR
THE RIVERSIDE PUB

She read the sign twice, wondering if her parents would have preferred a view of a mini-mall, before she looked up at the big white Colonial and read the law office sign: HAYES, SMITH, & ELLSWORTH. The firm who'd bought the house had been HAYES, HAYES, & SMITH.

"Kind of like our place," Mimi said. "I mean, Mother and Dad's."

"This was my folks.'"

"It *was?*" Mimi drove up the driveway. "You didn't know?"

The garage had been torn down; its space and the small backyard were a paved parking lot. "No," Snowy said. Aside from last Monday, she'd only met Jason Ellsworth once, when he represented Hurricane Farm's owner, Mrs. Penrose, at the closing at the bank, and she hardly noticed him because she and her Valium were concentrating on signing the papers without shaking, but later when Alan had said that switching from their Eastbourne lawyer to a Gunthwaite lawyer would simplify things, suggesting Ellsworth, she had agreed.

Mimi was saying, "I suppose Mother showed us on that tour, but I forgot. You stressed out?"

"I'm fine." Alan must have conducted any business over the phone, not recognizing the address.

"Nifty place for lawyers. Dad's office is in a high-rise. Sure you don't want me to come with you? Well, I'll do my shopping—and maybe buy a tan."

Snowy smiled at her and got out of the car. Instead of crisscrossed organdy curtains, drapes hung in the front windows. Had she ever entered this house by the front door? She'd opened the door from inside, to bring in the mail.

"Good afternoon," the receptionist said.

"I'm Henrietta Sutherland, I have an appointment with Mr. Ellsworth."

"One moment."

Snowy hadn't been aware that wall-to-wall oriental carpeting existed; the walls it stretched between were rearranged. Where had the living room stopped and the dining room begun? The receptionist lifted the telephone receiver and pushed a button. Was this desk where the sofa used to be? Behind the receptionist, two women tick-ticked at word processors, the new sound, their heads cocked at the new angle, different from typists.'

Alan's habit of tilting his head.

She couldn't take in typing, she didn't own a word processor.

"Mr. Ellsworth is expecting you," said the receptionist. "Second on your right."

Nowadays, a downstairs hall. On went the carpeting. This wasn't her parents' house anymore, that house was gone. But when Jason Ellsworth greeted her in his office and said, "Please sit down," and she obeyed, she looked out the window, got her bearings, and knew she was sitting in the rooster kitchen, where there had been no place to sit before.

He said, "I'm glad you felt up to coming here," and started talking. Although he was younger than she, he behaved paternally, as he probably did with elderly widows.

She interrupted, "I understand. I have to sell the store to save the house, or sell the house to save the store."

"It's more complex than—in a nutshell, yes. Now, since you haven't an income, and—"

She tuned him out, listening to this house which had been her parents' passion.

"—my advice to you is—"

"To sell the house," she said.

"You could rent a small apartment—"

She put her chin up. "I'll remodel the store's upstairs storeroom into an apartment; it's unused. Can I get a loan to do this now? I think I might have a buyer for the house."

"Don't grab at any offer. We'll put the house on the market and sit tight, and it'll bring full price, being a Woodcombe house. I'll arrange with the bank for a remodeling loan."

"Thank you. After the money in the checking account is spent, I'll need—electricity bill, phone bill, my daughter's allowance—"

He took out a large checkbook and said, "Will five hundred do for the time being? We'll settle up as soon as the house sells."

"Thank you."

Leaving, she prayed that Mimi's car would be in the driveway, but it wasn't. She walked along the river. Alan could have saved the store by selling the house; instead, he killed himself. Was the financial crisis an excuse he embraced?

When Mimi returned triumphant over having found the perfect muslin, Snowy asked to go to the bank, and after she had deposited the check at the drive-up window on the site of Sweetland, she said, "Where are you buying your wedding cake?"

"That bakery in Leicester."

"You've already ordered it?"

"I should've, but it's far down the menu, I'm making the other food and my grocery list is—"

"How about Fay Rollins's Indulgences? I bought my wedding cake from its downtown predecessor. Indulgences does catering too." Snowy then recalled Dudley's lettering Katy's Catering, but she didn't offer this alternative.

Mimi said scornfully, "Catering? Like Mother wanted, before the exam sidetracked her."

"For our wedding, I just ordered some hors d'oeuvres. We're here in Gunthwaite, you could order the cake from Indulgences now."

Mimi regarded her. "From Fay Rollins? Why not." As they drove off down Main Street, Mimi asked, "Where was your wedding?"

"In that house."

"Oh." Mimi hurried on, "Thanks for phoning the fire warden about the date and time and using the cabin."

"Remember, an outhouse."

"No problem."

The last time Snowy had been able to enter a mall, she had held Alan's hand to anchor herself while they walked past indoor trees and the plastic benches on which sat the old men who had sat on the wooden benches in the grassy square downtown, guarding or being guarded by a Civil War cannon. That park had since been bulldozed and on it built a parking garage, in an unsuccessful attempt to win back mall customers.

Mimi's brisk pace made the Abnaki Mall even dizzier. Snowy tried to think of the plastic promenade as Jane Austen's Pump Room in Bath; she failed. All these shoppers here, strangers, maniacs hiding shotguns in shopping bags. She couldn't go one step farther.

"There it is," Mimi said.

Bev would label Indulgences chichi, but it still smelled like Vachon's Bakery, overpoweringly sweet, like jumping into the center of a jelly doughnut. Fay stood behind a glass counter that displayed sheer sin, tying gold cord around a white box. In

330

Vachon's, you had had to take a number, unless you were a waitress on a daily mission, and the boxes had been brown, tied with string.

"Have a nice day, Laura," Fay said to the customer. "Snowy, you're up and about, how are you doing?"

"This is the Mimi you've talked to. I'm sorry you have had to cope with Ruhamah, I thank you."

"She and Jennifer are coping, I'm here all day and Martin's in a world of his own."

"Is she still seeing the psychologist?"

"Yes. I think Jennifer and other friends are providing therapy that's just as useful, if amateur. Kim stays overnight sometimes, too, and I can hear voices in Jennifer's room late."

Ironically, a pajama party for Ruhamah at last. "You must let me pay her board—"

"Goodness gracious, with three teenagers and their friends in and out, one more mouth isn't even noticed."

"But Ruhamah's such a fussy eater—"

"She seems to eat what the others do. It isn't any trouble, really, she's welcome to stay as long as she needs to."

Snowy thought: I've got to talk to Ruhamah about selling the house. "Her clothes, could I drop them off?"

"Of course."

"Mimi here is getting married, she'd like to order a wedding cake."

Mimi exclaimed, "Tourtière!", pointing to one of the white gold-lettered signs on the wall, pronouncing it the proper French-Canadian way, tootkay.

"Pork pies," Fay said. "A Vachon tradition we're carrying on. Well, Mimi, a wedding cake!"

"And tourtière, my grandmother used to make them, gotta have some at the reception, and," Mimi said, glancing at Snowy, "some hors d'oeuvres."

Driving home, Mimi mused, "Mother faces certain things squarely, doesn't she, like naming me and Leon after Grandma and Grandpa Lambert. I went through a phase of being

331

ashamed of being half-Canuck. A shrink would go wild over Dad."

"What else is on the menu?"

"I'll cook a turkey, and Lloyd's roommate and his wife are vegetarians, so a lentil salad and—"

In the kitchen of Hurricane Farm, the phone began ringing as Snowy and Mimi came indoors.

Mimi said, "Shall I?"

Snowy nodded and left the kitchen to walk through the dining and living rooms. So much furniture. Antiques.

"Snowy!" Mimi shouted.

She ran back.

Mimi said, pale, "Mother asked to talk to you."

"Snowy," Bev said, "I'm at the airport, I'm flying down to Mother's; she's worse but she is determined not to go to the hospital. She's indomitable. She won't permit a cancellation of wedding plans, I'll keep you and Mimi posted. How are you?"

"I've got to sell this house. Is it okay to use a lawyer instead of a realtor?"

Bev made a peculiar noise. Was she crying?

"Fsbo," Bev said. "For-Sale-By-Owner, realtors loathe that—*you're selling your house?*"

"Julia did it, I can do it. She sold her first farm when she had to, and her second."

"But she—hell and damn, my plane—yes, if you don't use a realtor, use a lawyer."

As they hung up, Mimi said, "She's going to die."

Snowy hugged her.

"She taught me to weave. Mother doesn't want me to go down. Wants me and the others to remember her like she was our last visit."

"I'll check the garden for woodchucks, and then let's have a Beck's Beer."

They sat on the porch, and Mimi said, "You're going to sell this house? Did that lawyer strong-arm you? I know Dad, I know pressure."

"It's a practical decision, Mimi." Would Ruhamah accept it?

"Dad—I hope Etta keeps Prancer out of the swimming pool this time. Will you stay in Woodcombe? An apartment?"

"Your wedding dress. Please, go home for another spell and work on your dress."

"I can bring my sewing machine here."

"You'll be like an old-fashioned bride who's never set eyes on the groom."

"This weekend I realized I was getting cold feet."

"Almost everybody does, I expect."

"Did you?"

Snowy remembered how her cold feet meant sweat pouring down her hands. "I sure did."

"Lloyd and I've got no reason to get married! We don't want kids—don't tell Mother."

"Alan and I nearly didn't have any, on purpose."

"But you had one."

Snowy saw Alan weeping at the hospital.

After Mimi drove away, she went to sleep in Alan's bathrobe, on his side of the bed, and finally she dreamed about him. They were at the Sleepytime Motor Lodge, drinking warm beer and watching an old movie—

The goddamned fucking phone. It was Cedric Barlow, who said as she stood groggy in the kitchen, "I've talked with my son, and he's ready to make an offer."

"I've decided not to sell the store. But the house is for sale."

"Only the house?"

"Jason Ellsworth is handling things. My lawyer, at Hayes, Smith, & Ellsworth, in Gunthwaite."

"Repeat that?"

She did, and he hung up.

Five o'clock. What had happened to the phone number? She found it amid Mimi's notes of messages, its handwriting insane, and she dialed. If he'd left on the dot—

Tom said, "Hello?"

333

"Your schedule, you're off now? Could you meet me at the store before you go home and tell me how to fix the upstairs storeroom into an apartment the cheapest way?"

"Are you okay? Is Mimi with you?"

"I've helped restore those Old Eastbourne places, but I don't know how to do this."

"You're going to remodel a storeroom to rent?"

"I'm going to move in."

"You're selling the house. I've been chasing ideas round and round, and that was the only one that made sense. But. Can you run the store? Agoraphobia?"

"I'll try to."

Snowy, living over a grocery store. "Meet you there in an hour."

"Thank you."

She put on her best Levi's and a pale pink shirt, despite the dust she would encounter in the storeroom. Morale boosting, like makeup.

Six o'clock, closing time, and some last customers were lingering on the store's porch. Indoors, Irene, looking frazzled, said to Snowy, "I gave that nephew of mine a scolding he won't forget."

"People managed."

"They're saying maybe keeping busy was what you needed. Busy! In the morning the rush is at eleven, when the mail goes up at the post office and the retired people come in. After five, it's the working people. I thought I was retired until you bought this place. Now I'm used to working again. The supermarkets in Gunthwaite, they're always advertising for cashiers; don't worry about me if the new owner doesn't want me."

"I'm not selling."

"You're not?"

"But I don't know if I can afford to—I might have to run it by myself—I'll be in tomorrow. What should I learn first?"

"The cash register," Irene said. "Yesterday, you rang everything up on 'Void.'"

Opening the door, Tom heard Snowy burst out laughing.

He was holding a clipboard and a measuring tape. Irene said, "You changing jobs, Tom, going into real estate? She isn't selling."

"Oh," Snowy said, "he's here about fixing the storeroom. The stairs are at the back—" She hurried off down the aisle.

Irene said, "I'll lock up."

"Thanks."

Passing by the office doorway, Tom observed, "I've got a desk like that. Almost. So, the bathroom's off there, the pipes."

As they climbed the stairs, Snowy could feel Irene's eyes on them.

"No junk," he said, "just dust. I figured it'd be a mess."

"Alan cleaned it out. He loved throwing things away." She looked around the low-ceilinged dark room. An attic. "If it isn't big enough for two bedrooms, I'll sleep on the sofa, I've got a—convertible type."

They thought of his sofa, his bunk bed.

He asked, "How soon do you want to get started?"

"Soon as I can hire a carpenter."

"Hiring a carpenter on short notice is damn near impossible. I'll do a general plan now, come back tomorrow, get the plans drawn up, get an estimate on materials, and after Wednesday I'll work nights, I've got the nine-day stint next. It won't be so fast as a full-time carpenter, but it'll be sooner."

"I didn't mean—just your advice—not your time, your days off, your days at home."

"David's capable," he said, though they were speaking about Joanne. He began to measure and jot.

Downstairs, she studied the cash register, not daring to touch it, wondering how he would explain his early return to Woodcombe, and then she practiced scooping a pound of hamburg and weighing it. Alan had replaced the old scale with a computerized one. Overextending. She turned on the slicer, turned it off in terror. Along the aisle behind the counter she walked, memorizing locations of batteries, Pampers, aspirin.

335

Tom came down the stairs. "Combination kitchen and living room like the cabin; two bedrooms, small; a bathroom, very small. You hate paneling? Wallboard painted white, to get light. A skylight itself would be too expensive, and anyway they lose heat. Um, about expenses, I can loan you money for materials."

"Oh, Tom. No. The lawyer's arranging it. But thank you."

They looked at each other. She took her keys out of her shoulder bag, unlocked the door and, when they went outside, locked it, saying, "Have a good trip home."

Where he intended to make up for his unconsummated birthday night—and his Saturday-night lapse. "See you tomorrow."

That night in Ruhamah's room she packed some clothes, considered the toy menagerie and chose the animal Ruhamah had bought for herself, the baby seal. At her typewriter she wrote:

Dear Ruhamah:
     May I ask you to drive us down to Eastbourne this
Sunday? We should visit your grandparents and
Margaret and Howard. The sight of you would help
them so much.

Would it, actually? Alan's eyelids.

     We need to discuss the future—the house, the store.
                                             Love,
                                             Snowy

Into the envelope she put a twenty-dollar bill.

During her lunch break the next day, following Irene's directions, she drove to the Rollinses' house, which, as Irene had told her, wasn't a typical Woodcombe Cape or Colonial but a barn. Well, if Ruhamah preferred a converted barn, maybe she wouldn't mind a converted storeroom. Martin Rollins opened the door and said, "Snowy. Come in."

336

"Thank you, but I have to get back to the store, I'll just drop this suitcase off. I'm grateful to you and Fay for taking care of Ruhamah."

"Glad we can help."

Tom had returned midmorning, and in the afternoon he went to Gunthwaite, buying lumber and having Snowy's store key copied. The next day he began framing up the rooms, and throughout the rest of the week he worked nights. Snowy sometimes hid from customers by going upstairs to look at the work he'd done the night before while she at home had been listing what to keep or sell, waiting for Ruhamah to call, dreading a call from Bev. Would Puddles ever phone her again? Mimi did phone, checking in, reluctant now to talk about the wedding, and Dudley phoned, offering more assistance in the garden, asking about setting out plants; she told him she was working and didn't have time. Jason Ellsworth reported that Cedric Barlow's son had made an offer on the house, a hundred and fifty, advising her to hold out for his suggested asking price of two hundred and fifty. *Thousand.* Doing relaxation breathing, she prowled the apartment-in-progress. Apartments. Going backward. Her views here would be of Main Street and her backyard would consist of a loading platform. But she'd be lucky if she could maintain this roof over her head and the head of her daughter.

From whom she hadn't heard by Friday evening.

Patience, she told herself then, in the kitchen reducing on paper her *batterie de cuisine* almost to a mess kit, yet she put aside her list and went out to the van and drove across town past the Rollinses' barn. Her Subaru was in the driveway. She drove into the village and parked beside the Jeep at the store. The second floor glowed golden, as if somebody already lived there. She let herself in and called, "Tom? Just me," took a couple of Budweisers out of the cooler and went upstairs. To supplement the overhead light, he had rigged up utility lights which cast giant shadows of lumber and sawhorses.

"Hi," he said. "It's coming along. Oh—thanks."

"The place is wonderful."

"Be pretty rough for a while. How are you and the store getting on?"

"I've learned the cash register. I can slice bologna without slicing my fingers. I'm learning stocktaking."

Downstairs, the door opened.

Snowy said, "I locked it."

"Irene? Who else has a key?"

Ruhamah, for emergencies. Snowy rushed to the stairs, stopped, walked down. Ruhamah stood beside the postcard rack wearing her own clothes, jeans and a puce sweatshirt which said above a huge insect:

The New Hampshire State Bird
The Blackfly

Ruhamah said, "You're driving now."

"But not so far as Eastbourne. Could you? Your grandparents—"

"The kids, I overheard, you're working here and somebody's building an apartment upstairs. Who's the Jeep?"

"The carpenter. Let's go home, my baby. Lots to discuss."

Ruhamah pushed past her up the stairs. Snowy followed, saying, "I had to decide, there's no time to lose—Tom, my daughter, Ruhamah. Ruhamah, the fire warden on Pascataquac, who's also a carpenter and an old friend."

Ruhamah's eyes and height, Tom thought, were the only difference. He said, "How do you do."

"An apartment," Ruhamah said.

Snowy said, "Let's go home."

"I was going home. Hurricane Farm."

"Then let's."

"When Kim's mother got divorced, Kim said the men came out of the woodwork. He's *building* the woodwork." Ruhamah kicked a sawhorse and ran downstairs.

Tom said, "I'll pack up and leave."

338

"That arrogant—"

The phone rang. As Snowy went down to the office, she could see headlights whirling away from the front of the store.

"Hello?"

Bev said, "Mother died this afternoon. Here in the bungalow, the way she wanted. I couldn't get you at the house; Mimi said to try the store."

Not yet.

"Mother took Seconal, but she didn't tell me. In case I couldn't act the innocent, I suppose. I put the bottle with my things after I found it, and I've acted innocent as can be."

"Ah, Bev."

"I haven't told Mimi and the other children this part, I won't until I won't cry. I almost didn't tell you."

"It's different from Alan, she was dying. You sound so tired."

"Mother was tired. That's why."

"She wasn't alone. You were there."

"I've got to sell her car, put the bungalow up for sale. Mimi said they can postpone the wedding, but Mother was adamant, and the honeymoon reservations are already made and to try to reschedule a European—if Roger can just cope at home, I can cope here. Mother was brave, wasn't she, Snowy?"

"Yes."

"I'll go cry now. You too."

Bev hung up, and in the office doorway, carrying his toolbox, Tom said, "Ask at Gunthwaite Lumber, they'll give you the names of carpenters." He put his key on the desk and was gone.

Driving home sobbing, Snowy detoured over to the Rollinses', to see the Subaru safely parked there again.

339

"HI, MIMI, LLOYD," Snowy said as Lloyd's pickup stopped in the driveway. "Happy is the bride the sun shines on, especially after this rain—"

Overalled Mimi ran around to the back of the pickup, leaned in, and straightened up clasping an enormous plastic-sheathed turkey. "I'm as bad as Mother, I forgot the turkey!"

"You're holding it."

Lloyd asked Snowy, "Lawn mower in the barn?"

"It even has a silhouette," she replied, falsely placid, reminding herself of *her* mother. Lloyd himself always spoke with such deliberate calm that she wanted to look over her shoulder to make sure there wasn't an uncaged lion around. She added, "I filled the gas can." She had learned to pump gas!

Mimi shrieked, "We don't have a microwave—you haven't got one hidden someplace, have you?"

"Nope."

"Then set your oven, three-twenty-five. I forgot to *cook* it, sometimes Mother forgets and leaves the giblets package in, but at least she cooks the damn bird."

"Oh God." Snowy went back into the kitchen, turned on the oven, clattered out the roasting pan. Her mother had always cooked the big Thanksgiving and Christmas turkeys, of course; her own off-season turkeys were for three. Three no more. "I've never cooked a turkey this large."

"Neither have I," Mimi said, clawing at plastic. "Twenty pounds, the cookbook says eight hours, less if unstuffed, I was going to do it unstuffed anyway—"

"Sage in the cavity? I'll get some from the herb garden."

"Thanks, nine o'clock now, it ought to be done by five, we'll probably be back by then, but it wasn't supposed to be hot, on a June afternoon!"

Returning with sage, Snowy said, "Cold turkey. How are the cold feet?"

"I hate to admit it but Mother was right about having the whole reception catered and relax, but that seemed too formal,

340

and besides, Mother would've taken over and chosen every-thing. *I'm* remembering." Mimi extracted the giblets.

"And at least you remembered to thaw it."

"But how could I have forgotten—I was cooking other feast fare all yesterday, so I was going to let the turkey cook over-night, that's why I bought a self-basting, I wouldn't otherwise, who knows what they're full of, and we were packing the car for Boston, and then our roommates came from the Inn for a reun-ion and after they left, well, we got distracted, our last night of being single." Mimi shoved the turkey in the oven, set the timer, and ran back to the pickup.

Snowy recalled Puddles's night-before-the-wedding, relieved that Puddles hadn't sent Mimi an acceptance, nervous enough about meeting Bev, who had phoned last evening from the Gunthwaite Inn to say, "We've arrived—so hectic, while I was in Florida, Roger phoned and said, 'We don't have any water,' and I said, 'Did you call the plumber to come look at the filters?' and he said, 'What filters?' and I said, 'The filters have to be cleaned or they'll clog up'—*that* happened, and Leon had a fender-bender—and I still haven't heard about the exam, a neighbor's going to collect the mail tomorrow and I'll phone her—I can't stand it! Yesterday in a gourmet fast-food shop I go to I ran into a woman who took the course and she'd heard, she passed, and she says others she's talked to have all passed. Why haven't I heard? Do they torture the people who've flunked?" Snowy said, "*Gourmet* fast food?" Thinking that Snowy's showing more interest in food than the exam might be insensi-tive but was a good sign, Bev said, "Chicken nuggets with salsa. I've phoned Mimi, she sounded farther away than from Con-necticut. *Why* can't she have a normal wedding without a Girl Scout hike? Goodbye, see you tomorrow!"

Jason Ellsworth and the accountant had allowed Snowy to keep Irene on past Snowy's "training," and Irene would be working alone today, Snowy having taken this entire Saturday off to ready the house this morning. As Mimi toted in two Igloo coolers, Snowy said, "I've vacuumed. Now I'll dust. You mentioned decorations? Flowers and—? You concentrate on the decorations."

"That wasn't the deal." Mimi transferred plastic bowls and boxes into the refrigerator. "I was going to do the housework."

"You're the artist."

Dusting, Snowy bade farewell to possessions. Hurricane Farm had sold, and the new owner was, after all, Cedric Barlow's son. "Barlow by a nose," said Jason Ellsworth complacently, "I had another full-price offer five minutes later." When Frank Barlow had come up from New York to look at the place before raising his offer, he'd asked Snowy if he could buy some of her things; she would sell the rest at an auction next Saturday, except what she was keeping for the apartment. Alan would have enjoyed the auction, one hell of a trip to the dump. Simplify, she quoted Thoreau into the girandole mirror, simplify. Then she paused and examined her reflection. Yesterday during a slack spell at the store she'd leafed through a magazine on the rack, a women's magazine which had a helpful hint: Check your makeup outdoors. So this morning, after dressing in housework clothes, old Levi's and broccoli T-shirt, she had put on her face and carried her magnifying hand-mirror into the backyard. She'd just decided she had done the best she could when she saw a gray hair in her bangs. White. Twisting her head, she saw white hairs everywhere, blending in enough to be missed indoors. Had this milestone been creeping up on her, age and heredity? Or had it been caused by recent events? No, she'd read that although stress probably didn't turn hair gray, it might cause hair loss. If so, she ought to have become bald.

The auction over, she would move into the apartment. Not Gunthwaite Lumber but Irene had located an available carpenter, one of the guys at the Fabulous Fifties party, and he and his helper had got the dry wall up and taped, the flooring down, the plumbing finished, so the former storeroom would be fairly livable. Dudley had appeared at Hurricane Farm one evening bringing, in his truck, wooden tubs planted with tomato, pepper, cucumber, *broccoli* seedlings, saying, "The Gunthwaite

342

Gardens clerk suggested these for apartment-dwellers," and she said, "Container gardening! I've read of it," and kissed him, and while they were having a drink on the porch she remarked, "This young carpenter who's doing the apartment, he keeps asking me about my 'role' in the Sixties and I disappoint him by telling him Eastbourne didn't have demonstrations, all I did was write letters. Old Eastbourne had demonstrations, still does, like how to restore old houses and how to carve scrimshaw." Dudley said, "Did you see on the news last winter that on a Hippie Day at some school the kids made a mistake and instead of a peace symbol they used a Mercedes logo? Eastbourne? Have you been back yet?" Impulsively she asked, "Would you drive me there next Sunday afternoon?" and explained her driving handicap, adding, "Alan's parents might get the wrong idea if you—I'm capable of driving from the waterfront to their house, it's near downtown, would you care to spend maybe an hour by yourself, sightseeing at Old Eastbourne?"

As they were leaving that Sunday in the van, Dudley asked, "Aren't you taking his folks anything?" "What?" "Anything of his?" She realized Dudley meant Alan's belongings, clothes, watch, cufflinks, tie tacks. "Oh," she said, "people do this." Other people, parceling out possessions. She said, "Someday." Dudley dropped the subject and told hilarious tales about his kids during the drive, reminding her of her attempts on the trip from Hanover to Gunthwaite with her father. At Alan's parents' house, she and Alan's mother and sister wept together in the kitchen, his father coming in only after they'd emptied a box of Kleenex. He asked, "Where's Ruhamah?" As she had to Alan's mother, she replied, "Ruhamah sends her love, she's studying for a big important test." And maybe she was, at the Rollinses'. Alan's father asked, "What are your plans?" Protecting Alan, Snowy didn't admit any financial plight when she said she had sold Hurricane Farm and would be living over the store. "Sensible," his father agreed without argument, in his long-lidded eyes a dull hurt. On the way home Dudley stopped at a non-chain restaurant and bought ice-cream cones at the take-out window, the first cones of the season. Able to eat her fudge walnut that soothed a throat hoarse from crying, Snowy suddenly wondered about another person's getting the wrong idea: Did Charl know about this trip and Dudley's visits, or had Dudley spared his emotional wife who might conclude that he made a habit of consoling widows?

"The caterer!" Mimi called outdoors. "Fay's delivering in person!"

Going back through the house, which had begun smelling like Thanksgiving, Snowy found surprisingly traditional white streamers and wedding bells festooning the dining room, and in the kitchen, above the harvest table, white paper lovebirds perched in a bower of white rosettes. There was also a mystery, a brand-new plastic garbage can. On the porch, more streamers and bells over the golden oak table. Outdoors, Mimi had tied white balloons to the porch railings, the lilac bush, the bird feeder, the birdbath, the pickup's antenna, the barn doors, the mailbox. Lloyd was guiding the lawn mower in an idiosyncratic fashion around the backyard, avoiding the buttercups and daisies at the edge of the woods but also leaving circles of brilliant green grass unmowed here and there.

Fay climbed out of the white-and-gold Indulgences van. "I gave the driver a coffee break and myself an escape from the shop. Oh, balloons!"

Mimi tied one to Indulgences' antenna and asked the question Snowy was steeling herself to ask. "How's Ruhamah?"

"Hard to say, the kids get so keyed up in June." Fay opened the back of the van. "Softball game after school yesterday, pajama party at Lisa Edgerly's tonight, I know that much. In fact, Joyce Parker—Kim's mother—and I have been talking about why should they have all the fun, why don't we have a pajama party for mothers sometime. Thanks." Taking charge of the cake carrier, she directed their conveyance of hors d'oeuvres and tourtière into the kitchen.

Snowy said, "She's well, though?"

"Ruhamah?" Fay inhaled, sniffing. "She's fine. Turkey—we

344

could have cooked one for you. Well, it's not a dead mouse."
She reddened.

Mimi stood gazing at the cake, as matrimonial in appearance as any airy white cake though a carrot cake beneath its frosting.

Fay asked Snowy, "The word is you've sold the house?"

"Does Ruhamah know?"

"Who can tell what teenagers absorb. You'll be living over the store? Living in the village will be more convenient—"

Through the noise of the lawn mower came the sound of another engine, and the florist's van pulled up behind Fay's.

"I'm off," Fay said. "Mimi, best wishes."

When Mimi didn't respond, Snowy said, walking with Fay to the porch, "Thank you so much, everything looks lovely."

"Yes," Fay said. "Er, Snowy, all the details of the mothers' pajama party haven't been worked out yet, but I'll supply the Indulgences and Joyce will rent the naughty videos, you're invited to bring your p.j.'s if you'd like to come, I'll phone. Bye!"

As the two vans maneuvered in the driveway, Snowy wondered aloud, "Is there a method to Lloyd's mowing madness?"

"Huh?" Mimi said. She ran onto the porch. *"Shit!* He's making butterfly gardens, he used to when he mowed his folks' lawn so some wildflowers would grow in suburbia—Lloyd!"

"It's okay, I was just curious."

"But Mother'll think he's even screwier than she already does. Lloyd! And he should be going to the store and getting the ice for the champagne!"

Suddenly Mimi bolted across the driveway into the barn, leaving Snowy to ask the florist's delivery man to put the flowers in the kitchen and, upon his departure, to wring her hands about what, since the refrigerator was full, to do with these other traditional surprises, a bridal bouquet and wreath of white marguerite daisies, which she finally laid in an Igloo. Hurried now, harried, she finished the dusting without farewells, getting more and more nervous. She checked the turkey and realized the mower had stopped, so she went outdoors and saw Lloyd ambling down from the orchard with Alan's pruner. He'd been wasting precious time pruning! She said, "Mimi says you have an ice errand?"

"I was going to prune that lilac next."

"I think perhaps the ice is more important."

"Will do."

He drove off, and she went into the barn. "Mimi!" Disturbed barn swallows were making passes over the hayloft. "Mimi, are you up there?"

Mimi's voice said, "You can't come up after me! Heights!"

"We're running late, we should be grabbing some lunch. I'll set out the buffet china and silver and glasses, but are you going to serve the cake in the dining room and other food in the kitchen and drinks on the porch, and what flowers go where and do you want decorations in the living room?"

Mimi didn't answer. Snowy considered threatening to phone Bev, and then, slapping at mosquitoes which along with deerflies had arrived for the occasion, decided that bugs would force Mimi down and returned to the house, in the bathroom taking the Valium bottle out of the medicine chest. She'd resolved to try to get by on her own. Cold turkey. But those reunions with Bev had been such flops! She put the bottle back. Throwing together a peanut-butter sandwich that she ate in frantic nibbles, she arranged the tables, the flowers, white streamers, remembering the Valium-free trance of a June wedding twenty-six years ago.

Into the barn she dashed. "Mimi, where is Lloyd buying ice, has he gone to the North Pole instead of the store?"

"Hope he has!"

"We're late! Come have a sandwich, I've got to change. Are you wearing something else to climb the mountain, jeans? Try relaxation breathing, deep breath, count—"

"I don't want to get married!"

"Mimi, people are almost due—" Sure enough, Snowy heard a vehicle, and it wasn't Lloyd's pickup which parked outside the barn. The car was a big new royal-blue American

346

car, but it should have been a veteran Land Rover because the woman stepping out of it was dressed for a safari in wrinkled khaki jungle fatigues, with around her neck a silken version of her prey, a leopard-skin print scarf. A Banana-Republic–type outfit! Snowy had seen many such in Gunthwaite last week while clothes-shopping. Unfortunately, the woman was so pale that the khaki was an unbecoming choice—Holy fucking Christ, the woman was Puddles.

Mimi said, "Kristin, my roommate, she has no intention of getting married until her biological clock starts ticking and maybe not even then, she's been test-driving some guy three years and they just broke up, simple, no divorce, and anyway, her job, she's got this fantastic job, okay, she has to live in New York but maybe I should be too, maybe my entire life is a mistake!"

The hesitancy with which the woman came into the barn made Snowy think for a second she wasn't Puddles. The woman spoke. "I understood the wedding was being held on a mountain, not in a barn, bird-shit flying."

"Puddles," Snowy said, pointing to an invisible Mimi, "meet the bride. Mimi, Puddles is here!" The snail-curls were gone; Puddles now wore her still-brown hair over-forty short and efficient, and for the first time Snowy could truly envision Puddles, white lab coat donned, ruling an office domain, her fragility thickened.

Another car arrived, and Mimi's head popped up. She said, "Oh my God, it's Lloyd's family!" Beginning to cry, she disappeared again.

"Nerves," diagnosed Puddles. She yelled at the hayloft, "At least you aren't moving to South Carolina!" and ran to the house. "Bathroom!"

Desperately, Snowy greeted the Quinns, introducing herself to Lloyd's mother, father, brother and sister-in-law and a baby acting ominously cranky. Mimi hadn't mentioned any baby. Then up the driveway came a station wagon with Connecticut license plates, followed by a Volvo with New York plates.

Although, Snowy told herself, I am again in rags in public, my underwear is clean this time and I've got my face on. But she was about to bolt, like Mimi. Mimi was actually doing what she'd gone in fear of doing! The cars braked. She would not faint, she wouldn't have a panic attack or a heart attack. Would she?

"Snowy!" Bev called, leaping out of the passenger seat of the station wagon. Snowy had expected her to be wearing the preppiest sporty attire available; she'd underestimated Bev, who had chosen stonewashed denim jeans and jacket, with a magenta shirt which Ruhamah would have coveted, collar up. "It's been *twenty* years!"

They hugged, and Snowy saw the sight gag happen again as it had two decades ago, doors of the station wagon emitting a seemingly endless number of people, but now the youngest was her namesake, red-headed Etta who was the Bev Snowy knew far better than this tall woman, stunning-looking indeed but unbelievably almost fifty years old. Snowy couldn't possibly be the same age.

"Snowy," Roger said. A mustache counterbalancing a receding hairline, he wore a striped dark blue rugby shirt with *his* stonewashed jeans, and Snowy pictured Bev still dressing him for work every day, the way she'd dressed the children when younger. He kissed her cheek. "Where's the bride?"

The young man and two young women getting out of the Volvo were, Snowy supposed, the roommates and Lloyd's roommate's wife. Was roommate Kristin the person to try to talk Mimi down, or Bev? "Excuse me," she said to Bev and Roger and ran over to the Volvo and asked, "Kristin?"

"You're Snowy?" said the woman clad in an outfit reminiscent of Bennington, jeans and a ruffly peasant blouse and dangling earrings. "I've got—"

"Mimi's having a panic attack, she's up in the hayloft. Could you talk to her? Thank you. Barry?" Barry wore jeans, a red knit jersey without an alligator or any insignia, and he also wore approximately two days' growth of beard, a style appar-

348

ently still in fashion. "Lloyd went off for ice hours ago and hasn't come back, did you see his pickup in the village?"

"Didn't notice."

Roger asked, "Anything amiss?"

"These mosquitoes, bugs," Snowy floundered, saying to Bev and Roger, "Why don't we all go have a glass of wine on the porch. I'm behind schedule, must change. Have you met the Quinns before? No? Lloyd's roommate and his wife? Could you introduce yourselves?" She fled into the kitchen, wedged a half gallon jug of chablis out of the refrigerator and carried it to the porch table, set it beside the wine glasses, champagne glasses, highball glasses, and then rushed into her bedroom to do relaxation breathing as she put on her light blue corduroys and a new shirt she'd bought in Gunthwaite's Lakeside Outlet Mall during a long lunch break. She had driven by herself to Gunthwaite, very slowly, with many stops to let cars pass, but she'd got there, and she had walked down the mall's indoor streets and hadn't keeled over, in and out of clothing stores she'd walked and at a virtuous discount she had bought this up-to-the-minute oversized shirt of pastel blue and pink flowers in which she had planned to meet Bev. Inhale, count to four—

The bedroom door opened, and Puddles said, "Hi. I'm snooping." She went to the bureau mirror and unknotted her scarf and stuck it in a back pocket. "I hate scarves, I never know how to tie them."

"Remember when we wore a red Woolworth-silk scarf in the back pocket of our dungarees? Freshman year?"

Puddles lifted a snapshot of Alan standing on the Pevensay jetty. "Even though I only met him that once, since he died I keep seeing his face."

They looked at the snapshot, Snowy feeling the surge of love always followed by desolation, like the waves against that jetty. The seventh wave is the big one.

Puddles asked, "Are we having Thanksgiving today?"

"Mimi forgot to cook the buffet turkey."

349

"She inherited Bev's memory! How's everything else? At Susan's wedding, the wrong tuxes were delivered."

"Bev's here—I've got to check the turkey—"

Cracking her knuckles, in the kitchen Puddles asked, "How does Bev look?"

"You'll say, 'It isn't fair!' "

"You're scrawny—sorry, and I'm sorry I hectored you." Puddles, contrite?

Snowy said, "I'm sorry I hung up." She shut the oven door. "Has Susan had the baby?"

"Guy James Cram Hammond! Eight pounds, nine ounces!"

"So you're a grandmother."

Puddles tapped the rooster memo pad. "I remember this."

"There's wine here," Snowy said, heading for the porch, "help yourself—"

"Puddles!" Bev sprang out of the crush. "You were able to get away!"

As Bev and Puddles hugged, Snowy saw Lloyd's pickup turn at the mailbox. She wanted to kiss him, she wanted to murder him, but instead when the pickup halted she ran to him and said, "I was about to call Rent-a-Groom. Could you go talk to Mimi, she's in the barn, panic attack."

"Will do," he said calmly. "Shouldn't I ice down the champagne first?"

"I'll take care of it." After, however, Snowy transported the bags of ice to the porch, where Bev and Puddles helped her lug them into the kitchen, she paused, at a loss. "Where would Mimi have put the champagne?"

A quest! Attempting to dispel awkwardness, they seized upon this as if the champagne were the Holy Grail. Puddles opened the refrigerator and said, "Not here," and Snowy said, "Yes, I know," and Bev said, "Down cellar, that's where Mother stored mine, in the old ice chest."

Snowy remembered how her mother had borrowed space in neighbors' refrigerators. "I don't have an old ice chest."

Puddles said, "I bet we all have sagging chests, though."

"Speak for yourself," Bev said. "I'm delighted that my busty friends are now complaining. Revenge! Oh, this garbage can, it's new? Did Mimi buy it? Some people use them for giant ice buckets. Why am I smelling turkey?"

The garbage can was empty. Snowy said, "Maybe Mimi put the champagne down cellar to keep cool until the ice," and at the foot of the cellar stairs she discovered a case of magnums. "Voilà!"

"Your kitchen," Bev said as they poured ice into the garbage can, "is exactly what I imagined from your description, after the wedding you must give us a house tour. I certainly can see why the place sold so fast, if I were a realtor I'd be drooling—I phoned home this morning and my neighbor says the exam results weren't in the mail, I am going mad!"

Puddles said, "Well, for Christ's sake, phone the examiners and find out—sold? Snowy, you're selling this house?"

Bev said, "Phone them and be told to my face I flunked? How humiliating! Is Mimi getting dressed, where's Mimi?"

Snowy looked out the window. Consumed by her own panic, she, the expert on panic attacks, had failed to aid Mimi, but out of the barn walked Kristin, with Mimi and Lloyd, arms entwined. "There she is."

"Good God," Bev said. "What has she been doing?"

"Rolling in the hay," Puddles said. "Snowy, you're *selling?*"

Snowy said, "I'd better wash the used glasses so there'll be enough later."

While Lloyd assigned people to cars, Mimi put the wreath and bouquet in her backpack and dismissed Bev's pleas to clean up—"No time, do it at the cabin"—and Snowy and Puddles raced around gathering glasses for the dishwasher and then got into the Lamberts' station wagon. The cavalcade moved out, led by the pickup in which Mimi and Lloyd went together to their wedding, to Bev's despair.

Roger said, "Quit harping."

On the middle seat between Puddles and Dick, Snowy imagined her household machines mutinying during her absence, like

351

Bev's, the turkey burning, wine glasses shattering. She glanced back at Etta on a jump seat. "Hi."

"Hi."

"You'll be starting junior high next fall?"

"Yes."

Leon tousled Etta's hair. "Unless she runs off with her riding instructor."

Snowy felt Puddles twitch.

Dick said, *"Rides* off. Into the sunset."

Leon said, "Into the swimming pool."

Bev said, "Stop that teasing this minute!" and the rest of the trip was made in silence broken only by the beeps of Dick's wristwatch battery going dead.

Cars lined the clearing, but there was still room for the wedding party to park. "Here's Joe," Mimi called, "the justice of the peace," introducing a man waiting there beside a Honda, garbed in a gray sweatsuit, and from under a blanket in the pickup she took a forest of walking sticks which she doled out, telling Snowy, "Lloyd wasn't working overtime, surprise, he was making these while I was with you, favors for the guests—except you, Michelle," she said to the baby of whom she would soon be the married aunt, if cold feet didn't recur.

In a baby carrier on Lloyd's brother's back, Michelle scowled. Lloyd's sister-in-law equipped herself with a diaper bag, Roger shouldered an L.L. Bean backpack, Barry a guitar case, and Lloyd asked, "Everybody ready?"

"Eek!" Bev said. She'd touched her ear, and her finger had come away red. She was wearing a crust of blood as a second earring.

Snowy said, "Blackfly bite."

"Damn," Bev said, digging in her denim shoulder bag.

"I've got some," Puddles said, whisking a Kleenex out of her safari bag, and while she tended to Bev's wound and Snowy offered fly dope from her pastel blue leather shoulder bag, the others began the climb.

So the triumvirate brought up the rear. At first they talked

352

as if they were on telephones, not looking at each other, speaking into the air ahead, Bev asking about Susan, Puddles announcing grandmotherhood, Puddles asking Snowy why she was selling the house, Snowy saying, "An economic necessity, I'm going to live in an apartment in the store," Bev asking after Guy, Puddles replying, "He's meeting a deadline, too busy, I flew to Logan at the last minute," but then they began to conserve their breath and any strength not needed for climbing and swatting. When Snowy stopped and pointed out the cellar hole, they stood shooting glances at one another.

Then Bev said, "Pant, gasp, playing doubles doesn't prepare you for this. Mimi. A minister in a sweatsuit! All right, justice of the peace. Well, Mother would have enjoyed that."

Puddles said, "Our first reunion since *my* wedding."

With her walking stick, Snowy prodded at a granite foundation block.

Puddles waggled a branch. "This spruce tree or fir or whatever it is, it smells like Noxzema!"

They inhaled and laughed. Bev said, "It does! How nostalgic!"

As they climbed onward, Lloyd's parents dropped back, and Bev walked beside them, acting gracious, making mother-of-the-bride conversation on this unlikely stage, and Puddles said to Snowy, "Ruhamah's still avoiding her home?"

"I've talked to the psychologist twice. She says to give Ruhamah time." But Snowy hadn't told the psychologist about the Tom episode; the psychologist hadn't asked, so Ruhamah mustn't've told her either.

Puddles said, "Have you talked to a shrink about yourself—okay, sorry." She pulled her scarf out of her pocket and mopped at her brow. "God, getting hotter than Tophet."

"Aren't you used to heat by now?"

"*Southern* heat."

Under the bear tree Snowy stopped again, and Bev turned from the Quinns and said, "How much farther? Mimi's going to give me another heart attack—hell and damn."

Puddles pounced. "Heart attack?"

"It wasn't a real one, just a potassium deficiency because of the diuretics I was taking. A false alarm! So, unnecessary to worry anybody."

"When?" Puddles said.

"A couple of weeks ago."

"In Florida? Right after your mother died?"

"I called myself an ambulance—" Fearing Puddles would order her down off the mountain, Bev curtailed the harrowing story. "Snowy, I've forgotten to ask, Mimi mentioned the fire warden went to school with us but she didn't catch his name."

Snowy stared. A second shock, slamming against the heart-attack news. She had assumed Bev knew. She had assumed they were both not referring to him out of mutual embarrassment, intending to behave as casually toward him as they would a stranger. She'd kept track of his schedule. He was on duty today. But he had been buying his groceries in Gunthwaite or someplace now, for he hadn't come into the store again. "It's Tom."

"Tom?"

Puddles said, "Tom Forbes?"

"Tom?" Bev said.

"I'll be fu-" Puddles recollected the presence of the Quinns. "He isn't a teacher? He couldn't hack it at Rumford? You've met him? What does he look like?"

"Shirley Temple," Snowy said.

"Huh?" Puddles said.

Bev curtseyed and made her Shirley Temple face and the Quinns exchanged a baffled glance and Snowy laughed, and Etta came skipping back to say, "Mimi wondered if you'd flaked out," and up and up they went, Snowy slowing the pace more, Puddles keeping an eagle eye on Bev, who, as the tower appeared, stopped and took her compact out of her shoulder bag and said, "Ah, a breeze up here."

Mother Nature's wedding present, it was a stout breeze that discouraged bugs, but nonetheless the wedding party which

Snowy and the other tardy guests joined had taken refuge on the cabin's finished screened porch, Mimi and Kristin and Lloyd out of sight, presumably indoors. Other hikers strolled around the summit, alternately snapping photographs and watching the privileged persons on the porch. Roger hadn't had a regular camera in his backpack; he held—Snowy whispered to Bev, "What kind of camera is that?"

"Video," Bev said. "I wish Mimi would let me help her—"

So nowadays Bev starred in her home videos, as she probably had in home movies.

Puddles asked, "Where's Tom?"

"The tower," Snowy said, "I expect."

"What," Puddles persevered, "did you *say* when you met?"

"Mimi asked about having the wedding here."

"I mean *you two*. Is he still married to Joanne? Where's she? Do they live in Woodcombe but you never ran into them?"

"Attention, everybody," Kristin said, appearing on the porch. "Mr. Lambert, stay here, the rest over near that edge, stand wherever you like, very informal, Mimi says anybody with a heights problem stand in the back near those bushes."

But Bev began assembling the families of the bride and groom semiformally, while Roger reluctantly relinquished the video-cam to Dick for father-of-the-bride duties, and Lloyd emerged wearing clean jeans, a white shirt, paisley suspenders, and perhaps the most unconcerned expression ever seen on a groom. These blueberry bushes, Snowy thought, wouldn't provide much of a handhold if she fell over the edge, which of course was only as dangerous as Bennington's Cliff, and she looked longingly at the woods and saw Ruhamah coming up the trail, wearing jeans and an unfamiliar oversized shirt of tropical flowers.

"That," Puddles beside her said, "has got to be your kid."

Kristin called to Barry, "They're set, hit it!" Barry struck up "Here Comes the Bride" on his guitar, and hikers gawked.

In white muslin and daisies, Mimi crossed the summit on the

355

arm of Roger to stand with Lloyd before Joe and mountain ranges.

Puddles passed Snowy a Kleenex.

As the ceremony began, Ruhamah, pausing, took the place on the other side of Snowy and whispered, "Mimi isn't a wedding-cake bride, she's just plain beautiful."

So was Ruhamah, to Snowy. "Puddles," Snowy whispered, "this is Ruhamah. Ruhamah, Puddles. Bev's in front, white hair."

Ruhamah said, "How do you do," and Puddles said, "At last," gave her a hug, and asked, "Are you going to try out for cheerleading?"

"No," Ruhamah said. Then she looked up, and Snowy followed her gaze. Tom was descending the tower stairs. Puddles nudged Snowy sharply, indicating Bev, who was also looking upward.

Puddles whispered, "That's him? I'd never have recognized him in the world."

Dick might be aiming the video-cam at the bride and groom, yet for the triumvirate and Ruhamah the center of attention was Tom. Tom, not Bev nor Mt. Pascataquac, had stolen, however briefly, the show from Mimi. He went into the cabin.

"—husband and wife," said Joe.

Barry began strumming the triumphant recessional. Whew, Snowy thought, it's done and Tom didn't attend, now back down the mountain without having to speak to him, but Mimi and Lloyd led everybody onto the cabin porch where Tom was pouring champagne into little plastic glasses.

"Well, well," Roger said. "What's all this?"

"A pre-reception," Mimi said, giddy. "When you were taping the view and my favorite fire warden was handing over his cabin to us, he told me there'd be a toast, compliments of Pascataquac. Isn't he nice? Look, a bowl of trail mix, isn't he funny?"

Bev said, "Hello, Tom."

Mimi exclaimed, "Ruhamah, I'm so glad you could come!"

Roger asked Bev, "You know him?"

Bev and Tom regarded each other's hair with amusement.

Tom said, "Hello, Bev." Bev, still bewitching. Still walking that hula walk. "Roger. And, hey, Puddles." He proffered glasses, the courteous host. "Snowy."

"Thank you," Snowy said.

Mimi said, "Some champagne for Ruhamah too; it's all right, Snowy, only a thimbleful."

Tom gave Ruhamah a glass. Snowy's was trembling. Ruhamah didn't meet his eyes.

Mimi said, "No, Etta, you're too young—"

"A toast!" proclaimed Barry. "To the bride and groom!"

Roger said, "Tom Forbes. Is that you under there?"

During the shouts of "To the bride and groom!" the baby finally began crying, so Tom asked the mother, "Need changing?" and showed her the bedroom, while Snowy introduced Ruhamah to Bev and Roger and said to Mimi, "The turkey, I'll go ahead and check it—oops, I can't, the car-pooling."

Mimi said, "I'll thank my fire warden and get going. What is his name?"

"Tom," Bev said, "Forbes."

"I'm keeping my name," Mimi said.

Bev asked, "Will you hyphenate the children?"

Mimi asked, "Where's Tom gone?"

Puddles had collared Tom indoors, and after the wedding party started down the mountain she reported, walking between Snowy and Ruhamah in the middle of the group, Bev the last with the Quinns, "He did teach English, up in Newburgh. Burnout."

"Oh," Snowy said. "You drove here directly from Logan? Are you driving back after the reception or staying overnight?"

"He and Joanne are still married, three grown kids, but if you ask me, this job sounds like a trial separation, partially anyway. Ruhamah, one of my twins decided against cheering too; her extracurricular love was the science club. What's yours?"

"Softball," Ruhamah said. "I'm the new relief pitcher." Off she went ahead, to say something to Etta.

Puddles said, "I was wrong, she's not your kid. Jesus, downhill is wicked on the knees. How's Bev?" She glanced back. "Diuretics!" Turning forward, she said, "Uh-oh, Leon has the hots for Ruhamah."

Leon retied a Reebok until Etta and Ruhamah caught up to him.

"He is," Snowy said, "five years older."

"Guy is nine years older than I am." Puddles splatted a deerfly and lapsed into silence.

And Snowy heard Ruhamah's chortle. Would Ruhamah come home before going to the pajama party at Lisa's Fay had mentioned? Down, down the mountain they went. In the clearing the Subaru was parked closest to the road, and since she'd last seen it, it had acquired a bumper sticker:

NATIVE

The emphasis technique! By herself, living with a family from Massachusetts, Ruhamah had discovered this!

Bumper-sticker-conscious Mimi said, "Gotta have one. I'm married to a native, does that count? Married," she said faintly, removing her daisy wreath.

Ruhamah opened the Subaru's door on the driver's side. "Need a lift?" she asked Snowy.

"Thanks."

Snowy put her walking stick in the back seat. Had Ruhamah brought her suitcase, was it locked in the trunk? The Subaru led the procession, the radio playing some God-awful music for which, for once, Snowy was grateful. They came to the village.

Ruhamah said, "When are we moving?"

"Next Sunday. There's an auction Saturday. I haven't marked anything in your room. The bedrooms in the apartment are very small. We have to do this, Ruhamah."

358

"We're broke."

"Selling the house bailed us out. The store will support us if we're careful, I'll go over the figures with you."

"Might as well get rid of my menagerie."

Snowy touched her arm.

At Hurricane Farm, they both sat for a moment looking from house to barn.

Snowy said, "We will see him everywhere at the store, too."

"I want to see him. Now." Ruhamah got out of the car and unlocked the trunk.

Her suitcase. But was it to pack other clothes for the pajama party or did it signal a permanent return? Snowy hurried indoors. The stove, the dishwasher, had remained docile. Blessing them, putting the walking stick in the closet, she told Ruhamah, "Mimi forgot to cook the turkey," and heard a sound like wind whooshing through leaves. She spun to the sink window and saw an enormous black dog tugging at a lilac branch which had been ripped from the lilac bush—that's not a dog, that's a—"Bear!" she screamed.

It went trundling off into the backyard at a rocking lope, carrying in its mouth the branch, a white balloon floating and the suet feeder swinging.

"A *bear?*" Ruhamah asked. "Right in the yard and I missed it?"

Snowy ran onto the porch and yelled at the people getting out of their cars, "Stay in your cars, there's a bear!" She ran back through the kitchen, looking out windows, into the woodshed and looked out the woodshed window and screen door. The bear had vanished.

"Goldilocks, Goldilocks," chided Roger in the kitchen. "This isn't Yellowstone. Where's the champagne?"

"The bear stole the suet feeder!"

He opened the new garbage can. "Aha, thought so. I'll do the honors. Come in, everybody," he called, carrying bottles out to the porch. "A toast! Dick, the video-cam!"

Ruhamah lifted the turkey out of the oven. "What else are we having?"

Testing her, Snowy replied, "Boiled onions," and tested the turkey with a meat thermometer.

"We're not!"

"No." Snowy let the turkey start cooling and arranged canapés on plates as Roger lengthily hailed Mimi and Lloyd.

Ruhamah volunteered, "The Rollinses, they put onions in everything."

"Roger!" Puddles said, bringing Snowy a glass of champagne. "His 'whereas-es'! Want me to pass some hors d'oeuvres around when he clams up—"

Leon came in, asking, "Can I help?" and Roger did conclude his toast, this time the echoes of "To Mimi and Lloyd!" not setting off the baby, but then, as Puddles and Snowy began serving, he said, "Now, another toast!"

"Dad," Mimi pleaded, "that's plenty."

"I'll keep it short and sweet." From behind a cushion on the glider Roger produced a framed certificate. "To Beverly Lambert, Real Estate Salesperson!"

Bev clutched her chest, and in a flash Puddles was at her side, scattering canapés. Snowy stood paralyzed.

"To Beverly Lambert!" everybody responded, and Snowy heard Dick say to Mimi while he taped, "Our dramatic mother," and a truck pulled into the driveway behind the last car, Dudley's truck, GOLD LEAF OUR SPECIALTY. When Snowy could move again, toward Bev and Puddles, people kept stopping her to select a canapé.

"She's okay," Puddles said as Snowy reached them. "She hadn't even told Roger about the potassium scare."

Barry's wife gagged. "That was *liver!*" she said and upended her champagne glass.

Roger refilled his glass and sauntered back over to Bev. "Surprised?"

"*When did the notification come?*"

"The certificate? Oh, when you were in Florida. I was going

360

to give you a surprise party, but then Julia died, so I decided to wait until now. Do you like the frame, the mat? I spent a half hour with the framer choosing—"

Puddles said, "Is that man—yes, it's Dudley! Bringing a plant?"

Snowy squeezed back past people and opened the porch door. "Join the bash."

"I didn't know, I didn't intend any gate-crashing." Dudley held up a hanging basket of red impatiens. "Last Sunday you mentioned you usually have some for the hummingbirds, I'll just drop it off, you could hang it out a window in your apartment and attract them—"

"Dudley!" Puddles cried.

"Puddles?"

Taking the basket, Snowy said, "A reunion, Dudley, our thirtieth reunion," and they tugged him indoors, Puddles asking, "Where's Charl?"

"With Darl, gone out shopping and dinner."

"Natch! Did Snowy tell you I have twins?"

Snowy said, "Help yourself, champagne, bourbon," went outdoors and hung the impatiens on the hook beside the hummingbird feeder, examined the lilac-pruning done by the bear, on the porch picked up some of the fallen canapés, and went into the kitchen where Mimi, barefoot now, and Kristin, blouse pulled to an off-shoulder position, were setting out tourtière and Mimi's cold spinach soup, cold salmon loaf, lentil salad, rice salad, tossed salad, and Ruhamah and Leon were not in sight. Snowy started unloading the dishwasher, asking, "What took Lloyd forever to buy the ice?"

Mimi said, "On his way to the store he saw they were having a lithographics display at the Historical Society."

Kristin said, "Thank God he didn't notice *after* he bought the ice," and the oven timer pinged.

"Rolls," Mimi said.

"I'll get them," Snowy said.

361

Kristin said, "Snowy, I've got a message for you from my boss."

"Boss?" Snowy said, a cookie sheet of rolls aloft.

"At the gallery, the owner—"

Mimi said, "Isn't it terrific that Mother hadn't flunked after all?"

Snowy tumbled the rolls into the napkin-lined basket. "Gallery?"

"In New York," Kristin said, "the gallery where I work. When I told my boss I was going to New Hampshire this weekend for my roommate's wedding, she said *her* roommate was from New Hampshire, and we got talking about our roommates and—"

Snowy cried, *"What's her name?"*

"That's what Harriet asked about you. My boss, Harriet Blumburg. She said to tell you she'll be phoning. Who knows from where, she was off again, to China, she's hardly ever in the States."

"Snowy!" Puddles said from the porch. "Tom's here, he drives an old Jeep, some come-down, remember his convertible?"

Mimi said, "I invited my favorite fire warden for when he was through work, but he wasn't sure he could—where's Dad, he's supposed to carve—"

Snowy went into the dining room. Harriet. She couldn't wait to hear from her; she dreaded it. Reunions. In the living room Leon was rolling up the rug. Not commenting, she suddenly realized she ought to tell Cleora about the bear, so she went upstairs, encountering Ruhamah carrying her radio-cassette player and a handful of cassettes out of her bedroom.

Ruhamah said, "Leon says there's always dancing at weddings."

"Of course." When Ruhamah had gone downstairs, Snowy peeked into Ruhamah's room and rejoiced to see a mess again, the suitcase spilling clothes. In her office, she dialed the Thornes' number. "Cleora? Snowy. Just to alert you, there was a bear here a while ago, it stole the suet feeder."

"The cows are in the barn. I'll shut up the chickens."

Music erupted. Snowy said, "Mimi's reception, I'm sorry, let me know if the noise travels and bothers you and Isaac."

"A beer."

"A bear?"

"This afternoon," Cleora said, "Isaac, he asked for a beer. He always used to like his beer more than I approved of, but ever since he took sick he ain't wanted a drop. I never thought I'd be happy to have him want a beer. I found some left over from his last six-pack, and I put a bottle in the icebox and got it good and cold and took it up to him and set it on the bedside table. He ain't touched it yet, but I'm still hoping. Thanks for calling."

The music was interrupted mid-blast, and out of the upstairs bathroom came Bev, makeup redone, holding a pink plastic bag that read CORAL CREATIONS. Her voice raspy, she said, "If he'd told me, I could have told Mother. Mother would have known before she died. She would have been so proud."

"I don't understand why he didn't."

"It just dawned on me. Giving me the certificate makes it his. He's bestowing it."

Snowy was speechless.

Bev said, "He ridiculed the classes. Sabotage, arranging to go out with clients the night before the exam. Snowy, this just dawned on me, too—can a man who secretly opened Christmas presents when he was a boy ever be trusted? What else has he done secretly?"

"But in high school, he broke up with you because you went out behind his back."

"Is this your office? I was going to leave these here for you, to keep. Mother's copies of your books, very reread, and your letters, and a photograph of her, one Fred took at the bog."

"Bev."

"Let's go get blotto."

In the living room, Ruhamah and Leon were watching television, Ruhamah looking abashed, Leon pissed off. Snowy said, "The cassette player kaput?"

"Mimi," Leon said. "She told us, Mother, you made her promise there wouldn't be any dancing."

Bev stroked the pedestal table. "This is a house of mourning."

Snowy said, "Well, Ruhamah, what do you think?"

"He wouldn't care, so long as *he* didn't have to dance."

"Then everyone else can. Alan," Snowy explained to Bev as Leon bounded to the player and some group began braying, "hated dancing, even waltzing." He also hated reunions.

"Such a lovely house. Mother left me her money, needless to say, and there'll be the money from the bungalow when it sells. You won't permit me to help you, will you. You'll put your chin up."

"Thank you, no."

Mimi ran in, shushing, but Snowy said, "It's okay, let the rafters ring," and Mimi said, "Great, I'll get Lloyd," and Hurricane Farm began to jump, Dudley asking Snowy to dance, Snowy saying, "I'm sorry, I've forgotten how; ask Puddles." After she checked the ice supply on the porch, where baby Michelle and mother had both dozed off in the glider, she armed herself with a buffet plate for a prop and set forth to question Kristin about Harriet's globetrotting life, finding her, however, in the living room dancing with Lloyd, Mimi with Dick, Ruhamah with Leon, Puddles with Dudley, and Bev dancing with Tom. Roger and his video-cam were recording it all. Snowy retreated, remembering that she hadn't collected today's mail.

The irises in the front yard had begun blooming a few days ago, so the swamp irises at the beaver swamp would be too, and at Julia's old bog, if the bog was still there. Her hands always started shaking as she opened the mailbox, though she had disciplined her mind to clamp down on hope. The mailbox contained one envelope, her manila self-addressed stamped envelope: her manuscript returned from the latest publisher.

If Isaac lived, Cleora wouldn't sell the cows. Snowy left the envelope in the mailbox and walked slowly back to the house wherein danced Puddles, ARNP, and Bev, Real Estate Salesperson. On the porch, she mixed herself a vodka-and-seltzer, and Dudley came out singing, "Buy me some peanuts and Crackerjacks," lowering his voice at the sight of the sleeping baby and mother. He said, "I've been dancing with your daughter, I really didn't mean to gate-crash, you'd said Mimi was getting married but I didn't know when—or who is manning the mountaintop and is now dancing with the fair Kristin whose ruffles seem to be descending farther and farther. Charl was wondering if you might be ready to come to supper sometime. Is this party a test? Charl kept crying when she saw other couples, so she—how about after the auction, Saturday night supper, I'll pick you up, Ruhamah too if she'd like."

"We'd love to. We can get there on our own, though. What time?"

"Six?"

"Fine."

He wanted to ask more about Tom than he'd learned from Puddles, but he said, "See you then," and kissed her cheek.

"Thank you for the impatiens. My thanks to Charl." Who, Snowy thought as she waved to his truck, had been aware all along of his whereabouts. Dusk was drawing close. She carried her drink into the privacy of the woodshed, but Puddles walked in with a glass of chablis and inquired, "Dudley still platonic?"

"Yes."

"No such thing, men being men, it's always in the back of their minds if not the front of their pants. All these woodpiles up here nowadays, even regular houses have them, used to be only farms. Hearth and home. I asked Calvin to come up with me for the weekend, a whole weekend together away from Helmsdale to sort things out. That snapped it. Back to his hearth and home he's gone, the end of the evenings in the mattress factory. I feel like he died—oh Jesus, not the way you must, but—so tonight I'll be flying back to my hearth and home.

Which I ought to be grateful for; we aren't in bankruptcy court. Yet."

"Driving back to Boston will make an awfully tiring day. You could spend the night here."

"If I did, I might never go back."

In wandered Bev, sipping champagne. "There you are!" she said merrily. "What a treat to see Dudley, I'd forgotten Tom is such a good dancer, I didn't flunk the exam, I am a real estate salesperson, I have a profession!"

Puddles yawned, and Snowy thought: It was better by telephone.

"Now, Puddles," Bev said, "Guy isn't with you, so where have you stashed Calvin, in a Gunthwaite motel? Could you find one that hasn't become a condominium? I was amazed, and all the new condos being built, selling real estate around here must be *fun!* Puddles? Where's Calvin?"

"He's history," Puddles said. "I'll trim my menopause classes to two nights a week again." She balanced her wine glass on the woodpile and unzipped her pants. "Here's the very latest I told you about," she instructed, pulling down her underpants. "The estrogen patch."

Snowy's and Bev's eyes fastened upon the small transparent disk stuck to Puddles's stomach.

"—directly into the bloodstream," Puddles said, "releasing—"

Snowy said to Bev, "Remember when she was the first of us to try a Tampax?" and they collapsed laughing, Bev saying, "Our pioneer!"

"Hardeeharhar," said Puddles.

Bev said, *"Eeeeek!"*

A bear rose on its hind legs and looked at them through the window screen. Huge head surrounded by bugs. Big eyes with fractured prisms. Moments passed.

Then the bear dropped to the ground, and Snowy carefully closed the outside door and stepped into the kitchen to see it nosing around the lilac bush.

Tom appeared in the dining-room doorway. "Did I hear an eek?"

"There's a bear," Snowy said. "It stole the suet feeder earlier."

Puddles ran out of the woodshed, across the kitchen past him. "Head-count, is everybody indoors?"

Snowy and Tom watched out the sink window the bear's search for more suet. Funny, Snowy thought, the illusion of cuddliness, a teddy bear despite its size. Like Tom.

Tom said quietly, "They're roaming. The game warden says the rains have disturbed their feeding patterns, I've been keeping my garbage inside. A hiker today told me his beehives had been raided."

"The porch!" Snowy said. "It could slash the screen, the baby—"

The bear waddled across the driveway into the barn.

Tom asked, "Garbage cans?"

"All this noise, all these people, why isn't it scared?"

"If they're hungry—"

Roger thundered in, video-cam on his shoulder, other guests at his heels. "Bruin?"

Bev said, leaning against the woodshed doorjamb, "It is not a performing bear. It is independent." Mimi looked at her.

But as Roger taped out the porch door, the bear rolled a garbage can center-stage in the barn, knocked the lid off, and sat down on its haunches to paw within.

Puddles raced into the kitchen. "Ruhamah and Leon aren't here, I checked upstairs, I'll try down cellar, Jesus Christ, young love—"

"Snowy!"

Ruhamah's voice.

The bear lifted its head toward the hayloft.

Tom asked Snowy, "Do you have a gun?"

"A twenty-two."

"Good enough."

Snowy ran through the house, past Dick and Kristin dancing

367

in a corner, grabbed the rifle out of the closet, and ran back to the kitchen.

"Thanks," Tom said.

"A gun!" Etta wailed piteously, just like her mother. "You're not going to shoot the darling bear?"

"Not unless I have to." Tom said to Roger, "Keep the door open, in case a hasty return is necessary. 'Exit, pursued by a bear.' "

Even consumed with terror for Ruhamah, for him, Snowy was disconcerted by his new references. Shakespeare, Tom?

"Honest to God," Puddles said, "that hayloft has seen more action today than it probably has in fifty years," and Tom started across the yard firing the rifle into the air. The bear observed him with interest and tore the lid off the second garbage can. Tom paused. A stand-off.

Baby Michelle began screaming. That did it. The bear lit out, and so did Tom, in opposite directions, the woods and the porch. A long shiny black car pulled into the driveway.

"The limo!" cried Bev. "We're late. Mimi, you and Lloyd cut the cake, and please refrain from smearing it all over each other's faces, no matter if that's the fashion—"

"*Limo?*" Mimi said.

"I don't suppose you have a going-away outfit here. The limousine will take us to your apartment, where you can change and pick up your luggage for Boston—there they are!"

Roger's video-cam recorded Ruhamah and Leon's dash from the barn to the porch, as Bev told him, "Come tape the cake-cutting," told Barry, "Apologize to the driver, we'll be right along," told Snowy, "I'll deal with Leon later," and herded people into the dining room.

At the porch, Ruhamah and Leon hung back.

Snowy said, "You're just in time for the cake."

"Oh," Ruhamah said. Then she said to Tom, "Thank you."

He grinned. "Glad to oblige, but thank the baby."

Going past Snowy, Ruhamah whispered, "I was only showing Leon the silhouettes, we ran up the ladder when we saw the bear."

"Quick thinking," Snowy said. "Get some cake."

Snowy and Tom were alone on the porch. In the driveway, Barry spoke to the chauffeur, took small bags of birdseed out of the Volvo, and jogged back to the porch. Stashing the bags, he asked Tom, "Is the bear gone?"

"Maybe."

"This country living!" Into the house Barry went, and they were alone again.

Snowy said, "Ruhamah is going to a pajama party tonight. I'll be going to one sometime too—the mothers of friends of hers are having a mothers' pajama party."

"Are you worried about staying here alone with the bear around?"

"Mimi's roommate, I learned she works for *my* roommate, we lost each other but now we'll get back in touch. Puddles's guess is that you're having a partial trial separation."

After a while, Tom said, "Not intentionally, but that's what it's turned out to be. Coming on for years, I suppose."

Indoors, shouts: "The bouquet!" "Kristin caught the bouquet!" "I didn't *mean* to!" "Subliminally—"

Tom picked up a bag of birdseed and juggled it from hand to hand. "I could move the business to Woodcombe. There's a vacant barn on Main Street, in the business zone. I could live there after the tower is closed for winter, fix up an apartment like yours. How is yours? From outside, looks nearly done."

The commotion swept onto the porch, Barry tossed bags of birdseed to guests, Puddles said, "If it was nowadays, I myself would've been on a softball team," and as Mimi bent to hug Snowy, Puddles skillfully pitched a handful of birdseed down the front of the muslin dress.

Mimi whispered to Snowy, "Thanks so much."

"And I thank you."

The bear momentarily forgotten, birdseed-throwers chased the bride and groom to the limousine.

369

Tom put his arm around Snowy.

She said, "Remember when you broke up with me, and you told me we should almost make a date for four years hence, after college was over? We couldn't have imagined thirty years."

"Listen to those spring peepers."

Frigate Books Order Form

(Copy form or remove from book)

Date: _____

To order books by check, send this order form to:

Frigate Books
285 Range Road
Center Sandwich, NH 03227

Direct your questions about orders to frigatebooks@earthlink.net

Number
of Copies _____ THE CHEERLEADER $12.95 (After 1/1/03,$14.95)

Number
of Copies _____ SNOWY $16.95

Shipping: $4.00 for one book. $1.00 for each additional book
             sent to the same address.

Total: $_____

Ship to:

Name   _____

Address _____

             _____

Phone   _____

E-mail   _____

If you would like your copies autographed by the author, please
indicate on the back of this order form how the book should be
inscribed. Please print names.

To order by credit card, visit the author's bookshop at
             www.ruthdoanmacdougall.com.